FLAMMEUS

FLAMMEUS

BOOK ONE
OF THE EMBERJAR

VERONICA GARLAND

VERONICA GARLAND

Copyright ©Veronica Garland 2019
Cover art ©Amy Yeager 2019
Cover design ©Veronica Garland 2019
All rights reserved.
The moral rights of the author have been asserted.

This is a work of fiction. Names, characters, places, events, locales, and incidents are the products of the author's imagination or used in a fictitious manner. Any resemblance to actual persons, living or dead, or actual events is purely coincidental.

ISBN-13: 9781073531950
Imprint: Independently published

FLAMMEUS

VERONICA GARLAND

For my children, and for you.
May the Emberjar of your mind
be sparked by love, fed with curiosity
and shared with compassion.

FLAMMEUS

THE SPARK 7

THE FLAME 164

FLARE 229

FANNING THE FLAMES 377

CONFLAGRATION 429

THE EMBERS 455

VERONICA GARLAND

THE SPARK

CHAPTER 1

My life began on Conflagration Day. I was born in the month of Fire to an unknown mother who survived long enough to leave me on the doorstep of the Temple of the Goddess's Blessing. Pinned to my makeshift blanket was a small gold brooch in the shape of a flower. This tale had been told to me, as a young child, by old Saphna, one of the Priestesses, all of whom saw me as a gift from the Goddess when I was young and a useful working Maid when I became older. No matter. Conflagration Day this year was different. By the laws of the Temple, all foundlings must be given an opportunity to claim their Choice when they reached the age of maturity. Not that the Priestesses had told me this.

They did not believe in extraneous information at the Temple. I learned the Aphorisms of Ashkana in all their translations. I was taught how to wash the feet of the Goddess, and which scented oils were used on which day; orange blossom for Aureus, cedar for Viridis, lavender for Lilavis and jasmine for Flavus. Each day of the week had a different scent and a different colour, and it was one of the duties of the Priestesses and the Maids to ensure that people knew what day it was by the scent which trickled round the Temple, almost liquid, and the coloured silks which surrounded the Goddess, hanging from the arch above her head and laid out around her feet. My own day, Flammeus, was the scent of cinnamon, followed by Hyssop for Indicus and the fragrant Rosemary of Azureus. The Priestesses alone knew and told us the days from the passage of the stars. While I cleaned, I had watched the astronomers who called upon the Priestesses explaining it, reading it from their scripts. The Priestesses did not concern themselves with me much by then. I was convenient and quiet, and they ignored me. They certainly did not know that I had taught myself to read and scribe. There was a lot they did not know, and I had no intention of them realising any of it especially until the moment during the Choice ceremony where I would be offered a choice of parchments in order to see what fate the Goddess has chosen for you.

It's a clever trick; the Maids cannot read or scribe and choose only from what they see. The Priestesses offer two parchments. If they wish to keep the Maid, they will write her contract of binding on beautifully ornamented parchment. Abssina is the Priestess Artist and she adds subtle pictures to the parchment of things which that Maid loves; for Lunaria she drew butterflies and rabbits moving about between the leaves of flowering plants all curling around. It was a beautifully crafted scene.

Lunaria stood at the feet of the Goddess, her head bowed, wearing her birth cloth of colour. She was given the day of Lilavis, violet purple and the scent of lavender swirled around us, at once sweet and astringent. High Priestess Asinte brought forth the Scrolls of Choice. In her right hand she held that beautiful parchment crafted by Abssina, so lifelike you could swear the butterflies were moving and that the rabbit twitched its nose at you. On this scroll was scribed 'Lunaria becomes a Priestess of the Temple of the Goddess and is bound to her service forever'. In her left hand, Asinte held another parchment; this one grey and scruffy. It had lines in dark blue ink drawn round it and some half-hearted curlicues. It was scribed 'Lunaria will leave the Temple and pursue a life in the Outer'. Lunaria bowed her head and I could see her lips moving with a prayer to the Goddess. Lunaria worked hard for the Temple and could sew exquisitely. Her cloaks and stoles commanded high prices from the merchants that came to the doors of the Temple from lands beyond. Her soul was drawn to beauty and ornamentation and she believed in the Goddess, and she believed that the Goddess would guide her choice. Having prayed, she looked up and you could see her believing that the Goddess was speaking to her through the Parchment. She reached out her hand and took the beautiful page. Priestess Asinte enfired the other parchment and the flames crackled and spat as Lunaria's alternative life turned to ash. Lunaria took the page to the Goddess and lay it on the altar. Asinte called forward the Reader, who took the page from the altar and turned to address us all, Maids and Priestesses alike.

'The Goddess has chosen Lunaria as her Priestess. Her devotion to the Goddess has been observed and the Goddess has extended the hand of benevolence upon her. She needs no family other than the Goddess; she will be content, for the Goddess will make it so.'

Lunaria's eyes widened and her breath stopped. Almost immediately she remembered the Goddess and again her lips moved in prayer. What she prayed for, I cannot tell you, but when she looked up she stood demure and biddable in front of Asinte, ready for the Consecration of her life to the Goddess. Asinte took the veil for Lunaria from a selection, pondering over which to choose, until finally she alighted on one of deep lilac shot through with gold. Around the edges of it was embroidered in dark purple small lavender heads interwoven with golden wheatsheaves.

'How special,' she murmured to Lunaria. 'I believe this exquisite work is your own stitchery, Lunaria.'

'The Goddess must have guided my fingers, High Priestess,' answered Lunaria, fingering the veil.

In my place, clad in the drab, I rolled my eyes at Lunaria being unable to see through such simple trickery. Could she not see that all these supposed signs were nothing but old conjuring tricks playing with her mind? The beautifully ornamented parchment, the colours and scents that were chosen for her consecration had so obviously been chosen to convince Lunaria that being a Priestess was her calling from the Goddess. Lunaria placed the lilac veil over her dark curls and went to join the other Priestesses of Lilavis. As she turned to walk to the altar, we could no longer see her eyes and her face, veiled as they were from our gaze. The veils worn by the Priestesses covered the whole head and all the hair, and only had a small woven area at the eyes so that the Priestess could see outwards, but others could not see in.

There had been another consecration some months earlier. It was on that day that I had finally worked out how it fell so well for the Priestesses, because it was on that day that I was seated near enough to read the words scribed on the parchment myself. The Maid on that day was Bellis. Bellis appeared to do hardly any work around the Temple, and instead of learning her embroidery, or growing plants for the physic, or even scrubbing the flagstones, which was my own particular speciality, she would gaze off into the distance, murmuring words of prayer to the Goddess. I once asked her what she was doing, when I had scrubbed my step for the requisite seven times, and she was still trying to finish her first pass. Her eyes had widened at me and she had told me dreamily that she was thinking of the Goddess and her generosity. Bellis had come to the Temple as an offering, like all of us. Her family had probably given her up to the Temple because she was no good to them either, even as a baby. She sang, but not beautifully, and her work filled no one with joy. She had no skill that I could see, and she ate absentmindedly of the labours of others. She spent her spare time mooning at the statue of the Goddess, and instead of cleaning the Temple or folding and tidying the cloths of colour, she would just sit and gaze at the statue of the Goddess, outwardly spellbound by her magnificence. When I asked her what she hoped for at her consecration, she turned to me wide eyed.

'Why, to worship the Goddess for the rest of my life,' she answered. 'I cannot think of anything I would rather do. The Goddess soothes my spirit whenever I spend time quietly with her.'

'May the Goddess grant you your wish,' I answered, politely, puzzled by Bellis's deeply personal connection with the Goddess and sure that the Priestesses would do all in their power to rid themselves of the burden of one who took from them but gave nothing back in terms of work.

At the consecration three days later, on the day of Flavus, we Maids assembled again, dutifully crowding into the stone Temple. Clad in the drab, we blended into the stone, as was the intention. Only the Priestesses stood out, in their coloured robes and veils. The statue of the Goddess, on her raised dais was in the middle, under the arch, and we were shielded from the other half of the Temple by an ornate, carved, wooden screen which went from ceiling to floor, preventing us from seeing those of the Outer who came to the Temple, and preventing them from seeing the Maids in the drab, though they could still see the Priestesses during normal services. Bellis wore yellow, the colour of Flavus, and the scent of jasmine filled the Temple. The Goddess was clothed in saffron yellow silk. Bellis looked sallow in yellow, but even I could see that she had a sort of glow to her as she approached the Scrolls of Choice. I squinted my eyes to read the wording and drew breath. As was customary, two scrolls were offered. One was written in dark blue ink, and one was written in golden ink. The dark blue one was ornamented carefully with orderly squares and geometric patterns, and the golden one was sprinkled with stars and flowers. Bellis looked at them carefully. The writing meant nothing to her, so she looked at the pictures. At once her mind made the connection and she chose the golden scroll. Of course she did. It was Flavus, the golden yellow day. She was clad in yellow and so was the Goddess. She was named for a starry flower with a yellow centre; surely the Goddess must be speaking to her. I, on the other hand, could read the words, and knew she had made the wrong choice. She took the Parchment tentatively to the Reader, casting a yearning glance at the veils from which she was sure she would be awarded her Priestess veil in a few short minutes. Temptingly, on the top, was laid a glorious yellow veil, sprinkled with tiny stars of golden thread and sprinkled with glass beads. She handed the Parchment to the Reader, breathless in anticipation of a life worshipping the Goddess, safe from the ills of the world. The Reader read the Parchment and her words rang out clearly for all to hear.

'The Goddess does not deem Bellis worthy to remain in the Temple. She must leave within the hour and may never see the Inner Temple again. Henceforth, she will live in the Outer and must make her own way without the special favour of the Goddess.'

Bellis gasped and swayed and turned frantically for the other Parchment but Asinte was already crumbling it to warm ashes. She sank to her knees, pleading to the

Goddess for mercy. High Priestess Asinte looked at her wordlessly and then beckoned two Priestesses to take her away. We Maids watched silently as the veils were folded and put away, and the Priestesses filed out, facing into the distance, away from Bellis. As we left the Temple, we saw Bellis, clad in the drab once more, being escorted to the gates. I had never been to the Outer, and longed to see it, but it was clear to me that Bellis had buckled under the news and was struggling to walk. The fact that she was so distraught made me wonder if that life in the Outer was very different to the only life I had known, in the Temple. If you were deemed unworthy of life in the Temple, you left in the drabcoat, deprived of the colours of the Goddess. You left with nothing, as you came into the world with nothing. What you had in the Temple belonged to the Goddess; her parting gift to you was the drabcoat; whereas if you were chosen to stay in the Temple you received the gift of colour in your robe and your veil. Poor Bellis, who so loved the Goddess, had been rejected by her. Although the Goddess seemed to have precious little to do with the decisions that were made.

When I got back to my dormit, I sat down on my sleeping mat and tried to work out whether the Priestesses would want me to go or to stay. I could not ask any of the Priestesses; they did not converse with we Maids, except in scholar; teaching us how to oil the Goddess's feet correctly, how to scrub a step by the Seven Step Rule, how to sew and how to till the land. Those who showed gifting were moved to other higher classes and taught to become physics, or needlewomen like Lunaria, or even artists like Abssina. The gifted were always chosen by the Goddess; in scholar we were taught to be grateful for our gifts and to work at improving them. I wasn't sure how much I wanted to be selected by the Goddess, though. It was the only life I had ever known, and I had never been permitted beyond the Temple wall, yet I was not worried about going to the Outer. On the contrary, I longed to leave the Temple. I didn't even mind that I would be clad in the drab for the rest of my life. I had decided to work at step scrubbing when I had made my choice of work. It pleased me to follow the old rhythms of washing; there was a musical nature to it, and it allowed my mind to tease out questions from the answers I had been shown. I did not know how this skill would aid me in the Outer, but I felt sure that it must be useful, for the Goddess was pleased by useful work.

I was nearing the end of the Third Age of childhood and the beginning of the Seven Ages of Adulthood. I reached the end on my birthdate, Conflagration Day, which auspiciously fell this year on Flammeus, the first day of the week, the day of red and cinnamon scent, powdery and woodily pervasive. In the First Age of Childhood, your birthdate was a day when the old Priestesses cooed over you, letting you play with small scraps of silk and chiffon, giving you drops of scented oil to add to the Goddess, feeding you darkberries, combing your hair and occasionally telling you stories of interest. In my case, Priestess Saphna loved to tell me about the day she had heard a slight sound from inside the Temple. She had found me at the BabyGate, wrapped in a blanket, with a note scribed on it with my birthdate. Saphna speculated that my mother must have had wealth in order to pay a Scribe to write the note for her, and in order to have possessed the golden flower pin with which the note had been pinned. The pin itself, I had only seen once, quite by accident, during my Second Age of Childhood, which spans from seven to fourteen. In the Second Age, we Maids commence Scholar and are used as a general skivvies and porters for the Priestesses, whose hands must stay free to do the work of the Goddess. I saw the pin in a case in High Priestess Asinte's room, where I had gone with Priestess Helvina, carrying some boxes of fabric for the needlewomen, in a whole host of colours. Helvina caught me looking in the case and rapped my knuckles sharply.

'And that's why the brooch is in the case, Talla,' she frowned at me. 'You are wasting the Goddess's time looking at it and it is taking a place in your heart reserved for the Goddess, Bless her Name.'

'Bless her Name,' I responded dutifully, and cast my eyes down, as Helvina bustled me from the room. I was never given duties to Asinte's room again, even though I volunteered for them. Sometimes I tried to draw the shape of the pin from memory, when I had parchment and charcoal, which I had to hide in the dormit, under a loose stone. It was a circular pin, with many interlinking petals, finely made in gold filigree, with a dark red stone at the centre.

'Possessions are only possessions if they belong to someone,' was one of the most quoted of the Aphorisms of Ashkana. Nobody had possessions in the Temple – at least none of the Maids did, and I knew little about the Priestesses and what they might possess. The Priestesses did appear to have two main possessions each which were their veils. On the death of a Priestess, her veils joined the many used to clothe the Goddess. The scraps of parchment I had taken were illicit possessions, as was the burnt stick charcoal. I knew that in the Outer, people had possessions, and that some people had more than others, because of the traders that would come to view the crafting done by the Priestesses.

Lunaria was apparently quite popular with the tradespeople, since she stitched so well, and she was useful to the Temple. I had never been chosen to sit with the goods for trading since my work was in cleaning, which could not be traded. The Priestesses kept a close eye on the interactions between the Temple and the Outer, and it was clear to everyone after Lunaria's Choice, that she was now no longer sanctioned to sit with her own stitchery when the merchants came to trade, but rather sat in her dormit, or in the physic garden, with her silks beside her, still stitching the finest work, but it was now being traded by other Priestesses and Maids. Any enquiries about Lunaria were met with a steady 'Priestess Lunaria serves the Goddess with joy,' and that was the end of it.

I tried to work out whether the Priestesses would choose to keep me here at the Temple of the Goddess's Blessing or release me to the Outer. Of course, there would be no difficulty if they chose to release me, for that was what I wanted. I had no special friends or close ones there, no one did, and I kept to myself, quiet and watchful. But I was the only one amongst all the older Maids who had never set foot outside the Temple, never been selected to go on one of the rare shopping excursions, never been allowed to sit with the goods for trading with the merchants from the Outer. I had never been chosen to sell the stitcheries or administer the physic. We were all brought up in the Temple, kept apart from the rest of the world, but as Maids grew close to their Choice time, they were occasionally selected to have some limited encounters outside of the protective shroud of the Temple. Priestesses did occasionally travel to other Temples, and some even brought older Maids with them to assist them, but none of these opportunities fell to me. The Priestesses at my Temple seemed irritated by my ways and yet they held back from being truly brusque towards me. I felt sure that they intended to keep me in the Temple all of my days and I felt equally sure that I wanted to leave and explore the world outside of the Temple.

There were many, I am sure, like poor Bellis, who would have been incredulous at my wish to leave the security of the Temple walls for an uncertain life on the Outer. I knew nothing of life out there, save what I had observed from the merchants or other visitors to the Temple. The Maids were not permitted to speak to the visitors except to make negotiations of price with the merchants, and visitors only spoke with those whom they came to visit. The only male visitors to the Temple were the tradesmen as far as I knew; it seemed that on the Outer, it was the male who did the trading and the selling; we very rarely saw women from the Outer. When they came to worship the Goddess, they came to their own parts of the Temple, where they could worship the Goddess statue without seeing us, or us seeing them. Sometimes we did see them vaguely through the ornate screen if the curtains had not been draped swiftly enough. Once, I saw someone with a towering headdress in a mass of bright colours. The Priestesses had always told us that only they could wear the colours of the Goddess, and yet here was someone from the Outer wearing colours to worship. I asked everyone if they had seen it too, but they had not, or at least, they said they had not.

And now my chance was fast approaching, and I tried to consider what I would do for every eventuality. What if there was some other trick I was not aware of, and even if I chose the right parchment, the reader read only what she was told to read? What would I do when I left the Temple? With only a skill at the Seven Step Stone scrubbing, I did not think I would have a lot to offer the Outer. Would the Goddess punish me for spurning the Temple? I was unsure if there really was a Goddess or not. Sometimes I felt sure I could feel her presence, like beauty or joy, ethereal but somehow obvious; at other times she seemed to me to only be a smooth stone statue covered in oil and silk. What would the Priestesses do to me? Would they give me the golden pin when I left?

On the eve of Conflagration Day, I was called to High Priestess Asinte after the evening worship known as The Quenching of the Spirit. Lunaria took me there, her eyes masked by her lilac veil. I knew that each Maid was addressed by the High Priestess before the Choice Ceremony, so I was not especially surprised, although I was unaccountably anxious as to what might happen. When I arrived, High Priestess Asinte beckoned me forward and I came forward and knelt, as was proper.

'Maid Talla, your Choice ceremony falls in the morning. I wish to pray with you to our Goddess for the right outcome.' She paused and leaned forward, and, for a moment, I thought I could see a flash of darker blue from behind her cornflower blue veil. 'I feel sure that the Goddess is aware of you and of all your work in the Temple. You have been a faithful Maid since almost the day you were born, after all.' A note of hard iron had crept into her voice, and I willed myself to focus on the stone flags beneath my knees. 'In fact,' continued Asinte dryly, 'I would be extremely surprised if the Goddess did not choose you in the morning. Make sure you concentrate well on the scrolls of Choice, Talla. The Goddess will reveal her choice to you in the Scrolls, and you must be guided by the Goddess in all that you do. She will ensure you live a long and happy life.'

I wondered if that meant that without the Goddess's blessing, I would live a short and unhappy life. I felt that I was being given a not very subtle push in the right direction and had to keep reminding myself that none of the Priestesses knew that I could write and even scribe in a fashion. It was a matter of reading signs and symbols and understanding their meaning, and here the Priestess was giving me her own sign. 'As the Goddess wishes,' I murmured obediently, still looking at the stone floor. Asinte beckoned to Lunaria and told her, 'Take Talla for her robe, Lunaria, and give her some time in the Sanctum of the Goddess to prepare for her Ceremony,' and then she rose to leave the room. Lunaria waited for me at the door, veiled and silent.

As we walked along to the Sanctum, I tried to speak to Lunaria, but she merely told me that the Goddess loved silence from her Priestesses. I asked her how it was to be a Priestess, but she said nothing in response, guiding me to the chests of robes before the Sanctum. In truth I was excited. This would be the first time in my life that I had ever worn colour, the first time I was not clad in the drab. Lunaria opened the Chest of Flammeus, and the scent of cinnamon was at once around us. I was used to the smell; after all, once a week it was the scent of the day, and it was linked with me, for it was Flammeus tomorrow and Conflagration day too. A day of fire and warmth. Lunaria judged my size and selected a deep red robe from the chest. She showed me how to wrap it around my drabcoat and tie it with the silken tassel. As soon as I put it on, I felt different. I felt strong and alive, surrounded by warmth and light. I smiled at Lunaria happily and I felt the glimmer of a smile in return, before she guided me to the Sanctum and left me with the Goddess.

The statue of the Goddess was made of a type of stone I had never seen anywhere else, although as I had not been anywhere else, it was not, after all, so surprising. The stone caught the light that shone in through the high windows and reflected it in many different colours. It took on the hue of whatever colour was near it, like a chameleon. When you were clad in the drab, it was like a polished sandstone or soapstone, flecked with greys and browns, but when the Priestesses and the HandMaids came near it in their robes and veils, it picked up on their colours and glimmered like a rainbow. As I drew near to the feet of the Goddess, she seemed to glow with a warmth and a fire taken from my own robe. It felt humbling, that the Goddess would take on my colour for herself, and I felt a rush of attachment for the Goddess and all that she stood for. The Goddess was rounded, posed in a seated position with her legs and feet tucked under her, looking calm and peaceful. Her arms were folded in her lap, and the slight contours on her face which gave her character had been skilfully carved so that although there were no distinctive features, her face seemed to shine with a placid patience and satisfaction. Around her face was a ring of stone which caught the sunlight as it came in through the high windows of the Temple. I took some drops of cinnamon oil from the crystal bottle on the stand at the side and rubbed the oil in to her feet, following the same movements that I used when I scrubbed the step, counting the strokes to seven before changing direction. The Goddess had been a constant in my life, all of my life so far. She moderated my behaviour and guided my actions, and now I was contemplating leaving her. I felt disgusted with myself that I wanted to turn my back on all that was good in my life and set my sights on everything unknown; to willingly remove myself from the Goddess. I wept, and my tears formed round droplets on the oiled stone. I tried to rub them in, but they rolled off the statue and soon evaporated off the stone floor. I had been left a mat to lie on and after some time I went over to it, planning to only think and go over my options again, but the warm scent of cinnamon and the cosy feeling from the red robe sent me to sleep quickly.

It was not Lunaria who shook me awake that morning but Centaurea, another Priestess. She wore a light blue robe, the colour of spring skies, and a veil flecked with darker blue. I was disoriented when I woke up, wondering why my dormit was flooded with light. Centaurea waited patiently for me to stand up from the mat, blinking in the red glow of the light. The whole room seemed to reflect the light of my robe. I felt like the Goddess was sending me a powerful message; that I should stay here with her; that I could do much good for her. Imagine the strength of how I felt clad in the colours of Flammeus. Imagine what they could do... But Centaurea seemed uncomfortable in my warm red glow and I wondered if I would feel the same if I were bathed in her cool limpid blue colour. I tried to strengthen my mind and concentrate on the discovery of what may lay beyond the walls of the Temple. She led me to a small room beyond the Sanctum to wait for the Priestesses and the Maids to arrive in the Temple. I could hear rhythmic singing from the polished stone pipes of the Temple, and the muted noise of footsteps proceeding up the central Linea of the Temple. Centaurea led me out and let me walk up to the centre of the Temple, to the High Priestess Asinte.

Asinte addressed me from behind her veil. It was a strange thing that in the dealings with the Priestesses one could not see the face and the eyes. Her voice seemed to come from all around me, as she offered me the Scrolls of Choice. I tried to focus my mind on the Scrolls, but I felt hazy with the scent of cinnamon and pleasantly relaxed and sleepy. The first scroll presented to me was full of enticing pictures. Abssina had really worked hard on these pictures; there were people of all kinds, new flowers and trees, bright colours and patterns woven around the outside. The second scroll was in only a few colours, drawings of plain buildings with square patterns. I had to concentrate my mind to try to read the Scribing which seemed overly elaborate. The attractive script was, as I suspected, the script with the choice to remain in the Temple. It was very cunning, the way that they had filled that script with the things I most wanted to see when I left the Temple. I read both scripts carefully, trying not to betray with the moving of my eyes that I was reading the script. Finally, I moved my hand and selected the dull parchment, the one which chose to leave the Temple. Asinte stayed her hand.

'We pray for the guidance of the Goddess,' she said firmly

'May the Goddess be praised,' I responded mechanically, willing myself to remain with the Script of Choice. Asinte held the other script in her hand, without condemning it to the flames as she usually did. I carried the Script over to the Reader, trembling. From behind her veil the Reader looked up sharply. She looked over to Asinte, but Asinte could do nothing, trapped as she was by the ceremony. The Reader began to read.

'The Goddess does not deem Talla worthy to remain in the Temple. She must leave within the hour and may never see the inner Temple again. Henceforth, she will live in the Outer and must make her own way without the special favour of the Goddess.'

Her voice crumbled at the end, like fine sandstone trickling to the sea and she finished the words, barely able to read. There were sighs from the Priestesses and a politely disinterested silence from the Maids. I looked around me. I could see nothing except a rainbow of coloured veils facing my way. It was so hard to know what the Priestesses were thinking all the time when you could not see them and often could not hear them either. How did they speak to one another? How was it that they could all be of the same mind and yet not converse about it? Having seen their attitude to the unfortunate Bellis, I was bewildered by their apparent distress. Asinte still held the rejected scroll of choice in her hand; I could see it shaking slightly. Abssina stepped forward and gently removed the scroll from Asinte's hand.

'As the Goddess has spoken, so shall it be.' She inclined her head towards the parchment, and I imagined that she must be looking at her careful craftsmanship for the last time. It was not often that her artistry had not worked its magic on someone, and it must have hurt her to see the hours of careful thought that had gone into the work go up in flames. She placed the parchment gently on the flames. The fire crackled as it took hold and the inks she had used in the parchment turned the flame momentarily into a spectacle of different colours; blues and oranges, greens and purples. In only a few beats, there was only ash left. Asinte still seemed unable to move, and Abssina gently took her arm and led her back to the other Priestesses. She beckoned to Lunaria to take me out of the Temple. I looked around it for the last time. It was carved out of a single piece of stone, the walls smooth and unlined except by the arches which ran from each of the six corners to the centre of the roof. It had been built by Angels, so we were told, and their skill and mastery were evident. This stone building had been the centre and the security of my life until now. I had taken it for granted. The Temple had offered me a roof, and food and care of a sort where none other had. Here were my only family since my original one had left me here at the Temple as a new-born baby. Lunaria led me away, out of the Temple, her head bowed, and took me to my dormit.

'When a Maid leaves the Temple, it is customary to leave her in her dormit until the moment she leaves,' Lunaria told me. 'I will return in a short while to take you to the gates to the Outer.' She lifted up her head, 'Priestess Asinte was certain that the Goddess had chosen you for some special task; I heard her talking of it in her room. No doubt the Goddess will unfold your life as it should, Talla.' I thought I caught in her consoling words a momentary wistfulness for my position, but it was quickly replaced by Lunaria's by now customary demure and humble stance and she left my dormit.

Sitting on the mat, I frantically tried to come to terms with what I had done, and what I could do in the Outer. I had imagined that one of the Priestesses would come to me and talk me through what I should do on the Outer, when I left the Temple, but I was left alone. I had no possessions to take with me except for the parchments and the charcoal sticks which I had previously concealed under the stone in my dormit, so I carefully rolled up the parchments around the charcoal sticks and put them into the underpocket of my drabcoat. The red robe I removed reluctantly. It was warm and well woven, and it held the scent of the cinnamon which had always felt to be mine. I felt lessened in spirit as I folded it carefully and laid it on the wooden stool. My drabcoat, comprised as it was of strips of grey and brown cloth patchworked together, felt flimsy and uncertain. I smoothed my hair with the metal comb which hung, as did all objects in the dormit, from a leather strap attached to a peg in the wall. From an early age we had been told that everything belonged to the Goddess, and this was a way of reminding us that it did not belong to us. I ran my hand over the stone, smooth as an egg, and every bit as full of mysterious life. I strained to hear the Goddess's guidance in my mind but the dormit and my mind were both silent. Lunaria returned and checked the robe on my stool. She counted the items in the room; the comb, the toothtwig, the clay cup, the sleeping mat, the chair and the soapball and then gestured towards the door soundlessly. We walked out of the Temple into the courtyard, past the turning to the physic garden. I could see the Maids, with whom I had spoken only yesterday, watching me leave, and I felt the eyes of the Priestesses under their veils. Lunaria led me to the gate. I felt such a feeling of panic and excitement. I did not know who I would see, or how they would treat me. I did not know how or where I would live or eat. As we neared the gate, Lunaria pulled me to one side.

Lunaria looked around us quickly, turning her head since she could not see otherwise due to her veil, and then pressed a small wrapped parcel into my hands. 'This is for you; the Goddess came to me in a dream the night before your Ceremony of Choice and told me to give this to you, for it is yours and goes with you into the Outer.' Her voice faltered a little, as if she might be doubting the Goddess. I doubted the Goddess visited anyone in their dreams, perhaps because she had never visited me in mine, but I took the small package in my hand and thanked her. Lunaria opened the gate to the Outer and gestured to me and then pushed me slightly through the gate, whispering, 'Go with the Goddess, Talla.'

'Bless her name,' I responded dutifully, but the gate was already shut. I looked around me, curious to see this Outer world. The high wall which surrounded the Temple stretched along the way, with only a break for the entrance to the Temple which was reserved for the Outer, and which was currently shut. There was a deep red sandstone boulder some way along the dust track, and I walked over to it and sat down on it to think. I realised that I was still holding the small package that Lunaria had given me. It was wrapped in a scrap of parchment, and I thought to myself that I could use that parchment to scribe on. When I had unwrapped the parchment and found the enclosure, I was bewildered, for it was the golden flower pin. I held it in the palm of my hand and turned it to the sun. It was fashioned of gold filigree, as I have said before. It was very fragile, and the pin on the back was worn and bent slightly out of shape. The central stone was the same colour as the robe which I had worn only hours ago, and seemed to be both translucent and opaque, if such a thing is possible. I only knew that this was the only thing that my mother had touched that I too could touch, and that I would keep it by me to remind me of that link. After I had admired it, and tried to deduce the flower, which was not one known to me from the physic garden, I carefully pinned it to the inside of my drabcoat underpocket and rolled the parchment around my other parchments and replaced them in my underpocket too.

CHAPTER 2

The Temple appeared to be situated some way from anywhere else where people lived, and was set back from the track, with no obvious indication of which way to turn. I stood at the track and looked first to the east. Far in the distance, I could see that the land rose up suddenly from the plain. These raised areas were a dark purplish colour, and small clouds hung in the air close to them. The track to the west seemed to remain flat, heading straight on into the distance where I thought I could discern some trees, though no evidence of habitation. I was intrigued by the raised land, never having been outside the Temple, but I decided to head to the trees in the west. They might be fruit trees or would at least provide shelter from the sun.

Everything that I saw seemed new to me. The Temple was enclosed by walls and had its own wells and gardens to grow food for the Maids and Priestesses. Cloths and threads were traded from the visiting merchants using offerings given to the Goddess by the Outer peoples or in trade for goods made in the Temple, like the fine stitchings. Remembering the visits of the Outer traders, I comforted myself with the thought that there must be human dwellings within walking distance of the Temple, at least, and continued to walk along the way. The path was worn out of the sandstone and coated with a fine reddish dust. By the side of the road grew long grasses and wildflowers and small thorny bushes, whose white thorns could be seen easily, and which could also be seen scattered on the ground where they had fallen after being shed by the plant. There was a humming sound of insects in the grass and the chirrup of birds. I was used to being alone with my thoughts from my time at the Temple and did not resent the quietude but embraced it as a conversation with the Goddess. I picked up one of the old thorns from the path and turned it in my fingers. It had split slightly and was a little wider than a finger, coming to a point at the end. It struck me that it was just the right size to protect my charcoal pieces so, I took them out and carefully pushed them through the slit in the side of the big thorn. They were less fragile now, and in fact the thorn acted as a sort of charcoal holder, which meant I had more control over the charcoal, without having to press down too far. Pleased with my discovery, I walked on for some time. I walked perhaps two or three miles before I reached the trees which I had seen from near the Temple. They were kosso trees, their red blooms hanging downwards, and under them was a small group of travellers; people from the Outer.

It was only then that I realised how little I knew about looking after myself amongst strangers. Until now, I had always had other people around me to make sure I did what was right; spoke to the right people in the right way, did tasks in the right way, thought the right thoughts and said the right things. The Temple had guided me for my whole life and shaped me into who I was and now I was going to have to do all those things for myself. As I approached the group, I became more and more conscious of my drabcoat and of how different it appeared to their clothing. Within the Temple I had been as anonymous as any other Maid in a drabcoat but here the very thing which had brought me that comfortable anonymity made me stand out. There were two women and a man, along with a small child who was earnestly sorting out pebbles under the tree, singing to herself. They were in robes woven from cream coloured cloth, embroidered at the necks and cuffs with many colours. They seemed almost polished in appearance and looked at me curiously as I approached the trees where they were resting from the sun.

'I greet you,' I said tentatively.

'I greet you,' they responded, looking at me with more open curiosity. I could feel the eyes of the women passing over my patchworked drabcoat.

'Sit, please,' said the man, gesturing to the woven mat they had spread under the tree. I sat down, folding my knees underneath me, and spreading my drabcoat decorously around me, as I had been taught, shielding my feet. No one spoke. The child drifted away from its pebbles and came to stare at me, and then squatted by me next to the edge of the mat. She took a stick from a pile by the side of the mat and began to draw idle patterns in the dust. I watched her trailing the stick through the fine dust and she caught my eye. Silently she offered me a stick and I bent to join her at her pastime. She drew curled patterns and crosses and I drew flowers and trees. She laughed and clapped when I drew a picture of a bird.

Her mother smiled at me, showing a mouth of cracked but shining teeth, and said, 'You should stitch those birds onto cloth for me; I could sell them at the markets when we travel.'

'I cannot stitch very well,' I stammered. 'I was not taught the stitches, I was taught to clean, instead.' They all laughed.

'For sure,' commented the older woman, 'you cannot sell cleaning at the market; there's no trade in that!'

I thought about it. I had not realised until now just how useless my skills were in the Outer. I had been taken out of any of the valuable classes; the stitching and the physic, the farming and the provisioning, and kept to the cleaning. At the time, I had felt it was the best thing, that it was an offering to the Goddess too, just as even a gift as the others, but now I realised, that here, in the Outer, it was not. I needed to think of ways in which I could serve or offer my skills to the people of the Outer, not to the Goddess. Although the Goddess had indeed cared for me and looked after my basic needs whilst I had been in the Temple, I could not help feeling ill-equipped for life on the Outer. Then I remembered that, if the Priestesses had had their way, I would never have left the Temple, and would never have known this. What a curious thought; that there might have been an existence whereby I might still be in the Temple, scrubbing steps and flagstones, anointing the Goddess with oils and being measured and guided by the cadence of the days. The older woman interrupted my thoughts.

'We are going to eat; will you join us?' I was aware then, how hungry I was, and that I had not eaten all day. These travellers were not wealthy, and yet they were offering to share their food with me. The man sensed my discomfort and reassured me that they expected nothing of me. 'Help my mother to build the fire, and to stir the pot and we will welcome you,' he said. I got up from the mat and began to lay the twigs and sticks that had already been gathered into a neat pyramid.

'I am Talla,' I ventured to the old woman, 'I was at the Temple before.'

'Aye,' she said, 'we can see that. Throw you out, did they? Ah well, there's many not deemed good enough for the Goddess who might yet find themselves good enough for something, I suppose. They call me Merula.' She straightened up and her eyes tightened with her cracking back. 'He,' pointing to the man, 'is Lashim, his wife is Sutera, and the little one is Gesarit.' She poked in the emberjar with a strikestick and blew through the cut holes in the side. Once it was flaming well, she held the kindling to it and waited for it to catch light. We used emberjars at the Temple, and whilst they took careful tending, they were worth it. They were dependable and easy to use to make a fire for travellers and those without easy access to other fires. You could carry the life of the fire in a small jar, as a glowing ember and bring it to life. The emberjar kept it warm and the holes in the side fed the ember with air. Merula sat down for some minutes by the fire as I tended to it by adding kindling and laying the sticks until it took a firm hold.

Sutera was sitting on the edge of the mat, working on stitchery. She had an unrolled leather pouch beside her where she kept her threads and needles. She was sewing an ornate pattern of crosses and curled leaves, which encircled the neckline of a heavy cream coloured tunic. I wondered how she kept her work so clean. All around us was fine red dust, and yet the work seemed pristine.

'Would you like to see?' She caught me looking at her work, and after checking the fire and making sure the pot of water was set to boil, I moved over and examined the work. It was fine work, not as fine as Lunaria's, and of a different style, but I saw from the clothes that Sutera herself wore that this would be in demand in the marketplace. I felt self-conscious of my drabcoat, and looked down, ashamed. Sutera smiled at me.

'Why not try to stitch yourself, Talla? I could sell your work at the market if you could sew as well as you draw.'

I smiled involuntarily at the compliment. 'Praise the Goddess,' I muttered under my breath. 'Praise her name,' responded Sutera, mechanically. In the Temple we were taught to praise the Goddess for our smiles, for they came from her. However, I knew that I could not sew. Priestess Atammi had been sure to tell me how useless my efforts were in my few weeks in stitchery classes before I had elected to cleaning as my speciality.

I explained my lack of prowess to Sutera who laughed but did not praise the Goddess for it.

'Anyone can learn to sew,' she said. 'All you need is fingers and patience, and an eye for pattern, which you must have or else you would not be able to draw in the dust as you do. Artistry, on the other hand; that is a gift. If I could make designs and patterns like yours and sew them, I could make more trades at the market.'

An idea came into my mind; I had watched the Scribers copying passages to parchments before, and I wondered if it would be possible to do the same thing for cloth. I was about to explain this to Sutera when Merula called us to the food.

'I am sorry I did not stir the pot, Merula,' I said awkwardly.

She looked at me, not unkindly, and said, 'Aye well, the Temple seems to teach one skill well and not the rest.'

I was unsure what to think or to say. Was she complimenting me on my one skill, or denigrating my lack of skill in all other fields? I was so accustomed to every part of my life being measured and accounted for, that I was not used to having to determine my own actions to any great degree. Lashim had set me a simple task in exchange for my dinner; to build and tend the fire, and to stir the pot of food, and I had not done this small task because I was thinking about Sutera's embroidery. I did not know if I was still welcome to share the food and waited for them all to take theirs. I had no experience of this way of eating together. At the Temple, we sat together as Maids and were each given a clay bowl and a spoon for our food. The food was served by the provisioning Maids, whose bowls always seemed to contain a little more food of a little higher quality than the rest of us. We ate in silence and praised the Goddess at the end.

'Come, come,' said Merula. 'You will soon learn what to do in this life here in Oramia, outside the walls of the Temple. Take some food and eat it. Talk with us.'

I took the flatbread I was offered and scooped some stew from the pot. It was quite spicy, with vegetables and roots mixed with some dried goat meat. I had not tasted this food before, but I liked the flavours; they were strong and filled my mouth with interest. Gesarit sat and stirred her stew with a finger dubiously. She crept a little closer to me, eyeing my drabcoat.

'What's your dress made of?' she asked, rubbing her grubby hands over the stitched patchwork.

'It's made from scraps,' I answered. 'Old pieces of cloth that nobody else wants or can use. You can put them together and make them into something useful, you see.'

Gesarit looked doubtful. She herself was wearing a simple cream shift, but even this, a child's dress was carefully ornamented at the neck and the sleeves. Unlike her mother and her grandmother, her dress was sleeveless and shorter, and she did not have the shawl around her shoulders. We didn't see many children at the Temple aside from the Maids, of course, for the small children and babies lived in their own large houses with the older Priestesses who cared for them and taught them as they grew. They did not come with the merchants, who were usually travelling men, who had made a life of travelling from one settlement to another, trading and exchanging goods. Children were forbidden from the Temple unless they were Maids and did not attend the services with their parents until they were able to behave appropriately in the presence of the Goddess. I did not know how to converse with them very easily.

'I like your dress,' I told her, and her eyes brightened.

'My mama made it for me,' she said proudly, 'and she stitched it too. What's your favourite colour?'

I did not know how to answer. I had lived my life, knowing that my day was Flammeus and my colour was red, and my scent was the scent of cinnamon bark. Could you choose a colour for yourself? Did not the Goddess choose for you by virtue of the day on which you were born?

'I am not sure,' I answered finally, 'My own colour is red, but the Goddess chooses all to their colour.' Gesarit looked puzzled.

'But I have lots of colours on my dress, and I like them all,' she said. 'Some days I like blue, the colour of the sky, and some days I like yellow the colour of sunshine and some days I like pink, the colour of those flowers.' I looked over to where she was pointing and saw some flowers blooming through the dusty scrub. It was a colour that was not red and yet was not orange either. It was like a faded red, bleached by the sun, with perhaps some purple added in. I had never seen this colour before, and I knew it was not one of the colours of the Goddess. Only dark and light were known as colours beyond the seven of the Goddess. One was like the darkest night, and the other like the bright light of day; like charcoal and parchment they were, and they stood for right and wrong in the Temple. Balanced, they held the world, and the Priestesses were careful to evenly use the colours of dark and light.

'It is a different colour,' I answered the child. 'I do not know it.' Gesarit looked at me wide eyed. 'How can you not know pink?'

I was tired of the child's questions. Everything she said was a question, and one to which I did not have an answer. In the Temple, questions were used as a simple way of exchanging information for organising things.

'Do you have the parchments?', 'Have you scrubbed the steps?', 'Do you need a new soapball?' These were familiar questions to me, and easy to answer, simply. I did not like these other questions to which there was not a given answer. How could I know if I was right or wrong? I remained silent and ignored the child who continued to gape at me. I felt irritated and hoped the Goddess would calm me. At the Temple, we learned to control our feelings, and to subdue them. The Goddess provided everything for us, and for everything there was a reason, which could be explained. Slight irritations were soothed by oiling the Goddess, and spending time with the day's scent. There was nowhere for me to go here, to escape these people who had, after all, shared their food and their time with me. I stood up from the mat and began to walk over to the bushes a short distance away. I could feel their eyes on me as I walked towards the bushes, and hoped they would leave me be, and assume that I was going to relieve myself. In my efforts to appear calm and unhurried, I failed to look where I was going and tripped over a stone which lay by the side of the path. As I fell, I realised that I had not tied my underpocket back up from before the meal, when I had been thinking of showing Sutera my idea for the patterns. The thorn and parchments flew out in front of me, as did the parchment wrapped brooch. Sutera and Merula came to help me up, and Lashim followed them, waiting for me to pull down the skirt of my drabcoat which had rucked up as I fell. Gesarit brought me the parchment and the thorn, looking at me curiously as she gave them back to me.

'And what is this?' Lashim asked, picking up the parchment wrapped brooch. I scrabbled for it, but he held it out of my reach.

'Strange thing,' he commented, turning aside to his mother Merula. 'I thought possessions were forbidden to the Drabs when they got rid of them out of the Temple.'

'They are only scraps of parchment,' I stammered, holding out my hand. 'They belonged to nobody.'

'Give them to her,' said Sutera, pityingly. 'It is only bits of parchment and an old thorn. She might be half crazed coming out of the Temple; that might be why they pushed her out.'

'Crazed enough to have a treasure like this?' asked her husband, unrolling the brooch carefully. Then he saw the full design of the brooch and pushed it back in to my hands. The women too stepped away from me as if I were a venomous snake.

Merula looked at me, angry now. 'You must leave now! Where did you get this?'

I didn't understand; I had been talking and eating with these people only minutes before, and now they wanted to rid themselves of me. I had thought that maybe they would want me to give them the brooch, or to steal it from me, but instead, they seemed to find it repellent. I was about to say that it was mine, that it had been left to me by my mother, but something stayed my words and I spoke calmly and quietly. Long years of practicing for the Goddess meant that I was able to do this, even though my mind was racing.

'I am to take it somewhere,' I said. 'I do not know where to go. Can you help me?' Sutera moved to Gesarit and beckoned to the child to begin packing up their things. Lashim frowned at me. 'I know nobody who would own such a thing,' he said. 'What do you take me for, one of them?' and he turned and went to his family. I did not know who he was referring to, nor why I should consider him to be one of them.

Merula sighed and placed her hand upon my arm. 'We cannot help you, anymore, Talla. You will have to find where you must take it, but you must do it alone.

There is no one in Oramia who will help you once they have seen that brooch. Take my words to heart, and do not show this thing to anyone else.' She turned to go too. I stood still, feeling as I had when I left the Temple only a few short hours ago. I was alone and bewildered and knew not where to turn.

CHAPTER 3

I walked away slowly from the small group of travellers I had met earlier, without looking back at them. I was beginning to understand Bellis's distress at the thought of living in this Outer world. I felt as though the world was an ever-shifting place, here in the Outer. In the Temple we all trusted each other, and we all did as we were told, without question. We could depend on each other to do our jobs, whereas here, in the Outer, the only one person it appeared you could depend upon was yourself. I walked back along the road to the Temple, away from the group and the direction in which they were heading. Lost in my thoughts, I barely noticed as I walked back past the Temple and onwards to the east towards the high dark mountains I had seen earlier. After some time, I felt weary and paused for a rest near an outcrop of rocks. I took out the brooch my mother had apparently left me and looked at it thoughtfully. It told me nothing new. I wondered what it meant, that it would cause such effect on ordinary people. It had no effect on me; it seemed to me to be merely an interwoven representation of a many petalled flower, with a red stone at its heart. From the wear on it, I guessed it carried some age, and may have been a family treasure which my mother had wanted me to have. I started to ponder on why my mother might have given me up to be a Temple Maid. She may have been young and poor, with few options – but in that case where did she come by this pin? Perhaps my father gave it to her as a promise and never came back to bestow that promise. Perhaps my mother came from some noble family and was promised in marriage to some other family of governance. And why had the Goddess appeared to Lunaria in a dream and urged her to give the brooch to me as I left? It had not brought me any luck so far, in fact quite the contrary. I resolved to try to find out more information about the flower, without displaying the brooch to anyone else, in the hope of finding out more. I had told Merula and the others that I was looking for someone just on a whim, and, until now, I had not thought that I was. I had no real plan for my time in the Outer, only that I knew I wanted to go out into the wider world, and to find out more about it and the people that lived in it. Well I had certainly found out something about them, I thought grimly. I had found that they were swayed by the sign on a brooch, that they could appear to be friendly and yet not be, that they could fill you with trust and later go back on it. I thought how close I had been to telling Sutera my plan for the patterns to stitch and resolved to think more carefully before I divulged my ideas to someone who appeared to be friendly to me. I wondered why it had not occurred to me that all people could be like this. After all, I had found out for myself that the Priestesses of the Temple were duplicitous too.

Night was falling quickly now, and I realised that I would not be sleeping in shelter tonight. Far in the distance I could see the lights of fires and dwellings, but it was too far to reach before sunsdown, and besides I was weary and not sure that I could manage more tricky encounters with the unknown people of the Outer. I wondered if there were wild animals around here which might find me but could do little to stop them from finding me if there were. It was a warm evening and I would not be cold tonight. I headed for an outcrop of rocks clear of the trees and settled myself leaning on one which faced in to the sunsdown. I sighed as I stretched out my tired legs and feet in front of me. There was a faint breeze stirring the dried seed heads on top of the grass and they swayed, rustling slightly. In the nearby clump of trees, the yellow weaver birds squabbled with one another, each laying claim to their own woven home, and keeping out intruders.

As I sat there, resting, I played idly with some pebbles lying at the base of the rock. I amused myself by building them into towers and walls and making patterns with them. Most of them were rough and dull but there were a couple which were rounder and smoother than the rest. As the sundown continued, I thought of the Temple where all would be assembled. Asinte would be leading the prayers to the Goddess, Lunaria would be sitting with the Priestesses now, and some other Maid would be sitting where I used to sit. I stroked the smooth pebbles, unconsciously using the Seven Step pattern we used to anoint the Goddess with oil. We did not spend much time talking idly in the Temple, and I had been irritated by Sutera and her family, earlier, but I felt suddenly very alone. There would be nobody in the world who would notice if I were gone. I knew I needed to find companions, but I did not know how to understand the rules of who to approach and how.

The dark had come up and the stars began to show up against the blackness. I looked for the familiar constellations of the Goddess's world; the ring of Lilavis directly overhead, Ignis, the fiery star of Flammeus, hung low in the sky and shining brightly just beyond, was the triangular constellation of Flavus. Over in the east were the glittering pair of stars of Aureus. I remembered learning the shapes of the groups of stars in the Second Age of Childhood as we learned to count, for each constellation had a different number of stars in it. The six stars of Indicus made the shape of a fish and the four stars of Viridis made a tree, while the stars in

Azureus made the pattern of waves. I was comforted by these constant familiars and slept.

I woke with the dawn and was immediately aware that I was very thirsty, and that I needed to get to the dwellings I had seen or at least find some water quickly. I wished I had a gourd in a net, like the one which Merula had, in which I could have carried water, or berries. I began to walk, stopping only to pick some greener grass to chew and suck to slake my dry mouth. The little green sunbirds were singing in the thorn bushes, and, although I was thirsty and hungry, I felt uplifted by their song, and it seemed no time at all before I came across a small settlement and tentatively approached the first of the dwellings.

It was made of a combination of reeds and smooth reddish mud which had been plastered on to a tall wooden frame of a dome. It reminded me of an ants' nest. There was a small window and a hole in the roof through which I could see smoke. All the buildings at the Temple were built of stone. You might have thought they were built of blocks of quarried stone, but there was not a seam anywhere in all the buildings. The whole Temple was built from one big block of stone. It seemed as if it was a part of the earth itself because it had been carved out of huge rocks. But this dwelling seemed so insecure by the side of the Temple buildings. What happened when it rained, I wondered? How did clay withstand heavy rainstorms, or was it treated with a kind of gum from a tree, to make it more waterproof? My curiosity was raised, and I ventured closer to the building to try to work out how sturdy it actually was. I had just raised my hand to touch the wall of the house, when a deep voice called out to me.

'Hey you! What are you doing to my dwelling?'

Startled, I turned around hastily and saw a man heading towards me with a large stick which had been roughly carved into a sort of a pike. He glared at me and I dropped my hand quickly away from the building and dropped my eyes respectfully to him, worried that he might be just as antagonistic towards me as the group I had met the night before.

'I meant no harm, brother.' I answered. 'I was admiring your home and trying to work out how it was made. It is very fine.' The man's face softened at the compliment, and he relaxed the arm holding the pike. 'Aye well, it takes many a year of practice to get that kind of smooth finish on your house. The smoother it is, the more the rain just runs off it!' His eyes dropped to my drabcoat. 'You'd know nothing about that though, would you, sister? I see plenty of your sort up and down this road as they leave the Temple. Not many get very far. They all get picked up by the OutRiders. Anyway, come in, I could do with some company for an hour or two. I sometimes get bored with the folks round here.' He pushed aside a door made of lashed wooden poles and beckoned me in. I followed him through to his room. It was dimly lit, but adequate, with a grass mat on the floor and gourds and herb baskets hanging on the walls, much like our combs and soapballs in the Temple. I was suddenly reminded how thirsty I was.

'May I drink some water, brother?' I asked. 'I have not drunk anything since yesterday and my mouth is parched.'

'Of course, sister,' he replied, and hastened to retrieve an earthenware beaker. He dipped it into his water jar and offered it to me. The water was cool and dark to taste. It tasted of the clay of the pot and the deep underground whence it had come. I drank it steadily and finished the whole cup. I had been ready for it, and I felt more awake and more alive for having had it.

'My thanks,' I said, as I offered him back the beaker. 'Your courtesy and kindness are most welcome.' We sat in silence for some minutes. I was not used to filling my time with idle chit-chat and he seemed content not to speak. I had seen other dwellings loosely scattered around his own, so I was aware that I was in a small community of some sort. I wasn't sure whether everyone grew their own crops, as we did in the Temple, or if they specialised in growing different crops and traded them. Just like in the Temple, perhaps everyone had their role to play. I looked at the man who had welcomed me into his home. It was my first real encounter with a man. He was of middle age, still muscular and strong from physical work, but slightly softened by the years. His tunic was a dirty cream colour and simply ornamented with blue crosses around the neck, cuffs and hem. His hair was close cropped, and you could see his scalp through it. He had a well-trimmed beard, speckled with grey, and lines around his eyes. He caught me appraising him and chuckled.

'Aye there's not much to my appearance at the moment, sister. I am wearing my old working robe. I am waiting until I find someone to make me a new design, something that makes me stand out.' He looked wistful. 'My wife, Velosia, was a good seamstress and had an eye for pattern. She died of the ague a year's passing since.'

'May the Goddess be blessed,' I responded, automatically. In the Temple, this was how we greeted the news of someone's passing. The Goddess was blessed for all life and all death. Like the charcoal to the parchment she balanced life with death. The Goddess was Mother to us all, and when she called us to her, we rejoiced in our return.

He looked at me blankly. 'Why should I bless the Goddess for taking away my wife, sister, can you tell me that? What use does the Goddess have for her? The Goddess is certainly no use to me. She takes from me and gives me nothing!'

I did not know what to reply. I seemed to have caused this man distress just by saying something which in the Temple had always brought comfort. I hoped that he would not hold this against me now and cast about for something different to say to him to move his mind away from what I had just said.

'What patterns did your blessed wife like to make?' I asked, hoping that this would redirect the conversation in a happier direction.

'Ahh, she was a marvel; trees and flowers, the shapes of rocks and grasses, and even animals. I used to sell her work in the market for a good amount,' Benakiell replied.

'Do you have the robe?' I asked, making a plan which might help me. 'I could show you patterns too, if you would like me to.'

'Do you have the skill, sister? And what is your name, anyway?'

'I am Talla,' I replied. 'I have a skill at making patterns and pictures, although I fear I have no skill as a seamstress. You will have to find a good seamstress to sew the pattern for you.'

'What did you do at the Temple?' he asked, looking interested.

'I did nothing, brother,' I answered slowly, not wanting to give anything away. 'The Goddess chose.'

'Did she indeed?' He raised his eyebrows. 'Well, I am Benakiell Dinashim. Draw your pattern, if you will. I will leave you the robe, for I must go and help my neighbour with his crop. If I like the pattern, you can stay here for the night and I will feed you.' He went over to a wooden peg set in the clay wall and brought down a simple cream robe, unadorned, and gave it to me and then left through the door. He was a man of few words, this Benakiell, but it did not worry me. In the Temple, we did not speak for no reason. Rather, we kept our counsel. It was perhaps this lack of talking that had led my mind to wander along its questioning path and led me to the Outer where I now found myself.

After I was sure that he had gone, I withdrew the parchment and the thorn and charcoal from my underpocket and began upon my plan. I first took a square of parchment from my small supply and drew on it a pattern of entwined leaves. I had limited supplies of parchment and I could not easily rub off the charcoal, so I had to work out a way of transferring the pattern to the fabric without wasting my parchment. I had observed the Scribers at the Temple on several occasions and I had seen them use a copying method using a needle and a pouncet box. I didn't have either a needle or a pouncet box, but I thought I could use the charcoal and the thorn in the same way. After I had made the pattern, I used the sharp end of the thorn to prick many small holes in the patterns I had drawn. I carefully placed the parchment onto the cloth of the robe, around the neck and took a small amount of charcoal and crushed it to a fine powder. I rubbed this gently over the holes in the patterns, and it transferred the picture through the holes to the fabric beneath. All I had to do then was move the patterned parchment round so it joined on to the other side of the patterns and continue transferring the pattern. It meant that I had only had to draw the pattern once and yet I could easily transfer it onto the fabric ready to be sewn.

By the time Benakiell returned, I had finished transferring the pattern to the robe and had packed my tools away carefully. It was not that I knew I could not trust him exactly, but I had already found out what it was like to be rejected by the people of the Outer and I was wary of disclosing too much. He entered the dwelling, accompanied by a small, plump woman. She wore a robe embellished with sarcelly crosses at the neck and interlinked triangles at the hem, which strained across her roundness, but she also wore a dazzling shawl wrapped around her shoulders and neck. I was struck by its complexity, by the rich colours, and, once again, I realised that there were many, many more colours and patterns in the world than I had been given access to. In the Temple we were taught of the purity of the seven colours. The Goddess provided the colours in the rainbows, and no other colours were mentioned or available to us. Even the plants we grew were of specific colours. Beans had red flowers, pumpkins had yellow flowers, garlic had purple flowers. It seemed as if everything we lived had been controlled. It is hard to suddenly find out that things exist which you never even spoke about because you did not have the words to use for them.

'This is Gladia Nariana,' said Benakiell. 'She is the seamstress amongst us. That netela that she wears was made by my Velosia. She will look at your work and tell you if she thinks she can stitch it for me.'

I examined the netela or shawl that Gladia was wearing. The embroidery was small and finely worked, and the design was intricate. Velosia had interwoven leaves and flowers in a pleasing pattern which looked tangled, but my eye quickly discerned that she had used the branching patterns to make the pattern more and more complex, simply by dividing and redividing the pattern. In some of the spaces she had stitched sunbirds, which were based on the same basic pattern but were sewn in different colours and some had longer beaks or longer tails, and some had crests of feathers on their heads.

'It is fine work, brother,' I remarked. I knew his name, but I still felt it right to maintain some distance from him by using the respectful but rather wide-ranging title I had chosen for him. I had had no real opportunities for meeting with men at the Temple, and I still found them strange creatures.

'Aye, that it is.' His eyes softened, and I knew he was thinking of his wife as he traced a leaf on the shawl with his thumb, abstractedly.

Gladia looked at me squarely, her eyes taking in every detail. She skimmed over my drabcoat quickly, as if she had seen too many before, or perhaps disdained it, and returned her eyes to my face which she examined closely.

'I hear from Benakiell that you have a gift for patterning? He wanted me to come along and cast my eye over your work and see if I could stitch it. If I can, I will be grateful to try and get him wearing something more interesting than the things that I can sew. I have no hand for artistry. It's the hand of a worker not a dreamer.' She spoke briskly, and almost proudly, as if it were a bad thing to be skilled at fanciful artistry that gave pleasure. I showed her the pattern I had traced around the neckline of Benakiell's robe. He also bent over it and examined the fine lines I had traced on it carefully. It was not as complex as the one his wife had made, but it was regular and even and pleasing to the eye, and I could tell that they were both impressed by my skill. I felt warm inside, as I had done when I was silent with the Goddess on the day of Flammeus, with the scent of cinnamon around me.

'Well, you will look smart in this outfit,' remarked Gladia to Benakiell eventually and turned to me with a little more respect. 'I can stitch this pattern, for you have drawn it very clearly and so evenly!' She appraised me again with that clear, open look. 'If you wish, I can set some more work your way, and we can trade.'

I was taken aback because I didn't know if this was what I wanted. Did I want to go into partnership with anyone? Would Gladia try to steal my patterning idea?

Benakiell turned to me and said, 'Rest easy, sister Talla, Gladia will not do wrong by you. There are many that would, but we are of the old ways and we have no quarrel with you. I thank you for the gift of the pattern, and, as I said, you may stay the night, and I will feed you well for it. I would also like to give you these.' He reached up to one of the many wooden pegs set in the walls of the dwelling and brought down a large gourd in a bark mesh, and a small leather pouch or bag. 'It's little enough that I have to share with you that you might find helpful, but you can carry water in the gourd, and you can store your things in the bag.'

I realised that I had made my first transaction, just as the Priestesses made at the Temple. I had shown a skill, which I did not even realise I had, and had been rewarded for it appropriately. I thanked Benakiell, who waved it off. I examined the gourd carefully. When I was at the Temple, I had taken these water carriers and the large earthenware storage jars for water, which were kept in the cellar where it was cool, for granted. Now, I was more interested in them and saw how cunning an idea they were. They carried a large quantity of water and yet had only a small neck and opening at the top which meant that even if they rolled over, only a little would spill out. Because they were wider at the bottom than the top, they naturally sat in the best position to preserve the water inside them, and the bark mesh around it meant that it could be easily tied to a belt or a string for carrying. You could stuff the top with leaves or bark to make a stopper. The leather pouch was well cured and supple, functional and basic, but to one like me, who had never had anything to call her own, it was something to be treasured.

Gladia left the dwelling promising to return the next morning to see if I had decided whether I wanted to work with her for a while on the patterning. Benakiell began to make the evening repast, and, although I offered to help, he seemed content to do things in his own way, so I wandered outside his home to take stock of where I was. I had now been away from the Temple for over a day, and, although I still felt ill equipped to deal with a lot of the obstacles in my way, I felt calmer and happier to have achieved something in my short time away. I looked out towards the other dwellings. There were around a dozen of them, each made in the distinctive beehive shape that I had observed when I first arrived. Each dwelling area had a small garden next to it where crops were grown and tended, and some of the homes also had a small fenced area where they kept livestock, mostly brown, scrawny goats or small flocks of chickens. There was no sort of centre to the settlement, and no community buildings. I walked over to the small garden by the side of Benakiell's house, my feet making quick puffs of dust as they landed on the earth. I had not learned very well when I had been in the physic and provisioning classes and had forgotten what some of the plants were named. I could see a stand of some sort of grain, and some sprawling vines with yellow flowers, like a pumpkin. There were a couple of trees, one a pomegranate and the other one may have been a Paradox tree. There was a large clay holding jar to one side, and I raised the lid to look inside, finding, as I expected, it full of water. I drew out a small bucketful and washed my hands and face and feet, enjoying the feel of the water on my skin. In the Temple, we bathed daily, in stone rooms where there were two large stone vats of water, one of which had a fire lit under it which kept the water inside it warm. You took your soapball with you and your drabcoat. As you arrived at the bath house, you picked up another drabcoat in the right size, and took it with you. You then entered the bath house and washed yourself and your drabcoat, thumping it against the rough rocks set at the side of the room, until all the dirt had gone. We used the soapball on both ourselves and on the drabcoats, it was unscented- we used no scent on ourselves so that the scent of the Goddess's day could permeate around us and remind us of our days and colours. I realised that some soap would be a useful item to acquire if I decided to stay here for a while.

'Come and eat, sister Talla,' called Benakiell, and I turned for the dwelling, feeling hungry again. The dwelling smelled of hot spicy stew, and I could see that Benakiell had prepared a good meal for us. A large flatbread was laid on a big circular tray, and a steaming mass of spicy stew had been ladled onto the middle of it. A clay bowl and a jug of water waited next to the meal, to wash our hands.

After we had washed our hands, I closed my eyes to thank the Goddess for the food but was aware that Benakiell had already started on his eating without pausing to thank the Goddess. When I had silently murmured the prayer of Ashkana's Grace, I opened my eyes and found him looking at me, with what seemed almost like pity in his eyes. I didn't yet feel that I could ask him about this, so I said nothing at all and silently tore off a section of the flatbread and scooped up some of the stew that had been piled up in the middle of it. The stew was very good, tastier than the one that Merula had made, but also spicier. There were chunks of goat meat in it, but also chickpeas and onions and many different subtle spicy flavours which I did not recognise. The food at the Temple was good and wholesome, but it was made as fuel for the Maids and Priestesses, not to fulfil any kind of sensuous desire, and we ate it as such. Some of the stews at the Temple were tastier than others, usually depending on which Provisioners had been called upon to do the cooking.

FLAMMEUS

'This food is very good,' I said, reaching for another section of the flatbread. 'The flavours are very pleasing to eat.'

Benakiell looked amused. 'They can't feed you very good food at that Temple, if you call this very good! It's just a simple stew, but Gladia taught me how to make it after Velosia was taken from me, and I have made the same one ever since! If you stay here long, you will soon tire of it.' I wasn't sure that I would. In the Temple I had not even been aware whether I was tired or bored of the food and had eaten it and thanked the Goddess for it habitually, so I felt that it might take me some time to tire of this interesting flavour. We continued to eat, mostly in silence. It seemed we were both people who did not need to speak over much, and we were both happy to hear the silence. As we neared the end of the peripheral flatbread and the stew, we arrived at the afterbread. The afterbread was often one of the best parts of a meal, for once the stew had been scooped up with the flatbread from around the outside of it, the central section of flatbread was left, which had soaked through with the flavours of the juices of the stew. At the Temple, the very young and the very old were usually given the afterbread, as it was soft and easy to chew and digest, yet tasty and full of goodness. Here, however, there were no old or young, and he and I enjoyed it. After the meal was over and we had washed our hands again, I stood and offered

'Let me wash the platter, it is the least I can do for such a handsome meal'.

Benakiell laughed. 'Be very careful, sister Talla, I will get accustomed to you being here if you offer to wash up my platter after every meal!' but he acquiesced and sat out in the evening air whilst I took the platter to the water vat I had found earlier and scrubbed it clean with a little sand that had been set aside in a pot for that purpose. One of the things I had pondered, as a Maid in the Temple, accustomed as I was to scrubbing and cleaning, was how we could use sand to scrub a plate clean, and indeed eat off earth-clay – and yet see the earth as dirty. I enjoyed cleaning the platter, and the cookpot. In the Temple, cleaning was how I found my worth, and so it felt good to be able to work again in a proven way. The patterning was more unpredictable, and I felt more nervous about it, but I had been cleaning well since the Second Age of Childhood, and I could do it whilst I was thinking. I knew that there were those who considered cleaning to be a lowly calling, but for me, it allowed me to think of other things and let my mind ask questions and understand things. When I was learning to read and to scribe, I used to practice my letters in the soapsuds and on the dirty platters and then wash the evidence away or trace them in the dust and then sweep them away.

When I had washed the things, I returned with them to the dwelling. The sun was beginning its setting, and Benakiell was watching it, smoking a clay pipe of fragrant tobacco. The wisps of smoke floated up towards the sky until they blended with it. 'I will sleep out here on the step,' said Benakiell abruptly.

'I do not understand,' I said. 'I am happy to share your dwelling with you, and I will sleep outside if it is more pleasing to you.'

Benakiell looked at me curiously. 'Do they tell you nothing of the world in that Temple before you are thrown out? I would not have it said that I took advantage of a young Maid of the Temple as she passed through my life.' I was still puzzled. 'The people in the village there would not take too kindly to reports of Benakiell sleeping in the same dwelling as a Temple Maid. Folks would talk, and it would be a hard life for you. Besides,' he said, his features tightening, 'I would rather be out here in case the OutRiders come by. They always seem to know when there's been a release from the Temple. Often wondered if the Priestesses tell them so they can come along and pick you all up.'

I was puzzled. This was the second time I had heard mention of the OutRiders and I had never heard of them before, although once when some Priestesses visited the Temple, I had heard the sound of horses riding with them. These OutRiders did not sound like good people, and I was grateful for Benakiell's offer to protect me, although I still did not understand why he could not sleep in the dwelling with me. I was tired, and he was taciturn, and I went back into the dwelling shortly afterwards to sleep.

CHAPTER 4

I awoke with birdsong floating on the dawn. One song was a sort of rasping scrape while the other was fluid and warbling. For some time, I lay there, on the mat Benakiell had provided and listened to the differences between them but eventually, I sat up and saw that Benakiell was waiting outside for me to emerge. I hurried up, guiltily, and asked him to come in as I went outside the dwelling and went to use the wastepit which was set some way back from the dwelling and around which Benakiell or perhaps his wife, had planted thorn shrubs and trees to shade it from prying eyes. When I returned, Benakiell was cooking small, oval flatbreads. He offered me one and sliced off a chunk of honeycomb which he kept in a clay jar, carefully sealed with a large leaf to accompany it. In the Temple we used honey only for medicine, for tonics for the old and the young, for sore throats and coughs and to sterilise wounds. I had tasted it before as a medicine but had never eaten it as a simple delight like this. I decided that there was no reason not to talk to Benakiell about this, so I explained to him how I was not used to eating honey for pleasure.

He smiled ruefully and said, 'We don't know very much of what goes on in the Temple, truth be told. We go to the Temple, as we must, and we give our dues. We see the colours of the robes and hangings and we smell the oils. Many of us pray to the Goddess for her blessings and thank her for them. But we never talk to anyone that comes from there. You are the first for many a year who has made it as far as here and stayed longer than a few minutes. Usually they head the other way towards Aderan over that way,' and he pointed the way in which I had set off the previous day. 'Sometimes we see them here, but they are in a hurry to get somewhere else. Of course, they stick out more in a big place than a small humble place like this. How are you planning to evade capture?'

I stared at Benakiell, wondering if I did not understand something, or if he was making a joke. I did not understand properly what he was saying to me. It sounded like he was saying that all the Maids that left the Temple ended up in trouble. I had never imagined that, when a Maid left the Temple, anything bad would befall her. Of course, we never saw the Maids who had left the Temple again, but we all imagined that they perhaps felt shame at not being chosen by the Goddess. Later, when I understood how the Choice ceremony worked, I thought that it was likely that the Maids who were chosen to leave the Temple took themselves far away from it, perhaps to explore the Outer, or to live a different life, perhaps something they may have dreamed of. I felt uneasy now, as if everyone else knew something which I did not.

'Whom should I avoid?' I asked, in the end. Benakiell looked at me sharply. 'Don't play innocent with me, Talla. You must know the OutRiders, and what they do to those clad in the drab. I am surprised you have not begged me for a robe to wear instead of that drabcoat.'

'I don't know who the OutRiders are,' I answered slowly, even while my mind was racing. Benakiell glowered at me. 'You surely can't have lived your whole life in that Temple and not seen or heard of the OutRiders; we often see them riding up there towards the Temple- sometimes with Priestesses. We never trade on those days.'

I thought back. On one day every week, the Maids were given leave to remain in their dormits while the Priestesses communed with the Goddess. It was on a different day each week, so that one week, it would fall on Flammeus, another week it would be on Viridis and so on. It meant that once a month, there was one day of your special days on which you did not attend the Temple, for there were seven days in a week, and, naturally, seven weeks in a month. I realised that we were told to remain in our dormits for personal prayer for the whole of the Temple Time, and that we always obeyed. I had never seen or heard what happened at those times and thought that the Priestesses communicated with the Goddesses at some higher level at these times.

Carefully, I said 'I have not seen any riders at the Temple, however there were times when we did not attend Temple. Could it be that they came at those times?'

Benakiell looked at me again, and his features softened. 'You really know nothing do you? It makes it all the worse, what they do. We of the old ways cannot abide it, and yet we cannot stop it either. I still do not understand why they have not come for you yet.' He looked at my face, which must have appeared bewildered, and said more gently, 'Come, child, I will tell you of the OutRiders in good time, but for now I need to go and visit with my friends and talk with them. Perhaps you could draw some more; I have got you some parchment.' And he thrust a roll of parchment in my hands. 'Gladia thinks she can make some goods with your patterning and her stitching that could be traded for cloth, and perhaps some flour, or more honey, and a new pot.' I took the parchment obediently and sat at the door of the dwelling, watching as Benakiell bustled off. I idly traced a few designs into the dust before I started one in charcoal on the parchment and chose to draw a pattern of leaves and vines. Here and there, I drew in an ant, or a bee. I had finished the design when I saw Benakiell and Gladia walking back towards the house.

'Ah, she is busy again, your little Maid,' said Gladia, 'What design do you have for us today?'

I showed her my picture, which I had not yet pounced, for which I was grateful. I still had no intention of sharing that particular skill with anyone, even those like Benakiell and Gladia who appeared to bear me no harm. She took in the pattern with a practised eye, and I could almost see her working out which threads to use where. I was still unused to this mixing of colours. In the Temple, colours were kept together, and not allowed to blend, and yet here on the Outer, it seemed that they almost preferred to blend their colours, not only with each other in multi coloured patterns, but also to change the tones and produce new colours. Her eyes narrowed slightly as she came across the small insects I had drawn into the pattern. 'You will have to take that out if you want to sell a robe with this design on it at market' she said, pointing to the bee. 'Nobody here will want that on their clothes, it's too obvious! How does a Maid who knows nothing,' and here she looked pointedly at Benakiell, 'know to put in the likes of these bees into designs? If she is not one of the OutRiders, she is certainly not one of us and she puts the sign of the bee in her work. Perhaps she is an OutRider spy!'

I felt more and more confused. With every day that I spent in the Outer world, I learned something new which upset the way in which I thought of the world. In the Temple everything was clear to me. There were ways of behaving and things which happened each day without fail. There had never seemed to me to be any hidden depths, or anything which I had failed to understand. I had, of course, known that the Priestesses were occasionally involved in meetings and trades with people who we Maids did not meet, but I assumed, or perhaps I was told, I do not remember, that these meetings related to the Goddess herself. It was as though in the Temple there was only one layer to see and to deal with, and yet here there were many different levels. Each person behaved differently towards different people; some people knew things that others did not know; some assumed they should know what you knew yourself, some seemed to know things but then on closer inspection knew nothing. I could feel an unfamiliar feeling bubbling up inside me and wondered if I was perhaps feeling unwell. Eventually I could not bear the feeling anymore and shouted out.

'I do not know what you are talking about! I do not know! I keep on telling you and telling you and still you hide things from me, and you pretend things to me. I do not know you! You do not know me! You think I know things I do not know!' Benakiell and Gladia looked at me, astonished by my outburst. I felt giddy and yet somehow powerful. I had said what I was thinking, and it had felt good to say it in this way. I felt calmer now, although my mind was still fizzing like an uncontrolled ember.

'They don't often come out angry, do they, Benakiell,' commented Gladia, looking at me with new interest.

'Indeed, they do not, Gladia,' he replied, stroking his beard thoughtfully. 'They are not trained to have any kind of extreme emotion.'

I spun around to face him, still full of this strange emotion. 'And how do YOU know so much about the Temple anyway? You are a man and men are forbidden except as worshippers. How would you know what happens in the Temple unless you yourself are some sort of spy?'

Benakiell looked at me thoughtfully. 'I cannot tell you that, yet, Talla. You will have to trust me when I tell you that I cannot tell you yet.'

'And why should I trust you?' I had not finished yet. 'You tell me to trust you, and yet you do not trust me. Why should I trust you any more than you trust me? How do I know that you do not intend harm to me?' My lip began to quiver, and I felt emotion, such as I had not felt since the first age of childhood. I felt hot tears roll down my face. Benakiell looked at me helplessly and then looked to Gladia. Gladia walked over to me calmly and put her arm around me. We did not make personal contact in the Temple; we were encouraged to work as individuals for the greater good of the Goddess. I found it suffocating, this closeness of another body next to mine, and I edged away. Gladia moved away a little and then encouraged me to go with her to sit on the edge of Benakiell's veranda.

'Just breathe, child,' she murmured, and sat down next to me. Neither of us spoke and Benakiell moved inside his dwelling. I could hear the noise of him moving around inside. It was getting hotter and my drabcoat was already damp with sweat. I felt the trickling down my cheek of tears and sweat combining in a fractured trail of salt and lifted my drabcoat to wipe it away.

Gladia gently pushed my hand down. 'Leave it, child. There is nothing wrong with feelings. That's all it is; just a feeling.'

'I do not understand it,' I muttered. 'I do not like it. In the Temple, I did not have these feelings. It was easier.' I shut my eyes and thought myself back to the Temple. I thought fondly of the last dormit I had slept in. We did not keep the same dormits for longer than a few months, or else, the Priestesses told us, it would become a possession and we were forbidden possessions by the Goddess. So, every so often, we would be told to move to another dormit. They were, in any case, all identical. They were small rooms, connected to the main Temple by passageways. They were rock walled and cool and had only a small window to let in air and some light. Each dormit contained the same things; a sleeping mat, a woven blanket, a soapball, a comb, a toothtwig and a hook on which you could hang your drabcoat. I felt as though life was easier for me there in the Temple, without all these layers and without all these feelings which I had never encountered before. I wondered if all people on the Outer felt this way all the time. How did they cope with all these strange and unsettling emotions all of the time? How did they ever know what was true and what was not? I tried to fix my mind on something else and watched as a bee crawled up the stalk of a piece of flowering grass. Why had Gladia reacted so strongly to my placing the bee in the picture? A bee was surely a good thing, for they made the useful and delicious honey, and yet it seemed that she too thought it had some hidden meaning. I concentrated on the little insect, trying to stop my mind from going back to the thoughts which had upset me in the first instance.

The bee placed its legs carefully as it manoeuvred its way up the stalk. The stalk swayed as the bee's weight, tiny though it was, put more pressure on it. As it got closer to the flower, it seemed to become even more focused on its job and crawled with careful determination to get to the flower. I had not really sat and looked at a creature like this much before. In the Temple we all worked at the times when we were told to work, and we ate when we were told to eat, and we slept when we were told to sleep, and we worshipped when we were told to worship. There was not time to sit and examine the life that was around us. We had learned something about bees when I was in the second age of childhood, and I knew they gathered honey from the flowers and stored it. The Temple only grew certain vegetables with correct coloured flowers and some specific flowers, again of the correct colouring were grown in order to be used to adorn the statue of the Goddess on their colour day. The bees came to the Temple gardens to those flowers. However, we did not cultivate bees, or indeed other animals at the Temple. They were regarded as too much like a possession, and we were not encouraged to think of the animals except in regard of the food they might bring to us and to the glorification of the Goddess. We only used honey, as I have told you, for its healing properties, and the Priestesses traded for it in small pots from the traders who came to the Temple every week. They also bought their meat from the same traders. We only had meat on the day that the traders came, as we had no means of storing it, and we looked forward to it as a change from the beans and chickpeas and pumpkins which we normally ate. The bee was now within the heart of the flower and was still, and yet you knew, just from the feel it gave to the air that it was intensely busy, sucking up the honey.

Gladia patted my arm, removing my attention from the bee. I felt a surge of irritation with her. She had not lived my life, and yet it seemed as if she thought she knew better than I what I should do. She was not a Priestess, not even a Maid and could not surely perceive my life better than I.

'How are you feeling now Talla?'

'I am watching the bee.' I felt obstinate and unwilling to be pleasant. I did not look her in the eye. We did not often look people in the eye at the Temple, and, of course, we could not look the Priestesses in the eye since they were veiled.

Gladia sighed. 'I know that you want to understand what we are talking about. We would also like to understand what you are talking about sometimes, because we very rarely have much of a chance to speak to the Drabs when they are released.'

I looked up. She had called the Maids Drabs. I had not thought that we might be called something else by other people. Inside my head, I was a Maid still. A Drab sounded like one who had been judged and sorted by the clothes she wore. A Maid was a position in the Temple, the definition of me by my role or my status, and a Drab was by how I looked, from the patchworked Drabcoat I wore.

'We are not Drabs. We are Maids,' I muttered sulkily.

'Maids, Drabs; does it matter what you are called? Isn't who you are more important than what others call you? You cannot be a Maid here in Oramia, outside your Temple walls. The only place where Maids are Maids, is in the Temple, and you aren't living there now, are you?' She got up fairly briskly and with fair agility, considering her roundness, and brushed the fine red dust off her robe, which was decorated with a series of triangles in different colours.

'Come and see me when you have adjusted your drawing, and I will give you the cloth for it; perhaps I can do a netela for that design.' She pulled her own shawl over her shoulders and set off down the path towards the other houses, showing no signs of being uncomfortable with me, even though I did. I knew I needed to make more trading opportunities and build up my supplies, and Gladia was my only hope of getting into the markets. If she knew that a design with bees in it would not sell well, then I supposed she must be right, and I began reluctantly to try to rub out the bee designs, feeling pleased that I had not pounced the pattern and thus rendered the parchment unusable. I used a small rough piece of sandstone and gradually worked on all the charcoal until it had gone, and then began to pounce the parchment with my thorn, having first checked to see that no one was around. My thorn was becoming blunter, and I really needed to get a new one, or find some other sharp object to replace it with. I wondered if I could persuade Gladia to give me a metal needle, such as she used for her stitching. Perhaps I could trade with her and do some designs for her in return for the needle. I also needed to remember that Benakiell was allowing me to stay here and that I needed to somehow pay him back for his hospitality, even though I was not especially well disposed towards either him or Gladia. I wanted to be on my own, but I knew I needed their support. I resolved to try and get some more work, perhaps helping with crops or in some other way with the other dwellings and their owners. I could not rely too heavily on Benakiell and Gladia, until I understood better what they were thinking and why. I rolled up the finished design and looked for some grass to tie it up with. As I picked it, I saw a golden yellow flower which reminded me of my mother's brooch.

 I walked towards the wastepit and squatted down behind the thorn bushes, opening up my underpocket by loosening the drawstring. I carefully withdrew the parchment wrapped brooch and looked at it again carefully. I could see that the petals were all the same shape, and that they were more angular than I had first imagined. I compared it closely against the flower I had seen but it now looked less like a flower to me. It reminded me of something else I had seen, but the thought was elusive, hovering on the edges of my mind, like a faint light in the darkness. I looked again at the stone which was carefully cut and shaped and which formed the centre of the brooch. It was a dark red, much darker than the stone from which the Temple was made, and translucent, cut with only a few facets so that although it caught the light, it did not shimmer and twinkle like some ornamentation I had seen. Rather, it seemed to draw you in. I turned it over and examined the underside of it again. The pin was worn and slightly bent, as I had seen before. I wondered if this had happened when my mother, for I assume it was she, had pinned the brooch to the blanket in which I was wrapped. I began to think about the story I had been told by the Priestesses. Was it a true story? I had lived my whole life believing this story about how my mother had left me at the gate of the Temple and how I had been found by the Priestesses. I could not understand why they would have concocted such an elaborate story to tell me if it had not been true. And yet, since I had left the Temple I had been besieged with new ideas and questions and feelings until I scarcely knew what was real and what was true anymore. I wrapped the brooch up again and replaced it carefully into my underpocket. I pulled the drawstrings tight and knotted it twice to ensure that it did not fall out and then made my way back to the dwelling.

CHAPTER 5

Benakiell was sitting on the raised step around his house, waiting for me when I returned. He showed no signs of being discomfited by my earlier outburst, although I myself was acutely aware of it, but instead called me over to him.

'Talla, have you thought about what you will do next?'

I looked at him blankly and then realised that he wanted to know if I planned to remain in Mellia, the small settlement where we found ourselves or to go on my way. I did not know what I wanted to do next or where I should go. Life on the Outer seemed much more uncertain than I had envisaged back at the Temple of the Goddess's Blessing. I did not want to stay here forever, but I thought I could perhaps learn some more from the people I had met here, who seemed friendlier than the first Outer people whom I had met. But I did not want Benakiell to sleep outside anymore, and I wanted to work for my keep, as I was accustomed to doing.

'I do not know what to do next, in truth,' I said. 'Would there be a place where I could stay here? I am grateful for your hospitality, but I must work hard to repay your kindness to me, if I can stay.' I was a little flustered at having to speak so directly and make such difficult choices.

'So, are you feeling like working hard today?' he asked.

'Of course, brother,' I replied. 'I am very happy to be able to work for my keep.'

'Well, and I hope that you won't have to do that for too much longer. I have spoken to Achillea down the way and she is willing for you to live in the old dwelling her mother Cassia lived in until she died, in return for a new netela with a unique design.' He winked at me. 'She's always trying to find an excuse for a new outfit! That old dwelling is going to ruin because she has done nothing to it in almost a year, and if nobody lives in it soon, it will be no more use than an old chicken pen!'

I looked at him uncertainly. Did he mean that I would have my own dwelling? I had only been out of the Temple a couple of days and already I was to settle down here for the rest of my days?

Benakiell laughed. 'Don't worry, sister Talla, we won't make you stay any longer than you wish! But stay some time until you feel better able to live and move around out here and until you know what you want to do. If you have your own dwelling, you can preserve your modesty and it will be easier to keep you safe from the OutRiders. Gladia goes to the market in Sanguinea in four days, and she will trade for you, and try and pick up news of the OutRiders. Come on now,' he added briskly. 'We have a lot of work to do, and Achillea will be doing none of it! I think she has someone in mind as a handy man, but she needs to learn to do her own work!' He laughed and handed me a leather pouch containing tools to carry, whilst leading the way to the east of his dwelling where I saw a large pile of thin canes and grass. He saw me look at it and said offhandedly, 'Oh, I asked Ashtun to bring those to me this morning.'

Benakiell led me down the path to the east for some time. The path led downhill somewhat and curved away from Benakiell's land, where there were some five or six dwellings loosely grouped together. I was interested in how and why people chose to put their dwellings where they did and asked my companion about it.

'This place has been called Mellia for generations. I am a newcomer here and have only lived here for the past twenty years or so.' He smiled when he saw my face. 'And why is that a cause for surprise to you, sister? For you have surely lived at the Temple for many years yourself. There are not many of us, in the end, who can spend our lives travelling and exploring our wider life and further lands. Many of us may dream of that, but few can withstand a desire for security and peace. I myself travelled some of the lands beyond Oramia before I met my dear Velosia at the market in Sanguinea. She came from this place,' he indicated the dwellings with a sweep of his hand. 'It was her wish that we should live here. And so we did.' His voice trailed away and he looked distant. 'There used to be many more dwellings here; over to the east there were more than a dozen houses, but in time they have fallen to dust. It will be good to repair an old dwelling for you to use, even if only for some weeks.' He looked at me kindly.'We will get used to one another, child of the Temple.'

Benakiell led me on to Achillea's dwelling, which had been newly sealed and where there was another bundle of canes and grass, which he told me Ashtun had left there earlier. It seemed that he would also be joining us as we sought to make Achillea's late mother's dwelling habitable again. Achillea herself was, it seemed, not at home, for no one appeared to greet us, so we carried on to the older dwelling. Benakiell frowned as he examined the deep red clay that formed part of its exterior. It had been allowed to swell in the rain and crack in the sun and was crumbling off. He looked inside, but it appeared that the inside was bearing up much better, as it was not exposed to the elements, and he suggested that I could begin by sweeping out the insect life and the small plants that were making their way through the packed earth floor. I went over to the small copse of trees on the right and looked for some twigs with which to form a broom. I gathered a good handful of long twigs and took some of the grass which Benakiell had brought with him and added the strong pieces of dried grass to the broom and then plaited a holding strip for them. I worked silently and quickly. I was used to making my own implements for cleaning and broom making was not something I had ever given much thought to before. Benakiell smiled when he saw how quickly and neatly I worked. I had used the Rule of Seven in my broom making; seven twigs, each surrounded by seven strong pieces of grass and a woven strap of seven pieces of grass to hold them together.

'It's a pleasing broom you have there, sister, they taught you well at the Temple. You could trade those brooms right here in Mellia! Achillea could do with one herself!' He smiled at me again and I could feel my own face creasing in a smile in return. I bent my head in modesty, and bustled into the dwelling, but I could feel Benakiell's smile even when I could not see it. I brushed down the spidersilks from the higher walls and swept out the old leaves and stones from the floor, along with the centipedes and beetles which had made their home in the cool safety of the dwelling. I mindlessly swept to the Seven Step pattern, and in only a short time, I had the inside of the dwelling looking clean and ready for living in again. I ventured outside, where the noonday sun was hot and relentless, and wished I had tarried inside a little longer. Benakiell had stripped down and was wearing only a rough tunic to work on the house. His robe was carefully folded and placed on top of one of the thorn bushes some distance away. He was building over the old Outer framework of the dwelling.

'What should I do next, brother?' I asked him.

'Dwelling building is not work for women, so you cannot help with that,' he frowned. I turned over what he said in my mind. Of course, I had never seen Maids or Priestesses doing building work at the Temple but there was really no building work to be done there, since it was made of stone. It was as if it had always been there. The Priestesses often told the story of how Ashkana had chosen the place and the Temple had been built overnight by an army of Angels, who had left the large stone statue of the Goddess in the exact place where we worshipped it now. I did not understand why there would be women's work and men's work. Surely there was just work, and that work was best done by those who did it best? Of course, at the Temple we did not have the choice of allocating some work to men and some to women, for we were all women, but we did all the work that was required. Indeed, we women worked all the time at the Temple, and I was sure that no man could have worked harder.

'You may want to see what crops Cassia had growing in her patch. They will have gone to seed I expect, but there may yet be some fruit on the trees, or dried chickpeas or beans. Go and call Achillea and ask if you may borrow a basket for your harvesting.'

I felt ashamed that I should have to go to an unknown woman and ask her for her help, especially as she was already allowing me to stay in the old dwelling, and I hesitated.

'Go on,' he waved his hand.' Achillea is nice enough and she owes me for all the work she tries to get me to do for free! It will be good for you both to speak to another of the same age. Achillea!' he shouted out, and a woman came out of the dwelling, blinking, with her netela round her shoulders. It seemed that she had been asleep, for she blinked like an owl in the sun.

'Oh hello, Benakiell,' she responded placidly. 'I did not know you had arrived; do you want some water?' She seemed not to have noticed me at all. Benakiell gestured towards me, and she turned, still blinking. 'Oh, is this the Drab who is going to make my new netela?' She looked at me with interest. I was still not accustomed to being called a Drab. It seemed derogatory, as if I were an inferior being. Of course, in the Temple we had all considered that we were the lucky ones and had thought mostly that those on the Outer must be lacking something.

I looked up at Achillea, although I still found it hard to meet the eyes of another, used as I was to the veiled ones, and said, 'Greetings, sister.'

Achillea looked back at me, her eyes wide open. She had a small sharp nose and once again, she reminded me of an owl, with her big eyes and her beak and I had to fight the temptation to smile. 'Greetings,' she responded, looking at my drabcoat with suspicion. 'Are you sure she can pattern, Benakiell? Because if she can, why is she still wearing that hideous drabcoat?'

Benakiell started to answer, but I answered her for myself. 'Sister, I thank you for allowing me to use your blessed mother's dwelling, and I promise to pattern you a netela of great interest. As for my drabcoat,' I smiled, 'it is what we Maids wear in the Temple, and indeed you would wear one yourself if you were there.'

Achillea's eyes widened. 'Oh, I could not bear it! To wear no colour at all, every day. It would be like being a grain of dust! We must make you a robe of your own to wear! You should wear oranges and reds and bright greens; they would tone with those amber eyes of yours!'

'Enough of your chatter,' said Benakiell kindly, for it was apparent that she meant no harm to me. 'Talla needs a basket so she can go and arrange your mother's old garden and see if there is anything worth harvesting. Take her over to the garden, and she can maybe show you how to make a broom, for she is adept at it.' I felt grateful to him for redirecting the conversation along a path which I was more comfortable with, and for telling Achillea that I too had my skills. Achillea obediently went into the dwelling and returned with a flat basket which had a loose handle.

'I can fix this handle for you, sister,' I murmured, and Achillea clapped her hands in delight.

'Oh, Benakiell where did you find her? She can do so many useful things!'

Benakiell frowned. 'Talla will not be here to do your jobs for you, Achillea. She will pattern you a netela, as we agreed. More than that, you will have to trade with her. She is of worth, and you must offer her something of worth in return.' Achillea's eyes widened again. I was sure they could not get any bigger, and was fascinated by them, and by her long, curled eyelashes which framed them.

'I will ask Ashtun for some pomegranates off his tree. Then I can trade them with her for her skills!' She smiled triumphantly at Benakiell and to my surprise, he threw back his head and laughed out loud. I had thought he would rebuke her again for trying to escape her responsibilities, but instead he was amused by her obvious attempts to avoid work. She laughed along with Benakiell, and her laugh was like a bird, fluid and cadenced. Her eyes sparkled at him mischievously and she flicked the end of her netela at him. 'Or maybe I will ask you, Benakiell! You have some pomegranates for me, don't you?' She turned to me and carelessly took my arm. 'Come on then, Talla, let's go do some work before this old Bossybird flaps his wings again!' and she led me down the path from the dwelling to the overgrown patch of garden.

'It will be wonderful to have a friend my own age in this place,' confided Achillea. 'I get awfully bored sometimes. I used to go with Mother to the market where she sold fruit and honey but now, I feel lonely going on my own, so I usually wait and go with one of the others. Mostly the men in the village come and give me a hand if I need them to, and I sometimes look after the children when their mothers go to market. Do you like children?'

I thought back to Gesarit and her curious eyes and her unending questions. 'That depends,' I said cautiously.

'Would you like to have them yourself one day? How many would you like?'

I stared at her curiously. She seemed to be saying that I could have children of my own. I did not respond to her but looked around and saw that there were indeed pomegranates still on the tree. 'Look, pomegranates,' I said, pointing to them, and luckily her mind went off on another track like a breeze changing direction.

'Actually,' she confessed, 'I did know there were pomegranates on the tree, but I couldn't get them down on my own. I was going to ask Ashtun to do it for me! Now we can do it together!' and off she went with the basket and stood under the tree expectantly. I cast about for a splitstick to twist them off the tree. There was an old one leaning against the side of a Paradox tree and I moved into position under the pomegranate and got the stem of it in the cleft in the stick. I wasn't sure why Achillea could not have done this herself, and I suspected that she had no need to do things for herself. It seemed, from Benakiell's attitude at least, that she was indulged and a little lazy. I flicked the pomegranate off into the basket and Achillea squealed with delight.

'Oh well done Talla, let's try and get some more!' I wondered if her mind was slightly addled. She seemed to take an almost childish delight in the simplest of things. She skipped under the next pomegranate and held the basket expectantly, waiting for me to get the next fruit down. I brought down a dozen fruit all told, over the next minutes and my shoulders were beginning to ache.

'Achillea, why don't you have a turn with the splitstick?' I eventually suggested. She looked at me, surprised. 'Do you think I can?'

'Well of course you can, sister!' I replied, again trying to fight this smile that kept trying to appear. 'Just take the splitstick like so, and then get the stalk in the split...' I demonstrated how to trap the stalk in the cleft, and she flicked off the pomegranate. Unfortunately, I was not waiting to catch it with the basket as I had been guiding Achillea's hands and the fruit fell onto the edge of a sharp rock.

'Well, Talla!' exclaimed Achillea. 'Fancy letting that good fruit go to waste!' I looked down aghast at the waste of the fruit, and ashamed that I had not foreseen this. I was about to turn to apologise to Achillea when she burst into peals of laughter. 'Your face! Don't be silly, Talla! It was my fault that I flicked it off so quickly, not yours that you weren't there!' She walked over to the smashed fruit and picked it up. 'Look, it's only squashed here. We can eat the rest! I'm ready for a break anyway. Come on!' I followed her to sit under the Paradox tree. I was still trying to understand all the things which were new to me in this Outer world. It seemed that they chose their own times to work and to rest. Without the bells in the Temple, I had to follow the course of the sun to try to work out how much time had passed. The Temple bells followed a set pattern. The first bell rang to wake us, the second for the start of work after breakfast, the third bell for attendance at the Temple, the fourth for work again, the fifth bell for our main daily meal, the sixth for evening work and the seventh for sleep. Sometimes it seemed to me that the time was longer or shorter for one or another. Work time was much longer than the time given for getting up and getting clean, and it was even longer than Temple time. High Priestess Asinte used to quote the Aphorisms of Ashkana to us when we felt that time was going slowly. 'If you have time to notice the passage of time, you have too much time on your hands, and not enough work to do.' Moreover, 'Time may not be traded, only what is made in time,' and 'The time you have belongs to others'.

We sat under the deep shade of the tree and found ourselves each a splinter of stick with which to pick out the hexagonal red jewels of juice. A red dove cooed above us as we ate. I enjoyed the fresh taste of the fruit as I pierced each small sac with my teeth and relished the sweetness before the bitter seed within.

'Do you have any skill with bees?' asked Achillea suddenly. 'My mother used to be a Beeguard, but she had not taught me what to do before she died. She was taken by the same ague that took Velosia.' Her wide eyes filled unexpectedly with tears. I felt awkward, never having known a mother, and not knowing what she was feeling. I patted her arm tentatively, remembering Gladia's gestures towards me the previous day. She bent her head down further to hide her face, and I felt better, to not see the open hurt in her eyes. Her tears rolled down her face and landed in the soft dust making little balls of mud. She did not make a sound but allowed them to drop soundlessly from her cheek. Her small, fine hand met mine and curled around it instinctively. I willed my hand to remain pliable and soft, instead of stiffening up, which was my instinctive reaction, and she grasped it as if I were rescuing her from a deep pit.

After some moments had passed, and the small muddy drops had sunk further into the dust, and no new ones had appeared, I asked her to tell me about the bees, and how a Beeguard did her job. Achillea explained that a Beeguard looked after hives of bees, which were usually based in fields close to trees and flowers. She told me that a Beeguard usually only started to learn the job at the age of maturity, much like we in the Temple made our Choice (or it was made for us) of improving ourselves in the service of the Goddess as Maids and then perhaps as Priestesses in later years. The job of Beeguard was passed on down through families, who shared the secrets of the hive with their descendants. Achillea's mother had just started showing her the first elements of Beeguarding when she had been gripped with the ague and had died from it. I likened her mother to Priestess Asinte and the other Priestesses in my mind. They too had secrets which they were bound to pass on, but only when they deemed those younger than them ready to shoulder the responsibility of that knowledge. I wondered briefly what secrets Lunaria might one day learn, as a Priestess, for this path was utterly closed to me now. I had no special skills to pass on to anyone, except for my pattern pouncing, and I felt a pang in my heart that I did not have this rope of connection with family that Achillea had.

'Why do you not ask Benakiell to help you learn about the bees?' I asked. 'He seems to be very knowledgeable about growing things and making dwellings; he may have some knowledge he can share with you.'

'Beeguarding is a job for women, not for men,' answered Achillea, smiling at me, her tears forgotten for now. 'Men may not know the secrets of Beeguarding, just as women may not construct dwellings. Just as there are only women in the Temple, so there are only women in Beeguarding.'

This interested me greatly. I had thought at first, when Benakiell had told me that making dwellings was men's work, that he was in some way addressing himself to me as superior in some way; that he thought women were not strong enough or sharp enough to construct dwellings, and I knew that this was not true, so I had felt insulted by his statement. Now, however, I had learned that here in the Outer, both men and women had unique jobs about which the other had no knowledge. Each had a set of skills of which they could be proud and which they could only share with others of the same sex. I asked Achillea to tell me more, but just as she started to tell me about where the hives were found, we heard Benakiell calling to us, and realised that we were supposed to have been harvesting and tidying up the garden. I sprang up and hastily began to pull dried bean pods from their yellowing stalks, thrusting them into the basket which contained the pomegranates. We had not completed the work we had been set, and I had spent my time sitting and talking to Achillea instead of doing the jobs I had been asked to do. Benakiell had been working hard on the dwelling for me and I had done nothing. Achillea watched me, apparently amused by my haste, and remained sitting on the rock. Benakiell came around the corner and saw us in the garden, me frantically trying to fill the basket and Achillea watching me.

'Sister Talla, slow down,' he said. 'I do not call you to chastise you; I have someone for you to meet.' Achillea sprang up and immediately started to pick the beans, as if she had been doing it for hours. Benakiell laughed a great loud laugh. 'Achillea,' he admonished, 'Ashtun knows how lazy you are, why are you trying to fool him? If Talla has been working harder than you all afternoon, then you should not pretend otherwise!'

'I have not!' I interjected, and then dropped my eyes quickly. 'We harvested the pomegranates and then we sat and ate the smashed one and then we talked about Achillea's mother, bless her spirit.'

'Did you now?' asked Benakiell gravely, but with a twinkle in his eye. 'Sounds like a good afternoon's work to me. What do you think Ashtun?' Ashtun came around the corner as he heard his name and smiled openly at us. He was a tall man, spare, and slightly stooped, as if he were tired of always bending his head. His hair was cropped close to his head, and he was a young man, though perhaps a little older than me. His dark beard was cropped close to his chin too, and there were fine droplets of sweat on his brow. His eyes lit up when they saw Achillea, but barely flickered when he saw me.

'And how is Achillea, Lady of Mellia?' he asked bowing low. Achillea laughed that fascinating, rippling laugh of hers, and his eyes followed the line of her jaw as she threw her head back.

'Oh, the Lady of Mellia is very happy, thank you,' she answered finally, 'because she has a new friend to join her! You are forgetting your manners Ashtun! Say hello to Talla! Talla this is Ashtun Silasim.'

Abashed, Ashtun turned around to me and looked at me finally. 'I greet you, sister Talla.' he said finally, formally inclining his head towards me. I was struck by the different ways in which he chose to address me and Achillea. He had an easy familiarity with her, as if he were comfortable and able to be open with her. I knew I was somebody new to him, but I suspected it was more to do with my drabcoat and my Temple upbringing than anything else. I had started to resent this drabcoat, for all that I was also attached to it. I lowered my eyes instinctively as I greeted him back, and then, through some spirit of mischief, raised them up again almost immediately, and looked at him straight in the eyes. He had eyes the colour of warm coffee with glints of gold, and as I caught his glance at me, it seemed to me that I saw a sort of pity or even contempt in his eyes, and I felt that feeling flare up within me again. My eyes must have flashed some sort of unspoken warning, for he lowered his own eyes quickly, before bending down to pick up the splitstick which had slipped over. It gave me time to compose myself, and I asked Benakiell how the dwelling work was coming along.

'Come and see it,' he invited, and I willingly followed him along the path back to the dwelling, leaving Achillea and Ashtun laughing over something as we left. I felt that Benakiell had an understanding of me, and that he knew how uncomfortable I was in social situations like this. When we arrived back at Cassia's dwelling, I was surprised by how well it looked now that he and Ashtun had worked over the frame with new canes and some thick thatch. 'We only have to smooth the sides with mud, and waterproof it,' he told me. I asked him to tell me about the process they used to build the houses and he looked uncomfortable. 'It is men's work, Talla, as I told you before. It is not work you need to know how to do. What plants did you find in Cassia's patch?'

I recognised a change in subject and began to list some of the plants that I knew like the pomegranate and Paradox trees, the barley and the chickpeas and squash plants. There were also some small fiery chillies. 'I don't know the names of all the crops,' I confessed, embarrassed. 'I was not good at gardening at the Temple, so I did not work in that.' Now it was Benakiell's turn to be interested.

'How do you know what you are good at and who decides what you learn to do?'

I decided to give him a vague answer, since I was dissatisfied with this secrecy about men's and women's jobs already. 'The Priestesses guide our choices,' I murmured. 'We learn what is appropriate for us to learn, for the greater good.'

But Benakiell was not satisfied and pressed me further. 'What jobs do you do in the Temple? Are there some things that no one does? Do you ask people from outside the Temple for their advice sometimes?'

I pondered his question and then decided to ask him the same question in return. 'Well, what of Mellia, Benakiell?' I asked. 'How many jobs are reserved for men and how many for women? Do you ever ask the Temple to do jobs that you cannot do yourself? Are there jobs that no one does?'

His eyes twinkled at me, recognising my tactic. 'I see we have the makings of a fine trader in you if nothing else!' he said. 'Let's trade information, shall we, sister Talla?' I thought for a moment and decided I could most easily tell Benakiell about my own job at the Temple and it would also mean that I would not be giving too much away.

'My job at the Temple was to help to keep it clean and pure,' I told him. He looked at me, surprised that this was in fact a job. I looked him back squarely. 'Maintaining the cleanliness of the Temple is pleasing to the Goddess,' I stated. 'The Temple is large and there is always dust to get rid of. The statue of the Goddess must be kept free of dust, so that she can be oiled every day. If there was dust around it would stick to the oil on the Goddess, and that would demean her.' I thought back to the hours of every day when I had swept and wiped and scrubbed the stonework of the Temple clean. I explained it to him. 'On the day of Flammeus, it was my duty to clean the inner Temple, where the statue of the Goddess is. There are seven steps to the cleaning process. First, we must sweep the dust out of the room, then we must scrub the stonework, and then we must wipe the window carvings and the other carved edges. Then we sweep again, scrub again and wipe again. The final stage of the cleaning process is to oil the Goddess with the Cinnamon oil. For each stage of the cleaning, we use the Goddess number to guide our cleaning, like so...' and I demonstrated with my hand in the dust the seven-step process I used to clean; three columns up, then three rows across and then a circular movement over the top. Benakiell looked at me, still baffled.

'But why do you do this, Talla?' he asked eventually. 'Why not just sweep the Temple normally and every now and again wipe it over to keep the insects away? Surely the Goddess does not need to be oiled every day? What a waste of time and effort!'

I felt that feeling welling up inside me again. It was as if he was mocking me, or my Temple, or implying that my work was neither useful nor important. I looked straight at him, unable to speak for a minute.

'Are you angry with me, Talla?' he asked, after a moment or so.

'What do you mean, angry?' I said finally, my voice beginning to quiver. 'I do not know what that even means. I did not ever feel like this in the Temple. Everything was even and steady and calm. This feeling arrives when everything is unbalanced. I feel like a pot of muddy water which was settled which has been stirred up with a stick!'

Benakiell frowned in thought for a moment. I thought back to my time in the Temple. We were encouraged to aim for the even path in life. The whole Temple ran smoothly because everyone knew their job, and everyone knew the expectations of that job and everyone knew that one did not fail in one's job. Because these things were clear and definite to us, and we all abided by them, no one ever felt that their life in the Temple was any more unfair than anyone else's. Here in the Outer, I did not know what anyone's expectations were; everyone seemed to have their own, so that you were able to disappoint people with regularity, because they did not always share with you what they expected. If Benakiell had told me how many baskets of food I needed to harvest with Achillea, I would have been able to judge it better. But, I realised, it was not Benakiell who was angry with me, it was I who was angry with him, or perhaps with myself.

Benakiell began to speak. 'Sister Talla, I do not know of how the Temple works or of how you were treated there or indeed of your daily life. I only know the things which we have learned from our own observations and from the information we have gained from others who have been forced out of the Temple, and from the OutRiders' behaviour. All that I say or think comes only from me, and I am sorry if I have upset you with my words. It seems that you may have feelings that are unusual to you in the Temple, even though we here, on the Outer, as you call it, find them to be normal feelings in a life, and certainly nothing unusual.'

'I cannot think of feeling stirred up inside like this every day,' I acknowledged frankly. 'I do not like the way it makes me feel inside. I do not know what anger is. You seem to recognise the feelings I have just from looking at me and that means you must have seen this emotion before. I have not, however. This feeling makes me feel like shouting, and throwing things and even hurting people, and that is not how we behave in the Temple. We do not need to raise our voices, because everyone knows what is expected of them.' My voice shook.

'Aye, well, anger is a powerful feeling, there's no mistaking that,' answered Benakiell slowly. 'But in the right hands, it can be a powerful tool. If we can see life through another's eyes, we can see the injustice of their life and our anger can make us fight for improvement.' His eyes glowed, and he leaned forward. 'Talla, you feel anger against me and against others here in Mellia, for small reasons, for things that can easily be acknowledged and talked through. If we have disagreements here, we try to resolve them through talking and through seeing things from another's viewpoint. Sometimes, it is hard for all of us. Anger can make us lose our reason; it lessens our fear of risks and we stop looking at things from the viewpoint of others. When we reach the point where we can only see things from our own viewpoint, we on the Outer go to see an Empath, who can help us to readjust ourselves.' There was a lot to take in and I began to wish I had not started this game of trading information with Benakiell. It felt uncomfortably as if he had more insight into my nature than I did. I thought through what he had said and tried to see the world through his eyes. In the Temple, we had been encouraged to understand that we saw the world through the eyes of the Goddess, and that was enough. If we saw the world through the eyes of the Goddess, what need did we have of seeing the world through the eyes of another?

'We can talk about this more another time, sister,' Benakiell assured me. 'Meantime, I intend to stick to my side of the bargain. What did you wish to ask me about life here in Mellia?'

'I would like to know about the men's jobs and the women's jobs,' I stated firmly. 'If I am going to live here in the Outer, then I need to know what work is closed to me, simply by virtue of being a woman.'

'I am not sure you need to see it like that,' he murmured, 'but I can tell you which jobs are reserved for men and which for women. However, I cannot tell you how to do the jobs which are assigned to men, because it is forbidden, and I cannot tell you the details of the jobs assigned to women, because I do not know them!' I laughed, and felt the anger ebbing away. How ridiculous it seemed to me that there was this division in people's working lives. But maybe it was the same for Benakiell, and he thought it laughable that we women did all the work in the Temple, and indeed, that no men resided or worked within the Temple at all.

'The works reserved for men are dwelling making, cloth weaving, metal-smithing, animal slaughter, astronomy, brewing and scribing. The works reserved for women are seamstressing, Beeguarding, pottery, animal care, songmaking and Birthmothering. All other works can be done by both men and women, except of course for bringing new life into the world, which comes from the Goddess.'

I pondered the occupations he had mentioned. I realised that we always traded for the metal objects like the combs and the needles and knives and the cloth we used, and we did not weave our own in the Temple. We had no dwellings to make, no animals to slaughter. We did not drink wine or beer and had no need of brewing. On the rare occasions when I had seen and listened surreptitiously to the astronomers who visited, I had noted that they were men, but thought nothing of it. However, it was the thought of the scribing which I was really interested by. I wondered if men were the only scribers, if that meant they were the only readers too.

'It was not so in the Temple,' I said finally. 'We have accomplished scribers and readers amongst the Priestesses.' I decided not to go into my own self-taught skills in reading and scribing, for although Benakiell had noted my drawing skill, he was not yet aware of my scribing and reading skill. This secret knowledge and skill of mine may yet prove to be useful to me in this Outer world.

'I have heard that,' said Benakiell. 'However, I did not know it for sure until you told me.' He looked satisfied as if a small piece of tangled thread had fallen loose of its knots. 'I cannot scribe myself,' he confessed.

'I did wish to learn how to read some scribing when I was travelling and trading, but there is little enough call for it here, and nobody to teach it. What need do we have of it? Most of the scribes live in the bigger places, and they make goodly trades for their skill. It is the only sure way of sending a message far away, for many will forget the exact words of a message. The OutRiders use scribing a great deal apparently.' He looked at me expectantly, as if waiting for me to add to his knowledge of the OutRiders, but I had nothing to say. I had heard of them quite a few times now since I had left the Temple where I had not heard mention of them at all in all the time I had lived there.

At that point, we heard laughter and the melodious sound of Achillea's voice as she and Ashtun walked up the path. The sound of her voice reminded me of something I had wanted to ask Benakiell.

'Who decides what path of work a person makes their work? Can you change your path once it has been set? In the Temple, your path is set from an early age. It is the Goddess's destiny for you, and it does not change.'

'Well, usually you decide for yourself, but many people travel on the path of work taken by their parents or another family member,' he explained. 'My father made dwellings, as did his father before him. When I was young, I became a traveller and a trader, and had little use for my dwelling making skills, but when Velosia and I settled here, my skills were able to be used, and even now, I find plenty of trade work both here and in other villages. Sometimes I travel to work on bigger dwellings over there to the west and am away from the village for some weeks. It is demanding work, but I trade for many useful items. Why do you ask?'

I told him hurriedly that I thought Achillea was ill suited to Beeguarding, and that I thought she had a very beautiful and unusual voice and that perhaps she might think about becoming a songmaker instead.

'Who should be a songmaker?' asked Achillea curiously, rounding the corner suddenly, before Benakiell had chance to respond to my suggestion. Flustered, I looked to the ground, unsure about how my suggestion might be taken. Once again, Benakiell helped me out of my dilemma.

'Talla was just saying that she thought you had a beautiful voice, Achillea, and she was wondering why you did not choose a path as a songmaker?'

Ashtun exclaimed triumphantly and looked at me with something approaching respect, as he said, 'You see, Achillea, I am not the only one who loves the sound of your voice! You are like a nightingale.' Achillea laughed again, and I watched Ashtun as he gazed at her, seemingly mesmerised by her.

'What would I sing about, Talla?' she asked simply. 'For a songmaker must not only sing, but also tell stories in their songs, and I am no good at that.'

'Tell the story of something you know, Achillea,' suggested Benakiell. 'Sing of your mother and how she was and what she did for you. If your song is good, it will be remembered and so will your mother, Cassia. Perhaps you can try it out on us later. For now, I must go with Talla back to my dwelling and get my Paradox oil for the dwelling and bring Talla's things.'

'I do not have possessions,' I said, half still in the Temple, in my mind. 'Possessions are only possessions if they belong to someone. I only have my drabcoat.'

'And your water gourd and pouch,' Benakiell reminded me. 'And your parchment, and charcoal. And I have a small basket of goods for you to cook with.'

I looked at him, horrified. 'I am not a provisioner. I cannot cook food. I will have to eat fruit and roots.'

'Here in Oramia, men and women cook food equally,' said Ashtun. 'We all learn from an early age how to cook food.' It sounded like a rebuke to me, but before I could answer him, Achillea interrupted.

'We will cook together, Talla, until you have learned some small things. Benakiell will teach you how to make his stews, and I can make good flatbreads, and Ashtun will teach you how to make his spicy sauce, won't you Ashtun?'

Ashtun acquiesced reluctantly. It seemed to me that he did not like me and yet he scarcely knew me, so it must be because of my being a Drab, as they called it. But Achillea liked me, and I knew that Ashtun liked Achillea, so she offered him little choice. Benakiell and I walked back to his dwelling, and left Achillea and Ashtun sitting in the shade of the Paradox tree, talking quietly.

'It's good to leave them alone sometimes,' said Benakiell.

'Why?' I asked, interested. He looked at me, puzzled by my question.

'Well, so that they can spend time together alone, and ... you know...' his voice ebbed away as he saw my bewildered expression. 'Well, maybe Achillea can explain it to you better than I can,' he said hurriedly. 'Let us get the things we need now, sister Talla, for we have work to do.' As soon as he mentioned work, I realised how much time I had wasted in frivolous conversation and felt ashamed that I had not tried harder to get my tasks completed, although I reminded myself, that yet again, I had not had a given set of tasks to complete, so I had no way of knowing whether I was doing them well or not.

'Work is given for pleasure,' I murmured, almost inside my head. I found the Aphorisms of Ashkana fascinating, and I often turned them over in my mind, as

FLAMMEUS

I worked in the Temple. They sounded so simple and true, but the more you tried to tease the words apart, the more unsure you became about their true meaning.

CHAPTER 6

When Benakiell and I returned to Cassia's old dwelling, Achillea and Ashtun were nowhere to be seen and Benakiell wanted to finish the dwelling, but I could see he did not want me there observing what he might do with the Paradox oil. I had already guessed that he used it to waterproof the mud on the outer of the dwelling, so I raised no objection when he suggested I could go and work in the overgrown garden again. It was peaceful working out there in the sun. The bright starlings chattered sporadically, the crickets hummed, and I set myself my own goals. Benakiell had brought back a hoe and I used that to clear away some of the creeping vines that threatened to strangle the old plants. I wondered how on earth Achillea did not feel ashamed of the garden. I knew it was her dead mother's garden and not her own, but it seemed disrespectful to me to have let it go to weeds like that, especially as I had seen how deeply affected Achillea had been by the death of her mother. But perhaps the garden made her think too much of the loss of her mother. I, who had never had a mother, struggled to understand how that might feel.

I cleared away the weeds and vines, working steadily in the heat, stopping occasionally for a drink from the water gourd which Benakiell had given to me before. When I had cleared the weeds, I could see that the garden had been portioned out into four main areas. One was planted with chickpeas and beans, one was planted with barley and millet, one was planted with pumpkins and gourds and one was planted with herbs and spices, like the small chillies I had spotted earlier. In between these plots were planted trees; pomegranate and Paradox, figs and some other small fruit which seemed to attract the insects. After I had cleared the ground of vines and weeds, I turned my attention to the trees to see what was left on them. In truth, Achillea and I had harvested all the decent fruit. There were a few hard, green pomegranates left, the size of a lemon which were never going to ripen, and little else. The Paradox pods had not yet ripened, but as I looked upwards at the branches of one of the trees, startled by the scampering of a small, mustard coloured squirrel, I saw there were hollow logs hanging from the upper boughs of the tree by ropes. The squirrel sat above them, on a thin branch chattering indignantly at me.

I tried to look inside the logs, but they were too far up, and even though I tried to climb part way up the tree, there were no real footholds, and I was reduced to puzzling over them. I glanced up at them absently from time to time but still could not understand what use they might have, until I happened on a small group of bushes right at the back of the garden, near the Paradox tree. It was only as I brushed past their furry greyness that I realised that they were lavender bushes. The sharp, sweet scent filled my head and I immediately thought it must be Lilavis, for the scent of lavender denoted that day in the Temple. I tried to work back the days...I had left the Temple on Flammeus, then slept the night outside so the next day would have been Aureus, and then Flavus and... I stopped, puzzled. It could not yet be Lilavis by my reckoning and yet here was the scent of it filling my head. I shook myself and realised that although we in the Temple observed the days of our lives with colours and distinctive scents, people here on the Outer did not seem to. It felt somehow wrong for me to crush the leaves of the plant, and to pluck a stalk of its flowers and allow the rich scent to invade my mind, but I did. When I looked again at the bush, I could see it was crawling with bees, busily foraging in the flowers. I watched them as they worked steadily at their tasks, and then followed them upwards with my eyes as they flew off and realised that they were flying in and out of the hollow logs I had seen earlier.

Of course! Cassia had been a Beeguard, and these must have been her beehives. I wondered that Achillea had not mentioned them when we had been in the garden, but I supposed that they were so much a part of the scenery for her that she did not notice them, whereas for me, coming as I did, from the Temple where we did not keep bees or gather their honey, they stood out. It was a curious thing that we did not have hives for honey at the Temple. If it was a job demarcated for women here on the Outer, it did at least mean that there was nothing that a woman could not do relating to it, and consequently it might have been ideal for the Maids and the Priestesses. Instead, we had traded for our medicinal honey, and I had gathered, from listening to Helvina complaining about how many figs she had had to trade for just one small jar of honey, that it was a valuable item.

When I had spoken to Achillea earlier, she said that her mother had kept flowering shrubs and trees at the edge of the garden, but I could only see this one lavender bush which was crawling with bees, all busily trying to find a free floret. Looking more closely however, I spotted that under what was, I thought, just a mound covered in bindweed, was a row of other lavender bushes, half choked of light and covered with thick bindweed. A few brave bees had tried to make their way to these plants, but it was hard work for them, and of course there were not many flowers because they had been so starved of light. I took the hoe again and began to clear away the vines from the lavender. The scent was strong and filled my head. Every time I used the hoe to pull off more creepers, a fresh waft of scent was released. The bees which had been on the first lavender bush flew around me, but they did not sting me. They seemed both curious and grateful, if a bee can be grateful.

I murmured to them under my breath as I worked, 'Be still bees, I come to give you flowers of lavender, not to hurt you.' When I had finally cleared the creepers off, there were a dozen or so lavender bushes interplanted with some other flowers underneath them which I had not seen before. It was quiet there in the garden now, and I stopped to sit under the Paradox tree in the shade, to catch my breath. I watched the bees idly as I rested and saw how they seemed full of purpose. Each one proceeded with its task diligently, and they reminded me for all the world of we Maids, going about our work at the Temple, each focused on her task, and giving it her full attention. I was loath to return to Benakiell in case I offended him by viewing his waterproofing technique with the Paradox oil. It seemed odd here in the Outer that they were so concerned with keeping these secrets from one another. I had never felt, in the Temple as if I were keeping my work a secret from anyone, although I had never been asked the details of my cleaning job before. The Provisioners and the Physics and the Seamstresses did not know how to do my job, and I did not know how to do theirs, except for the essentials which we had all learned in Scholar before our paths had been chosen. Choice, in the Temple, had been largely something that other people did on our behalf, I reflected.

Later, when Achillea had returned and Benakiell had finished the dwelling, I sat in Cassia's old dwelling and thought what a strange feeling it was to be so responsible for something. Although I did not really own the dwelling, I felt as though it were almost mine, and I felt the need to clean it over and over and to make minute adjustments to the way in which my water gourd hung on the wall, or the place where my leather pouch and parchments would be stored. Achillea had provided me with a piece of woven cloth for her new netela which was the price of my having her mother's old dwelling, and I was determined to make a good job of it, so, once Benakiell had gone to visit Gladia, and Achillea had gone back to her own dwelling to cook (for both of us, for which I was very grateful), I started on the design for her netela. At first, I had thought to include the flowers of her mother's garden and the bees, but then I remembered the curious reaction I had had to my drawings of the bees before. I had not spoken much to Benakiell about the bees and the hives and clearing the bushes for them to feed on, but I saw his eyes drawn to the lavender bushes and then to the hives in the trees. I wondered why bees were such a delicate subject of discussion here, when they also seemed so much a part of their everyday life. I figured a design of flowers and birds instead, surrounded by spirals which made me think of the song coming from the birds. I was still convinced that Achillea would make a great Songmaker and determined to talk to her some more about it over our meal. Benakiell had told me that he would walk by on the next day to see how I was getting on. I tried to express my gratitude to him, but he brushed it off.

'It is better for you to live in your own dwelling. It means both you and I can sleep inside on a sleeping mat and will help to protect you from the OutRiders if they ride through this way. They have not been through Mellia for some time and it is surely time for another release from the Temple soon, since they seem not to have come out for you, for some reason.' At this he shot me a sharp glance, as if I should know why the OutRiders had not looked for me. I did not know anything about them except that I felt increasingly glad that they had not come looking for me as I did not know what I would have done if they had.

Over the next few days I worked carefully on the pattern for Achillea's netela. I was conscious of how little parchment I had and decided to try to make a small bank of different components of designs which I could freely mix and match together in a range of ways. So, I cut the parchment into small squares, leaving only one large piece which Benakiell had given to me. On one piece I drew an open flower, on another the spikes of lavender. On the next piece it was a nightingale, and on the next a sunbird. I made drawings of leaves and spiral forms. It was pleasing, soothing work. When I had pricked the holes in the patterns (with a new thorn which I had found on a bush in Cassia's garden), I began to lay them out on the length of cloth for Achillea's netela. I had decided to embroider each end, as was traditional, and have a small pattern of spirals like the tendrils of a plant or the music of a song along the edges all the way round. It took me a lot of time to put all the different parts of it together in a manner that was pleasing to me, and Achillea sometimes complained that I was altogether too fond of working but she enjoyed seeing the pattern emerge. I made sure that she did not see me pounce the pattern, and she believed that I drew it straight on to the cloth and marvelled at how cunningly I could reproduce the patterns. Over these days too, she taught me how to make a basic flatbread from flour and gave me my own flatbread starter. When I thought about it later, I thought it was a good way of sharing; to use some of the starter to make the flatbread rise and then to use some more of it to save again; continually replenishing it with new flour and water and continually saving it. It reminded me of an emberjar, which worked in the same way; use the embers to build a fire and then save some embers from that fire to build the next one. They are not the same embers, but they are part of the same thing.

Learning to make the flatbread was hard for me. For Achillea, and for Ashtun and Benakiell and Gladia who all stopped by at different times to witness my efforts, it was almost laughable that a woman who had reached the age of choice could not feed herself or make a flatbread. They all learned from their mothers and fathers at an early age, and it was second nature to them. Every night they would check there was enough starter and feed it with a little more flour and water. Then in the morning, they would mix it up with more flour and water until it made a creamy batter. This was then left until the time for the main meal of the day and would rise. It was cooked on a flat metal platter – Achillea lent me one to use – and you first rubbed this with salt before pouring the mixture on to it to cook. It took some attempts before my flatbreads were edible, but eventually Achillea pronounced them adequate. It seemed very hard work to me, and I found cleaning and tidying much easier, but Achillea assured me it was absolutely no effort at all for her whereas cleaning and tidying made her feel quite exhausted.

By my reckoning it was five days since I had left the Temple when I finally finished the design on the netela. I had tried to do my best work on it since Achillea had been so good to me. When Achillea had looked at the final design and clapped her hands in delight, we went to Gladia's dwelling, so that she could begin on the stitchery. She was sitting on her dwelling step when we walked up, fanning herself idly in the heat. I was still surprised by the amount of time which these Outer people spent in doing nothing, and yet they appeared to do sufficient work to be happy. I once asked Achillea why she sat so long, doing nothing, and she assured me that she was thinking, and it was very important. I found this hard to believe, as most of my thinking in the Temple had been done whilst I was working, and it was a strange concept for me to think without being busy at the same time.

Gladia looked at my drawing on the netela carefully and consulted with me about what colours I thought were most appropriate. This too I found difficult, as in the Temple the only colours with which I had had any kind of close association had been the deep red of Flammeus. I asked Achillea whether she wanted the pattern to look realistic or not, and she laughed her musical laugh and said she thought it might be lovely in whatever colour I wanted. On a whim, I asked her what day she had been born on, or what day her Coming of Age was.

'I have no idea,' she said. 'However, I know I am just a little older than you, Talla, for my coming of age was the day before we laid my mother to rest a year ago.'

Gladia looked sombre. 'Aye, it was a terrible time,' she confirmed. 'First Velosia, and then Cassia. We laid Cassia down on the day of Lilavis; seemed so fitting after all the love she showed those bees with the lavender. That means your Coming of Age was on Indicus.'

Indicus seemed to suit Achillea. Her laugh reminded me of dark river water or the deepest dark dusk when you heard the nightingales. I suggested to Gladia that she sew the leaves and vines and spirals in deep indigo blue and then sew the birds in whatever bright colours took her fancy. This idea pleased her, and she went away to find her threads to get started straight away. She also gave me some other lengths of fabric so that I could draw on them some more designs for her to stitch some netelas. She had the plan to take three with her when she next went to the market in Sanguinea. I wanted to go to Sanguinea too, but both she and

Benakiell counselled against it and suggested to me that I should bide my time, as the OutRiders had still not come to Mellia and they did not want me to be seized in Sanguinea. I was disappointed because I wanted to see this place which was so much bigger than little Mellia but was beginning to learn that Benakiell and Gladia knew much more than they told me and was grateful for their care, even whilst I found it exasperating.

CHAPTER 7

Over the next few days, I began to settle into life in Mellia, although I was still not sure how long I would remain. I was introduced to some of the other residents and met a family of five who lived near Gladia. The mother was called Karula, and the father, Verach. They had three children who varied in age between a daughter of crawling age to a boy called Avech who was in the Third Age of Childhood and was learning his father's skill of weaver. I saw them from far off sometimes, wending their way to the weaving shed they had built of sturdy wood to shield them from the prying eyes of the women in the village. I did not, personally, think there would be any great mystery in weaving cloth; I had looked at cloth often enough to know that it was made by weaving threads in and out of one another. There was a girl of around nine called Argania, who stuck to her mother's side and seemed barely able to speak- at least not to me, whom she eyed with silent suspicion. Her sister, Tilia, was a happy child and spent most of her time creeping around in the dirt outside the dwelling picking up unsuitable objects and taking great delight in shovelling them into her plump cheeks. Her mother spent most of her time removing these objects and admonishing the child who took the scoldings placidly and waited until her mother's back was turned before making yet another attempt. In truth, this child made me smile, for she had an indefatigable, sunny nature. Sometimes I would sit with her for a few minutes while her mother went to wash clothes with Argania, and I would present her with a peeled stick which she liked to chew with her new teeth. I had not had much contact with small children since I had left their ranks myself, and although I found the older ones unsettling at times, this small creature was more like a goat kid or a bird, and I found myself enjoying her company, such as it was. She made no particular demands of me, and I was free to sit and think. She had made a pet of a small tortoise, and I enjoyed watching her following it around, trying to bribe it with leaves and fruit, and decorating its shell with flower petals. Once, I used some damp clay to set whole flowers on its back, and it trundled around like a moving flower garden. This amused both of us, and Tilia clapped her chubby hands in delight.

I had not made any progress in finding out about my mother's brooch and what it meant, and why there were such reactions to the pictures of bees and to the OutRiders, and I wanted to find out more about these things without making provoking suspicion. The people here in Mellia seemed to bear no ill will towards the bees which flew around the village, and regularly traded for honey, so it seemed to me that the bees must symbolise something strange to them. They were not frightened of the bees themselves, so I thought it must be something about what they stood for. I had asked if anyone else in the village knew anything about the beehives when I talked about them to Achillea. She professed no real knowledge of how they worked, or how to remove the honey from them, only saying vaguely that her mother had not thought the time was right to show her what to do. I thought that Cassia had perhaps been right. Achillea, for all her natural cheerfulness and mischief, showed no real interest in the bees. However, she did introduce me to an elderly couple who lived a little distance out of Mellia, along a dusty track. Their names were Chavich and Rupicola, and Rupicola had also been a Beeguard, before Cassia. They were of advanced age, being in the First Age of

Wisdom, and were both a little deaf. Achillea introduced me to them and told Rupicola that I was interested in her mother's beehives and in Beeguarding, and promptly disappeared, leaving me sitting awkwardly on a mat, talking rather loudly to Rupicola, after she had told her husband to leave the room, so we could discuss the bees.

Rupicola repeated herself many times, but I could see the value of that for me, especially since it was a subject about which I knew nothing. She told me, rather unhelpfully, that everyone developed their own way of dealing with their bees, and that although she herself had been someone who had used smoke to cause the bees to leave the hives, Cassia had had a different gift which meant that the bees left her alone when she came to take the honey. Rupicola talked to me as if I should know some things, and I did not like to tell her that I had not even looked inside a hive before. She told me that some honey could only be harvested at certain times of the year, on special days, depending on the hive. That reminded me a little of the Goddess and the way in which we had only used certain colours and flowers and scents to worship her on certain days. She told me the names of some shrubs and flowers which attracted the bees, and I assured her I would try to plant them. At times, Rupicola was confused and vague. She seemed to think I was Achillea and told me several times how pleased she was that I was following in my mother's footsteps finally. It was easier, and quieter, to just pretend that I was Achillea, as I could not countenance explaining the complexity of my situation to her in a loud clear voice. She instructed me to check the hives for honeycombs and to make sure that I left some of it in the hive. I asked her how to reach the hives and she looked at me, bewildered. I sensed that she was tired of answering questions, and I suspected that her mind was tired too, for she seemed to keep falling asleep with her eyes open. At length, I stood up and made my excuses to leave. As I left the room, her sleepy eyes snapped open and were suddenly sharp and clear.

'Come here child,' she instructed, and obediently I went to her and bowed my head respectfully. She took my hand and held her own hand over the top of it, hovering so closely that they almost touched. I felt a warmth like soft warm honey between us, even though nothing was touching me, and she moved her hand sharply away.

'Are you the one?' she murmured to herself. I did not think that I had heard this right, or rather, I was sure that I had heard it right, but was bewildered as to its meaning, and asked the old woman to repeat what she had said. But her eyes glazed again, and she motioned me away irritably, leaning her head by the side of the dwelling as if preparing for sleep.

CHAPTER 8

After I left the old Beeguard, I walked slowly back to Gladia's house, where I was going to see if she had yet returned from the market in Sanguinea, where she had taken the worked netelas. It was not yet clear to me what traded goods I could expect for my contribution to the netelas. After all, it was Gladia who had the cloth, and Gladia who had sewn the design, and indeed Gladia who had walked the long walk to Sanguinea and sat in the market with them. She had asked me before she left what she should try to find for me. I had much of the food I needed already, and only asked for salt. Achillea had looked meaningfully at my dirty drabcoat and then at Gladia, and, embarrassed, I had asked for a soapball too. I was not used to this idea of working for one's own gain. For me, work had always been my life. This is no complaint; work filled my time, and although I had precious little other time to pursue my curiosities, especially when I knew the value of scribing and reading, I did not have to use much of my mind for cleaning, which left it free to think on other things. Here on the Outer, they were much occupied with aspects of life from which we Maids had been shielded during our time in the Temple. Since I had left, I had become more aware of feelings inside me which seemed to have been suppressed during my time at the Temple. Perhaps we had no time for them, or perhaps no need for them. Our pleasure, if indeed that is what it was, was to serve the Goddess in whatever way was deemed most appropriate for us by the Priestesses. Out here, I was more aware of how other people's actions had their effect on my feelings. In the Temple, there were no definitions of feelings, except regarding the

Goddess. So, we were told that worshipping her made us feel joyful, or that our lack of work would make her feel angry, but we had no understanding of what it meant. Since I had come to Mellia, I had found out that some feelings came from my interactions with others; Achillea's singing lifted my heart, Benakiell could make me smile with his wry observant asides, and Gladia emanated a sort of sturdy security, like the pillars of the Temple itself. I wondered what effect I had on the feelings of those around me. I was unsure of Ashtun. He seemed suspicious of me and guarded his time with Achillea jealously. I often caught him studying me when he came to visit her, and whenever I caught his eyes he looked away. I pushed at my hair and realised that I should have asked Gladia to try to trade a comb for me. Now I would have to wait until the next trip to Sanguinea and continue to use the comb of sharpened twigs laced together with grass blades I had made.

I looked across the land as I walked to Gladia's dwelling. To the west of Mellia, somewhere, there lay the Temple, hidden from outside eyes. We saw the sun and the sky, and the gardens where our food and the flowers to praise the Goddess were grown but I had never realised until I left the Temple how big the world was, and how much there was in it. I felt almost frightened that there was so much I did not know, and so much which I had not yet learned. More and more, I felt what Gladia called anger. I was angry that I had not, until now, even known anything about this different world where it was possible to live, or of different ways of living. I was angry that the Priestesses had kept so much from us and was unsure of why they had done so. I felt like I wanted to go back there, and ask Asinte those questions, and shake Lunaria by the shoulders and ask her why she had accepted her fate so willingly. I pulled up some long grass as I walked past and tore it into small pieces, full of my own anger.

Across the plains, I could see the columns of dirty charcoal clouds massing. The rains had not yet reached us here in Mellia, although the air seemed full of moisture. The bees in the gardens were more active than usual and more intent upon their gathering tasks. The dark purple mountains which ringed the flat, golden plain frowned down, and I felt irritable and then anxious to see Gladia and hear her news. I arrived at her dwelling and saw that there were others already there, so I knew she must have arrived back home. I hung back at the doorway, unwilling to push in where there were others with more calls on her time and her bags of traded items, but as I arrived, the busy talking and muttering stopped, and they all turned to look at me.

'Come in, Talla,' called Gladia briskly, motioning me in firmly and directing pointed looks at a few of the other villagers who had been talking busily until I arrived. They took their leave, until all that were left were me and Gladia, Benakiell and Achillea. Ashtun took his leave reluctantly, shooting me sharp looks as he left as if he resented me for some unknown reason.

'How was the market?' I asked, unsure about why we were all sitting inside on this hot day.

'Ahh yes, it was very successful,' answered Gladia cheerfully. 'I traded your netelas for some good items, Talla, look what I have got for you.' She opened a cloth bundle and showed me a soapball, a cone of salt and a bone comb. I was surprised that she had managed to get them all for me and did not think I deserved them. I was especially touched that she had seen my need for the comb and had traded for it for me. I thanked her gratefully and promised to get to work on the next project she might have for me. I also opened my own cloth bundle and gave her the small tied bunch of chillies I had harvested that day from Cassia's old garden.

Benakiell interrupted Gladia's pleased responses to my gift. 'Gladia, we don't have much time. Tell Talla what else she needs to do and what you heard spoken in Sanguinea.' Gladia turned and frowned at him fiercely. I was puzzled. I had been looking forward to hearing all about Sanguinea and maybe sharing food with these people who were becoming important to me, but apparently an event had occurred which meant I would have to wait for that.

Gladia turned to one side and took out a package from her basket, handing it to me. It looked like more cloth for me to put my designs on but when I unwrapped it, I saw it was a dress. It had been embroidered inexpertly round the edges with a slapdash design and was obviously not new. I didn't know what Gladia expected me to do with it.

'Talla, I know that you are attached to that old drabcoat of yours, but you will have to take it off and get rid of it, as soon as possible. You need to get changed into this dress now, and we will have to work hard on you; we only have a few hours before the OutRiders get here.'

I looked at her dumbly. My drabcoat was, I knew, tatty and old and dirty. It was made of strips of patchwork fabric and had been worn by many before me. But it was, apart from the hidden brooch, my only possession from my time at the Temple, and I had only received the brooch from Lunaria when I left. I felt that I was carrying with me all my life when I wore the drabcoat. It helped me to remember who I was, and even though at the Temple I had only been one of many, I wanted to cling on to it. Without it I felt like I would be a nobody; someone who did not belong at the Temple, but who also did not belong in the Outer, even if she wore the clothing of the Outer; someone who seemed to be part of both worlds but unable to claim either.

'Hurry up Talla,' urged Benakiell. 'We must be rid of the drabcoat before they come or terrible things will happen. If they find the drabcoat or find you wearing it, they will know you are from the Temple. We need to show them that you are of Oramia, not the Temple.'

'It's not that bad, Talla,' offered Achillea cheerily. 'That old scrap of patchwork is falling apart anyway, and although this other dress is badly stitched, you and Gladia can unpick it and make it better later.'

I continued to stand silently. Gladia took hold of my arm and pushed the folded dress into my hands. 'This way,' she said firmly. 'You can get changed in here where I sleep,' and she led me through behind the reed screen.

'What will happen if I do not change?' I asked finally. 'What terrible things will happen?'

Gladia looked at me sharply. 'The OutRiders will stop at nothing to achieve their goals. When I was in Sanguinea, I heard from the other traders that the OutRiders had been there, searching for you. They knew your name and your birthdate. They said you had stolen something of great worth from the Temple, and they will stop at nothing to bring you back.'

I tried to ask again. 'But what will they do?' I was not sure about any of this. Surely it could be explained to these people that I had only got the brooch because Lunaria had given it to me, and that I had freely chosen to leave the Temple. Then I started to think about what might happen to Lunaria if it was found out that it was she who had helped me with the brooch, and how I could explain that I was able to read the scripts of choice and make my own choosing, beyond the influence of the Priestesses. But what could the OutRiders do?

Gladia sighed in exasperation. 'Talla, we do not have time for me to explain to you what the OutRiders might do, except to say that some people have said that it is better to be dead than to be found by an OutRider, and not only that, but they will do the same thing to anyone that is found to have helped you at any time. You will need to trust me on this, for now. They leave us alone, on the whole, to get on with our lives, as long as we take goods to the Temples to trade, but they will stop at nothing to achieve their goals.'

I thought of those who had helped me since I had chosen to walk out of the Temple. Lunaria, Merula and her family, Benakiell, Gladia, Achillea, and even the others; Ashtun, the old couple and Karula and her children. I realised suddenly how much my life had been changed by them already and the choices they had made to help me, and I realised that it was time for me to help them too. I had to trust them.

Then I remembered the brooch in my underpocket. I did not want Gladia to see it, but I had to protect it before the drabcoat was destroyed. I thought quickly, and feigned modesty.

'I will do as you ask,' I answered Gladia, lowering my eyes demurely. 'But I ask that you let me disrobe in solitude. It is hard for me to take off this drabcoat and I prefer to be on my own.' And, in fact, I did prefer to be on my own. I was accustomed to the sight of other women disrobing from our time in the Temple, but we did little observing of others, as our time was limited, and we focussed on bathing and washing at those times.

'Of course, sister,' murmured Gladia, leaving me behind the screen. Hurriedly I untied the ties at the side of the drabcoat and slipped it off me. I untied the underpocket from the main part of the drabcoat, feeling it quickly to ensure the brooch was still there. I tied the underpocket round my waist again first, making sure that it hung down low and could not be seen. I slipped on the dress. It felt very strange to no longer be wearing the drabcoat. The fabric of this dress was very smooth compared to the drabcoat, whose patchworked ridges I had got accustomed to, and the brightness of its creamy colour looked sharp against my skin. The needlework was a combination of greens and yellows, and it felt wrong for me to be wearing those colours until I remembered that the OutRiders had known my birthday and would expect me to dress in the colours of Flammeus, if any. My arms felt naked and exposed, since I had no netela to act as a shawl. I took a moment and then walked out from behind the screen.

'You picked a good fit, Gladia,' commented Achillea. 'It looks well on you Talla, even if it doesn't have your clever designs and Gladia's special stitchery. As I said before, you can always change it later.'

Gladia looked a little uncomfortable. 'I would have given you one of my own dresses, Talla, but I had traded all my goods almost by the time I heard the news and needed to get a dress for you, so I had to make do with what I could find.'

'I am grateful,' I reassured her. 'You have thought kindly of me to help me so much.'

'Where is the drabcoat?' interrupted Benakiell anxiously. 'I need to hide it before they get here. Gladia was told that they were making their way back to the Temple, stopping at every habitation on the way.'

'How do they know I did not go the other way?' I asked, puzzled.

'They will go down there too, Talla,' confirmed Benakiell. 'But we can only concern ourselves with what happens in Mellia. Did you go that way at all? I thought you only came this way from the Temple?'

I had not told them about Merula and her family, because of the brooch, but now I hastily told them about my encounter, leaving out all reference to the brooch and merely saying that I had then chosen to go the opposite direction.

'I wonder if they have yet found them,' mused Benakiell. 'It may be that they have already got this information from them.' My mind moved on quickly from that and I realised that if they had indeed spoken to Merula and her family, especially to her son Lashim, they would know all about the brooch. They would also know that I could draw and had parchment and charcoal with me. They would know that I had told Merula and her family that I was searching for someone in connection with it. I hoped that none of that family had taken too much notice of my appearance. The drabcoats had this effect on people here in the Outer; their eyes skimmed over your face and returned to the drabcoat with a sort of fascination as if there were nothing else interesting to them.

'I must do something with my hair,' I spoke my thoughts aloud, 'and I must hide my drawing things somewhere safe.'

'I can take your drawing things,' said Gladia comfortably. 'I have some things that I have tried to draw patterns on before, and they can just go in with them.'

'I will do your hair straight away!' said Achillea, excitedly. 'I have been longing to do something to it since the day you arrived!' She pushed me eagerly so that I was sitting in front of her and seized the comb which Gladia had traded for me. She began to drag the comb through my hair. While she tended to my hair, which I found strangely soothing, Benakiell talked to me, giving me the information that I must say to the OutRiders if they questioned me. He told me that I was to say that my name was Allia and that I was his niece from the village of Lacteus, far to the south. I had come to live here when my mother had died and had moved into Cassia's hut after she too had died. He told me that the OutRiders would travel through the settlement and ask questions where they saw fit. If all appeared normal, they would leave quite quickly, but if anyone told them something which seemed untrue, they would remain in Mellia until it was resolved. Gladia then suggested to me that I should remain quiet and demure, with my eyes cast to the ground when they spoke with me, and that I should be doing a normal activity for the village when they arrived. In my case, it would be best if I could attempt to persuade them that I was a Beeguard, as they were known to be uncomfortable in the presence of bees. I wondered how Benakiell knew so much about the OutRiders, and where they got their information from, but there was no time for me to ask questions as they prepared me for my role as Allia.

I did find time to ask what of the other residents of Mellia; Karula and her family, and Rupicola and the other families with whom I had had little enough contact although we each knew of the other's presence. Benakiell sought to reassure me. 'There's no love here for the OutRiders,' he replied grimly. 'We live with them, as we live with the Temple, for they both control us in different ways. We seek only to live our lives in peace, to trade and to be free to do as we wish.' I found it hard to imagine that the Temple controlled the lives of the people of the Outer; High Priestess Asinte had assured us that the people of the Outer only attended the Temple through choice and came in such great numbers because of the manifold blessings that the Goddess brought to their lives. They had certainly appeared to me, as a Maid snatching swift glances at them through the holes in the carved screen, to be happy to be there; to have entered the Temple dutifully and with reverence. Perhaps it had all been play acting after all.

'And whatever you do,' added Gladia, 'don't do that thing where you look at the floor and mutter Praise Her Name whenever anyone mentions the Goddess. It will give you away immediately.' I felt the flame of anger grow inside me again. It caught hold of me so swiftly sometimes that I could not stop it gaining a foothold. I had tried over the past days spent in Mellia to mute the angry feelings I sometimes had, and at least push them down so the flames did not shoot so high. I had imagined my anger as a fire partly because of my own day's name Flammeus and my connections to fire through my birth on Conflagration day. I reasoned that perhaps it would help me to see my anger as a fire spark and my mind as an emberjar. I could keep the glowing coals enclosed in my mind and use them safely sometimes without the fire gaining control of the whole landscape. This was the image I had decided upon but so many things had happened that I was losing control of my inner emberjar. I held my tongue, for I knew they were only trying to help me, even though it seemed they did not understand the Goddess, nor yet understand that it was so very difficult for me to stop myself from responding in ways I had been responding since I was a very small child.

Eventually, Achillea finished combing my hair and braided it away from my face in the style of the Outer women. We were never encouraged to do more than comb our hair in the Temple to keep it tidy, for spending more time on personal adornment than on working for the Goddess would have been disrespectful to her. I felt over my head with my hand. I felt somehow naked, dressed as I was now, even though I was wearing less flamboyant clothes than Achillea and Gladia. I felt that my face was too much on display. I was used to not showing my face and habitually lowered my eyes or bent my head to the ground, as we had been taught to do as Maids, in preparation for wearing the veil as Priestesses.

Achillea smiled at me triumphantly. 'I knew there was a lovely face under that hair. You look very fine, Talla!'

'Perhaps too fine,' worried Benakiell. 'She needs to get that dress a bit dirtier. Achillea, her hair looks very good, but can you try and make it look a little less cared for, as if she had it done a few days ago?'

'No!' objected Achillea. 'Benakiell, doing hair is what we young women like to do. It would be unnatural if Allia,' and she turned and smiled at me, 'did not want her hair done by me, her only young friend in this dull place. Trust me, it would be much stranger if she did not care for her hair!'

'I think she's right,' agreed Gladia, also smiling. 'Now come along, you need to go and get started on working in the garden. I have organised for Rupicola's old bee ladder to be brought to Cassia's garden, Talla, so that it will seem more as if you are a Beeguard. The OutRiders know little enough of how to deal with bees, so, as long as you listened carefully to Rupicola, you may fool them yet.'

I followed on behind her and Achillea as we walked to Cassia's garden, which I still could not think of as being mine. I kept telling myself that I was Allia, Benakiell's niece as we walked along. It seemed too beautiful a day to be feeling such anxious anticipation. I could not imagine the OutRiders coming here, much less what they might look like, and I did not want to ask Achillea or Gladia any more questions. Instead, I walked along quietly, listening to the toooo-wup-tooooo of the doves in the Paradox tree. The sky was a bright clear blue, the colour of Azureus, and the air was clear although yet again in the distance, I saw the pillars of rainclouds building up in the distance. As we passed my dwelling, I remembered my drawing things and parchments, and quickly went to get them, tying the covering parchment over the rest of my pattern pieces and hoping that Gladia would not undo them and find my pounced patterns.

CHAPTER 9

Benakiell had taken my drabcoat off me and left before us. I had no idea what he was going to do with it. Perhaps he would bury it or burn it. While the people on the Outer disdained those of us clad in the drabcoat, I had grown more attached to it since I had left the Temple. Perhaps it was because it was almost my only link with the place where I had grown up, but perhaps also, I liked the way in which it had seemed to render me invisible in the Temple and longed for that anonymity again sometimes. There, I could blend into the background, and people forgot I was there. It was made of many different strips of earth coloured cloth, which all felt slightly different. It made me feel as if I was carrying with me small pieces of other people's lives. I resolved that one day, if I was able, I might wear a drabcoat again. I mused that although in the Temple the drabcoats belonged to none of us and to all of us, since I had left the drabcoat had become mine, and with ownership, came attachment.

When we arrived at the garden, I spotted the bee ladder that Gladia had brought down from Rupicola's dwelling. It had been made from the trunk of a medium sized tree which had regular branches off both sides. It could be leaned against a taller tree and ascended easily enough. I leaned it up against the tree from which the hives all hung and, having checked that it was stable, planted my foot on the first branch and began to ascend, albeit with a degree of caution. Achillea laughed nervously. 'Don't go too high, you might fall off!' I assured her that I would come down if I felt unsteady, but privately my heart sang. It was wonderful to be up here, higher than anyone else. The tree was lightly leafed, and I could see through the dappling light across the plains to the mountains. I had placed the ladder quite close to one of the hives, and I was curious about what it would be like in the hive and how the bees would behave.

The hive was made of a hollowed log, hung from the tree with a thin bark rope. As I was up close to it, I could hear the tiny noises of many bees inside, moving around, their wings vibrating, the buzzing noise amplified by the log. They ignored me as I stood close to their home and flew in and out busily. I reached out to the hive and rested my hand on its surface. It was warm from the sun and you could feel the grain where it had weathered. It felt like when I had oiled the feet of the Goddess; you could feel a kind of ancient spirit humming beneath your touch. I looked out again over the plain, wondering if I might see the OutRiders coming but there was nothing in the direction in which I looked.

'Allia!' called Achillea, suddenly. 'Allia, these Riders would have speech with you.' I looked down and saw that there had entered three riders into the garden, silently. How they had managed to get there so quietly and yet so swiftly tantalised my mind. I had hoped that my mind would have had some few minutes to prepare, and yet here they were, already.

'A moment only, sister,' I replied as I parried for time to prepare myself. 'I need to secure the hive.'

I reached out to the hive and pretended to tie the knot of rope more firmly to the hive. The bees inside grumbled as I made the hive sway this way and that way, but they settled. Covertly I looked down and was gratified that I had given myself a little extra time to prepare myself, for what I saw took my breath away.

The OutRiders rode sturdy, steel grey horses. They had long legs and delicate arching necks which were festooned with leather bridles and harnesses upon which metal discs had been attached. The effect was to make them shimmer in the sun, like fish scales. From the crupper were hung soft red tassels. They stood quietly, their ears twitching with the flies, their tails moving likewise. They showed no evidence of strain from the weight of the armoured Riders on their backs, which must have been considerable. Achillea stood calmly to one side of the garden, with her basket balanced artfully on her hip. She had put some pomegranates in it that she had been given by Ashtun and it looked as if they had just been picked. One of the OutRiders and his horse stood near her, one stood at the pathway to the garden, and one stood under the tree which my ladder leaned against. Of course, they would be especially interested in young women, I thought to myself, and wished that I had considered this and asked to have worn a man's robe.

'Hurry up.' The OutRider under the tree spoke. The voice was the voice of one who expected to be obeyed immediately. It was not raised; on the contrary, he spoke in an ostensibly polite manner, with even tones, but his voice was devoid of feeling. I did not want to obey him, and yet I found myself moving hastily towards the ladder. As I scrambled down the ladder in a rather ungainly fashion, my mind was blank of any ideas to save myself, and I concentrated on trying to come down in a modest fashion. When I had finally got my feet on the earth again, I looked up to the OutRider on the horse. I wondered if he ever dismounted.

He wore a dark brown polished leather armour. It had been ingeniously jointed in different places to allow for the smooth and unfettered movement of his body. Each piece looked as if it had been specially made to fit exactly. The shiny leather carapace reminded me of insects; beetles and ants and scorpions who also seemed to have a kind of jointed armour. There was no way to view the face, for that too was guarded by an intricate filigree net which shielded his face, and by a leather and red cloth helmet which covered his head. It reminded me of the veils worn in the Temple, and I was not intimidated by it, but rather, in a curious way, felt comforted by it. I guessed that he must be very hot under the armour, but he showed no signs of discomfort.

'Who are you?' he questioned.

'I am Allia, of the village of Lacteus,' I replied, demurely casting my eyes to the ground. 'My uncle Benakiell invited me here to stay since Achillea's mother Cassia died.'

'What do you do here?'

'She helps me in my mother's garden,' answered Achillea before I could answer myself. 'My mother was a Beeguard and I know nothing of the job. Allia is a Beeguard too and has come to help me with the bees. You saw her up there on the ladder adjusting the hive.'

The OutRider grunted. His horse stood poised, ready to move at his master's wish. The Rider by Achillea smoothly dismounted and went over to her. I did not know what he might do. Now that he had got off the horse, I could see he was very tall, a good span taller than most of the men of Mellia. I could not see the person at all though, only that shiny, oiled leather armour. He stood over Achillea menacingly, and she cowered as he came nearer.

'We did not ask you, woman.' He spoke quietly. 'Keep your mouth shut or we will shut it for you.'

The Rider near me looked down on me. He was considerably taller than me, too. As I have said, they seemed taller than the men of Mellia, and I was smaller than the women of Mellia. It was like being next to a tree.

'Answer the question.' It was an order like no other I had heard. It reminded me of how Priestess Asinte made an order; very quietly, but with such implacable hardness behind it that you felt you would rather obey the order than find out what might ensue if you disobeyed it.

'It is as she says,' I answered in an equally quiet tone. 'I am a Beeguard. Achillea knows nothing of Beeguarding and took no knowledge from her late mother Cassia. Since her death, the village has been without honey because they no longer have a working Beeguard and my uncle Benakiell invited me here to help.'

The Rider looked at me intently. At least I assume he did for I could not see his face. He gestured to the Rider who was standing mute and stationary at the path to the garden. This Rider moved over so that he too stood next to me. I felt stifled by my nearness to their horses. I had never been near one before, and the size of them and their muscular power was intimidating. I could not help glancing at the silver discs which had been fitted to the bridles, for they did not make a sound as the horse moved and I could see that they had been backed with some soft leather or vellum so that they did not chink as they hit against each other when the horse was moving. There was a shield mounted off the saddle, with its back to the horse, so you could see the holding bar inside it which was made of wood, and the underside of the shield which seemed to be made of a tough sort of hide which had been coated in some sort of substance, possibly Paradox oil. I quickly lowered my eyes to the floor when I realised that I might show too much interest in these Riders. However, I was still curious about them, and although Achillea was obviously frightened of them, for her hands shook, as she stood, holding her basket of pomegranates, I did not know what to expect. I had no experience of anyone hurting me or punishing me, except when I was in the First Age of Childhood, for minor transgressions, for we Maids did not disobey. It was not within us.

'What are you looking at?' Again, the question, almost mildly put, yet somehow menacing.

'Your horse, brother,' I answered without thinking, and answering honestly.

'I am no brother of yours,' answered the OutRider, sharply. 'And I am not convinced you are a Beeguard either, are you Talla?'

He had slipped in my name very casually, and I was grateful that I had looked to the floor in deference when I spoke with him, so that he did not see my eyes widening in response.

'I beg your pardon,' I said, in response. 'I am Allia, not Talla, perhaps you heard it wrongly?'

'I heard nothing wrong,' he answered. He gestured again with his hand and the OutRider to the left of me took out his arrows and his bow. I felt sick, and did not know where to look, or what to do. I kept my head bowed and saw from the corner of my eye that Achillea too had her head bent to the ground.

'A test of your skill, sister... Allia, was it?' said the OutRider pleasantly, as if he were wishing me a good day as I walked past his dwelling. He dropped his hand down abruptly and the other Rider notched his arrow into his bow and aimed up into the Paradox tree near the garden which was festooned with hives. The arrow flew through the rope that had been holding up the hive which I pretended to secure earlier and the hive at first jangled down on one string, jerking awkwardly before the whole thing dropped to the floor.

'You do not appear to have secured it very well,' murmured the OutRider who appeared to oversee this small force of three. 'Show us your skills with the bees, so we can see a real Beeguard in action.' He kicked me casually in the back while he sat on the horse, and I stumbled forward towards the hive. I felt sure that he would find out that I was an imposter, for I had never even been near to a hive before. I could feel everyone watching me, including Achillea. I had to stay calm, for Rupicola had told me that the bees could sense anxiety and anger in a person. I made myself think of the seven-step process of cleaning and encouraged my mind to concentrate on it. I bent down to the hive. There was an angry, grumbling buzzing coming from within. Instinctively, I placed my hands over the hive as I had done before, and then hovered them over it, just as Rupicola had hovered her hands over me. I could see that at the end was a board through which a small hole had been made, and which could be raised to gain access to the hive. Taking in a breath, I lifted it up to reach in for the honeycomb, as Rupicola had instructed me. When I had listened to her earlier that day, I had never imagined that I would have to prove myself so quickly and with no practice, in front of a hostile audience. But I had no option; there was no way to talk myself out of this and I knew that if they divined that I was not a Beeguard, my whole story would collapse, and their casual brutality would be visited upon the other people in the village. I waited patiently after I slid the slat upwards but could hear the mounting noise of the bees within the hive. I imagined what it must be like to have been thrown all about in the fall from the tree and to know nothing of what was going on outside. Perhaps a little like me when I left the Temple. And so, believing I knew how they felt, I moved a little way from the hive.

'The bees will be angry with you,' I stated matter of factly to the OutRiders. 'You may wish to be wary of them.' Of course, I feared that they would be angry with me too, but I hoped, from what Benakiell had said earlier of the OutRiders dislike of bees, that they would be on edge. They did not move, but the horses' legs tensed. It was as if the horses were connected to the Riders in some unseen way, for they seemed to reflect their inner thoughts. With this in mind, I decided to watch the horses rather than the Riders.

'I look forward to a demonstration of your skill,' repeated their leader. He sat easily in his saddle, confident, but his horse's legs were trembling slightly. The OutRider near Achillea shifted slightly in his saddle and his horse sidestepped quietly. The one who had shot the arrow sat implacable in the saddle and his horse too seemed more relaxed than the other two. I stood silently, waiting for the bees to emerge from the hive. They came out like water, first in drops and then in larger groups and then in a stream or a waterfall. There were hundreds of bees there and they flew as if they were one creature with many different parts but with one mind. The sound was like rushing water too. I stood quietly near the hive, dumbly waiting for them to start attacking me and wondering how many times I would be stung before I called out in pain, or before they moved on to the OutRiders. Rupicola had told me that the bees consented to coming out of the hive at specific times of year, when the honey could be harvested easily, and at other times, their ire was raised, and they fought against intruders. These bees had not had their honey harvested since Cassia's death and were quite unused to human contact. It seemed unlikely that they would not sting anyone, especially given the violent manner in which they had been removed from the tree.

They flew over to the leader of the Riders and hovered over him and his horse in the same way that my hands had hovered over the hive and that Rupicola's hands had hovered over me. He did not move a muscle, but his horse was so braced that I thought it might collapse. I watched it as the sweat ran down its legs, and its sinews quivered with the stress of the bees' visitation. The one with the bow and arrows leaned forward intently, watching for any sign from his leader that he should take action, though I did not know what he might plan to do except loose his arrows at me or Achillea. The atmosphere felt like a taut piece of rope being stretched to the utmost, and as the bees hovered angrily over the leader of the OutRiders, I knew I still had to prove myself to them, so I closed my eyes and silently offered a prayer up to the Goddess for protection before I held my arms up and out, so that I looked like a cross. I stood motionless, and as I waited, I heard a low and tuneful sound. Achillea, for all her evident fear, was making a low and musical humming noise with her lips closed. The music ebbed and flowed and rippled through the still air, picking up on the vibrations of the hundreds of bees until I was unsure about where the bees ended and where Achillea's humming began. As she hummed, the bees turned and flew straight towards me.

The OutRiders leaned forward on their horses, following the passage of the bees towards me with interest. I closed my eyes and waited for the bees to land on me and sting me. They flew so close to me that I could feel the fanning of their many wings moving the air against my face. Their bodies whirred with the effort of hovering in one place, but hover they did, for some time, just above my skin, as they had done to the OutRiders. The air hung still and then they landed on me. My arms were heavy with the weight of them. They covered me completely, save for my face. Achillea told me later that I looked as if I had been turned to clay because of the thickness and the stillness of the bees on me. Their activity made me hot; it was as if I had been wrapped in a blanket of bees. The OutRiders said nothing, but the leader gave a sign, and it seemed that I had passed some sort of test, for they turned as if to leave the field. The bees dropped off my body suddenly and flew into the hive as if they were one creature, except for a small cloud of them who hovered over my head as if awaiting a command. As the OutRiders turned to go, this small fighting force flew towards them, menacing in their direct flight. There was nowhere to sting the OutRiders themselves, for their armour was well crafted and secure, but the bees seemed to know this and aimed instead for the flanks of the horses, each horse receiving several stings at the same time.

I had dropped my arms to my sides and was watching the OutRiders as they turned to leave. When the bees stung the horses, they reared up, and although the Riders quickly regained control of them, I could see it had unsettled them. They wheeled round to go, saying nothing, but instead lifting their shields up, as if to protect them from the stings of the bees, as they galloped off silently, leaving only small puffs of red dust behind them. When I saw the shields, I was shocked enough to sit down abruptly on the ground. Achillea rushed over to me and put her arm around me, congratulating me on having passed the OutRiders' test, and praising my calm handling of the bees.

'They must have taught you to do that in the Temple,' she said. 'It takes years and years of Beeguarding to be able to call them like that.'

'It was your singing,' I mumbled, still in shock from what I had seen on the shields. 'You must have told them what to do in your singing.'

'I learned it from my mother,' she said, sounding pleased. 'I never knew what the tune meant; my mother just said it would be useful to me one day, and so it has been. Why, Talla, you are still shaking; be still and be calm, they are gone now.'

'I will try,' I replied, unsteadily. It was not the experience of the bees coating me that had unsettled me, however strange and ominous a feeling it might have seemed to be. It was the emblem embossed upon the shields and picked out in shades of red and yellow. It was the very same design as my brooch!

CHAPTER 10

Achillea and I sat in the garden for a while, unsure of what to do next. We did not know if the OutRiders were still in Mellia or if they had passed through already, and we could not go and look in case they were still there. Achillea cracked open one of the pomegranates from her basket, and we ate it, licking up the sweetness of the juice. I asked Achillea if the OutRiders often came to the village looking for things or people, and she told me that they did ride through the area quite regularly, but usually left the smaller villages alone, preferring to spend time in the larger settlements like Sanguinea and Aderan where they searched for traders, who had the goods they wanted, unless they had someone else to search for. I asked her what she meant by that.

'They come by to pick up the Drabs,' she said, matter of factly, forgetting that I was one of them. 'Whenever one is released by the Temple, they seem to know, and they come out after them, often less than a day later. It seems that you are different to all the rest, for although we expected the OutRiders as soon as you came to Mellia, yet they did not come until today, and when they came today they were intent on finding you and knew you by name.'

I listened to her speak and felt a deep and hot anger growing within me. This time, I did not want to keep it within the emberjar of my mind, but I did want to find out the truth behind what happened to the Maids who left the Temple. We were never told what happened to those who left the Temple, understanding only that it was the will of the Goddess, that the Goddess chose those who remained and those who left. I, of course, had worked out before I left the Temple that it was more the will of the Priestesses, or at least their attempts at influencing the result of the Choice ceremony which decided the outcomes of the Choice. But I had only learned that fact through teaching myself how to scribe and to read the parchments. We did not use written words very much, and it had taken me a long time and some observation and practice before I could grasp what the symbols on the parchments meant. There were only a few Priestesses who could read and scribe, and the Maids were given no lessons in it. We learned what we learned of the world through the words of the Goddess spoken by the Priestesses. And now I wondered how much of that came from the Goddess herself, and how much came from the mouths of the Priestesses.

'What happens to them, after the OutRiders take them?' I asked, my thoughts turning to those I had known who had not been deemed worthy by the Goddess of remaining in the Temple. Those who had not worked hard, or had not been skilled at anything, or who had talked out of turn. I thought of Bellis, for whom I had felt nothing but mild curiosity when she had been chosen to leave the Temple, and bewilderment at her upset. What had the OutRiders done with her?

Achillea looked at me, bewildered in her turn. 'Do they not bring them back to the Temple? I always thought that they took them back there.'

I thought back over the years that I had seen Maids leaving the Temple and knew that not one of them ever came back. The only input of new Maids came from a steady supply of infants who were gifted to the Goddess or abandoned as babies on the steps of the Temple, like me.

'No,' I answered, slowly, trying to understand. 'We never see them again.' A thought occurred to me. 'Why do you protect me, Achillea? You and the others in

Mellia. Benakiell and Gladia? Why do you protect me, and not the others who are picked up?'

Achillea looked embarrassed. 'Normally they don't get this far. If they do, they usually ignore us and walk past us as if we are not here. They never seem part of this world and make no effort to be part of it. They seem to have no goal or aim, and usually try to head for Sanguinea. You were different. You spoke to Benakiell and have always tried to work and be part of us. You are different because you seemed to want to be outside the Temple. Even though the other Drabs are frightened when the OutRiders catch them, they seem to go willingly in the end; I just thought it was because they told them they could go back home.'

She stood up and extended her hand towards me to help me up. I walked over to the hive, where I could still hear the bees, and examined the ropes which had held it to the Paradox tree. I would need to find some more rope before I could put the hive back in the tree, but I thought that the bees might prefer to stay put than be moved around yet again today, and I wasn't sure how well my luck might hold out with them. We could hear no noise coming from the rest of Mellia although this did not really tell us anything, since, as I had found out, the OutRiders were very skilled at being both quiet and threatening. As we approached the turning of the path back towards Achillea's dwelling cautiously, we heard someone coming along the path, but it was the sound of footsteps not horses' hooves, so we knew it was unlikely to be an OutRider. It was Benakiell who was hurrying towards us. His robe was covered with the fine red dust that surrounded us, and there was a cut to his cheekbone. He looked relieved to see us both.

'Are you alright?' he asked, looking us over. I do not know what he must have thought, looking at us, for I had been surrounded by bees and kicked into the dust by the OutRider, and Achillea's face was grimy and tracked with tears.

'We are fine, Benakiell,' Achillea reassured him, laying a hand upon his arm. 'But what of you? What did they do to you? And what of the rest of the village?'

Benakiell frowned. He explained that mostly the OutRiders had quietly visited each dwelling area and asked questions. No one had spoken of me to them, but when they asked if there was anyone else in the village, one of the children said Achillea's name and then Karula had had to explain that Achillea was harvesting, along with Benakiell's niece. They had asked Ashtun the way to the field and he had not answered quickly or respectfully enough. One of the OutRiders had hit him across the face with his crop and knocked him to the ground as he rode past him and had caught Benakiell with his crop too.

When Achillea heard this, she flinched, and Benakiell sought to reassure her by telling her that Ashtun was at Gladia's house being cared for there, and that we could hurry back to Gladia's house together, now that he was sure we were both alright. As we hurried down the path towards Gladia's house, I saw that Benakiell's cheekbone cut was still bleeding and that he winced as he wiped the blood away.

We arrived at Gladia's dwelling, to find Ashtun lying under a tree, his head propped up on a mound of soft baskets and cloths. Achillea rushed to his side and they reached for each other in affectionate embrace. Once they had assured themselves that the other was alright, they talked and told one another of what had befallen them. I could hear Achillea telling Ashtun how brave he was and how safe he made her feel. Gladia came out of the dwelling with a wet cloth, and Achillea took over the care of Ashtun, while Gladia bustled over to us. I was fine, although I felt sure I would be bruised in the morning from being kicked over by the OutRider, but Benakiell was by now in obvious pain from the cut to his cheekbone. Gladia looked over Benakiell's wound and tutted.

'I may need to stitch that wound,' she said finally, and went back inside to fetch a needle and thread, for she apparently intended to sew the raw edges of Benakiell's skin together. I must have shown some horror at the thought because Benakiell chuckled briefly and assured me he could manage the pain.

'Tell me again about what happened with you and the bees,' he said. 'It will take my mind off it all.' So, I told him what we had seen and heard of the OutRiders and of how the bees had swarmed around me and yet not stung me, and of how they had directed themselves at the OutRiders' horses at the end. As I was talking to him, Gladia returned with a needle and some fine thread and a jar of honey. She cleaned the wound with the honey first. I was fascinated by this and asked her about it.

'Why, that's one of the reasons why the Beeguards are so useful, isn't it? They help us to get the honey from the bees which we can use for so many things. It stops a wound from going bad, and helps it heal. And the taste of it helps with the pain too. From what I hear from Achillea, it sounds as if you have the BeeGift yourself, Talla, which means that even if you want to carry on making the patterns for me, you will always be able to have a trade for yourself, for honey is always in demand. Why, I am sure even the Temple and the OutRiders use honey, although they do not have the Gift, and they do not try.' She gently poked the needle into Benakiell's skin. His eyes were shut, and aside from a tensing of his jaw, I saw no evidence of pain from him. I watched the tenderness with which she tended to the cut and saw that Benakiell was soothed by her doing the task, painful though it may be. Glancing round I saw Achillea and Ashtun, she with her hand laid across his head, and he reaching for her other hand with his. The crickets sawed in the grass, and I sat, motionless and somehow unable to move.

I felt very much alone, for I could see that my friends were preoccupied with each other, and with caring for those they loved, and at that moment I too longed for someone devoted to me in the same kind of way. I could feel my lip trembling, and my hip throbbed where I had hit the ground when I was kicked. I felt hot and dirty and tired, and at that moment I wanted to be back in the Temple. When it was hot outside, you could be cool in the dark rock hewn building where the Goddess statue was, or in walking through the narrow labyrinthine passageways between the different parts of the buildings. When you were unwell you were tended to by the Physic. Each Maid in the Temple and each Priestess was surrounded by others who knew and understood what it was like. We knew our jobs and we knew our world. Everything seemed so safe and secure. And here I was, only weeks after I had left the Temple, unsure of my place in the world, unable to understand what my past life had really meant, or why it seemed so important to them to get me back from the world of the Outer, and indeed where they would take me if they found me. If it were not for what Benakiell and the others had told me, I would have almost given myself up to the OutRiders, because the lure of returning to a fixed world was so strong. Sensing that my place was not here, at this moment, I got up and told Gladia I was going back to my dwelling. She nodded abstractedly as she concentrated on her job and I trudged off down the dusty path.

As I reached the fork in the path to the garden which was Cassia's but which I now thought of as mine, I hesitated and decided that rather than go back to my dwelling, I would go back to the garden. The path was scuffed with the marks of the horses' hooves. For some reason, I expected the garden to look different when I returned to it, but it was exactly the same, except for the beehive which still lay on the floor where I had left it. The sun was lower in the sky and there was a breeze stirring the leaves. Achillea had left the basket of pomegranates and I took one from the basket. I had not realised how hungry and thirsty I was until now, and I enjoyed the red jewel like seeds of the fruit, thinking how much they reminded me of the shape of the honeycomb in the beehive. The bees were by now returned to their work, busily getting on with the thing which they lived for; the building up of their hive and the feeding of their young and the protection of their home. They foraged happily in the flowers as I sat and watched them, eating the fruit and musing on the things which had happened in that day.

I felt in my underpocket for the brooch and re-examined it. There was no doubt at all that this was the same sign which had appeared on the tanned hides of the shields displayed by the OutRiders, but what could it mean? The OutRiders were all men, as I had found out from Benakiell. Had my mother been wed to one of them? How had my mother got hold of the brooch? Had my mother been taken against her will? Or perhaps it was an ancient heirloom from hundreds of years ago. Or, perhaps, again, my mother had been nothing but a common thief who had stolen it from an OutRider and paid the price for it. The design on the brooch reminded me of something I had seen quite recently, which hovered elusively in the edges of my mind like a fish in the dark shallows. I threw the finished pomegranate shell onto the pile of rubbish in the corner and got up again. Even though I was exhausted, I could not be still, and was restless. I wandered over to the beehive on the ground and rested my hands upon it once more.

The hive was made from the hollowed-out branch of a tree. I lifted the side of it up again. The sounds of the bees within grew in intensity, but they did not emerge. I saw that there was a small lever to one side of the top of the hive, which I had not noticed before. I slid it to one side and that allowed me to slowly prise off the lid of the hive and let me look inside. I could see much more clearly than I had been able to this morning when I had only found the side entrance to the hive which Rupicola had described to me. It seemed that Cassia had developed a new way of accessing the hive which allowed her to get the honeycomb out more easily. I placed the lid of the hive to one side and peered into it. The bees were crawling busily over the honeycombs. I saw that Cassia had hung five strips of wood onto grooves inside the log. I lifted one out carefully. The bees which crawled upon it moved a little but in general seemed to have no care that I was examining them with such interest. As I looked at the honeycomb, I saw that it was made of many six-sided wax chambers which ingeniously fitted next to each other. I realised then what it was that the brooch design reminded me of.

The brooch was made of a group of seven six-sided shapes interlocking with each other like beehive cells. The central shape was the red stone which had also been cut, with great craftsmanship into the same six-sided shape, with facets accurately cut at exactly the points at which the filigree overlay would have gone, to make it look as if the central stone had on it a six-pointed star or six petalled flower. I held it in my hands, trying to understand why the OutRiders would carry the badge of a design which showed a honeycomb, when I already knew, from what my friends in Mellia had taught me, that they had no tradition of Beeguarding, nor any affinity for bees. In fact, from what I had observed earlier, the OutRiders seemed to be quite anxious and wary of them – or at least their horses were.

I was unsure of whether I should talk to my friends about the brooch. I remembered the reaction of the first people I met on the Outer when they had seen the brooch, and I knew it was not yet time to reveal it to them. First, I needed to find out more. I had always wanted to find things out. As a child in the First Age, I was forever getting into trouble for asking too many questions or pushing things beyond their snapping point, whether clothes lines or people's kind natures, and I had done a lot of learning for myself through my third Age whilst I was a Maid, learning the Seven Steps to cleaning. I had taught myself to scribe and to read script by observing and remembering things and by putting patterns together, and I was good at fitting patterns to pounce together. Surely, I could untangle this mystery if I had enough knowledge. I sighed and was about to drop the slat with the honeycomb back in the hive, when I realised that the bees which had been on it had moved off it completely. Holding my breath, I slowly withdrew the full honeycomb on the slat from the hive. The bees showed no sign of being disturbed by this and continued to ignore me as I slid the roof of the hive back on again and slowly moved away, still holding on to the honeycomb. Achillea's basket still lay on the ground with the pomegranates in it and I lay the honeycomb carefully on top and made my way back to the dwelling that I now supposed to be my home. When I got back, dusk was falling, and I felt it unlikely that my friends would return for the day. I drew up a gourd of water from my waterjar and found a flatbread to eat. I broke off a little of the honeycomb and ate it with the bread. Its sticky sweetness and its heavy fragrance on

FLAMMEUS

my tongue melted me towards a tired calm, and I curled up on my mat and slept.

CHAPTER 11

That night I slept an exhausted sleep. I had not bathed, nor removed my dirty clothes the day before, and had fallen asleep as quickly as I lay down my head. The night was filled with dreams, although they did not disturb me. My dreams seemed more like watching an interesting story than ones which involved me directly. I dreamed of the OutRiders who had been with us in the fields. The one who had spoken to me was speaking to me again, and yet he had the face of Benakiell, and I did not fear him but rather listened to his message. He entreated me to travel further afield than Mellia, to Sanguinea and beyond. In the dream, as he spoke to me, Lunaria came walking down the path towards me, her face unveiled, as I had known her as a Maid, not with a veiled face like the Priestess she was when I left the Temple. Lunaria stood beside the OutRider and stroked his horse. She looked me in the eyes and told me that I should look for the truth, and that the Goddess had sent the bees to protect me.

When I awoke, I felt bewildered by this dream, and quickly dismissed it as the imaginings of a tired and busy mind full of questions. One of the Priestesses, Amagna, had frequently told us of the dreams sent to her by the Goddess. She had many lessons to take from these dreams, and although I had found myself questioning them more than once, it did seem to me that they were dreams which had a purpose and were useful. The dreams I had were merely a jumbled mess of unfinished messages or words. If my dream had ended by proving one of the Aphorisms of Ashkana such as 'Every person has a given place. The Goddess gives the person to the place,' or 'Fulfil your work and you will be fulfilled,' I could have understood it better.

I was aching and bruised from the events of the day before and I took care to wash carefully, using the soapball which Gladia had brought back from the market only the day before. It seemed like a long time since I had been so grateful to see those little possessions. I looked ruefully at the dress which Gladia had brought back for me. Because it was a light colour, it showed up the fine red dust that I had fallen in, and I thought of my drabcoat with real affection, for although it was plain and boring, you could not see the dirt and dust on it as much. When I had washed and eaten the last of the flatbread and a little more of the honey, I was ready for the day, and I decided to walk to Achillea's dwelling to see how she was. I broke off some of the honeycomb and put it in my carrying gourd. This had been made from a wide flat gourd and had some bark netting strapped around it so that you could carry food in it easily, either by holding the straps, or by lashing it to other gourds or by carrying it in your hands or on your head. Achillea, however, was not at her dwelling but had herself gone further up the village towards Gladia's house which was, fortuitously for Achillea, close to Ashtun's house.

It was there that I found them, with Ashtun apparently none the worse for his encounter with the OutRider's crop and kick. As she saw me making my way along the path, Achillea rushed out to greet me.

'Talla! I am so happy to see you! You crept away so quietly last night, and I was worried about Ash so I stayed for longer than I should have done. I came by your dwelling to tend to your bruises with some of Rupicola's honeysalve, but you were sleeping already, and I did not want to wake you!'

I noted her unconscious use of Ashtun's familiar name, and her joy, and smiled back at her, in some way lightened by my friend's happiness. A strange thing this, that in the midst of difficulty and high drama, of anxiety and pain and suffering, the opposite emotions of happiness and peace could be more keenly felt. If Ashkana had been more occupied with the feelings of people rather than their ability to work, she might have made some aphorism in that regard.

I offered Achillea the gourd with the honeycomb in it which I had taken from the beehive the day before and she looked at me wide eyed. 'Where did you get this?'

'I took it from the beehive yesterday,' I confessed, a little worried that I had done the wrong thing in harvesting the honeycomb.

'But how did you manage to get it out? I tried often after my mother died to take out the combs like she used to do it, with a smoking torch and my head well covered, but they never let me near it, and in the end, I left it be. I got tired of being stung by those nasty bees! I can sing to them, but they still don't like me!' Achillea bit her lip petulantly, but also in jest, and I laughed, as did Ashtun.

'They are just jealous of your beauty,' said Ashtun fondly to Achillea. Then he realised that his implication was that I was not as beautiful as she and that the bees could not be jealous of me and looked abashed. It did not bother me. I was not accustomed to being judged for my appearance anyway and would have been more insulted if he had made comment about my laziness.

'I just took off the lid,' I said simply, 'and the bees moved off the honeycomb for me. None of them stung me or threatened me; it was as if it was a gift.'

'I think you are the one with the gift,' said Ashtun. I was surprised to hear him say this to me for I think it was the first kind thing he had said to me, but perhaps, like Achillea, he was merely relieved and happy to be safe.

'She has the BeeGift,' exclaimed Achillea. 'Only someone with the BeeGift can make the bees do their will.'

I looked at her, surprised. I had certainly learned a lot about the bees in the short amount of time I had been in Mellia. Rupicola had mentioned that Cassia had a gift for dealing with the bees and had been almost resentful of it. I was certainly grateful that I had not been stung by a bee. In fact, I had never been stung by a bee, and although they came to the Temple gardens and the flowers, they never seemed to stay long enough to sting anyone.

'Rupicola said your mother, Cassia had a gift with the bees,' I responded, eager to know more. Achillea laughed her rippling laugh.

'Poor old Rupicola; she always thought she should have been more successful with the bees, but her honey was never as good as Mother's. She tried to explain it away to everyone by saying that mother had the Gift and that it was some sort of magic thing, but really, we all knew that my mother worked harder at growing better flowers and cleaning out her hives better than Rupicola. Rupicola really wanted to believe that Mother had the BeeGift. It was something to do with some dream that she had. Gladia!' She called over towards Gladia's dwelling, and Gladia bustled out, her sewing in her hand, to see who was calling her in such a peremptory fashion. She started out with an irritated frown but when she saw me, her face eased, and she smiled at me.

'Hello Talla. I trust you are feeling none the worse for yesterday?'

I assured her that I felt much better and showed her the honeycomb that I had brought with me to Achillea. Gladia broke off a bit of the honeycomb and put it in her mouth, as if savouring a fine wine. Her eyes closed, and she sighed happily.

'Ah Talla, I hope you did not get too stung getting this out of the hive, I have not tasted honey this sweet for many a year. Is it from one of Cassia's hives?' At this point, Achillea broke in and told her my story. I was content for her to do so, for I saw no point in revisiting old ground. When Achillea had finished explaining and had triumphantly told Gladia that she was sure I had the BeeGift, she demanded that Gladia tell the story of Rupicola's dream to me.

'Ah well, such a story demands a good telling,' answered Gladia, smiling. 'I will make coffee and invite Benakiell to come and sit with us too; I'm sure he can add some details to the story.'

We sat under the shade of a Paradox tree near Gladia's dwelling. The tree, like all Paradox trees had a rough, cracked bark and lots of bright green, glossy leaves. You could see the small, brown Paradox nuts growing from the little branches. I was slowly getting more accustomed to these strange breaks in working that the Outer people were so fond of and growing to appreciate the things which they gave to me. Just sitting and breathing in the fresh air of the morning mixed with a faint, drifting haze of wood smoke, listening to the insects in the grass and watching the clouds move lazily across the sky, I felt much as I used to feel when I would oil the feet of the Goddess.

Here in the Outer, there was something of a ceremony about the making of coffee. Not so in the Temple where it was made efficiently and in large quantities and then stewed all day in large pans. It tasted rich enough and certainly made us more eager to work, but it was also decidedly bitter by the end of the day, and not something I had looked forward to very much. The coffee here was much different; lighter but richer. Each time they made coffee, they roasted the beans first and then ground them just before they made the coffee. In the Temple they roasted all the beans in one go and then ground them down and filled large sacks with it. Now I had tasted the freshness of this coffee, I never wanted to taste the Temple coffee again. I had watched coffee being made several times since my arrival in Mellia, but I still liked to watch carefully so that when it came to my time to make coffee for others, I would know what to do and when to do it.

Gladia put some coffee beans onto a flatbread skillet and turned them as she gradually roasted them over her open fire. About halfway through the process she brushed the husks away. As we sat, sniffing the aroma, I wondered why coffee was not one of the scents the Goddess had favoured particularly. The scents for each day at the Temple were all rather heavy scents, but they were all based on plants. Perhaps it was because coffee was edible. They could have had honey too on another day, I mused. When Gladia had finished roasting the beans, she put them in a small mortar and ground them with a stone pestle. By this time Benakiell had arrived, sporting a very neat scar on his cheek, but looking otherwise unscathed by his encounters the previous day, and he too took his turn at grinding the beans, asking me about the bees and the honeycomb. Achillea ended up telling most of the story to him again, occasionally checking with me that she had all the details right. She told a fine story, I must admit, better than I could have told myself. I was still not used to this embellishment of fact in order to deliver feelings and atmospheres. In the Temple the only one whose feelings we considered were the Goddess and mostly we were occupied with pleasing the Goddess so that she blessed us. Once the beans were sufficiently ground, Gladia put them in to the black clay coffee pot which had been already filled with hot water.

She poured the coffee into small clay cups for us all, and we took the first sips of that rich, almost acrid flavour and waited for her to begin the story of Rupicola's dream.

'Rupicola had this dream many years ago, probably before you young things were born, I don't remember when. But it was unusual because Rupicola was, until then, always one of those very sensible, down to earth women. She did her jobs and she tended her bees and looked after her family. After she had this dream, she still did all those things, but it was as if she was always searching for the one in the dream. She told me about her dream when she had it. I was about your age or a bit older, I suppose.' Gladia settled herself more comfortably on the step she was sitting on and took a sip of her coffee. 'I will tell it to you as she told it to me, for it has almost become part of our village tradition, we have been telling it for so long, and perhaps,' she looked at Achillea, 'you might be right about Talla and the BeeGift.' She began to tell the tale, polished by many years of the telling.

'It was darkness all around her although she could hear from every direction the sound of battle. She could hear the sound of horses, and thudding, of metal and whips cracking, of arrows and swords and the sound of pain and death. She felt as if she had been encased in a dark woven cloth, so thick she could not see where I was going, and yet fine enough to let her breathe and hear the sounds. She was being carried on a strange kind of wheeled cart and felt as though this part of the dream might last forever and could not wake up from it.'

'Rupicola said she felt like she was being bound with creepers too,' Benakiell reminded Gladia. 'She said she felt how she imagined a Paradox tree might feel when a strangler fig encases it.' Achillea shuddered and inched closer to Ashtun. I could understand why. I did not like the idea of being bound in such a way either and had always disliked the feeling that I got from being in one of the many twisting narrow passageways in the Temple, where there were no windows and little light. My mind began to imagine the sounds that Rupicola had dreamt, and they were all the more real to me since I had seen the OutRiders' horses yesterday and heard their whips and arrows.

'When she could finally open her eyes and see, Rupicola said it was suddenly very different. She said she was in a warm stone home filled with glowing coloured light. She said it reminded her of the Temple, but that instead of just one colour, all the colours were there, mingled. There was no sound, except what Rupicola described as the sound of the colours. She felt very warm and protected and she moved as if she was on a boat on a slow flowing stream, without any effort from her. She was taken along through this gentle tunnel of colours and lights until she reached an inner chamber where a voice spoke to her. And it was these words which made such an impression on Rupicola. The voice was that of a woman, and she said "In Mellia one is coming who has the BeeGift. She will come from one to another to overcome. She will sting like a bee and soothe like honey. She is the one who has been chosen. You will know her for her gift. She will bring forth honey as she pleases; she will be protected by the bees themselves; the bees will not sting her, nor will they leave her in peril. She will come, and the old Queen will be gone. You will know her by her sign." And then she woke up.'

Achillea looked at me triumphantly. 'My mother could never get honey out without being stung at all; even though she was gifted with the bees, I don't think it was like the dream.'

I pondered on what I had heard Gladia say and remembered the warm feeling as Rupicola had held her hands over me, and what she had said to me, which I had dismissed as the mutterings of an old woman whose mind had turned against her. 'Are you the one?' she had asked me. But if I was the one, then why had I been chosen? And what was the sign? And how could I be sure I had the Gift? I must have looked puzzled or confused, for Benakiell leaned forward, placing his cup down carefully as he did so.

'I do not think you need to overthink this, Talla,' he said. 'If you are indeed the one with the BeeGift, it will become apparent to all of us as the time goes by. Rupicola's dream happened a long time ago, and we do not even know if it has any import, for she refuses to go to the Empath who might be able to sense better than us if she truly had a dream which foretold the future or if it was just a story she made up to gain attention, and to direct it away from her bumbling with the bees.' He smiled at me, and his eyes twinkled. 'Achillea loves a good story as much as the next person and she may well have built this up into something and nothing. It does seem as if you have a talent with the bees, but it may just be that they sensed your help and were grateful that you cleared away the vines off the flowers and tended to them. And we have not seen any special Sign that you have brought. You look much the same as any woman of Mellia, especially now that Achillea has braided your hair like that, and you are wearing the clothes Gladia got for you. I would expect the next Queen to come with some Outer sign; a difference in how she looks, or a token of royal birth or some such thing; but you are a Drab from the Temple, and you came with nothing.'

As Benakiell spoke, I realised that I did indeed have a token with me; the brooch. I had been told by the Priestesses from an early age that the brooch belonged to me and that it had been pinned to my infantcloths when I was left at the Temple. But now I was unsure what to do. Having seen the emblem on the shields the day before, I thought that somehow, I must be connected to the OutRiders, although I did not understand in what way, when they were all men. But if I showed the brooch now to these people, what would I do if they too turned me away having seen it? I knew that they wanted to protect me from the OutRiders, but I did not know whether that was just because they did not like the OutRiders any more than they seemed to like the Priestesses of the Temple, for it seemed that they were controlled by the OutRiders and by the Temple in equal measure. And yet, if I did not show them the brooch, they would not be able to help me with the task I had set myself of finding out more about my origins. And who was the Queen? I had never heard tell of a Queen before, in all my time at the Temple. I decided to try to find out more before I committed myself to something which I could not reverse.

'Tell me about the Queen,' I invited, looking at Gladia, for I felt sure she would be the one who would know the most.

'What do you want to know, that you could not already know?' she answered me.

'I know nothing at all,' I assured her. 'I did not even know there was a Queen until you mentioned Rupicola's dream and what it meant.'

'How can this be?' burst out Ashtun, springing up from his place next to Achillea. 'Does she take us for fools? We all know that the Temple is in the pay of the Queen! Surely, she does not hope to make us imagine she does not know of the Queen. Maybe she has even seen her with her own eyes! I heard that when the Queen travels, she travels like a Priestess, veiled so that no one will know of her presence!'

I gaped at him. These people from the Outer were incomprehensible. How could it be that Ashtun could assume that he knew so much about what I knew? He was attacking me mindlessly, knowing nothing. He knew nothing of the Temple; how could he, when it was inhabited solely by women? I felt the by now familiar glow inside my mind. I wanted to hit him with my fists and push him over and stamp on him. Benakiell must have read something in my face for he stood up too and laid a restraining hand on my arm, as I fought to get up.

'Ashtun is as much of a hothead as you, sister Talla, leave it be. Nothing was ever solved by anger with no direction.

'My anger has direction,' I muttered grimly. 'It goes to him, who knows nothing of life in the Temple and nothing about what I know and yet assumes he does! His mind is full of nonsense he has heard from other people and taken for the truth and yet he cannot take anything I say for truth!' I pushed Benakiell's hand away from me and stood up, facing Ashtun, looking straight at him, even though it felt very hard for me to do this still. I had observed that the people on the Outer looked into one another's eyes when they wanted to see the truth, even though we Maids had been taught that to look into the eyes of another was disrespectful and would teach us nothing about the person, and might, in fact, seem to give us information about them that was wrong. Ashtun's eyes blazed at me as he looked down at me. He was considerably taller than me and well-built and muscled and he reminded me at that time of the OutRiders I had seen the day before. His eyes, which were normally warm like coffee, were flinty, sparking stones now.

'And what do you know of life outside your precious Temple?' he mocked. 'You expect us to believe that you are innocent and ignorant of everything on the Outer.

You take our goods as offerings to the Goddess and use them yourselves. We must work every day and give half of everything to the Queen; did it never occur to you in all your time at the Temple to ask where all that fine cloth came from? And all those scented oils? Where all the goods you use come from? Why only the OutRiders have horses and weapons? You cannot expect us to believe that you are so stupid, Talla! We have seen your skills on the Outer and you must know some of this!'

Achillea, Gladia and Benakiell looked at me. Achillea looked embarrassed, Benakiell looked grave, Gladia looked straight at me, as if trying to read my mind. None of them seemed surprised by Ashtun's attack. I did not know what to say to them. They could not believe of me that I did not know the things they were telling me and yet it was true. I had only ever lived one life; that of a Temple Maid. They had their lives in the Outer and they attended the Temple and they encountered the OutRiders in their everyday dealings. What would they know of my life? And yet, as I asked myself this question, I realised that they would not know anything of my life. They had told me themselves that the Maids who left the Temple were rarely in the Outer for very long before the OutRiders picked them up and had acknowledged that I was unusual. Benakiell had asked me a lot of questions and I had not answered all of them, guarding my knowledge close to myself. If I wanted them to understand me and to believe me, I was going to have to trust them too, and I was going to have to share with them the details of my life so far. I needed time to think, and I wasn't sure if I had much time before they too would lose patience with me and drive me out of the village. I was sure that Benakiell and Achillea would want me to stay, although Achillea had loyalty to Ashtun, and Benakiell had loyalty to Gladia, who seemed so suspicious of my lack of knowledge, although she too had helped me and protected me. I did not know what to do, and stumbling slightly, I walked away from them. Achillea made to follow me but Ashtun held her back.

'Leave her be,' he said, grimly.'She has no answer for me, and that is answer enough!'

I turned to face him. 'I will answer your questions,' I said firmly,' but I will do it later, when I have attended to the bees.' I did not know where my sudden desire to spend time with the bees had come from, but I knew without question that I needed to spend time on my own in the company of the bees and the flowers, and that they would help me find the right path in the same way that they helped one another to find the right path to the flowers which bore the sweetest honey.

CHAPTER 12

As I walked away towards my garden, and my flowers and my bees, I resisted the temptation to turn back and see the expressions on the faces of those I had left behind. Instead, I guarded the anger spark in my mind's emberjar. Each time I started to calm down, another thought intruded and made me ask more questions of myself and become more and more irritated. Luckily it did not take very long to get to the garden since I was walking rapidly and with purpose. My aching limbs from my fall the day before were overridden in my desperation to get somewhere where I could allow my tangled thoughts to unwind and be made straight again by purposeful but mindless activity. In the Temple, the act of cleaning had been soothing. Although I did not ever feel anger in the Temple, there had been times when I was calmed in my spirit by the act of the seven-step scrubbing. In the Temple, I had not had many feelings, when I thought of it. We all seemed to understand what was required of us, and we were able to fulfil it. During the First Age of childhood, there had been more times when one had felt emotion; when Priestesses had raised a smile from us and for us or when we had attacks of pique on being told we would never make good Physics or that our scrubbing left something to be desired. I mused on the Temple and my fellow Maids as I headed down the path. I had carried out my interests in scribing and in reading on my own and was not aware that any of the other Maids were at all interested in anything outside of working for the Temple and the Goddess. We knew the days of the week by the scents of the oils, and by the colours with which the Goddess was adorned. We knew that at the time of

Choice, Maids would go on to either become Priestesses, or they would be rejected by the Goddess and forced into the Outer. When I was at the Temple, I had congratulated myself on my acuity at deducing that the Priestesses were the ones that chose, and that the idea of Choice was, in fact, an empty one unless you had the skills of scribing and reading which were only given by the Goddess to the Priestesses. I realised now how foolish I must appear to those on the Outer. They were skilled in interactions, in the interplay between one and another. They read the faces of those around them as I could read a scribed parchment. This reading for feeling, emotion or guile was not something we had ever been taught or had any experience of in the Temple. In the earliest age of Childhood, we were corrected if we dared to look in the face of a fellow Maid, and it was, of course impossible to look into the faces of the Priestesses. It occurred to me suddenly that I had never realised the power that this gave the Priestesses, for they of course could look into the eyes and faces of we Maids, and divine our thoughts, whereas we could not see anything of what they thought and knew nothing of it unless they told us. They quoted Ashkana to us 'Your life is written in your work not in your face'. I could feel the emberjar in my mind damping down, and the smoke of my anger, which had clouded my thought, ebbing away, so I could concentrate on the issues ahead of me. I had to decide whether to trust these people or whether to leave them. I had learned a lot of what being a member of Outer life was like, and I thought that I could probably manage on my own, if I kept quiet, and travelled sensibly. Where I would go, I did not know; I might head for Sanguinea and try to trade some of my meagre possessions for cloth to pounce and sew.

The hive that had been shot down was still resting on the ground, and the bees were busily flying in and out of the side entrances to it. I knew that I needed to hoist it back into the tree so that the bees could return to their normal patterns of life, and so that the honey could be protected from the onslaughts of any animal thieves who might wish to destroy the hive in order to get the honey. I sat down on a rock and unpicked the bark rope from the side of the hive and examined it to see how I could put it back together again securely. It was pleasant, and the sound of the bees comforted me as the chanting in the Temple had comforted me. I did not understand the meaning but in the cadence and the rhythm and the rise and fall of sounds, my blood settled to its own steady beat. The arrow had split the bark cleanly and I could see, from unpicking the other end of it slightly how the rope had been made by braiding strips of bark around a central core of bark strips. I wondered idly who had made the rope and if it was a man's job or a woman's job before picking up the strands and knotting them firmly back together and fitting my own braiding around the bark. It was not a tidy job, but it was strong, and it did what it needed to. Before I went to pull the hive back up to the high branch it had hung from, I lifted the panel again to look inside. I couldn't stop myself from wondering if I had the BeeGift. Inside my heart, I longed for it to be true, for it would mean that I was special. It would mean I was not just a Drab, not just a Maid, not just Talla whom nobody loved, and whose mother had abandoned her, but Talla the BeeGifted, the one who could understand the bees.

I murmured to the bees; little nonsense murmurings mimicking their humming. I watched them as they moved from chamber to chamber of the new honeycomb they were building; they were always working, building up the chambers with wax, feeding the grubs with honey, signing to each other in insect ways. As I watched them, I saw that one bee, slightly larger than the rest was crawling from new chamber to new chamber laying eggs in each one. This must be the Queen Bee of whom I had heard from Rupicola. Suddenly I wanted to know more about the bees; about how they lived and their society; about how long they might live and why they made honey and how a Queen was chosen. And in recognising this, I realised two things. Firstly, that my curiosity about the bees was the same as the curiosity that Ashtun, Gladia, Achillea and Benakiell had displayed in my life in the Temple. Secondly, that I really wanted to find out more about the bees. If I wished to do so, I would need to stay here, with the hives and with the knowledge of the village, as well as that of Rupicola; for all her addled wits, she may yet retain useful knowledge. With this decided, I began to thread the rope through the holding loop on the hive. I would answer the questions they had for me about the Temple, and I would ensure that I asked questions in return, for I did not intend to give up my knowledge for nothing. I also did not intend to reveal my brooch to them yet. I needed more time and more knowledge before that.

I propped the beeladder up against the tree and threw the mended ropes over the lower branches of the tree. I climbed down and, pulling the ropes down, raised the hive up into its former hanging position. Now, I needed to secure the ropes to the tree again, but I could not do that without letting go of them to hold on to the top of the BeeLadder. I looked around me desperately, trying to work out a way in which I could complete this task before returning to the others.

'It looks as though you need the help of others there, sister Talla,' came a voice, as Benakiell walked around the corner. It seemed that there were some tasks that did indeed need more than myself, and Benakiell held the ropes tight until I was up at the top of the Bee

Ladder and could secure them. When I was satisfied that the hive was back in its rightful place, I descended the BeeLadder to finally meet his eyes, and I think that in some strange way he understood what I had decided, for he walked beside me back up the path in companionable silence.

When we returned, I decided that I would try to behave as they did in the Outer and looked my companions fully in the face. However, they looked away from me, as if ashamed, and it seemed as if there were many rules about when and why to look at peoples' eyes and faces. It was all very complicated. Ashtun looked studiously into the distance, concentrating his vision on a pair of doves who had landed in the thorn tree and were cooing to one another, sidling up and down the branch; Gladia started to move the coffee pot and the skillet out of the way, and Achillea fiddled with her netela idly tracing the pattern that I had designed for her.

'I have come to answer your questions,' I said. 'I will try to answer you what I know and what I do not know, and what you would like to know, but I am ignorant of much. I truly did not know of the existence of a Queen of this land, and there is much I do not understand about your lives here on the Outer too. I hope that I can also ask you some questions.'

Ashtun did not respond, and neither did Gladia. But I was never so glad of Achillea and her sweet, light nature. She rubbed her owlish face with her hand and then asked, perplexed, 'How do you bear wearing those awful drabcoats every day without cease? I could never do that!' Benakiell smiled good-naturedly at her, and then looked to me for an answer.

'We do not have choices in the Temple.' I began, trying to put into words the knowledge which had rested inside my head for so long without being voiced. 'Until I entered the Third Age of Childhood, I did not even know that people of the Outer wore clothes of different colours.'

'How could you not know that? All around us we see people wearing different costumes and colours and they all attend the Temple,' pointed out Gladia.

'Maids do not attend the Temple while the Outer attend until they reach the Third Age.' I answered, remembering the time when I had first attended the Temple with the other Maids of a similar age to myself. We had been told to keep our eyes to the floor as we listened to the chanting to the Goddess and kept silence for meditation. The people of the Outer attended the Temple through one chamber in the Goddess's atrium, and we Maids were seated in another. The Outer people were already sitting in their chamber when we filed in, our faces obediently turned to the floor, but I caught sight of some of the gowns and the headdresses out of the corner of my eye through the screen, and something inside me urged me to peep at them. They reminded me of colourful birds or butterflies. Each time I attended the Temple from then on, I would steal tiny glances at the people of the Outer. As I got older, I sometimes saw them as they attended the Trading Days, when the Temple opened its gates to the merchants of the Outer, who came in bringing their goods for trade. I explained all this to the two women, who listened attentively.

'Trading Days?' burst out Ashtun scornfully. 'There is precious little real trading goes on at those! Why we could get four times as much for our goods if they were fairly traded in Sanguinea, but we of Oramia are forced to attend those days every month.'

'Who forces you?' I asked. It did not seem to me that any of the Traders looked forced or beaten into attending the Temple. The Trading Days occurred, as Ashtun had noted, every month. As with everything else at the Temple, the day on which Trading Day fell was important in that it determined the colour of the traded goods. Aureus was a day on which oranges and saffron and frankincense, pumpkins and carrots and peppers could be traded. It was also a day on which anything of a deep brownish orange was traded, so it was the day on which we acquired any clay pots we might need. Green goods were traded on Viridis; lettuces and cabbages, beans, melons, green cloths and netelas. Some items appeared to have been given an honorary status such that white and cream goods like soapballs and goats milk were allocated to Flavus, and metal goods were traded on Indicus.

Ashtun again looked at me incredulously, as if to say that I was a fool. I was learning how to read faces too, and that my own face could be read, so I looked openly into his scornful eyes and he searched mine as if looking for the truth. Finally, he answered my question.

'When we go to trade at Sanguinea, we never know whether we will be forced to go to all those Temples. We set up to trade our goods and if it is one of those days, then the OutRiders will select traders to escort there. They make it plain that there is no negotiation and that we will be expected to trade whatever the Priestesses want. We must accept whatever they offer us in trade, even if it means we lose, or end up with some scrappy vegetables or half put together sewing! There is no point in resisting, for the OutRiders would take the goods for nothing, if we did.' He looked at me indignantly, and I felt angry again. I thought of Lunaria's beautiful pieces of embroidery and her skills with the needle, and of my fellow Maids who worked tirelessly in the fields to grow crops, and the physics who made the tonics and the other work which we all did day after day. It was as if Ashtun had decided to dislike all the goods simply because he had been made to trade there. But I still didn't understand why he blamed the Temple. To me it seemed more as if it would be the OutRiders who he should be feeling this resentment towards. However, I chose not to respond to this part of what he said, for he had said something else which had interested me very much, and which I needed to know more about; he had said Temples, as if there were many of them.

'How many Temples have you visited?' I asked Benakiell, surmising that he might be more inclined to answer my question calmly, and hoping that Ashtun's curiosity and desire to find out what I knew would keep his temper in check. Benakiell had spoken the truth when he compared the two of us. I thought that perhaps it was because I was unaccustomed to some of the feelings which I seemed to be discovering since I had left the Temple. The longer I stayed away from it the more I felt like a pervasive influence was gradually being removed and a clouded screen was slowly being withdrawn from my eyes. I could not, however, think of any similar excuse for Ashtun who seemed to speak before he thought on many an occasion. Perhaps Achillea was drawn to his impulsiveness.

Benakiell inclined his head as he considered my question. 'Well, when I was journeying and trading, in my younger days, I must have traded at a dozen or more, although I do hear tell that there are many more, over the mountains beyond Sanguinea.'

My surprise must have shown on my face. I had never imagined that there would be so many other Temples anywhere, nor even that the world was big enough to hold them. From the Temple we could see into the distance but there seemed little there, and I had always thought or perhaps been told that there was just a community of people who lived on the Outer and with whom we traded from Sanguinea and that beyond that were only mountains and nothingness. Other Temples sometimes sent their Priestesses to visit ours, but I had always assumed there were only a few.

'She really did not know!' exclaimed Gladia. 'The poor child knows nothing of the world beyond what she has learned here and in the Temple. And it doesn't seem like they taught her much there either!' She looked at me with pity. I felt indignant, that my lack of knowledge might be so disdained, for I had thought that I was reasonably knowledgeable; after all, I could scribe, and pattern, and I had devised the pouncing of my patterns, and I could clean very well, and I knew the Aphorisms of Ashkana. I could mend things adequately. I had taught myself to scribe (although they did not know that) and I had listened to the astronomers talking about the stars.

Achillea replied, 'Talla knows a lot of things, and what she does not know, she learns quickly! She is far better than me at tending to plants, even though she did not do that at the Temple, and she can clean well, and she works very hard! And she has the BeeGift!' She looked at the rest triumphantly, blinking her large, open eyes at them. Benakiell nodded his head in agreement and reminded Ashtun that they also wanted to learn about my world and my work in the Temple as much as I wished to learn about life on the Outer, and that they might also learn things or understand things of which they had no prior knowledge.

'Are they all the same as my Temple?' I asked, fascinated by the thought that might be more of them. Perhaps the Maids who were sent out from the Temple were moved into other Temples by the OutRiders? But we had, as Maids, always been assured that our Goddess was the only one. I could not comprehend how there could be more than one.

'Why not tell us about your Temple' suggested Gladia, 'and then Benakiell and Ashtun can compare what you describe with what they know.'

I began to explain to my companions what life in the Temple was like. That each day held few surprises and that we worked for most of the day, interrupted only by food and prayers and sleep. I described to them how we had an allotted time to bathe and that we had no possessions. I described the days of the week and their associations with colours and scents and confirmed to them the different jobs undertaken by the Maids. I did not touch upon the Priestesses complicity in the Choice ceremony, or on the fact that I could scribe. I still felt that this knowledge was something which might one day be very important to me.

'Tell us about the Goddess,' invited Achillea, 'for what you see and believe may be different to us.' Her eyes looked dreamily into the distance. 'I always loved listening to the singing in the Temple when I used to attend with my mother. I wanted to take part in it, but of course we were forbidden from joining in with the singing, since that was reserved for those of the Temple.'

I remembered the beautiful singing of those who had been chosen by the Goddess to glorify her through song too. We Maids joined in with the rhythmic chants and the rise and fall of that was pleasing in its way, but the soaring notes of the singing touched me, even as a Maid whose feelings seemed to have been dull in comparison to how I felt now. I wondered how I might feel if I heard it again, and then Achillea began to sing. It was a song of the Goddess and her Creation. I had heard it many times before in the Temple and the voices had risen and fallen like waves. Here, there was only the pure note of Achillea's singing, but it too rose and fell, like a swooping bird. She sang of the days of Thoughtfulness before the world began, and of the Days of Creation when all things were made; things of joy and things of pleasure, things of work and things of life. She sang of the birds and the fish, of trees and fruits and flowers. I had never taken in the words, in all my time at the Temple, merely enjoyed the sound and the music in the song without applying the words to myself. But now I had seen and experienced these things. Now I knew joy, and anger and I had seen colours I never knew existed and had met people of all types, and the words about the Goddess rang through me like the sound of a bell and I sat, and I wept because Achillea had made it real for me through her singing. The others sat back and enjoyed the song too, but it did not have the effect on them that it had upon me, and when she had finished the song, Achillea smiled at me sunnily, and offered me her netela to wipe my eyes.

'They say that a songmaker is skilled if she can turn words and sounds into feelings,' she remarked. 'I am happy that the song was so powerful for you; it is one of my favourite songs from the Temple.'

With some effort, I returned to the question which Achillea had originally asked me, about the Goddess herself. From the First Age we were brought up to know and understand the Goddess and her role in the life of the world, and our role in the life of her world. I had, of course, never considered if the same were true of all the people on the Outer. And now that I knew there was more than one Temple, I suddenly wondered if there was more than one Goddess. However, I knew it was time for me to answer a question, even though I felt sure that I had many more questions for them than they had for me.

'The Goddess is the Mother of the world,' I began. 'You sang it yourself in the song. She brought forth the world and all that is in it. We who live in the world must work, as befits our skill, and our work glorifies the Goddess and gives life to the world. You have seen the statue of the Goddess in the Temple, and through our oiling of the statue with the daily scents of plants and flowers, and the dressing of the statue with colour, we please the Goddess with her creations and so she blesses us with life and work.'

Ashtun curled his lip and snorted derisively. 'And who has told you all this about the Goddess?' he asked. 'Does the Goddess herself come to you as you sleep in the Temple and speak to you through dreams like Rupicola? Does her statue speak to you in words that only you can understand?'

'No,' I replied calmly, even though there were already sparks inside my head. 'We have the writings of the Priestess Ashkana, who wrote down the messages of the Goddess while the world was yet young.'

'Hmmm, and I suppose this Ashkana was given the gift of scribing from the Goddess herself?' Ashtun sneered.

I almost retorted that scribing was not so tricky, and that I had taught myself to do so and I supposed that Ashkana could have done the same thing, when I remembered that my scribing was not to be disclosed. If they discovered my clever little pounce patterning, I could manage; after all, it now seemed that I was more gifted with bees than with pouncing, but my scribing and reading were my only weapons and I guarded them jealously.

'I do not know,' I answered politely. 'I am only a Drab from the Temple with little learning after all.'

Benakiell cast me a sharp glance when I said this, but the others accepted it naturally. I continued to explain. 'The Maids only learn from the Aphorisms of Ashkana. If you stay in the Temple after the Choice and become a Priestess, then you learn the Anticipations of Asmara.

Only the Priestesses may hear and read the Anticipations of Asmara, who came before Ashkana. Her writings are too difficult for those other than the Priestesses to understand.'

'Hmm,' Benakiell appeared deep in thought. 'It may be,' he addressed Ashtun, quite as if we women were not there, which vexed me. 'It may be that the different levels of the Temple are kept separate in their knowledge from the rest.'

I tried to pick up on the links I had been offered in this conversation.

'It is related to age,' I began, hesitantly. 'You cannot become a Priestess until the Choice ceremony, and then you begin your learning to be a Priestess.'

'Were you close to any of the Priestesses?' asked Gladia. 'It must have been strange for you, not having an older person around you to talk to about their life's experience. What if you had not wanted to become a Priestess?' I could not betray my reading and scribing abilities, so I pretended innocence and said merely, 'The Goddess decides.'

'Well something must have caused the wrong decision to be made by the Goddess then!' said Achillea. 'Otherwise why would they be so intent on finding you by name? It must have been meant for you to stay and become a Priestess and somehow things went wrong.' I did not look at her, for she had come uncomfortably close to the truth. I thought about Lunaria and her life at the Temple. Like me, she had been abandoned on the steps of the Temple, and taken in by the Priestesses, grateful for the gifts of the Goddess. She had been left at the same sort of time as me. She was quiet but strong and calm, and her embroidery showed her keen eye for detail. I wished now, that I had taken the time to talk to her of her sewing and ask her questions about herself. I thought of her generosity towards me on that final day of mine at the Temple, and of the risks she had taken to give me the brooch, and I thought how wonderful it would be if I could see her again. Of course, I would not see her, but only see her in the veiled costume of the Priestesses and would know her only by her voice or by her veil.

If, as the Outers suggested, the OutRiders and the Temple shared information at some level, then I wondered if Lunaria might now be in trouble. She had, after all, come to me with the brooch, and it may be that somebody had spotted her. I presumed that the loss of the brooch had been discovered and that was the reason that the OutRiders were eager to find me. Perhaps they only wanted the brooch and not me? I toyed with the idea of walking past the Temple and leaving the brooch there to help Lunaria, but concluded that this would be a hazardous undertaking, and probably one which might lead to Lunaria suffering more. I realised that I did not even know if Lunaria was still at the Temple, or if she had been punished and removed from it by the OutRiders too. It was all becoming muddy and churned up, like a riverbed when you walked along it, but I sensed that, unlike the riverbed, it would be a long time before any of these swirling clouds settled and presented me with a clear picture. It was all very well to sit and talk about these questions, as they were fond of doing here in the Outer, but I was of the Temple and I was used to resolving problems through working.

I stood up impatiently. 'When do you next go to Sanguinea, Gladia? For I intend to come with you to trade. I can find out about some things myself and observe the town and choose what to do. I may need to go to the Temple somehow. Everything is a puzzle and I cannot just sit here talking about it!'

Gladia looked at me, astonished by what she saw as stupidity but Achillea clapped her hands in delight, and turned to Ashtun, 'Don't you think that's a good idea? We could all go together and travel away from this boring place! We could find out the news, and Talla and I could look at the goods for trading and maybe Talla could take some of her honey to trade, for it is excellent honey. Oh, please say it is a good idea! I long to travel to Sanguinea again, and since my mother died, I have had no one to go with.' She looked pointedly at Gladia here, who sighed in exasperation. Ashtun was, I could see, more interested in this idea of mine than he had been by any other, and it occurred to me that he felt, like me, that sitting around talking was not going to achieve very much. I looked to Benakiell. He was the first of the people in Mellia that I had met and had seemed to keep my safety and wellbeing important. He considered things in a measured way and I believed that he might make good choices. He stroked his beard reflectively and his fingers strayed to the stitched wound on his cheek; an obvious reminder of the dangers that we faced. It seemed an uncertain journey, I acknowledged silently; there was no reward aside from knowledge and that very knowledge might lead us deeper into danger.

'I think it may be a good idea for us to travel out of Mellia for a while, after yesterday. I do not think the OutRiders will be gone long before they return to ask more questions. However, I am not sure that Talla is ready for Sanguinea. She needs to learn our ways more, and to talk and trade easily with others.'

I frowned at this criticism, and the holding back of my plans. I felt sure I could acquit myself in the world of trading, and I had managed, after all, in a short time, to learn a great deal of Mellia and its inhabitants.

'The town folk are not like us, Talla,' he told me mildly. 'They are not kind or polite and they will hesitate at nothing if they think a trade can benefit them more than you. If any of them suspected that you were the Drab the OutRiders had been searching for, they would inform the OutRiders straight away. However, perhaps we could go and find out some more for you?' He looked around at the others, and again I felt myself excluded and cast out. Would I ever feel like I belonged anywhere? Knowing what I knew now, I could not return to the Temple and work mindlessly anymore. But neither, it seemed, could I be part of this world of the Outer. To my surprise, it was Gladia who responded first, and her response surprised me too.

'I agree that it will be hard for Talla in Sanguinea, especially.learning to trade. However, I do have another suggestion for us all. If we allow ourselves a few days to ready ourselves, I can get more sewing together, and Achillea can do some work and harvest the gardens.' She looked pointedly at Achillea who pouted, but for once, no one was paying her any attention. 'Talla can try to harvest as much of that honey as she can, and Benakiell and Ashtun can bundle their building materials up. We can all travel to Sanguinea and Talla can see the market and the town. But for this first time, it will be a good thing for her to merely watch the trading. After a day or so, we will leave you in Sanguinea and trust that you will trade our goods for us while I accompany Talla with her honey to the Empath Erayo. Talla is not yet used to our lives and she is not accustomed to the burden of feelings. The Empath can help her to understand her feelings and her dreams and perhaps direct her path. The honey will pay in full for the visit to the Empath and more besides. I feel the need to unburden my soul to the Empath after these past weeks.' She sighed and I realised how tired she looked, and how hard she must have found this upheaval in her life. Her suggestion intrigued me and learning about the Empath might help me on my journey to discover more about my mother and the brooch, and about the Temple and the OutRiders.

'I agree with Gladia,' I said, and they all looked at me, surprised.

'So do I!' said Benakiell. Achillea looked mutinous, for this meant that she would be expected to do the cooking for Benakiell and Ashtun once Gladia and I had left to go and visit the Empath. I had noticed that although both men and women seemed equally skilled in cooking here in the Outer, if there was a woman in a group, she was expected to do the cooking even whilst still doing the same amount of work as the men. I wondered if there was some similar skill which worked the other way around.

'At least you can show me the market,' I reassured her, 'and perhaps advise me on a new robe.' Mollified, she turned her attention yet again to Ashtun and began chattering about what she would take to trade, and which market would be the most suitable one to take me to. He smiled at her indulgently and stroked her hand and I mused that somehow Achillea had a way of making even Ashtun seem warm and friendly. We all agreed that we should leave for Sanguinea on the next day of Flammeus and separated to go back to our dwellings and prepare for the journey and the trade.

THE FLAME

CHAPTER 13

My senses were assailed on every side. My eyes were wide with trying to fit in every part of this many-coloured spectacle of shape and size and texture. My ears were full of the noises I heard all around me and my mouth was full of the smells, so strong they had become tastes in my mouth. The market at Sanguinea was truly a sight I had never imagined.

We had spent the past days preparing for this journey and for this destination, although Gladia and I also had some way to travel after Sanguinea in order to reach the Empath. I had taken the time to climb the bee ladders and inspect the rest of the hives which Cassia had left hanging in the tree and which I was now in charge of. They were not mine, in truth, but I thought of them as mine since I was the only one harvesting the honey from them. There were nine hives altogether, and each one seemed full to bursting with sweet fragrant honey. From each hive I withdrew two large honeycombs, and each time the bees moved almost politely off the honeycomb. I became more confident each time I handled them, and when the bees crawled on my bare skin, I no longer flinched, expecting them to sting me, but allowed myself the time to be still and wait for them. Sometimes, Achillea accompanied me down to the hives and sang as she harvested the pomegranates and figs to take to market. Her singing always made the bees drowsier and they seemed lulled by it, like small children being sung to sleep. Each honeycomb was placed in a gourd container, whose top was then stuffed with wadded leaves to preserve the honey from the taint of the air. As I withdrew the honey, I marvelled at the construction of the little wax rooms, one for each bee grub and was once again reminded of my old life at the Temple, where, like bee grubs, we Maids were each placed in a small dormit and provided with food in the expectation that when we grew we would be sent out to work for the hive. Each bee worked all the hours of the day, collecting from the flowers, protecting the hive and cleaning it assiduously. I wondered why they did not stop a while to rest, when the combs were full of honey, but they seemed unable to stop themselves from working.

Ashtun and Benakiell concerned themselves with collecting building materials to take to trade in Sanguinea, and to use to ply their building trade within the city. They explained to me that many of the people who dwelt in Sanguinea were traders rather than crafters and had moved away from the old ways of learning a craft. Consequently, the skills of such as Benakiell in waterproofing and repairing dwellings were in high demand, and they could always make good trades, for both materials and services. They collected long, whippy sticks and poles for roofs, bundles of fine long yellow grass for thatch, split reeds and big pots full of Paradox oil. They sharpened their thatching knives and their plating slabs, ready for work. Gladia had asked me to draw my patterns on more netelas which I was happy to do, creating geometric patterns, and ones of interwoven flowers and leaves, always being careful to leave off the bee symbol. I understood now that the symbol of the bee was associated with the OutRiders and that this brought fear to the people of the Outer, but I struggled sometimes with the knowledge of my possession of the brooch which matched the symbol on the back of the OutRiders' shields. I felt affection for the bees and the way in which they had seemed to take me into their hearts, and I did not feel the same fear of them that others did. It seemed a strange paradox that whilst their honey was much in demand, the bees themselves and the symbol which depicted them were so feared. Achillea grumbled her way through harvesting the fruit and husking the dried beans from Cassia's garden, and Gladia encouraged her to pick the small spicy hot chillies which grew in the garden and dry them in the sun, for they too fetched a good trade and were often used in spicy stews.

It had taken us two days of walking to reach Sanguinea, for we all had bundles to carry and our pace was slow. The sun was hot overhead and we walked in the early morning and in the evening, stopping under thorn trees or by the sides of rocks to rest in the heat of the midday. As we neared Sanguinea, we began to climb out of the valley floor in which we had been, and the air became fresher and cleaner to breathe. There were more plants growing here where it was cooler, although the dust was still fine and red, and the sun still soaked quickly into my skin. My bundle was an awkward shape, being a knobbly mass of gourds containing honey, all of which had to be kept upright. I tried to stack them on top of each other, but they slid around, and I seemed to be always stopping to check on them or shift them around. Achillea carried her fruit and vegetables in a large cloth bundle which she carried on her back supported by a wide strap around her head. For all her apparent laziness, she walked stoically, and rarely complained. The men carried huge bundles of sticks and straw on their heads, balancing them with a sturdy pole. The sticks were rested on a small bound nest of cloth which they placed upon their heads to rest the heavy load on. Gladia had in fact the lightest and the easiest bundle to carry, but she struggled with it even so. She was a plump lady, and she puffed and panted her way along the path with her neat light bundle of threads and netelas, exasperating me with her grunts and groans even while I admired the capacity of Ashtun and Benakiell to stride along with their enormous loads.

Sanguinea itself was a large collection of dwellings perched on a flattened outcrop of rock about a third of the way up the side of a mountain. The dwellings were close built, with no gardens, although the odd one did have some chillies growing in an old clay pot by the entrance. I was most interested in the dwellings which appeared to be placed on top of each other such that two dwellings fitted into the space of one, with one dwelling on top of the other. The upper dwelling had a wooden ladder propped up the wall so that the owner could climb up to their dwelling. I gaped at them and Benakiell smiled to see my astonishment.

'It makes sense, if you think about it,' he said. 'Sanguinea itself cannot grow outwards much further or it would fall off the side of the mountain, and yet more people wish to come here for trade. To me, it is like an anthill which grows bigger and taller with every passing year. There is more wood here than in Mellia and the other villages on the plain, and they can use the wood to make a strengthened roof for the lower dwelling.' He stopped abruptly then, and I sensed that he had told me too much of the secrets of building, which was, as he had informed me on numerous occasions, a man's job.

There was one main route into Sanguinea, and a constant stream of people moved along it in both directions, all carrying bundles such as ours. The path on which we walked was made of worn clay hardened by the footsteps of many. We walked alongside others, all of whom were busy with their own bundles and thoughts and who moved along mindlessly, ignoring this amazing arena which assaulted the senses. We made our way towards the market on the southern side of the settlement, where Gladia and Benakiell knew of a good place to set up and trade our wares. I had never been among so many people, nor indeed been anywhere which felt as anonymous as I had done in the Temple, wearing a drabcoat.

The market was a large open space, where the clay dust had been trodden and rained and polished into a hard surface. Some of the traders who were there seemed to have a permanent stand or table constructed out of bits of wood. Presumably, these were the ones who could always find trade; those who traded food and provisions, everyday utensils like water gourds and soap balls, and tidy bundles of kindling. All the other traders settled themselves down higgledy piggledy, on grass mats or tough woven cloths and displayed their goods for trade. As I looked around, I realised that it was a complicated task, this trading. There was no set tariff for anything, and each person traded for the things they needed most. A person who already grew tomatoes in their garden would not trade much for a selection of round fat tomatoes but might be willing to offer much more to someone who could trade them a fine piece of cloth. Another who lived within Sanguinea, where little grew, might be happy to trade their cloth for a basket of tomatoes. When we had found the place to set up, Gladia waved me and Achillea away.

'You can get your things out in a while. Achillea, show Talla the market stalls, and watch out for the OutRiders. Talla keep your netela over your head. Go on, off you go!'

Achillea clapped her hands with glee and put down her baskets. She took a small gourd of chillies with her, in the hope of finding a good trade. Benakiell and Ashtun were talking on the corner to a knot of people who were already clustering around them, eager for their skills. Achillea led me through the bustling scene, showing me some of the sights. In general, it seemed that the traders set up their wares in close proximity, so that if you were looking for food, you might go to one part of the market, and if you were looking for gourds and pots, you might go to another. Each trader tried their best to show off their wares, with fruit and vegetables piled in fanciful towers and mounds, and ground spices and herbs temptingly displayed in open baskets or folded leaves. There were pyramids made of tomatoes and pomegranates and flat open pots full of glossy darkberries. We paused by some of the stalls selling netelas and robes. I examined them and was secretly pleased to see that none had the consistency of pattern and regularity that my pounced patterns had. Achillea, however, whisked me on to a small stall which sold oils and perfumes in small gourds and clay vials. They were firmly shut at the top with carved wood stoppers, but the trader would open them up so that you could smell the oils before you chose them.

'What have you to trade, sister?' she called to Achillea. I realised then how difficult it must be if you wanted an item whose owner did not want the item you wanted to trade. I supposed you would have to trade several times over in order to get the thing you required.

'I have these spicy hot chillies,' replied Achillea, taking out a handful of chillies from her bundle. 'Freshly dried in the sun, and perfect for your stews.'

The trader cast a critical eye over the chillies. 'I have enough chillies, I am looking for Paradox oil, or lavender blossoms, or pomegranates.'

Achillea, who had looked momentarily downcast, brightened at the mention of pomegranates. 'I have pomegranates too, sister,' she responded. 'How many do you need for one of these?' Achillea picked up one of the small clay vials of oil. At the Temple we used at least one a day of these oils as we oiled the Goddess's feet, and I could not imagine how many pomegranates, chillies, or finely embroidered netelas that would amount to.

'A full three weeks' worth.' At first, I was bewildered by this phrase and then I realised that this was the way in which this woman counted. She did not count with number names, but rather used the number of days in a week as her guide. It seemed a lot of pomegranates to me for such a small vial of oil, but I started to work out in my head the things which had to be done to produce the oil...the making of the clay vial, the wooden stoppers, the Paradox oil and the flower blooms that were soaked in it to release their scent. Achillea pondered the trade.

'I will come back later with them,' she offered, 'and then I will trade you for this scent. Smell it, Talla!' I bent my head to inhale the scent and was instantly transported back to the Temple, for it was a lavender scented oil, sweet and yet tart, fresh and yet musky. I closed my eyes and for a moment, it was as if I was standing at the feet of the Goddess once more, rubbing her feet with oils. It reminded me of Lunaria too, for her day was Lilavis, and her colour was the purple of lavender, as was the embroidery on her veil. The thought of Lunaria brought me back to the reason for coming to Sanguinea, and whilst I obediently followed Achillea around, looking at the animals and the flour, the wood and the clay pots and the metal jugs, I was wondering about the OutRiders and where they might be.

'Talla, hmm,' the perfume trader looked up at me briefly. 'Now where have I heard that name before?'

'Oh!' Achillea started and laughed brightly, before I could begin to think of an answer. 'It's so annoying, isn't it, Talla? That Drab who went missing a while back? That was her name too! It's a good job that Talla

FLAMMEUS

obviously isn't her, but people keep on remarking on it! I told her she should change her name, but they've probably found her by now, haven't they?' She dipped her head to one side like a curious bird and looked openly at the trader who laughed with her.

'Aye, sister,' responded the trader. 'Why I remember when the very same thing happened to me some years back. Took a lot of persuading to make those OutRiders understand that it wasn't me. They've got to be stupid! I mean as if a Drab wouldn't stand out a mile in those ridiculous clothes they wear and that unearthly look they all have when they leave. Good job they are all picked off, if you ask me,' she continued. 'For what earthly use would they be to us, here on the Outer?'

I bent my head to hide the sparks were leaping in my mind. I could not afford for my reaction to be spotted by the trader, and yet her words made me feel angry. I picked up one of the clay vials and sniffed at it appreciatively as Achillea had done. It was the scent of Viridis, green and acid and cedarwood scented, smelling crisply of trees and leaves, sharply verdant.

'It's a popular one, that one, Talla,' offered the trader, keen to make another sale. 'Or perhaps,' she cocked her head at me, appraising me in some sort of hidden way, 'perhaps this one?'

I inhaled the familiar scent of cinnamon bark, rich and dusty, the scent of Flammeus. It crept up my nose and entered my mind, stilling my anger and filling every part of me with peace. I knew that if I could get this small bottle of scent, I could begin to control my temper better.

'What have you to trade?' asked the trader, sensing an exchange.

'I have honey,' I replied. 'Honey, and honeycomb too that you might use the beeswax from for your scented salves.' The trader's eyes lit up and I knew that would be able to bargain my way to a small vial of perfumed oil in exchange for some of my honeycomb. Achillea told her where we would be sitting, and the trader nodded her head approvingly when Achillea told her that Gladia was there too, for it seemed she was someone who had traded with Gladia before. We walked back to Gladia, past the pyramids of carefully arranged melons and figs, past the pomegranates and the ears of corn and the sheaves of millet. We walked past the batches of cloth and of silk, past wooden boxes of spices and great bundles of wood and straw. My head was alive with the sights and the sounds, and the smells. There was the faint pervasive scent of coffee, and the dusty scent of spices wrapped around with the smell of fresh wood and vegetables and the overriding smell of sweat mixed with perfumes of every type. I felt quite giddy by the time we arrived back to where Gladia had set up her goods.

Gladia had carefully laid out the robes and netelas so as to best display her fine stitching. I felt proud to see my pounced patterns displayed so prominently and realised that I had helped Gladia too, for the more she traded of her stitchery, the more she would be able to exchange for supplies of more cotton cloth and embroidery threads. She was engrossed in trading with an elderly woman when we arrived back and only indicated vaguely where we should put our goods before turning back to her customer. I had brought eight small gourds and four large ones with me to the market. Gladia had told me that I would need the large ones to exchange with the Empath. As I looked around me covetously, at the wide variety of goods on offer, I hoped that the Empath would be worth this vast expenditure. I had decided that I needed to get myself some more flour and salt, and coffee, and some more gourds. I had already fixed my mind on the perfume but had not yet decided on what else I should trade for. The afternoon pressed on and Achillea helped me to make good trades for my honey, whilst making canny exchanges herself for her pomegranates and chillies and dried beans, pouting prettily at the male traders who invariably gave her what she wanted, and chatting easily with the women, who seemed to see in her a kindred spirit. I found the trading arduous, personally. I had no patience with the convoluted and complicated dance of words with which we encircled one another, and instead longed for a simple exchange to be made briskly and efficiently. I understood now what Gladia had meant by her remarks earlier about how hard I might find it to trade and regretted that I had thought ill of her.

As it neared the end of the day, I had three gourds of honey left, for I had traded one of the remaining ones for some parchment. I had it in mind to make some more patterns to pounce for Gladia, feeling that this would be my best way to assure her of my support. I wanted to trade them all on this first day, for whilst my head was swimming with sensation, I also felt the need to remove myself from the busy mass of people everywhere. I wondered how the bees lived in such close proximity with each other, and fancifully imagined that they took some moments of calm at every flower they visited on their own. A trader stopped; his wares wrapped up in a rough cloth. He was tall, but not overly so and he moved with a lithe agility, swinging his wares down off his shoulder in a single movement.

'Can I interest you in something rare and unusual to trade for that honey of yours, sister?' he asked, eyeing the gourds with apparent interest. 'I have just the thing for you which I would be willing to trade for a gourd of honey, and I am drawn to trade with you.'

Achillea and Gladia were talking, next to Gladia's wares, discussing what items they still needed to trade, so I had to talk to this man on my own, without their comfortable support. I still felt awkward in the back and forth talking that was done here on the Outer. In the Temple, talking was a tool; it was used for working, for communicating. There was not really a pleasure in it, as such. Out here, they could spend immense amounts of time talking back and forth. The trading was like a game; where one made an offer, another countered it, back and forth, like children rolling a ball of leaves from one to the other in the dust. There was no point, and yet it was enjoyable to them. In the right circumstances, I too took enjoyment from talking, especially with my companions from Mellia, who I knew better than others. Talking to strangers made me nervous. However, there was no choice, and his proposal had filled me with curiosity about what he might think was especially appropriate to me.

I tried to look him in the eye, as Achillea and Gladia did, and was surprised when his eyes crinkled up at the corners. His eyes were the colour of honey or amber, and an unusual clear, light brown. His mouth above his neatly trimmed beard curved upwards in a smile.

'Show me what you have then, brother,' I said, trying to return the smile. 'For my honey is the best honey you will find in this place.'

'Many make that claim, sister,' he warned, wagging his finger at me playfully. 'Be careful who you make it to, for I am an expert in the tasting of honey and many others would say that their honey was the best honey in the place too...'

I flushed, concerned that I had said something that might not be true, or that I might have to defend, but the trader laughed pleasantly. 'Oh, don't worry!' he said. 'I am not going to judge your honey against all others. I have a hankering for some good honey to carry with me on my travels and,' he travelled his eyes over me, 'if the honey is as sweet as its trader, it will indeed be good.'

Embarrassed, I looked down, but then, determined that I would manage this trade, and that I would learn to banter and trade in conversation as well as goods, I looked back up at him and said pertly, 'Well the honey is certainly sweet, brother, would you like to try it?'

I had seen other traders offering customers small samples of their wares, especially if they were edible, to assure them of their quality, and it made sense to me that someone might wish to be sure that they were making a good trade. I unstopped one of the gourds and dipped a freshly peeled stick in it. The honey was almost the same colour as his eyes. I proffered the stick to him and he took it from me, brushing his hand across mine as he did so. He raised the stick to his mouth and parted his lips to lick the syrupy goodness. I found myself opening my mouth slightly too, as if it were me who were tasting my own honey. He ran his tongue thoughtfully over his lips, and I felt a strange feeling inside me, as if I had honey running through my veins instead of blood.

'You are right, sister,' he affirmed finally. 'Your honey is the best honey I could hope to find in this place, and perhaps as far as I travel. Now I know I want to trade for some of that wonderful honey, the question really is, do you want what I have to offer?' He arched his eyebrow at me quizzically.

'Show me what you are offering,' I suggested. He reached into a sack and drew out a small wrapped package wrapped in a dark brown cloth. Inside it was a cinnamon box. It was just a box, quite plainly made. I did not really need a box, for I had nothing to put in it, and yet I wanted to trade my honey with this man, for he appreciated the honey that my bees had made, and he had eyes like honey and he interested me in a different way to my companions from Mellia. He looked at me, and reading my indecision, urged me to open the box. His voice was low in pitch but enticing in tone. Carefully, I prised open the lid and looked inside. In the box, strung on a length of fine leather was a cunning metal pendant of a bee. I had never worn jewellery in my life before, for it was not worn in the Temple, and indeed it was unnecessary to me now. I could have traded the honey for more flour, or for figs and dates and salt and spices, but I was suddenly possessed with a fierce desire to own this beautiful thing for no other reason than for its beauty. I did not know the metal, for it looked like a mix of silver and bronze, but the bee was correct in every way, from the fine tracery of the wings to the six legs, to the slightly hairy look of the body. I lifted it out, admiring the craftsmanship that had gone into making such a dainty thing.

'It will look well on you, sister,' coaxed the trader. 'For you must have the BeeGift to produce honey like that, and I am sure you, above others, can appreciate the workmanship.' In an instant, I made the decision, and offered him the gourd of honey. He bowed theatrically and exchanged the box for it. His eyes twinkled at me as he said, 'A beautiful bee for a beautiful Beeguard.' And then he turned to leave, having seen that Achillea and Gladia were bustling over to me having realised that I was trading without them. I felt irritated with them, for I wanted the trader to stay and talk a while and I knew that they would take over my conversation with him. But before I could turn to him to say anything more, he melted quietly into the crowd, winking at me briefly before he left.

'What were you trading for?' asked Achillea, noting that I had only one gourd left. Gladia skimmed over the small bundle of things which I had traded for with a swift and practised eye.

'I knew we should have come straight over!' she exclaimed, exasperated. 'She's gone and made some foolish trade with one of those merchants that wanders around persuading people to part with valuable stuff like that honey and giving nothing in exchange! She doesn't have the skill to pick them out! You will learn how to trade, Talla, don't worry,' she said as she turned to me. 'We should have looked after you better instead of gossiping.'

'But I have traded my honey for something beautiful!' I replied. 'It is small, but it is so cunning and well made.' And I opened the lid of the box to show them my bee necklace. Achillea drew it out of the box warily to look at it. Gladia frowned at it. I was puzzled by their reaction to it. Achillea, I knew, loved jewellery and treasured the pieces which used to be her mother's, even though she had been forced into trading some of them away when she needed food, and, after all, her mother was a Beeguard herself, so she already knew that the bees could only bring good things to those who tended them. I supposed that Gladia was wishing I had traded my honey for something more useful, but I had thought she would have praised me for trading the honey for something which was so obviously valuable and beautiful.

'Aye, well, if you must have it and wear it, put it under your robe, Talla,' said Gladia eventually.

'I do not understand,' I said. 'If I put it under my robe, nobody will see it. I thought you would see how lovely it was, just like I did. And the trader was very nice,' I added, as if this made a difference.

'Why could you not have traded for a flower necklace, or a bird, or a circlet?' asked Achillea. 'Nobody likes to see bees and honeycombs on pictures or drawn or engraved on anything, even though we love their honey. It is because it reminds people of the OutRiders! You have seen the picture on their shields! The OutRiders and their Queen control us and if you wear anything related to the honeycomb, like that bee necklace, people will see you as one of them and not one of us! Gladia told you this already!'

I recalled the reaction of the first group of people I had met when I left the Temple when they saw my mother's brooch, and Gladia's reaction to the pattern I had made for her to embroider which had bees on it. I closed my hand around my necklace, feeling angry that I should have to be bound by these beliefs. I put the necklace round my neck, and then dutifully slipped it under my robe. Gladia and Achillea looked relieved to see me complying with their instructions and began to talk of where we would spend the night, for the evening sun was lighting up the sky with a red glow. It looked almost as if the sky were on fire, and the colours melded into each other like the colours of oil on water.

As I bundled up my goods, including the last remaining gourd of honey, I could feel the little bee touching my skin. It had been cool to the touch when I first put it on, but now it had taken on the warmth of my body. With every move I made, I could feel its little legs tickling me, and it reminded me of the day when the OutRiders came, and I had stood, covered in bees, who had protected me. While I followed Gladia and Achillea to the place where they had agreed to meet Benakiell and Ashtun, I turned over the recent events in my mind. It seemed that everyone enjoyed and appreciated the goodness and the virtues of honey. Even in the Temple, honey was used in a medicinal capacity, and there cannot have been many young Maids who had not exaggerated their cough in the hopes of getting a spoonful of honey to treat it. The OutRiders had the design of a honeycomb on their shields and armour, and knew of the BeeGift, and although they seemed wary of the bees themselves, I was sure that, like the others on the Outer, they enjoyed eating the honey produced by the bees. The ordinary people of the Outer valued honey; they used it every day to sweeten foods and to add to tinctures and unguents. The more I learned about the bees and their way of life, the more I admired them, for it seemed to me they worked together harmoniously for the good of the hive. They produced a substance which was universally useful and appreciated, and yet people were fearful of them and of some hidden meaning which related back to the OutRiders and their mysterious Queen.

Later, as we sat and ate our evening meal by a fire in the courtyard, I asked Benakiell if he had ever seen anything crafted like the necklace. He had obviously been told by Gladia of my purchase, for he showed no surprise when I withdrew it from under my robe and brought the leather string over my neck.

'It's a well-made thing, Talla,' he said appreciatively, turning it over this way and that so it caught the glow off the fire. 'I have not seen anything quite like this before. Can you describe the trader to me? I may know him from my travels.'

When I closed my eyes, I could still see the trader's honey eyes and hear the warmth in his voice, but I was not sure that that would help Benakiell, and I truly did want to know who he was. For, now, I had so many new questions to ask of him; had he made the bee himself? If not, where did it come from? What was it made from? And what was his name? I cast my mind back to what he had looked like.

'He had light brown eyes, and I think he wore a dark blue or grey robe. He had a beard, and dark brown hair. He smiled a lot and talked well.'

Benakiell looked at me, twinkling his eyes, and he reminded me of an older version of the trader we were talking about. 'Seems to me, sister Talla, that you have a good eye for the detail of this trader; he must have made quite an impression on you.' My cheeks grew hotter, perhaps through the warmth of the fire and Benakiell sat silent for a while, deep in thought, his mind flicking through the names of traders who were skilled in this sort of metalwork.

'Perhaps his mother was a Beeguard,' he suggested, 'I remember many whose sons were taken long ago.'

I did not know what he meant by 'taken' and thought to myself that perhaps it was a kindly way of saying that the child had died. Many children died out of the many who were born; they lived brief lives some of them; like insects. The Priestesses told us when we were young Maids, in the First Age of Childhood, that the Goddess herself chose those who shone the brightest to finish their life's work early, and to rest. In fairness to the Priestesses, they tended to their charges well and not so very many of the foundlings died in the Temple. However, every day of every week would see some bereft mother from the Outer weeping at the feet of the Goddess, kissing them and pleading for the return of their child. As a youngster, I did not see why they would want their child to come back to spend the rest of its life working when it could rest for all eternity with the Goddess, but then I had no knowledge of this other world of the Outer, where it seemed work was not the touchstone for existence, but rather it was people, and the threads they wove between themselves of work, and belonging, and family, and love for one another. And I could see, now, how the loss of one of those threads might make the whole fabric of one's life collapse to holes. Absently, my hand strayed to the little bee, and I touched its smooth warm body.

'In the meantime, you really should keep the necklace hidden beneath your robe, in case it should cause any trouble to you, especially since you and Gladia set out on your own tomorrow morning at dawn to see the Empath,' added Benakiell as he prepared to stand up.

I had forgotten that I was going to see the Empath, and now wished that I was staying in Sanguinea for longer, so that I could try to trace the mysterious man who had traded the little bee with me. But I had been assured that the Empath would give aid to both me and Gladia, and it was another opportunity for me to explore the land of the Outer. We retired to sleep shortly after this, and as I turned about on the grass mat, I thought of the words of the trader as he had called me beautiful, or so it seemed, and his words melted into the comforting drone of bees in flowers as I finally slept.

CHAPTER 14

We awoke early the next morning with the first soft rays of the sun and Gladia and I shared some coffee, hastily brewed, and a flatbread with a little taste of honey on it, to give us strength for the journey ahead. Benakiell and Ashtun insisted that we leave behind the goods we had traded to return with them to Mellia so that we did not have more to carry than necessary. Benakiell bade us goodbye and spoke quietly to Gladia before we left. I guessed he was telling her about our conversation, but he may have just been wishing her well.

Gladia and I set off down a path which led to the east, directly into the rising sun. There was a chill in the air and the distinctive smell of heavy dew on dry, red dust. We did not speak a great deal as we walked, but rather looked about us. The path led us through an area of scrubby trees growing from the dust, with thorn bushes sprinkled around. The path was flat and stony and for a while it seemed an easy walk, but we soon began to climb again, and as I looked back towards Sanguinea, I realised that we were beginning to ascend the foothills of the purple mountains which I had first seen on the day that I left the Temple. The air was tight as we climbed higher, and the scrubby trees gave way to taller greener trees. After some hours, as the sun had risen further in the sky and was shining full into our faces, we stopped by a large rock under a tree and sat down gratefully to rest ourselves. We drank some water from the gourd, and chewed on some dried figs. There were interesting plants growing nearby with long sword like leaves on tall stalks and other small plants with insignificant yellow flowers and furry leaves like the ears of a small animal. I did not think the bees would like it here, with so few flowers. Although the land seemed greener and more abundant, the lack of the bees and other insects, and the additional lack of birds made it feel lonely. I wondered if there were any small animals which lived here, perhaps in the trees or in the thorny thickets. There were a few small bunches of people walking up and down the trail and we spoke with them as they passed us. Some of the travellers seemed to recognise Gladia and asked her about the market trading in Sanguinea, and others were strangers to us both. Some of the clothing seemed different too; the netelas were thicker and less ornamented, although the decoration round the cuffs of the gowns was more detailed and complex. Many also wore hats or turbans on their heads, and sleeveless jackets over the top of their robes. It was much cooler up here on the mountains, so the thicker clothing made sense.

When we stood up again to carry on walking, the sun had passed overhead and now warmed our backs. It made it easier for us to walk, without squinting against the sun, and although Gladia puffed and moaned, she seemed invigorated by the fresher air, or perhaps by the prospect of seeing the Empath. It was a good thing that I was used to hours of physical work from my days at the Temple because, although we worked hard, we rarely walked for long distances. The people on the Outer walked all the time although they worked less than we had done. The air was beginning to cool again when we arrived at a sort of clearing where some dozen people were gathered around a fire, and where Gladia told me we would spend the night before seeing the Empath in the morning. She told me that all the people who were waiting were there in the hope of seeing the Empath too, but that the Empath only chose those she wished to see. I was surprised, for I had thought that we would definitely see her; Benakiell and Gladia had seemed quite certain. As we rested, I asked Gladia to tell me about the Empath and what work she did.

'An Empath is born. And although most of us follow in the footsteps of our parents and our ancestors in our paths, the Empath does not always follow thus. For an Empath rarely meets a soul mate or has a child because of the burden which they carry on our behalf,' started Gladia, settling herself more comfortably against her pack.

'I do not understand,' I interrupted, 'how another person may carry the burden of someone's heart or mind within themselves, for it has no substance, unlike your pack.'

Gladia smiled, a little smugly, 'I would not expect you to understand. We all know that the Drabs from the Temple have no feelings or seem to have no feelings. Although,' she looked at me speculatively, 'your feelings certainly seem to have emerged since you have been living in the Outer! Perhaps it is the company, or something you ate!' She chuckled.

'Have you been to see this Empath before?' I asked, trying to ignore the spark which always flared in my mind when Gladia talked about Drabs in the scornful way that she sometimes did. Occasionally, I wanted to tell everything that I knew and had been taught to show her that I was not just a meaningless drudge, but something more than that, but I held my tongue. It would not serve me well to tell her everything about myself. It could yet be that I would need to use that information for some other purpose. And now, having thought about this, I became concerned that somehow this Empath would be able to read my mind and divulge the secrets within it to Gladia, so I asked Gladia to tell me some more about how the Empath worked.

'I have seen Empath Erayo six times now,' she reflected. 'And each time I have seen her, she has given me strength to look forward instead of backward. She has taken my burdens from me and given me time to set my face towards the dawn again. We do not realise what heaviness we carry with us, Talla.' Her eyes, usually brisk and sharp, dulled somewhat, as if reflecting on her own burden, of which I knew nothing.

'But how does she do that?' I asked, still not understanding.

'When I have visited her before, I have gone in to see her, and sat on a mat on the floor,' replied Gladia. 'She has held my hand, or touched my head or my shoulders, and you can feel everything leaving you to go to her, and all that is left is lightness.'

'Does she read your thoughts as well?' I asked, desperate to know, for I needed to be able to work out how to deal with this, if so.

Gladia didn't seem surprised by the question. 'I was worried myself about that the first time I went to see her,' she admitted. 'I didn't want someone I didn't know reading inside my thoughts, but it seems she does not read thoughts, but only feelings. She does not need to talk to feel your feelings and she does not need to know why you have those feelings.' She sighed again. 'It must be a strain, bearing all the weight of everyone's feelings. Since I find it hard enough to deal with my own, I cannot imagine how she must feel sometimes.'

'But she must feel happiness too,' I pointed out. 'There must be people around her who are happy and whose happiness she can feel in the same way. Perhaps her family or companions come to her with their happy thoughts and feelings too, to share them with her.'

Gladia looked surprised by this, but made no comment, except to say that she now felt tired and would be going to sleep. Long after she was snoring comfortably by her pack, and the small group of people who were also camping had gone to sleep, I sat by the orange and black embers of the fire, thinking about how feelings which had no physical weight to them could become so heavy, and yet could also lighten one's mood. It was a curious thought, and I pondered on it until my thoughts became confused by sleep.

The next morning began at dawn. I stirred, moving my cramped leg under my rough cover, and feeling the sharp stone under my mat which had bothered me all night. Already the camp was bustling, and people were rolling up their belongings and hoisting their bags, apparently ready for the Empath. I got to my feet dully, unsure what to do. The night had been a restless one, beset with strange dreams which had no meaning to me; dreams of children and small babies, of elderly and sick people, of arguments between people I had never met. Through the clamour of preparation, I heard insistent bells ringing, and getting louder, and turned to view where it came from and who was making it.

The Empath Erayo arrived in the camp, escorted by two motherly women who stood close to her, and who were the ones ringing the bells. She was a fragile looking woman, small and spare. I could not easily tell her age, but she may have been in the Seventh Age. There were no grey flecks in her hair, but she wore it cropped close to her skull, with a grey netela wrapped over it, much the same as the Priestesses wore their veils in the Temple, except of course that we could see her face. As she entered the camp, we all fell silent. She stood still, seemingly scenting or tasting the air, from the way in which she moved her head this way and that. The women either side of her were carefully essaying what might have been brought to trade with the Empath. It must be difficult, I thought, to live so far away and to be so reliant on the gifts of others. For it may be that no one ever thought to bring her a soapball, or a comb, or a set of new gourds, but instead brought her things they might value for themselves; fine spices or parchment pictures, or carefully embroidered items.

I wondered how she chose who to see, and whether some people were regularly turned away for not passing a kind of unwritten test. Erayo tilted her head as she viewed us, standing awkwardly in the fine dust, our paltry campfires struggling to keep alight with their lack of attention. There were not very many of us, so I was not surprised when the women who seemed to guard the Empath started telling people to get out their trades and to be ready for their time with the Empath. I had, for some reason, thought there might be something more of the ritual about it, used as I was to the traditions of the Temple. In the Temple, there would have been the presence of sweet scents and colours, the acts of chanting and of meditation, the hearing of the Aphorisms of Ashkana and the moment in which we awaited the message of the Goddess presented to us through the Priestesses. This, however, seemed quite prosaic; the gathering up of tradestuffs for a meeting with someone who had a special gift. In the Temple, I felt sure, they would have ascribed her talents to the Goddess, and she would have been told that it was her life's work, rather than a tradeable commodity. There again, I mused, she would have had no need of things to trade in the Temple for we fed and clothed ourselves. My mind flitted back and forth between the Temple and the Outer, at once thinking that each one had attractions and each one had detractions. Engaged as I was, I was unaware that the Empath guards were standing in front of me, waiting for my trade until Gladia poked me sharply. My mind's emberjar flared briefly, and I felt like poking her back in her warm, doughy arm and watching her reaction, but I cast my eyes down to the floor momentarily, as we were taught in the Temple and then, my mind cleared, looked up at the guards.

'What have you to trade with the Empath?' one asked in a desultory fashion, apparently finding the whole process tedious.

'And please,' interjected the other one, 'please, don't say you have brought Empath Erayo a scented oil or a wooden box! We have quite enough of those!'

I was just about to answer when Gladia interrupted me. 'We have honey,' she answered quickly and firmly. 'There are two of us, myself and my companion, Talla. We both wish to see the Empath and we have brought this fine honey, two gourds of it to trade for her time.'

'Two of you?' said one of them sharply. 'Two visitors mean two trades!'

Gladia was not put off. 'As I told you, sister,' she said firmly, 'we have two gourds of honey, one for each of us, and when you have tasted this honey, which Talla here has coaxed out of her bees, you will know its worth.' I began to feel pleased that Gladia was there with me, and my earlier urge to poke her quite disappeared. I would not have been able to hold my own with these women, but Gladia was not intimidated by their frostiness. She gestured towards me for the gourds of honey and as I fumbled for them, she looked about her for a twig to peel to make a tasting twig. The Empath remained standing in the middle of the clearing, turning her head this way and that, as if to try to rid herself of some annoying invisible swarm of flies. The stick peeled, Gladia dipped it in the honey and offered it to the slightly larger, and consequently, I thought, greedier of the two. As the guard tasted the honey, her face softened somehow, and a small self-satisfied smile crept to the edges of Gladia's mouth. She turned to me, and her face was uplifted by her smile. I understood then, that this trip was every bit as important, if not more important, to Gladia than it was to me, and I felt pleased that my honey, or rather, my bees' honey would allow her to see the Empath. The guard nodded her head to us both and took the gourds. The other guard looked wistfully at the gourds and I felt a pang of pity for her since she had not tried the honey, but there was little I could do. We went to sit down on a mat laid down under a tree, and the Empath paused to look at us all before she moved back towards her dwelling. In the time she had been amongst us, she seemed to have aged, and she walked carefully, as one does who feels dizzy or light-headed. The large guard came up to me as they went past and hissed, 'The Empath will see you last.' I wondered how she had made that judgement, and what it might mean.

It was an interesting process to watch. The guards would come and take one at a time out of the dozen or so and lead them through the trees between our clearing and the small dwelling of the Empath. Everyone who had been anxious about being seen had now become calm, and there was less fretting and more a resigned, patient waiting. Some talked quietly amongst themselves, but most of them just sat and waited their turn. As each was beckoned forward, I noticed how quiet and peaceful it was; there was none of the frenzied bustling there had been earlier; no one battled to be the first to be seen by the Empath, but just waited patiently, knowing that they already had what they wanted. I wondered if I had been placed last because somehow the Empath knew something about me; that she knew I was a Temple Maid and that she would send for the OutRiders. I tried to feel anxious, but instead I felt calm, my feelings dulled and pacified. As each person went to the Empath, I noted the expression on their face and tried to see how it changed when they returned. They seemed to return a little lighter and brighter, and ready to move on with their lives, packing up their belongings quietly and moving on out. Nobody spoke to another about their experience, which frustrated me, for alone out of all of them I felt that I did not know what to anticipate. In the Temple, we did not have worries. The Priestesses did not accept their existence, frankly, and work was the salve which was applied to everything. But then, in the Temple, we did not have feelings like I had encountered on the Outer. Here, feelings could threaten to overwhelm you, could take over your mind and even your body and cause you to say or do things which you might not ordinarily do. Each session lasted only a short time, and it did not seem to be long before Gladia and I were the only ones left sitting on the mat. As Gladia heaved herself up off the floor, she patted my shoulder in a friendly way and ambled down the path, following the guard, and then I was left on my own.

It had been some time since I had been alone; we had been travelling to Sanguinea together and, in the town itself, we were surrounded at all times by people. At times like that I longed for my small dormit in the Temple, a room that I could call my own, with no possessions to occupy my mind. For all that we worked so hard in the Temple, the quality of our peace was high, and the time spent on our own was valuable. It was harder to achieve that with all the social pressures of the Outer; people to trade with, to keep links with, people whose help you required. But then, this association and friendship with people brought its own rewards. I turned my face towards the sun and sat, with my legs stretched out in front of me, enjoying the moment of warmth and light.

Gladia returned with a spring in her step. The twinkle was back in her eye and the wrinkles that had seemed more pronounced recently, especially since the visit of the OutRiders to Mellia, were softened. She was accompanied by the guard who waited to take me to the Empath. Once again, Gladia patted my shoulder, as if to give me comfort or succour, and yet I did not feel in need of it. I remembered Benakiell telling me that one of the reasons to go to the Empath was to help a person to deal with uncontrollable feelings which threatened an imbalance in life, such as my anger, which seemed to flare rapidly and which I found disconcerting, although in the Outer it was not so very unusual. He had also mentioned the Empath when he had been telling me about Rupicola's dream; that Empaths could take on those dreams and perhaps interpret them for people. I do not recall ever dreaming in the Temple. Sleep was a solid block of rest for the body and mind, and there were no feelings within it at all. Since my arrival in the Outer, I had found my dreams unsettling, occasionally strange and sometimes even funny. I tried not to think that the Empath might become aware of all my dreams, including the one in which the merchant who had traded the bee necklace with me had featured. I felt for the bee with my hand just as we arrived at the dwelling of the Empath.

CHAPTER 15

The dwelling itself was nondescript, of mud smoothed over a wooden frame. The floor was smooth too and there was a crisp smell of an astringent herb which I could not place. Empath Erayo sat on a mat, sipping from a small gourd. She smiled as I walked in and said, 'I greet you, sister, I am drinking some of your excellent honey mixed with my water here. It soothes my throat wonderfully.' I smiled tentatively because I did not know how else to respond; I had expected portentous words and possibly incense, and yet this was just a simple dwelling with a normal person in it, talking to me without artifice.

'Come, sit with me and let me try on your feelings,' she said simply, and I moved to sit with her. She turned to face me and then reached out her hands towards me. They did not touch me and yet I felt a warmth between us flowing like warm honey. It was not a rushing feeling of relief or enlightenment but the sweet encouragement to give my feelings to her which seemed impossible to resist. Gratefully, I gave in and sat, as her hands moved gently, hovering over my skin. As I yielded to her, I recognised the feelings as they left; the anger I felt over the Temple and the OutRiders, the conflicted feelings I had toward the Temple and the Outer, the tiny things which angered me like the way in which Gladia called me a Drab, my impatience with Achillea and Ashtun when they sat indolent for so long. All these things I felt trickle from me, leaving behind them a space smooth and clean, like the floors of the Temple after I had cleaned them according to the Seven Step Rule. As I felt my mind clearing, I looked at the Empath who looked back at me candidly.

FLAMMEUS

'You are not who you say you are,' she began. 'I have never taken on these kinds of feelings before. You concern yourself with different things to people here on the Outer. Don't worry,' she said, as she saw my rising concern. 'I do not read your thoughts; but your feelings. I do not know who you are, or where you came from, but only that your feelings are different from many others. You concern yourself greatly with work, and your work has kept your feelings within. The feelings I take from you are almost those of a child, unhoned, and uncontrolled when they escape.' She reached out her hands again to me, and my tongue was stilled before it began. 'Your dreams come from another place, from another one. She is powerful and is trying to reach you. You are searching for one that you cannot find, and your search will take you to places of danger. But you are a Beeguard; that will serve you well. Go to the bees; they will listen to you and absorb your feelings like an Empath. They will sweeten your pain and bring forth honey made all the sweeter by the bitterness of your tears.'

I had no words to speak to her, so I reached out my hand in a gesture of thanks to her. As my hand touched hers, I felt a sudden flood of feelings. Where mine had flowed out of me slowly, inexorably, towards her, these feelings broke through like a river in flood. But these were not my feelings rushing out of me, but the feelings of others rushing into me. I felt a jumbled mess of feelings, I felt utter loss and grief, and felt the tears roll down my face, and yet before I had chance to feel the grief in any real sense, it was replaced with feeling of betrayal and disbelief that a friend could treat me thus, and again, before I could channel the feeling, it too was replaced with a feeling of sad resignation, and with it came the flash of Gladia's face. I opened my eyes abruptly and moved my hand from the Empath hastily. She gave a start and tried to focus her eyes on me.

'What was that?' I asked her harshly. 'Why do I have these feelings? They are not mine.'

Erayo looked up at me, and in her eyes something was lightened and there was gratitude, along with a profound pity and a knowing look which made me feel uncomfortable.

'You have the gift,' she murmured. 'I have never felt my gift as another feels it. And yet, you have the gift. What you felt was my own burden of feelings, those feelings I have eased from their owners. When you touched me, the channel which usually only flows one way was opened and my feelings flowed into you, in the same way that yours flowed into me just moments before.'

I sat back, suddenly utterly exhausted. Erayo called for one of her guards to bring the gourd of honey, and she dipped a peeled stick in it and gave me the stick to suck as I sat there. I felt like a child given a treat, but the honey did calm me, and fed my mind until I stopped feeling so shaken and was able to ask more questions.

'Why did this happen?' I asked finally. 'You said I had the gift of being an Empath, but I do not understand other people's feelings, let alone feel able to take them unto myself. How can I when I do not even know what many of the feelings are nor how I should react to them? And why has this only happened with you and with no other? For I have touched others before, and this has not happened.'

Erayo pondered my questions. 'Perhaps it was only because I took away some of your own feelings and that opened up the channels of feelings within you that have been closed for so long. It may be that if you had not come to see me, then you would have never known you had this gift. '

I was horrified but curious at the same time. 'Does this mean that I will always know what my companions are feeling towards me and others?' I asked, wondering if I would be able to cope with living close to other people on the Outer if I were to be bombarded with their feelings all the time. Gladia had told me herself that most Empaths lived simply and alone, because of the burden of their gift. Erayo looked thoughtful.

'I do not know. It may be that you can only bear the burden of an Empath. It is so unusual for one who has the gift to not be aware of it from an early age. And I have never heard of any other who can do this. Once, we believed the Priestesses of the Temple might have had the gift, and that it may be given by the Goddess, but others believe that the Priestesses feel only for their Temple and for their work.' She tipped her head to one side and scrutinised me, and there was in her face some sort of inkling that she was working out where I came from. After a pause, in which I dropped my eyes and my feelings downwards, she continued. 'I only heard of one other way that people can take on the feelings of others, with the gift of the Empath, and that is from the ancient writings, before the Age of Ashkana. It was said in those writings that the bees can communicate and sing to one another in ways which we do not understand. It was said that if you had the talisman of a bee made from honeygold, then you could sense the feelings of others just as the bees can sense the feelings and moods of their brethren. You do not have such a talisman, do you?' she asked suddenly, turning towards me. I tended to the ember in my mind, heaping dull ashes upon it to keep it hidden, and gazing at the floor again, as we had done in the Temple, trying to keep my feelings in check.

I shook my head, and quickly asked Erayo what she thought I should do. She suggested I should meet my travelling companion and see if I felt anything from her, and then perhaps I could go on my way. She cocked her head to one side again, reminding me of Achillea and her bird-like ways, and I felt a surge of feeling toward Achillea. I missed her chatter and her gurgling laugh and the sound of her beautiful singing voice, her idleness and her fondness for eating sweet things whilst sitting in the shade. I wanted to get back to my other companions. Erayo had been helpful and pleasant, and yet whilst I had shared all the feelings which she had taken on herself from her visitors that day, I did not feel her own feelings. It was as if she were an empty gourd or water jug through which feelings were poured, this way and that, and yet left no trace. My companions from Mellia had shared their feelings with me, and willingly listened to my questions and misunderstandings and there was a mutual care there which this woman seemed to lack. It seemed a curious thing that one who seemed to care so much for others could leave one feeling so underwhelmed. I wanted to move away from her as quickly as I could, because of the bee talisman which she had mentioned, which hung under my robe and touched my bare skin with its honeygold feet. I wanted to take it off and keep it somewhere safe. Some time it might be to my advantage to use its power, but for now, I just wanted to see Gladia and leave this place to travel back to Mellia. I asked if I might go to relieve myself and Erayo asked one of the guards to show me where to go. Once there, I hastily removed the bee necklace and placed it carefully in my underpocket then returned to Gladia who was sitting waiting patiently for me.

'How did it go for you, Talla?' she asked curiously. 'You have taken a fair time in there. Was the Empath explaining your dreams to you? Did she help you by taking away your anger?'

I looked at her, and, in my mind, I saw the flash of feeling I had had from her and I knew that the feeling of sad resignation had come from her, and that she wanted something that she did not think she could have. I had also felt a deep heartache which I knew came from her, but which I could not explain. I paused for a moment, wondering if Erayo had been wrong, and if it was nothing to do with the little bee pendant after all, but no more feelings came to me from Gladia, so I knew that I was just recalling the feelings which she had given to the Empath and which I must bear now, in turn, for I could not let her know that her feelings were known to me.

'I found it strange and somewhat alarming,' I explained tentatively. 'It took a long time for my feelings to emerge and then I was a little shaken by it all. But she did tell me that my dreams were sent to me by another, a powerful one who sought me.'

Gladia's eyes lit up with an interested, slightly smug light. 'I knew there was more to you than met the eye!' she exclaimed triumphantly. 'Perhaps your Priestess can send dreams, and is looking hard for you? Who else could it be... perhaps even the Queen! But why the Queen would be searching for a Drab...' Her voice tailed off as she pondered about who would consider me worthy enough to search out. I gritted my teeth and was grateful that it was not Gladia wearing the little bee talisman for she would have surely felt the full force of my anger and irritation with her for her careless remarks. I should stop reacting so much to them, but since I had recovered my feelings from wherever the Temple had banished them, it was rather difficult to always present a calm demeanour. I fiddled with my pack and tied and untied a few knots.

Gladia waited for me impatiently, having apparently recovered all her energy. I pondered on how it was that so much seemed to go into these feelings that went so deep, and I thought of how much energy we had put into our work at the Temple. It seemed that somehow, they had harnessed that energy which in the Outer went upon feelings both bad and good and managed to get us to put it all into our duty and responsibility of work. I still did not know how I felt about this; I often needed to focus solely on doing some work, whether it be cleaning or weeding or pricking out patterns on my parchment, though the Goddess knew how little time I had spent upon that recently. As I felt again the feelings which had surely come from Gladia at the time that everything rushed from the Empath to me, my irritation with her dissolved away. She carried her own burdens, and she bore them cheerfully for the most part, and patiently. I resolved, not for the first time, to maintain my patience for longer, and engaged her in conversation about patterning and what sorts of patterns she had seen at Sanguinea; which ones were selling well, and which colours seemed to be most desirable. Her eyes lit up and I realised that I did not try very hard sometimes to have small and gentle conversations with my companions. They were easy and restful and gave pleasure to both parties.

'I saw a beautiful netela at the market,' explained Gladia, quite animated. 'It was unusual because it was all patterns; there were no flowers or leaves in it, and yet it gave the impression of leaves and flowers. It was stitched quite finely.' She paused for a small sniff which seemed to imply that she could stitch it finer, 'And the colours were all in blues and pale greens and the odd splash of bright yellow.' She continued to describe it to me, and as I asked her questions about it, I could begin to picture it in my mind, and resolved that something similar would be my next project to pounce on the parchment. If I worked hard on it, then Gladia would be able to make good trades on her next visit to Sanguinea.

We continued talking as we walked, and truthfully, it made the time pass quickly. Gladia had assured me that she knew the way, and we were heading down off the mountain where the Empath Erayo made her home and back towards Mellia on a more southerly path which meandered down the mountainside like a stream, curving round boulders and scrubby pockets. There were not many other people about, and we contented ourselves with nodding and politely greeting those we came across until the sun became quite hot and we both felt the need for some rest. We propped ourselves up against a smooth stone and had some water from our water gourds. The water tasted brackish and was tepid, and I looked forward to arriving back in Mellia to the taste of fresh sweet water from the stream. Gladia took out some flatbreads, which were slightly tough and yeasty, and we ate the last of the figs I had brought with me. Of course, we had our other traded goods too, but we did not want to start on them until we got back.

'I wonder who your mother was,' mused Gladia as she finished her flatbread, picking bits of fig out from between her teeth with a small stick. I looked up, startled. In all the time I had spent out of the Temple, nobody had ever discussed this with me before.

'I do not know,' I responded honestly. 'The Priestesses told me that my mother abandoned me at the doors of the Temple, like all the others. Why do women do that, Gladia?'

Gladia looked at me sharply and seemed to fight some battle between her head and her tongue before she eventually said, 'Not all women have a choice, Talla. Life is hard on the Outer, especially if a child is born without a father. Many children are born to those who have no use for them; they are accidental and unwanted. It is better for some babies to go to the Temple than to die, after all. And some mothers have no choice about their babies, especially when they are young.'

I thought on what she had said, and it unsettled me. What if the Priestesses had told me the romantic story of my abandonment and the tale about the brooch just to make me feel like I had been loved? Perhaps I was just an unwanted child who had been in the way; perhaps my mother had hated me and had never known my father. And, if that were the case, then mayhap I had stolen the brooch from the Temple, even whilst I was sure it was mine. And Lunaria had brought it for me anyway, I reminded myself. I felt the shadows cross my face like the swift passage of clouds over a field on a windy day. Gladia seemed not to notice my discomfort and carried on talking, almost to herself.

'Of course, they don't get as many as they used to that way. And yet still the Temples are full. The OutRiders used to come through the village looking for girl babies and youngsters and take them away! Sometimes they tried to buy them from the poor ones; offer them trades for the children and say they would be well cared for. And in the end, I suppose they were,' she mused sadly.

I looked at her, aghast at what she had said so matter-of-factly. The Priestesses had stolen the Maids? They were not unwanted after all, but rather taken from their mother's arms. Or even sold to them like objects of trade? I did not know what I would rather believe; that I was unwanted and abandoned or that I had been stolen from my mother's desperate clutch. I would rather have had the story I had been told since I was in the First Age of Childhood, but it felt more and more as if it could not be true. Gladia caught my eye eventually, and I glimpsed, again, a flash of what seemed to be pity in her dark eyes.

'Did you never wonder where all the Maids came from?' she asked curiously. 'For they are not born of you, since the Maids and the Priestesses do not birth children, and yet the Temples are replenished all the time.'

'I never thought about it,' I answered truthfully, feeling shallow, as if this were something that I should have bent my mind to. Looking back to my time at the Temple and teaching myself to scribe and to read, listening at the door as Astronomers told their truths to the Priestesses about omens and foretelling, but also of weather and good growing times, I wondered that I had interested myself in so much that was outside of my life, and yet had never contemplated fully the tangled nest in which I lived. I stood up, briskly brushing off the crumbs of flatbread, and, taking my cue, Gladia did the same thing, and hoisted her pack onto her headband.

We walked on, both of us thinking our own thing. There were few others on the road, and after some time, we stopped seeing other travellers completely. The land stretched around us, the mountain of the Empath Erayo now seemed far away, and when I looked back behind me, it looked as dark and mysterious as it had looked when I had first seen when I left the Temple. Gladia had told me that the mountains were called the Osho mountain and were the highest in the land. The dried yellow grass on the plain waved in gently moulded hills, stretching far into the distance. Here and there, the landscape was broken by small tufts of dwellings; all a bit different to the ones in Mellia, their thatched roofs steeper and lower over the walls. Around each set of dwellings were Paradox trees and other trees; figs and pomegranates and dates, and small gardens growing fresh food for the dwellers. Sometimes there were steep rocky outcrops which were occasionally crowned with stone buildings. Gladia told me that these too were Temples, but they bore no resemblance to my Temple. The path to them must have been both steep and treacherous but winding upward rather than downward.

These Temples stood high, looking out over the plains, able to view the land for miles around them, whereas my own Temple was invisible from the nearby track, dug as it was into the rocks below it.

The Temple where I had grown up was built by the Angels of the Goddess in the long distant past. It was hewn out of the rocks of the earth, so that you descended to it down steep pathways through the terraced gardens which surrounded it. There were endless passageways around the Temple, from one part to another; from the Temple up to the dormits, to the trading area and the gardens. The building was seamless, pure rock; the same rock that the statue of the Goddess was made of. As we passed one of these Temples, I had an urge to visit it, to reconnect myself with the Goddess. To smell again the scents of the days, and to oil the feet of the Goddess in the prescribed way. In the Temple was order and routine; work and duty. I longed to be back in my dormit cell, just big enough for me to sleep, with my soapball and my comb and my drabcoat, and although I was enclosed with smooth seamless rock, yet there was a space around me for myself in which to think. Gladia must have detected my wistfulness in the way I looked back toward the Temple on the hill, and took my arm, a little roughly.

'You cannot go back to the Temple, Talla,' she said. 'For you would give yourself away with your longing; you know too much, and it is still too near you for you to hold your feelings in.' I saw that she was right, and it was a curious thing to think that I had feelings about a place in which I was encouraged not to have feelings. My mind twisted this way and that like a cat chasing its own tail.

We fell silent again, absorbed in our thoughts and neither of us were aware of any other travellers. All we could hear was the sawing of the crickets and our own breathing and the slap of our feet in the thick red dust. Suddenly, Gladia grabbed my arm again, in exactly the same place, pinching my flesh so that I could almost see the bruise already.

'Why do you keep doing that?' I grumbled at her, snatching my arm away and rubbing it fiercely. I looked up, expecting to see her either looking remorseful, or looking brisk and confrontational. Instead, when I raised my eyes, I saw the reason for the pinch. Lounging on some boulders under a thorn tree right next to the track were two OutRiders and their ash grey horses. Gladia looked around wildly, but behind us we could see a cloud of dust rising and heading towards us. Only men on horseback could leave such a trail, and the OutRiders were the only men on horseback. It seemed that we must be trapped, for we could not outrun a horse. We were trapped between these OutRiders and their comrades whose dust cloud we could see heading to the same place. The last time we had encountered the OutRiders, the bees had come to my rescue, and the rest of my companions had been close at hand. Here, in the middle of the grassy plains, there was only me and Gladia, neither of us equipped to fight an armed man. One of the figures on the rocks stretched and, catching sight of us, slid down easily. His horse turned to look at us, prickling his nose up at our scent. The OutRider wore full leather armour, oiled and tempered by years, and a helmet which obscured much of his face. The other one too, approached us. For our part, we both stood still, holding on to one another like small Maids in the First Age. Just like the others, these two seemed to move silently. The one with the helmet stood in front of us, relaxed, but alert. His fingers moved swiftly as if speaking to his companion, who moved behind us. I felt constrained and frightened, even though not a word had yet been uttered.

CHAPTER 16

'Greetings, sisters,' spoke the first. 'Where are you going, all on your own?' The words were spoken mildly, but I wondered what the correct response was. Was this path prohibited? Had Gladia brought me down some old route which had been taken over by the OutRiders?

Gladia answered briskly and cheerfully. 'Just heading back down to Mellia. We have been trading in Sanguinea.'

'Why go such a long way around?' he asked. 'This is not the way to Mellia from Sanguinea.'

'Is it prohibited now?' asked Gladia, brightly. 'If only you would tell us when you change the rules.' The OutRider did not respond to this effrontery and instead turned his attention to me.

'Why are you so silent? Is she touched?' He turned to Gladia as I struggled to contain myself.

I had to try even harder when Gladia, entering the conversation, tipped her head to one side and said slowly and speculatively, 'Well, you know, she seems quite normal, but occasionally I do think her mother dropped her on a step when she was a child...' The OutRider laughed, ambled in front of me and appraised me.

'She looks alright to me. What do you think?' He turned to his companion, who was squinting towards the approaching dust cloud of yet more OutRiders. Suddenly, I felt quite tired and all the fight fell out of me. All I wanted was to go back to Mellia, to tend to the bees, to talk with my companions and to drink coffee. I was tired of travelling and of speaking to people I did not know, tired of keeping up a façade to them all, and longing to just be myself. The other OutRider pulled his eyes reluctantly away from the dust cloud and looked at me. At least I assume he looked at me, for he wore a full faced helmet. It was, like the rest of his armour, made of dark brown polished leather, perhaps from some sort of buffalo hide. It had been tended and oiled over many years and now resembled a fine-grained wood. Over the face ran a strip which led from the top of the helmet down over the nose to the chin. Across it was a mouth guard with a metal grille to allow him to breathe. Over the eyes were fine slats of leather and metal grilles like the one over his mouth. You could not see his eyes at all and yet when I heard his voice, I gave a start of recognition.

'A fit enough looking Maid,' he confirmed, dismissively. The tone was more abrupt, but the timbre of his voice was unmistakeable. It was the voice of the trader who had traded with me for the little bee, which now resided in my underpocket, along with my brooch. I did not understand, nor know what to do. He turned back to the other OutRiders, now nearing us, and then made more hand movements to his comrade. My mind was trying to make sense of what I had just heard. How could he be a trader and an OutRider? How many people were there, who pretended to be one whilst really being the other? And how could I have ever felt like he could be trusted, and that he had my interests at heart, if he were one of these OutRiders who imposed the law of the Queen by brutal force on the people of the Outer? Whose own comrades had terrified us in Mellia not so many days before? And what implication did this have on the cunning little bee that he had traded with me? Erayo had said that it was made of some rare metal that had power; could that hidden power have led this false trader straight to me, or had he been watching me all the while, waiting for a moment when none were around to make his move? Achillea had told me some of the stories she had heard of what the OutRiders would do to people if they went against the laws of the Queen, and I shuddered that I may have taken us into such a position of danger.

The horses started and looked alert. The sounds of the oncoming OutRiders were getting louder. We had no hope of running away from them and we would be swiftly overpowered by them. I noticed the bows and arrows slung on the saddle, and the long, wickedly sharp looking swords that each man wore. Their armour would protect them from just about anything, except bees which could, I realised, crawl between the leather joints and sting them. How I wished I was back with the bees now; I would have felt safer. The OutRiders both approached us and swiftly threw their arms around our necks, twisting us backwards into them. My feet scrabbled at the dirt as I fought to breathe. Gladia reached out her hand to me and pleaded with me with her eyes to say nothing to get us into further trouble. The trader with honey in his voice bent down to my ear and very quietly told me that I was to ride with him on his horse and that he would put me up on the horse. The other one must have said something similar to Gladia. Gladia was no willowy child, but the OutRider lifted her and tossed her onto the saddle barely drawing breath as he swung himself up in front of her. Before I could prepare myself, I too was launched onto the saddle of the horse. I had never been so close to such a large creature and I was terrified of it, and awe-inspired at the same time. Its hair was so close to its skin that it rippled like the silken cloths we used for the Goddess in. As soon as I was on, the trader OutRider mounted it too and passed a rough loop of leather around us both, presumably to hold us together and to prevent my jumping off.

FLAMMEUS

Despite my fear, I was strangely fascinated by this turn of events. I was helpless in the face of the power and aggression I felt from these men and their animals, and yet it excited me, and I did not fight or kick against him.

'Hold on,' he told me and spurred the horse. Our horses took off, galloping along the trail, keeping ahead of the oncoming OutRiders. I wondered why they were leaving now instead of waiting for their comrades, and then, as we turned a steep bend, they veered off the path and galloped instead over the long, waving, yellow grass towards a small range of knobbly hills. Gladia was puffing and panting and squealing as the horse bounced her up and down and the OutRider on the same horse swatted at her irritably as he tried to control the horse.

The heat of the sun came down in waves as we rode on. I glanced behind quickly, barely daring to move my head lest I fell off the horse and saw that at first sight there was no sign of the following group of OutRiders. I became accustomed to the rhythm of the horse, and its rise and fall became predictable as we rode on. The OutRider did not speak except occasionally to his horse, finding it unnecessary to speak with me. For my part, I had many questions; I was convinced it was the same man who had traded his bee for my honey, but I did not feel I could ask any contentious questions, and contented myself with staying on the horse, and taking in the ride. I watched the movement of the OutRider in front of me; how his legs grasped the horse, and how he moved his body, so it moved with the same rhythm as the horse. His armour was so cunningly jointed that it did not restrict him but moved smoothly, like the carapace of an insect. I started trying to make my own body rise and fall at the same time as him and found that it was indeed a deal more comfortable than the jolting crash which occurred if you landed on the horse's back at the wrong time. Watching Gladia brought a wry smile to my face, as she grasped her OutRider, whose patience was eroding as she huffed and grunted and swayed from side to side.

The OutRiders drew alongside each other, and I looked at Gladia, trying to look calm and confident. She looked back at me stoically, and I felt her strength where the previous day I had felt her weakness and vulnerability. Gladia's rider spoke. 'What do you think to a stop, brother? The horses need a rest, especially mine,' and he looked meaningfully behind him at Gladia. My rider looked back but there were no signs of the other group of OutRiders and I wondered again why they had not waited for their comrades.

'Let us get to the outcrop over there, where there is shade,' he replied, and, as I heard his voice again, I knew that I had not dreamed it, that he was indeed the same man who had traded me the little bee. But the little bee had so far only allowed me to feel the feelings of the Empath, and I had not had it resting on my skin since then, for I had put it in the underpocket of my robe. As I recalled what Erayo had said, I remembered her theory that a channel had been opened with our contact. She had asked me about the bee, or at least about a talisman made of a precious metal and that it might be the cause of this opening of channels. And now I thought that if I could put on the bee again, it might help me to at least understand the feelings of the OutRiders, if the channel were indeed open. I wriggled with frustration; not knowing what caused the detection of feelings I had felt, not knowing who the OutRider-Trader was, not knowing or understanding our situation. The OutRider turned to me.

'Stop moving about on the saddle. It makes the horse uncomfortable and he is bearing a heavy load. We will stop soon, and you can get down while we eat and rest.'

FLAMMEUS

His voice was surprisingly calm and kindly, and in contrast to the manner of those other OutRiders I had seen and heard. Should I tell Gladia that this OutRider was the one who had traded me the bee? She had not been happy about my acquiring the bee in the first place, so I thought that she might be both smug and victorious, and decided not to tell her. Besides, nobody had ever mentioned to me that the OutRiders might sometimes be clothed as ordinary people of the Outer, and I was not sure that this was common practice. Everyone associated them with their armour and their horses and their brutal ways, and I was trying to put the differing stories I had heard together with the evidence I had seen but still came up with no explanation for the turn of events.

Eventually, the OutRiders drew the horses in towards a large stone outcrop which stood proud of the flat grasslands around it. The sun beat down on us from a resolute blue sky, but there were some small shrubs around the base of the outcrop, and the stone cast a shadow of deep shade. The OutRiders swung themselves easily out of the saddle and brought the horses' bridles over their heads and led them towards the bushes in the shade with Gladia and I still mounted.

'Dismount then!' said the OutRider to Gladia peremptorily. She half lay across the horse as she struggled to get her leg over to the other side, her skirts rucked up. It made the sides of my mouth twitch, but I understood it was my turn next, and it was more difficult than the OutRiders made it look. They were both sitting on a rock watching us lazily, speaking in that quiet sign language that they had. I straightened myself up after I had landed on the ground and began to try to walk to the edge of the other rock, but my legs would not obey me, and began to quiver and shake. Gladia, meantime, had plodded on, without appearing affected by the long ride. My legs were so accustomed to sitting on the horse that for a while they would not obey me and remained rooted to the spot. Eventually, I managed to walk, very stiffly, towards the rock, but on lowering myself down on to it, got up again swiftly. Riding on the bony back of a horse with very little padding meant that it was painful to sit down on anything hard, and instead I lowered myself down further onto the grass, and gingerly stretched out my legs. Gladia looked at me and smiled mischievously, 'You see, there are, after all, advantages in being well padded!' and I laughed. We did not know where we were, nor where we might be going, or what lay ahead of us, but in that small, simple moment, I felt happy to be there, with my friend, having ridden a horse. Back in the Temple, I had not even ever imagined being near to a horse, let alone riding one, and here I was, surrounded by the air and the space and the sun of the Outer. Even if the OutRiders killed us, I thought, I had done something interesting with my life.

The OutRiders moved towards their horses, giving them water to drink and once more conversing in that strange unspoken language of theirs. I looked across to Gladia.

'What shall we do?' I hissed, 'Where are they taking us? What about Achillea and Benakiell and Ashtun?'

Gladia looked at me, a stoic expression on her face.

'We cannot do anything, Talla. When an animal is caught in a snare, the more it struggles to free itself, the more it tightens the trap. If you do not struggle against that which contains you, sometimes, you can find a way out. We do not want them to know that we want to escape them, so be polite, and give them no reason to suspect us. Benakiell will go back to Mellia with the rest, it was already decided.'

'Already decided? You knew this would happen?'

Gladia looked uncomfortable. 'Well,' she said finally, twisting her netela, 'It was always likely that they might find you, so we had talked about what might happen if they did.'

'But they haven't found me! They only think I am some ignorant woman who did not know which way to go, don't they? They do not know that I escaped from the Temple,' I dropped my voice down to a low whisper, 'nor that I am the one their Queen searches for. Otherwise they would have surely killed me by now. Wouldn't they?'

Gladia shook her head, baffled. 'They do not know who you are,' she confirmed, 'and yet they are treating us too well. The OutRiders do not treat people like people, more as numbers and sticks of wood to move around as they will, into whatever pattern they choose! Maybe they think we will tell them more if they treat us well. By now, we should be at least beaten, if not...' her voice wound down to nothingness as she contemplated what could be happening to us. Instead the two OutRiders continued to tend to their mounts, evidently unconcerned at their prisoners talking to one another. I got up and immediately the OutRider who had ridden with Gladia strode over to me, obviously not quite as unconcerned as we may have thought.

'Where do you think to go, sister?' he asked.

'I am uncomfortable with sitting in the saddle,' I admitted to him, 'I have never been on a horse before and my body aches in places I did not think I had. And,' I paused, and cast my eyes modestly to the ground, 'I need to relieve myself. All that bouncing about...'

'Aye,' he responded amiably enough. 'I can see you might feel that way. You can go behind that bush,' he gestured towards a shrub which grew close to the rock outcrop, 'but don't think to run, for there is nowhere for you to go.' I nodded and walked over to the shrub and squatted behind it. I quickly drew out the fine little bee pendant from my underpocket and placed it around my neck, making sure that it was well hidden from view. I felt the curious metal warm to the touch. I had no idea whether the bee would help me but because the OutRider had traded with me for it, I surmised that there must be something important about it. I returned to the rock where Gladia was waiting, and she took her turn. The OutRiders tossed us a gourd of water and some flatbreads and dried dates and we ate and drank thankfully.

After the hot time of the day had passed, the Out Riders once more climbed to the top of the outcrop and frowned into the horizon, scanning for evidence that they were being followed. Satisfied, they motioned for us to remount the horses. My skin underneath my robe was nearly rubbed bare and it hurt as I lowered myself down onto the saddle. The OutRider noticed my wince and commented mockingly, 'You are a novice in the saddle, sister.'

'And no wonder,' I answered. 'For there are no women riding horses in this land, and no men either, only OutRiders!'

'For every job, there is a person,' he chided me, 'and whilst I may master a horse, some women can master much smaller creatures – like bees for instance.'

His tone gave nothing away, although his remark felt pointed directly at me, and he himself must recognise me, even if he did not yet know that I recognised him too, and he turned back to the horse, once more slipping the leather strap around me, and taking the reins in his hands. We then had to wait patiently as Gladia hoisted herself into the saddle with much effort. I was quite sure that she was doing it as slowly as possible, but the OutRiders seemed to have a lot of patience. Again, this was not the impression I had previously encountered, especially those who came to Mellia and who shot down my hive. Their casual aggression had shocked me and made me fear them, and yet these two seemed little different from Benakiell and Ashtun.

We set off again eventually and had been riding for an hour or so when the OutRider pulled the horse to an abrupt stop, and I fell into him. I reached around him instinctively to steady myself and felt the warm channel I had felt at Erayo's open up again. I could not discern any ill feelings in what came to me; some impatience and tiredness but no anger or aggression. Indeed, what I felt most was a sense of security. He drew back almost instantly from my touch and addressed himself to conversing with his companion. There was a cloud of dust heading towards us and it would appear there were more OutRiders approaching. Tentatively I edged a little close to the OutRider, for the little bee of empathy seemed only to work with the human touch. I managed to edge my hand so that I could touch him through the armour, and immediately became aware of a change in his feelings. They rushed through to me; anxiety and anger, and yearning and something which felt like hatred, until I moved my finger away. What could it mean?

The two OutRiders spoke in that silent sign language for some time and then both dismounted and drew a short distance away.

'What is happening?' hissed Gladia. 'Are they going to kill us now? Why would they do that? Waste all this time and strength and then kill us here?'

'I don't know,' I confessed, 'But I feel that they will not kill us.'

Gladia looked at me sharply. 'You can feel them, can't you? Just like Erayo. You can feel them!' My lack of answer was answer in itself to her. She breathed out. 'What will they do with us?'

'I cannot read their minds,' I answered, frustrated that I could not. 'I only know that he,' and I pointed to my OutRider, 'is somehow trying to protect us from something. I do not know anything else! I wish I did!'

'So why have they stopped because of those OutRiders?' asked Gladia.

I clenched my teeth together. Did she ever listen to what I said? 'I cannot read their minds,' I started, speaking slowly to her in the hope that she may retain what I told her.

'I am not a halfwit,' she retorted primly, pursing her lips at me. 'In any case, your Empath feelings might not be working properly. Temple Maids are not Empaths, so it might be telling you the wrong thing.' She looked at me triumphantly, and I had no response. She might be right; although I was sure she was not. The other OutRiders were getting closer and we could see now that there were three of them, riding at pace towards us. Our escorts returned to us and remounted the horses grimly. Mine turned around and said to us both, 'Keep quiet with your heads bowed. Do not speak out or you will surely die.' He moved his hand away from the reins, even though the horse continued to move forward without skipping a step and put his hand to rest, superficially casually, on his sword. His companion, equally casually, moved his bow within easy reach.

The oncoming group slowed as they approached us. Their armour glinted in the sun like the shining silver scales of lizards or snakes. The leather was so highly polished and the silver discs which ornamented it so fluid that my eyes ached. I focused my attention on the armour of the OutRider right in front of me and compared his armour to that of the new OutRiders who had just arrived. His looked older and more worn close-up but no doubt was just as glorious from a distance as theirs – or at least had been at some time in its past.

CHAPTER 17

The group of three OutRiders drew in their horses and stood in front of us. The sun was shining directly on my face and it was no hardship to keep my head firmly bowed down behind my OutRider.

'Hail!' The oncoming group greeted ours peremptorily. The horse beneath me shifted uneasily and I inched my finger to close the gap between myself and the man in front of me, so that I could try to understand his feelings.

'Hail,' returned Gladia's rider, just as brusquely. There was a moment which might have seemed awkward on the Outer. Nobody spoke and the silence oozed between us. There were many such silences in the Temple, and I had learned to make use of them, to gather my thoughts in them and to make plans. I could not see, since my head was bowed, and I thought again, how complicated life was, with the need to constantly judge people by their faces and their slight inclinations of the head. The immoveable rules of Temple life had simplified my passage through life; that much was evident. Then, I felt my rider move in small bursts and I realised he must be using the silent language to communicate with the OutRiders in front of me. It became more and more urgent and my finger touching him could feel both his frustration and his fear. The three OutRiders came closer to us until I could feel them looming over me, like deep shade from a granite overhang. I kept my eyes to the ground, clenching them shut to avoid looking at them.

'What do you want with this old bird?' one jeered, looking at Gladia. 'She is no good for anything.' Gladia twitched, and shuffled, and I knew it would not be long before she could not hold her tongue anymore. He rode even closer to our horses until he was firmly between the two horses on which we rode, and withdrew his sword, idly.

'Although we could have some sport with her,' he mused, and flicked the point of his sword under Gladia's netela. It was the one which she had stitched from one of my design, and his sword poked a hole in it as he lifted it up. 'Why would our Queen, bless her name, want a dried-up old woman like this? But,' and the smirk in his voice broadened here, 'I am sure our Queen, bless her name, would want her faithful soldiers to enjoy some sport. This one,' he leaned over me and I smelt the sweat and leather and the sharp odour of his breath upon me, 'we can save for some real sport; she will be a good worker in all ways.' His companions laughed meaningfully and the two OutRiders who had been taking us along laughed too, although more awkwardly. I did not dare to look sideways towards Gladia but wondered if this was going to be our end. Perhaps all the effort in getting us here was merely so there would be no interruption in their activity, and, as Gladia suggested, my empathy was not a true reflection of the feelings of the man whom I had trusted.

'Let me look at you,' suggested the OutRider, and with one easy movement of the sword, he flicked Gladia's netela off her face and let it fall like water off a knife onto the saddle in front of me. I fixed my eyes upon the stitching, thinking of the patience with which Gladia had stitched the pattern. I recalled her delight in it, and her eagerness to stitch the new design, and naturally take it for herself. I remembered the pleasure in her eyes as Benakiell complimented her on it.

'Take her over that way, brother,' he advised my OutRider, gesturing at me. 'She can watch the sport. It will no doubt make her more biddable when she arrives at the Queen's Court.' The horse turned, obedient to the pressure of the OutRider's heel, and he led me a short distance from the group and pulled me roughly off the horse. He took the long leather rein off the horse and bound me tightly with it, so tightly I could scarcely breathe. I glared at him, and even though he still wore his masked helmet, I knew he could see the contempt in my eyes, and he turned away. Then he bent down to pull the knot tighter and whispered very quietly, 'Do not move for they will surely kill you. I will see your friend comes to no lasting harm. Trust me.'

I almost snorted with laughter, in the manner of Gladia, for what he said seemed so ridiculous, but as he touched me while he knotted the reins, I felt only concern from him, and again, a simmering rage. He sauntered over to the other OutRiders who were taking it in turns to flick at Gladia with their swords and laughing as she flinched a little more each time. One of them came up on the other side of her and pushed her hard so that she fell off the horse awkwardly. I could not bear to watch and yet I had no choice. The three late arrivals jostled around her with their horses as she lay panting and moaning in the soft red dust, her familiar face shining with sweat and anxiety. They began instructing their horses who joined in with their game, stepping over Gladia, hopping over her as she rolled from one side to the next. One of them even raised its hoof as if to bring it down upon her and then moved it at the last moment.

I cannot explain now how I could sit and do nothing, only that it was as if I was carved out of stone. Eventually, they tired of playing games with their horses and allowed Gladia to raise herself up to a sitting position. She looked straight at me, as if searching for help and guidance, and I was lost. For all my scribing and reading and watching and learning, there was nothing within me that had ever encountered this. Punishment in the Temple was written down and followed a strictly acknowledged path, with sanctions for almost every misdemeanour written down so that there could be no discussion, merely the following of the laws of the Goddess. I had never seen this lazy fascination with the pain of another.

And still we did not speak, her and I. There was no reason we could not have spoken our minds and yet we did not. It was as if we knew that it would just be another way in which they could torment us, and so we said nothing and remained, the two of us, stubbornly silent. The three OutRiders who had come later came up close to Gladia and murmured obscenities in her ear. I could not hear them but could only tell from the expression on her face that their words were upsetting and disgusting to her. They dragged her to her feet and pushed and shoved her as she stood, passive and yet still strong. I wriggled in my straps of leather, but the OutRider had bound me so fast in a sitting position that I feared I might fall over if I moved too much. I kept trying to catch Gladia's eye, willing the little bee of empathy to jump the gap between us and show her that I was feeling for her, and even allow me to take from her all the pain she was in. But the bee brought me no help and I continued to watch her, helpless. Eventually, one of them looked over at me and suggested that I be brought closer, so I could better observe what was happening. My OutRider (as I had begun to term him in my head, for I had no name for him, and indeed I did not know if OutRiders had names) came over to me and dragged me roughly to my feet.

'Stay silent,' he whispered to me, his breath tickling my cheek. 'Whatever happens to her, stay silent.' I stared at him and opened my mouth to speak, but he held his gloved hand over my mouth so that I could not.

The combined scent and taste of the leather made me retch and I closed my mouth obediently. In the distance, the heat made the dust above the grass wobble almost so that I thought I could see a group of figures walking closer, but when I blinked, they had gone.

'Hurry up,' ordered the one who seemed to be in charge. 'Don't think you are getting that one to yourself; we all want a share!' and they all sniggered. My OutRider walked back to them with little or no haste, dragging me behind him, like a goat on a string. They waited until I was quite close to them and then motioned the OutRider to make me sit again, against the rock outcrop. Once more the air wobbled in the distance. They took Gladia and bound her hands together with a restraining rein and then, to my horror, they tied her behind the horse and the leader of the three swung himself into the saddle with such ease that I admired it with part of my mind, even while I was horrified with the other.

'Help me,' begged Gladia in a voice which quavered and cracked, sounding very different from her usual brisk and cheerful tones. She looked at me pleadingly and my mouth wanted to speak but struggled to say anything. And when I did say something finally, it was not a scrap of use to her, but the words came out of my mouth before I could think about them.

'Think of the bees, Gladia, the bees can help. And the Goddess will guide you.'

My OutRider strode towards me and slapped me hard across the face. His eyes felt flinty even through the helmet. 'I told you to be silent,' he repeated. And, to my shame, I fell silent.

The OutRider began by walking the horse up and down as if he were in a parade of some sort. The horse walked very slowly and proudly, as if it were putting on a display and Gladia walked behind the horse, her bare feet shuffling in the dirt, her clothes dusty and torn. He then nudged the horse with the toe of his foot and the horse began to dance. It lifted its legs high with each step and performed an elaborate set of movements, increasing its pace as it did so until Gladia was jogging to keep upright with it, scurrying this way and that. The OutRiders guffawed at her, and again the rider upped the pace, so the horse was now trotting and Gladia had to run with it. I willed her on and prayed to the Goddess that these OutRiders would soon tire of this, and turn their attentions to me, for then at least I would not feel so helpless. Gladia tripped over herself eventually, as they must have known she would. Gladia was not a young woman, nor an agile one and she had no chance of righting herself as the horse continued, barely pausing to regain its trotting rhythm, dragging her behind it on through the dust and over the gritty shale that lay about us. Gladia began to whimper, like a small animal in pain and I could not bear it.

'Stop it!' I shouted. 'Stop that! Let her go! She does nothing wrong! Why are you doing this to her?' The OutRiders ignored me and mounted their horses so that they could run as a pack with Gladia still being dragged behind them. My eyes filled with tears again, the atmosphere seemed to wobble, and I really did see figures approaching. The OutRiders had not seen them, occupied as they were with demeaning my companion in every way they could. They dragged her back and forth in front of me so that I could see the grazes on her body oozing with blood and caked in dust. I did not know whether to look at Gladia or the OutRiders or the approaching figures. Surely there could not be more of these horrible people arriving, for nothing could improve this.

I cast my eyes down to the earth, determined that I should not see this spectacle which they were putting on; whether it was for me or for themselves, I could not tell, and again felt ashamed that I could turn away from it. Gladia's cries had descended into whimpering and gasping, and still they pulled her about, seemingly not bored of their play. I tried to concentrate on the tiny grains of stone and sand which glittered in the dust. These sharp and beautiful crystals were the cause of Gladia's stripped flesh, and I thought with longing of the smoothness and the rounded curves of the Goddess. It is a strange thing that we can call something by the same name as another thing and yet it can be so different in character. A rock can be hard and sharp and painful or smooth and curved and comforting. A person can be a Temple Maid or an OutRider or one of the Outer. Somehow the same and somehow different. As I looked down at the dust, I saw, crawling along in the dust, in a determined fashion, a bee.

I had not seen a bee since I had been in Mellia. The bees which I tended had been my soothing balm, my honey, if you like. Tending the hives and the flowers on which they fed had been the thing which had anchored me and calmed the rage which sometimes built up in me, and I missed them, even while we had only been gone for some days. I could not stretch out my hand to it, as I did in the garden, for I was bound so tightly with the leather strapping, but I inclined my head slightly until I caused my shade to fall upon it. It moved to the sun. I inclined my head again to make the shade come upon it, and this time it flew up to me, and rested on my shoulder. I twisted my head around, to try to look at it more closely, and saw the figures approaching were now quite close, and still had not been spotted by the OutRiders, who were now in some sort of circle around Gladia with their backs facing out, the shields, made of some kind of dark hide with the emblem of the Queen etched upon them. It was my emblem; the brooch of my birth, and yet it was on these accoutrements of war.

It was then that I heard the sweet singing rising above the silence. It was a song of sweetness and beauty, an innocent, lilting song, such as a young woman might sing as she travelled a path. There was only one I had heard whose voice was like this, bubbling and rich and yet light-hearted and wistful, and that was Achillea, but Achillea was away in Mellia, far from this terrible day. The OutRiders stopped their activity and wheeled around, aggressive and ready to fight, their hands to their bows and swords. They moved their horses in front of Gladia's body, which lay, by now unconscious, behind them. The singing stopped abruptly, and I raised my eyes from the dirt. It was Achillea. It was Achillea and Ashtun and Benakiell. I felt joy and pain in equal measure. For my companions, my friends, had come to find us. They had missed us and come to find us. The OutRiders had come to find me to take me back to the Temple, but my friends came to take us home. And in that sweet realisation there came also the knowledge that by doing this they had unwittingly placed themselves in danger and the likelihood of more sport for the OutRiders.

'Go!' I called to Achillea, my voice gruff and harsh. 'Sister, go on your way. There is nothing here for you.' I hoped that she might understand what I was trying to tell her, and would walk on quickly with the others, and save themselves from what lay ahead.

'Shut your mouth!' came the command from the OutRider, he who had trailed Gladia behind him with such carelessness. Achillea's big eyes widened as she saw me and realised who it was. She rushed over to me, and as she came over, Ashtun and Benakiell followed her, their hands at their belts. Achillea had no thought for the danger she was in and rushed to me. She still had not seen Gladia's prone body.

'Leave her!' ordered the OutRider. 'Or you will be the next!'

Achillea spun to face him, her normally placid eyes flashing with rage. 'She has done nothing to you! Nothing! She has been trading and she has lost her way, and you have taken her! Leave her!' And she turned to me, worrying at the leather knots with shaking hands, her back turned to the OutRider with such contempt that I feared for what might come next. He strode towards her impatiently, his hand grasped about his sword, but somehow insouciant, clearly used to getting his own way and not really having to fight for it. His horse stood patiently in its place, in front of Gladia. The OutRider raised his hand to Achillea, in the same way that my OutRider had raised his hand to me, and I caught the glimpse of a ring on his hand before he flashed it across Achillea's face, and the noise cracked in the stillness. A drop of blood landed on my hand. Achillea turned from me, towards Benakiell and Ashtun, and, at the same time, the OutRider reached for his sword. Ashtun ran forward to Achillea, shocked by the blood on her face, and furious. He pushed forward to get to Achillea, barely glancing at me, as I sat, still mute and wriggling against my straps which had been slightly loosened by Achillea's brief efforts.

The OutRider drew his sword and the other OutRiders moved towards us on their horses, leaving the one horse which still had Gladia tied to it behind, standing, waiting patiently for its orders. At this point, Benakiell rushed forward too, catching sight of Gladia on the ground and groaning in the pain of what he saw. The three later OutRiders drew their swords, for it was too close to use their bows. Ashtun had a sturdy stick with a sharpened point on the end, and Benakiell had a stick with a knob at the end. They launched themselves in fury at the OutRiders who laughed patronisingly at them and waved their curved, honed blades in front of them. It did not seem to occur to the OutRiders that they could fail, for after all there were five of them and only two men here, one of whom was past his prime. There were three women; one lay unconscious on the floor, occasionally thrashing her head from side to side, one had a face that was covered in blood and the other, myself, was strapped to a point of uselessness. The two OutRiders who had originally taken Gladia and I wheeled away from the back of the group and urged their horses to move further away, drawing their bows as they did so. I guessed they were giving themselves distance in order to get a good shot with the bow. Achillea bent to the knots again.

'Talla, speak to me,' she urged. 'What have they done to you? Why did they take you? Where is Gladia?' She tugged on the straps; her hands bloody from the cut on her face caused by the OutRider's ring.

'Over there,' I whispered. Benakiell and Ashtun were doggedly trying to fight the OutRiders but were at a disadvantage. The OutRiders were on horses and had a height advantage, and they had their swords which they slashed in the air, keeping the space between them and my friends.

'You will pay dear for this old man,' one of them warned Benakiell, who was trying to beat his stick against the horse's flank. The OutRider glimpsed the other two OutRiders who were wheeling off to a further point and called out to them.

'Good thinking, brothers, one man each! We can make great sport of this! A prize for the one with the cleanest shot – we shall have two fine young things to play with afterwards, and the winner can pick first! We'll drop back to give you the shot!' The two mounted

FLAMMEUS

OutRiders directed their horses backwards with the same high stepping movement they had used before when they had started with Gladia, and the third backed off with them, on foot, his sword held out in front of him. Benakiell and Ashtun stopped where they were, uncertain by the turn of events, and not quite understanding what was about to happen. Achillea continued to wrestle with the knots, pulling and dragging at them as she loosened them. I watched as the bee flew around her hands, for all the world as if it were trying to help her.

'Be still!' called my OutRider and there was a zithering in the air as the arrows left their marksmen. Two left at almost the same time; their dull thwacks echoing one another as they hit their targets, and then came a third, just as the OutRider on foot turned towards the two bowmen. The arrow hit him in the neck, and he fell, crumpled to the floor. I saw that not only had he been felled, but that the other two arrows, which we had assumed were meant for Ashtun and Benakiell, had taken as their mark, instead, the other two OutRiders. Both had been skilfully shot in the neck.

The air screamed with the silence. I could only hear the murmuring of the bee, and the thudding of my own heart for what seemed like hours but must have been only the blink of an eye. Achillea continued to fight with the knots frantically, unable to grasp what had happened and why. Ashtun and Benakiell gaped at each other in disbelief and then Benakiell ran to Gladia's side, and Ashtun turned to Achillea whose face was streaked with dark red blood and tracks of sweat. He gently pulled her from me, and she leant into his comfort and wept, soundlessly, her body heaving with the effort of being so quiet and having so much to express. And so it was that those who loved one another were comforted by the presence of their dear ones, and that I, who had never yet been loved by another person, nor, until recent times, even been aware of the existence of love, felt alone and empty.

I was still weak and powerless, my leather bonds still taut against me. I closed my eyes, feeling light-headed and exhausted and somehow apart from all others. I could hear the pairs murmuring to one another, Gladia now apparently conscious. I felt a sawing at my bonds, after some minutes, and opened my eyes, expecting to see Achillea back again. Instead I met the liquid brown eyes of my OutRider, who had inserted the point of his sword under the leather straps and was sawing through them. When he realised that my eyes had opened, he stopped the sawing and gently touched my cheek. As soon as his skin met my skin, I felt the channel of feeling between us flow again, and I felt concern, and anger and exhaustion, flecked with relief and anxiety. But by now I did not trust the little bee of empathy. My mind was too enwrought by the things I had seen him do, taking part in the torture of Gladia, tying me up, capturing us in the first place. He drew his fingers away slowly as if he too felt the channel of empathy between us and had become aware of my distrust and my fear. He continued to saw at the leather vigorously without speaking. As the bonds finally shifted and I was able to move, I saw that my friends were together, watching me and the OutRider. Bewildered, I felt their distrust too. Even though my bonds were now loose, and the severed straps had fallen to the ground, I did not feel that I could take the first steps towards them, for if they rejected me I would have nowhere to turn. Not for the first time, I questioned whether I should have stayed in the Temple, away from these complicated feelings of love and hate, anger and peace. There was, in that uniform dullness, a certain attraction, especially now that most of my feelings were so uncomfortable for me.

FLAMMEUS

The OutRider gestured to his companion, and his companion moved over to the group of friends and gave them some instruction. They sat down where they were; Gladia was by now propped upright against Benakiell's shoulder, and my OutRider took my hand and led me patiently, as one might do to a child of the First Age to sit with them. I sat without speaking, hurt by their inability to see that I was not any different to the person that they had known before. Ashtun glared at me, Achillea looked to the ground, Benakiell avoided my look and looked vacantly into the distance. I knew that I had to do something, and so I got up and went to Gladia's side. She looked at me wearily, but there was no resentment in her eyes, only pain and exhaustion.

Gladia's face was already swelling where it had been grazed against the shale and grit of the earth and was powdered with fine red dust which had mixed itself with blood and tears. Her eyes were both darkened by bruising already, and she squinted in the sun. Her lips were cracked and bleeding, and her clothes were torn to shreds. One arm hung loosely to the side, useless, and I saw that it had been dislocated. Instinctively I reached out for her hand and held it, willing the channels of empathy to awake between us. I closed my eyes before I could see what the others' reaction was and concentrated on willing the little bee to work. Having only a few minutes earlier distrusted it regarding the OutRider, now I found myself hoping and trusting in its powers toward my friend. Gladia sighed a deep shuddering sigh and gave her hand up to me. I felt her fear rush into me, my mind was full of whirling, disjointed feelings of pain and terror, and other mixed feelings, brief snatches of hope and even a sort of peaceful contentment. The feelings were fuzzy and blurred, as if seen from far away, in the same way that the colours were blurred when you viewed them across the long grass in the heat of the midday sun. I took away my hand as the feelings ebbed between us and realised that she was looking at me. There was no suspicion in her eyes, and I understood that there would not be, for she had been with me all the time and knew that what had happened was not my doing, whereas the others had doubts, especially because of the strange behaviour of the OutRiders.

'Forgive me, Gladia,' I whispered to her and she nodded her head and patted my hand without speaking. As I lifted my head to finally look at my friends, I was met by the even stare of the OutRider with the honeyed eyes. His companion looked at me too, but his was more of a questioning look, and only hovered on me briefly before returning his full attention to the OutRider standing before us, who began to speak, finally without his ornamented helmet. Ashtun gripped his stick and I could imagine him calculating how easily he could leap towards the OutRider and beat him now that his guard was down.

'Be still, friend,' said the OutRider, sensing the tension. 'I take off my helmet as a sign of trust. I also lay down my sword.' He bent down and loosened the leather strap which held the sword to him and dropped it to the floor. Ashtun subsided.

'What is it that you do?' asked Benakiell, and I was surprised by the harshness in his voice. 'For you have nearly killed this woman here who has done you no harm, and you have betrayed your fellow soldiers and shot them in the back. What manner of man are you?'

ID
FLARE

CHAPTER 18

'Let us begin by explaining ourselves,' said the OutRider. 'Then, when we have settled down, we can move to a better place, out of this hot sun, and where our sister,' and he indicated Gladia with his hand, 'can be tended to.'

'She is no sister of yours,' growled Benakiell. 'You did not rush to defend her, and you obviously abducted them both. Now you no doubt wish to try some new devious trick on us to achieve your aims.'

'Listen to him first, father,' said the other OutRider, the one who had carried Gladia. 'And at the end, you can judge us both.'

Benakiell subsided, and Gladia shifted uncomfortably. The OutRider who had first addressed us looked at her with some concern. I did not understand how one who had taken part in the painful treatment of someone as harmless as Gladia could then be concerned about her. These feelings of the Outer confused me at every turn, and I turned to look at Ashtun and Achillea, who sat next to each other, evidently taking strength from their relationship, both exhausted but happy to spend time together, even if it were here, in the middle of waving grasslands punctuated only by rocky outcrops and small, gnarled stands of trees.

'My name is Ambar,' began the OutRider, 'and this is my comrade, Tarik. We cannot tell you any family names, as we have no family, for we were OutRiders of the Queen.'

I noted his use of the past tense and wondered if he would explain further.

'How do we know,' asked Achillea quietly, 'that you are not simply lying to us. For this could all be a plot to make us believe in you and then for you to do something even more wicked to us. How can we trust you?'

Tarik turned to Ambar and they spoke again in that flashing sign language. I was suspicious of this wordless language and resolved to watch them carefully to try to decipher it. It had taken me many months to understand how to scribe and to read the scribing and this language would take just as long, especially if they did not want us to know what they were saying to one another. Maybe it was a completely different language from some other far-off land which I would not be able to understand. But it was intriguing, and I could see how useful it might be. Perhaps the Priestesses had some similarly silent and incomprehensible language of their own.

Ambar began again, leaning forward towards us, his brown eyes fixed upon us all steadily, without shifting his gaze. 'You do not know much of the OutRiders, except what you have seen and experienced of them. And what you see of them is a fair picture, I warrant. But which of you here has ever sat to talk to an OutRider, nor yet made acquaintance with one? You may not know about our lives any more than you may know about the lives of a Temple Maid.' He looked pointedly at me at this juncture. 'But there are amongst us those who would uphold the old values of duty and honour, and loyalty to our Queen and those who would bring about shame and suffering. In the same way, in the Temple, there are those who worship the Goddess, and those who use the Temple as a front for more wickedness than you can imagine.'

FLAMMEUS

Benakiell leaned forward, obviously intrigued despite himself, at the prospect of learning more about the Temple and the soldiers of the Queen. 'Go on,' he said slowly.

But then Tarik spoke, his quiet voice commanding our attention. 'It is more important to tend to our sister,' he said. 'For she is in pain and she needs rest and comfort.'

'You made her like that!' burst out Achillea. 'You made her like that, and now you wish to heal her? I would not trust either of you near her!'

Tarik looked uncomfortable. 'We could not refuse to join the sport,' he answered. He waved his hand in the direction of the three sprawled corpses, 'Those others would have killed us straight away and then taken their way with our sisters. We would not have let them give her more pain than she could take.'

Gladia spoke. Her voice was worn and cracked, broken in its way, just as her skin had been. 'Let them guide us,' she said. Gladia's normally feisty spirit was quelled and calm. 'My wounds hurt me, and I need to rest. That one, called Tarik, he carried me on his horse and did not harm me before, when he had the chance to, and so I trust him a little. Let him carry me again, if he wishes to help.'

Immediately, Tarik sprang forward, and Ambar went to his aid. Together they assisted Benakiell in half carrying, half propping Gladia up until they got back to Tarik's mount, and after no small amount of heaving and pushing, managed to get Gladia sitting on the saddle.

'What of your brothers?' asked Ashtun, pointing at the dead OutRiders. I had not seen a dead person before, for the Maids never saw or dealt with the dead in the Temple, only the Priestesses. I did not even know what they did with the dead, for we were told that they had gone to be with the Goddess. The OutRiders looked unreal. In one sense it looked as if they were merely sleeping in the sun, and yet, in another sense it was as if they were the chaff or husks left after winnowing; empty of being.

Ambar looked at them dispassionately, and then with increased interest. 'We will take their armour, and their horses,' he concluded, 'and leave the rest by the rocks. You will need to help me.'

Ashtun came forward, rather mutinously at first, for he did not like being told what to do. He began to help to remove the fine leather and metal armour from one of the bodies. Benakiell remained at Gladia's side, as did Tarik, supporting her. Achillea moved towards one of the other corpses and began to gingerly remove the armour, shuddering at every movement.

'Go to the horses, Achillea,' I said, and they all turned to look at me. I had been mute for so long, they may have thought my tongue had gone. 'Speak to them or sing to them to soothe them. I will help here.'

I bent over one of the dead men and began to remove the armour. I concentrated on unbuckling the chestplate and sheath from his corpse. He was heavy to move, and it took some time. Ambar and Ashtun worked more quickly on the other two. I reached to remove the helmet and as I did, the OutRider's face rolled towards me, his eyes open and dull. I could see the fine growth of stubble on his chin, and his long eyelashes now fringing emptiness. And yet I could not feel for him in the way I felt for my companions. I did not know him, nor did I admire him. He had been a cruel man and had died a swift and mercifully short death. I knew that for Achillea, her sensitivity to life meant that she could envisage the face of her dear Ashtun beneath the helmet and be moved by that, but I could not. I admired the craftsmanship in the helmet; the burnished leather and the dancing discs of metal, before handing it over to Ambar, who was buckling it all together with one of the long leather straps that had been used to bind me. He and Ashtun dragged the bodies to the rocky outcrop before returning.

Achillea was standing near to the horses singing to them softly. I noticed that she did not stand too closely to them and realised that she had never been on a horse, like me, and that the nearest she had been to one had been that awful day in the garden when the OutRiders had upset the bees. I walked over to her and went to the horses. They whickered softly as I got nearer, and I reached out my hand to stroke the neck of the nearest one. It looked at me a little blankly, incurious about this new person. I wondered if it felt the loss of its master, or if it was merely trained to respond to fixed commands.

'You will have to ride that one; he has chosen you,' commented Ambar. 'You rode well enough behind me, you will manage. I will buckle his rein to mine so that he will not bolt with you.' I looked up at him, and his eyes crinkled at the corners as he smiled wryly at my face. I suppose I must have looked shocked, or perhaps excited. Either way, I felt as if it were not quite the right feeling, and silently I cursed my lack of understanding. He turned to Ashtun and, having ascertained that he had never ridden a horse before, told him that he would still have to ride the second horse with Achillea. Ashtun looked excited at this opportunity, and I wondered if he were planning to gallop off with Achillea away from us all. Ambar must have wondered the same thing, because he showed him how the horse would be buckled to the other side of his own horse. I wondered how the horses would move smoothly together. He led the third horse over to Benakiell. It was a dappled grey horse, its tail held high and proud, its mottled patches of white like patches of lichen on a grey stone. 'Do not worry, father,' he said kindly to Benakiell. 'The horse will do as it is told.'

'I am not worried,' retorted Benakiell, to my surprise. 'I have ridden a donkey before, on my travels in other lands as a merchant. Never an OutRider beast though.' He almost spat as he said this, and I tried to catch his eye, but he kept his face averted from me. Tarik linked Benakiell's mount to the horse on which he sat with Gladia and urged his horse to move forward. The horses moved as if with one mind and I had little to do save make sure that I was sitting comfortably and moving with the rhythm of the horse. I felt the aches and pains of earlier and hoped it would not be a long ride.

CHAPTER 19

We rode through the dusk as the changing light of the evening brought shadows and a welcome coolness. We stopped once, to drink water from the water gourds, but we did not dismount, and it seemed that Ambar and Tarik were eager to get to a place of safety. I wondered where we might be heading, and if they could be trusted. Trust was not something I had had to understand in my Temple days. In the Temple, there was no choice regarding trust; we lived a life of facts. If a Priestess told you to do a task, then you did it, without asking why you should have to do it or what the asker might be getting out of it. Looking back, even now, not so very long after entering the world of the Outer, I questioned why we had all been so willing to never question, and to do the bidding of the Priestesses so obediently. It occurred to me that trust came from the ability to question, from the sense that you could never be sure how people's feelings and emotions would drive them, and whether their words and actions were a true reflection of themselves. And having answered that question, we chose, or did not choose, to trust them. It was a complicated dance, and reminded me of the ways in which the bees seemed to dance with one another when they met, first this way and then the next; should I trust him, should I not? In the Temple, I would merely have been told whether to go with him or not, and I would have done it. We were often told that we should place ourselves into the hand of the Goddess and that she would guide us. I wondered briefly what the Goddess gained from this, and then felt ashamed that I had questioned the great Mother of us all.

My companions were silent on the journey; there were some small murmurings between Ashtun and Achillea, and the odd moan from Gladia as the horse bumped her bruises and grazes, but aside from that, nobody spoke. I wanted to speak to Benakiell, but I could not think of what to say. I could not bear that he might ignore me and turn his head away again, as he had already done, so I said nothing and lapsed into a mindless observation of the changing colours as the night drew near. There were high dark clouds in the sky and the deep blue of the earlier hot sky melted into a purple colour, the colour of Lilavis. I had lost count of the days since I had left Mellia, and I no longer knew which day it was. In the Temple we had observed each day scrupulously, celebrating each colour with its scented oils until the whole Temple was redolent with it. The hangings for the Goddess were changed each day by the Maids. It meant that we were familiar with the scent of our day, and its colour. The hangings were very thinly woven and richly embroidered by those who were gifted seamstresses in the Temple, like Lunaria. We Maids always felt it was a special day for us, when it was our day, for we could oil the feet of the Goddess and watch as the stone with which she was made took on the hue of the day. Looking up at the sky, there were tinges there too of Flammeus, Aureus and Azureus – in fact most of the colours of the Goddess – were painted on the sky by the changing brush of time.

Shortly afterwards, Ambar called the horses to a walk and led us to a small grove of thorn trees. Next to it was a shelter made of thorn bushes and clay, cunningly disguised so that, unless you knew it was there, you would ride right past it. He and Tarik dismounted their horses, leaving us still buckled to them, and stood a little distance away, using the sign language, and then returned to us. Ambar came over to my horse and helped me to dismount. It had not been easy to ride the horse, wearing the robe, and I was grateful to unbend myself and to stand on the land again. Next, he helped Achillea down, who stood rubbing her thighs ruefully and exchanged a weary glance with me. I noticed that they left Ashtun and Benakiell mounted until the end and guessed that this was to keep them in a position of weakness.

'Come and help your sister,' said Tarik, gesturing to Gladia, who was dazed and in pain from the ride. Tarik had bundled cloth around her to cushion her wounds, but it was clear that her pain was deep. Achillea and I went over to the horse to try to help her down, but her size and the way in which she was sitting made it awkward, and Tarik called to Ambar to come over. Tarik bent over to make a step and Ambar stepped on him to more easily get to Gladia. He lifted her arms around his neck and lifted her from the horse down to the land. I was amazed at their strength, for they were no bigger than many men, and yet they hardly noticed the considerable weight of Gladia. Once they had got her down off the horse, they wrapped her arms around their shoulders, and half supporting, half dragging her, took her into the shelter, and called Achillea and I to tend to her while they went to fetch the others.

The shelter was cool and dry inside and there were gourds of herbs and spices hanging on the walls, along with deep clay pots of water and dry goods like flour and figs. It seemed well equipped and must have been regularly maintained and used. There was a grass mat on the floor, and we helped Gladia to lie down on it. Ambar came in with Ashtun and Benakiell and the shelter felt very full suddenly. Tarik came in too, having tied up the horses and let them drink and feed well. Benakiell ran his hand approvingly over the smooth interior of the shelter and said, rather gruffly, 'Fine workmanship here. Just the right amount of Paradox oil.'

'Aye,' answered Tarik. 'I have learned to make these places from watching those with skill. You have the skill yourself, do you not? And you, brother?' He turned to Ashtun who conceded that he and Benakiell were indeed dwelling makers. There was a silence, and then Tarik said, 'We need to tend to our sister here,' and he knelt at Gladia's head, and began to examine her wounds. Benakiell started up, indignantly, but Ambar calmed him.

'He has the skill of a Physic,' he said quietly. 'He will not harm her but make her better.'

'He has already harmed her!' burst out Achillea, indignantly. 'How can a person harm another and then heal her?' Benakiell's face darkened again, but Ambar lay a restraining hand on him. It was a firm restraining hand, and there was no argument.

'Come here, sister Achillea,' called Tarik, from Gladia's side. 'If you wish to help your sister here, I have things that you can do.' Achillea immediately got up and went over to Gladia and Tarik. I felt the emberjar of my mind begin to flicker. They were behaving as if I were not there, as if I had nothing to offer. Nobody had spoken to me or asked me to help.

'I want to help too,' I said. I spoke quietly, but my words seemed to echo through the shelter, as the rest of the group looked at me.

'You didn't want to help when Gladia was being hurt!' retorted Ashtun, scowling at me. 'You are younger than her, and you owed her your loyalty. She has done so much for you, and you,' he looked at me contemptuously, 'you have done nothing for her. What help have you offered her?'

My heart hurt with his words, more truly than the stinging of the cuts where the tightly bound straps had cut into me. I thought of the designs I had done for Gladia to embroider and with which she had made such good trades. I thought of the honey I had coaxed from Cassia's bees and the garden neglected by Achillea, and which I had willingly given to Gladia, who had a taste for sweet things. I thought of the times I had carried baskets for her, and the times when she had spoken to me sharply for no good reason, and I thought of how much pain it had cost me to take on her feelings and her worries when I wore the little bee of empathy. But I could not say any of this. I saw it and I felt it but there was none here who felt my feelings as an Empath could.

Benakiell remained silent, and Achillea continued to bathe Gladia's wounds with the herbwater that Tarik had given her. She too was shutting me out. I wondered if it would have been better to have been taken by the OutRiders on the first day I left the Temple, and to have never lived these days. I got up and silently withdrew from the shelter, first wrapping my netela around my head and neck against the cool wind and the even colder looks. I walked from the shelter and went to the horses, who stood quietly by the thorn bushes, their tails swishing against the flying creatures of the night. I stood next to the horse on which I had ridden and leaned into its warmth, stroking it, running my fingers along the length of the hair, over and over. The rage in my mind subsided, for I did not know who I was angry with, except perhaps myself, and the fire of rage, fanned by others, extinguished itself with my tears. Tears were not common in the Temple, except of course with those in the first two ages of childhood, and even then, after the first age, children became less emotional. Besides, we had no need of tears. The Goddess looked after us, and we worked willingly for the Temple. Sometimes, if there was an accident and someone was hurt, tears were shed until the pain was relieved with coffee or honey. I rested my face against the horse and breathed in its warm life, letting the tears melt into its hair. It stood there, amiable enough, letting me comfort myself with it.

'He does not need bathing, sister,' said an amused voice behind me, and I turned to see Ambar looking at me curiously. These OutRiders moved and spoke with each other so silently, I could see how they were effective in their job. I turned my head away from him and said nothing. He came towards me and began to stroke the horse on the other side, and then reached down to the saddles which were piled on the ground and took out a brush made of wood and leather.

'If you are intent on grooming the horse, then you must do the work properly,' he added, talking to me as if I had not just turned my head away. He picked up my hand in his and slid it through the leather strap on the brush, and holding my hand with his, he moved the brush in overlapping arcs on the horse's back. His hand was warm and dry, and he brought with him the sharp, crisp smell of herbs and the scent of wood smoke. I felt the warmth of the little bee between us, and I took from him exhaustion and anxiety, determination and anger, much like my own. He did not seem aware of the passage of feeling between us, but he relaxed into the grooming of the horse with me, in silence.

'You cannot blame your companions for their anger,' he said finally. 'They expect you to behave as one of them would, and you are not one of them. In any case, there was nothing you could do. It is I and Tarik they should be angry with, but they do not dare to show their anger in case we injure them too. You were not much hurt, and Gladia was, and so they blame you for not being hurt. They know her better than you and would rather you be hurt than she. It is simple to understand.'

'Simple for you,' I muttered ungraciously, still brushing the horse, but on my own now, Ambar having lifted his hand off mine as he spoke.

'It was not always so,' answered Ambar. 'Two years ago, I was like you, a stranger in a land I did not understand. I have listened and observed and travelled.'

'You are an OutRider,' I said, 'You fight for the Queen and against ordinary people who do you no wrong. I have heard their stories too.'

Ambar grasped my shoulders and turned me around, away from the horse, facing him so that I should see him. There were streaks of grimy sweat trailing down his face; his honey coloured eyes looked at me and flashed a warning fire at me and my words. 'You will find out who I am, and for whom I fight, sister Talla,' he said. 'And you will know my worth through what I do, whether it is hurting your friend Gladia, or saving her life, and you will judge for yourself which one was more important.' I looked up at him, and with the edge of his thumb he wiped my face where the tracks of my tears had run. It was so gentle and so lightly done that I did not feel the little bee's warmth again, but I felt my own warmth, a warmth within me as I responded to his kindness.

'Come, sister,' he said, 'for you have work to do for your friend. I came to find you, for only you can help me with the physic that brother Tarik needs. Do you have any honey still with you?'

I reached towards the gourds hanging from the tree branches, found the last gourd of honey which remained to me of my precious harvest, and followed Ambar back inside. Gladia was still moaning through the pain as Achillea did her best to wash out the grit from her grazes, and Ambar spoke to her as he knelt beside Tarik, who was tending to her wounds.

'It will sting, that is true, but no more than a bee stings and then it will ease. Meanwhile, your sister Talla will help you with her honey.' He beckoned me over to Gladia's side, and she scrabbled for my hand, as I tried to follow Tarik's instructions to mix the honey with a bitter bark water. I spooned the mixture into her mouth and she drank it greedily, for the honey was sweet and the taste of it soothed her. I put down the cup after she had finished, and I reached for her hand, which I had avoided until now. I did not want to know her feelings towards me, but I could not take off the little bee without drawing attention to myself, and so I reached for her hand and braced myself.

There was no angry feeling, nor even disappointment that came flooding through our touch. In fact, there was very little; some warmth, tiredness, pain and a sort of acceptance. In truth, I did not know what some of the feelings were. In the Temple we did not talk about our feelings, mainly because we did not seem to have them. So, I look back in hindsight when I talk about these feelings. I did not always recognise what they meant, and perhaps even now, I am interpreting them as I think they were, for who can tell us later what our feelings may have been? In the moments after we encounter them, the feeling is pure, acute, like water or the sound of a bell. As time passes on, we tell ourselves stories and try to touch the feelings again, but life is never the same, and these days I firmly believe that every feeling is new and unique. I held Gladia's hand as she drifted off to sleep, even while Achillea was still washing her wounds. Tarik came to look at them and asked me to bind them with some strips of woven bark cloth, wondrously soft. I had never seen such things before, and I examined them carefully before doing as I was instructed and coating the wounds with honey before putting the dressings on.

'The honey will prevent the wound from rotting,' said Tarik. 'There will be no scars. The herbwater I gave her to drink will make her sleep for some while, strongly, and will let her mind rest.'

'How can you tend one whom you hurt?' asked Achillea, again, unable to understand this. I was not aware enough of how simple things could appear in the world of the Outer. It seemed to them to be unthinkable to hurt someone and then care for them, and yet, to my mind, they were hurting me now and yet had cared for me. Perhaps it seemed more reasonable to care for someone and then not care for them, than to hurt someone and then care for them.

Ambar did not respond to her plaintive question but spoke instead to Tarik with his hands, moving them so quickly I did not have the chance to even try to see what some of the movement were.

'We will eat,' announced Tarik and went to the large pots and gourds in the shelter to find food. He took out a flat plate and some flour and made a flatbread, quickly and efficiently. He added oil, and onions and herbs to the centre of it and set it to cook. Gladia was now snoring peacefully, her flesh wobbling with every outbreath, and she had lost her grasp on my hand. I stood up to move to the fire where the flatbread was cooking and started to feel dizzy. I reached out to Achillea to steady myself and collapsed at her feet. I heard voices as if through a fog, swirling around in my mind, but was unable to reply to them. I was aware of Ambar feeding me sips of the same honey and bitterbark mixture he had given to Gladia, and then I slept.

I did not know what Ambar and Tarik had said to the others whilst I slept, but they must have explained my inability to fight on behalf of Gladia. It may be that Ambar explained that he had tied me up, or that there was no choice. In any case, when I awoke, it was to friendlier faces and to the smell of coffee steeping in a pot. When I sat up, Achillea came to me and asked me how I was feeling, explaining what had happened. Gladia still lay sleeping and the men had apparently gone to feed the horses or to find them fodder. She brought me coffee and dates, and we sat together. I asked her how they had come to find us, and she explained that the route that the OutRiders had taken us on was an old path from Sanguinea to Mellia and that they had set out when Gladia and I had not returned. It had been nothing more than chance, she said, that they had come across us. I told Achillea that we had been forced to spend the night waiting for our turn to see the Empath Erayo, and that had been the main reason for our lateness. I told of how Gladia and I had been captured by Ambar and Tarik, and how they had been taking us to an unknown destination when the other OutRiders joined them.

'Ashtun says they are not to be trusted,' said Achillea. 'How can we trust OutRiders? They are not like us, and they do not have the same ways as us.' I held my tongue, understanding that I too, even after all this time, was not one of them either, and that I was perhaps not trusted either. Achillea searched in her pack and found a comb.

'Come Talla,' she said, awkwardly, 'we are friends, are we not? Let me do your hair.' I saw that she was trying to make peace, and that this offering was to show me that there should be no more unease between us. Normally, I had no patience with my hair being done but Achillea loved to sit and make hairstyles and sing, so I submitted myself to her ministrations and allowed her to braid my hair. I was beginning to understand the virtue of this small ritual, and to understand that there were things in life that could not be forced into words.

FLAMMEUS

Perhaps, even, words complicated life. If Achillea had tried to explain the myriad emotions that had run through her heart and mind since she had seen Gladia being pulled behind the horses, the words would not have made me understand any better. I understood that she wished for us to be friends again. Friendship was not a simple black and white choice of life in the Outer but rimmed with uncertainty and muddied by doubt and memory. Achillea's hands ran through my tangled hair; the comb scraped my scalp and the small repeated movement of her hands in my hair warmed me. I felt I needed to offer her something in return for this comfort, but did not know what to offer, other than not complaining at her for taking so long with my hair. In the Temple, hair was not something to be glorified, but rather something which was hidden away when you reached the first age of Adulthood. We all had our hair cut in the same way as children, and who knew what the Priestesses' hair looked like since it was always hidden beneath their veils.

Achillea had just finished my hair when the others returned, with kindling for the fire. There seemed to be a truce between the two pairs of men, and they had worked to get the materials we needed. Ambar smiled at the sight of us by the fire together. It was the first time I had seen him smile properly since he had persuaded me to trade the honey for the little bee pendant in Sanguinea.

'Women have to do their hair even in the most desperate circumstances,' said Benakiell gruffly. 'You look better, Talla.' I wondered if that meant I looked bad before but dipped my head in acknowledgement.

'Do you like it, Ashtun, do you think Talla looks lovely?' asked Achillea, standing up to join him, linking her arm into his, tilting her face with her big eyes up to his. He looked down to her, and, in a gesture which reminded me of Ambar the night before, he ran his thumb gently along the line of her chin.

'There is no better hair braider than you, Achillea,' he affirmed, smiling, stopping short of making any remark on me, and bent down to put some kindling on the fire and replaced the coffee pot on the fire. It would be well steeped but maybe it was just something to do.

'Talla is a lovely woman.' The voice was weak and a little cracked, but there was no doubt that it was Gladia's voice. Benakiell hurried to her side, as did Ambar, and they helped her up into a sitting position. She was stiff, covered in bruises and grazes, but her eyes were bright in her face, and those eyes were fixed on me.

'She must have really hit her head hard,' muttered Ashtun, lapsing into silence after Achillea poked him. Gladia continued to look at me and then began to speak.

'Talla has done all that she could do for me. How could she have taken on those animals? She was better off keeping silent as she did. Look at her in front of you. She is very fair, who knows what those beasts had in mind for her when they were done with me? And if she had brought attention to herself, they would have left me alone to be sure, but they would have moved their attention to her. We have all heard what they do to women. Imagine that happening to her, who has not ever even had a conversation with a man until she left the Temple! Imagine what that would do to her! You should be ashamed of yourselves for your suspicious minds! As for these two; well I knew they were playing some devious game. Tarik here was trying to protect me with his horse from the rest, and he,' she gestured to Ambar, waiting patiently by her side,' he told me not to lose heart.' Her voice broke a little with the effort of speaking, and Ambar pressed a gourd of honey water into her hand which she sipped gratefully. 'Come to me, Talla,' she urged, and I went to sit by her side, as Ambar moved gracefully out of the way for me, his robe brushing mine as he went past.

'I won't break,' she said to me, a trace of her old acerbic nature reasserting itself. 'I may have nearly been broken, but I will mend. That honey of yours is magic; no wonder Erayo spent such extra time with you!'

'What did the Empath say to you, Talla?' asked Achillea excitedly and the others turned to me with interest, awaiting my answer. I guessed that for them it was a new kind of experience; a Temple Maid going to an Empath; what might she have taken from me, or given to me? I was unsure about what to say to them about my trip to the Empath and about the effect of the little bee on my feelings. Ambar had traded the little bee with me for the honey, which was now healing Gladia, and the little bee had caused me to take on the Empath's feelings. Following our departure from the Empath, there had been trouble of all kinds. I could not help but think that the little bee and the Empath had caused me much difficulty, and not eased any of my troubles. Since Erayo seemed to have opened up the channels within me that the little bee used, I was slowly becoming more accustomed to detecting the feelings of others, and the closer I felt to them, the more I seemed to be able to empathise with their feelings.

'She told her of her dreams, didn't she, Talla,' encouraged Gladia. The others turned to me expectantly and I felt that I should tell them too of what Erayo had said to me. I had placed it to the back of my mind after I had become focused on the bee and the passage of feelings and had almost forgotten that it may be important information. There seemed to be no reason why I should not share it with my companions. Perhaps it was my training in the Temple; the constant memorising of aphorisms and chants, prayers to the Goddess and responses to the Priestesses which meant I could remember exactly what the Empath Erayo had said to me, and so I repeated it exactly as she had said it to me.

'Your dreams come from another place, from another one. She is powerful and is trying to reach you. You are searching for one that you cannot find, and your search will take you to places of danger. But you are a Beeguard; that will serve you well. If you cannot find an Empath where you travel, go to the bees; they will listen to you and absorb your feelings. They will sweeten your pain and bring forth honey made all the sweeter by the bitterness of your tears.'

Ambar and Tarik gave each other meaningful looks and began their silent language again. It infuriated me and yet I did not wish to make it an issue. Just as in the Temple, when I taught myself to scribe, I wanted to learn their language without letting them know I knew it. Benakiell looked at me appraisingly; for perhaps the first time, I believed he was not feeling antagonistic towards me but rather that he was curious and interested in me again.

'She knew you were a Beeguard then,' he mused. 'It must be your calling, after all.' I shifted impatiently. It seemed to me obvious that the Empath could have divined I was a Beeguard purely from the honey which I had brought her, but I did not point this out, welcoming the thaw in Benakiell's attitude.

'She was right about the danger,' chirped Achillea. 'You have already done that bit! But who are you searching for? And why is someone powerful looking for you? Unless it is the Priestesses who want you back in the Temple! Or the Queen... but why would the Queen want you?'

This was the question to which none of us knew the answer. The Temple had little to do with the Queen, worshipping the Goddess as we did, and keeping to ourselves; the people of the Outer feared the Queen but never seemed to see her or know much about her; the OutRiders were the obvious ones who should know more, but were Ambar and Tarik real OutRiders? What did they know about the Queen, and if it really was her who was looking for me?

I looked around at my travelling companions and thought about how much they had been endured on my account. Gladia had been injured and abused, Benakiell and Ashtun too had been injured by the OutRiders when they visited Mellia, and Benakiell, in particular, had stood up for me and supported me when no other had. Achillea had shared with me her knowledge and her friendship, her loyalty and of course her mother Cassia's dwelling and bees. The two OutRiders who had ridden with us had saved us from the other OutRiders and had taken grave risks on our behalf, and what had I done for them? I decided to tell them of the brooch my mother had left pinned to my swaddling when she left me at the Temple, and the importance it seemed to have for those pursuing me, but before I could formulate a way of telling them this, Tarik spoke.

'It is time now for us to share our knowledge and our thoughts. There is trouble growing in this land, and whilst we come at it from different paths, we can all see the trouble and we can all see what it does to us. Let me start by telling you my story, and my knowledge and then we can talk about what import, if any, it has. But first we should eat, and drink coffee. Ambar will make the flatbread and perhaps our brother Benakiell will make the coffee, for I see that Talla's honey and Ambar's herbs are healing our friend, and food will make her even stronger. Talla and Achillea will attend to you, Gladia.'

For all his quiet demeanour, it seemed that Tarik was a man who organised people well and I wondered if he had organised his fellow OutRiders in the same way. I couldn't help but notice that his arrangement had left him and Ashtun with nothing to do, however. Tarik sat next to Ashtun who, despite the apparent thaw in relations between us and the OutRiders, continued to carry a suspicious look on his face. As Achillea and I helped Gladia upright so that she could go outside, I heard him asking Ashtun his opinion on the different kinds of woods used in building, and I admired his way of bringing everybody together, with no one left out. After Gladia had finished outside, we helped her to clean herself somewhat, and gave her more of the honey and herbs. Although she still needed help to walk, and was bruised and swollen, her eyes were clear and her interest in getting back to eating and drinking coffee confirmed to Achillea and I that Gladia was returning to her old self.

The flatbread was good; warm, chewy and flavoured subtly with some herbs. We ate it with some dried dates and figs and drank the strong gritty coffee to which I had so quickly become accustomed. Tarik began his story.

'I would like to tell you what I know, and I hope that, together with your knowledge, it will assist us in understanding the dangers which face us. I am an OutRider by upbringing, by which I mean, I am committed to serving the Queen, by virtue of having been brought up to be a soldier and a servant of the Queen. Just as the Temple is full of unwanted girls, so the OutForts are full of unwanted boys. Or at least so it appeared to me, as I grew up. I knew nothing of the Temples at that time, nor indeed much of the Outer. I learned to practice the crafts we used in the OutFort; leatherworking and metal working to make the armour and the weapons, animal handling, horse riding and the skills of archery and sword handling. As I left the Third Age of Childhood, I had to choose my path.'

So far, Tarik's story sounded much like my own. In his case he was brought up by the OutFort and in my case, I was brought up by the Temple, but they sounded very similar establishments. I wondered again about how so many children were abandoned by the people of the Outer. Of course, Benakiell had told me that the OutRiders used to come and take children from the villages, but that did not seem to explain the ready availability of children. There was usually one every couple of months or so. The babes were left at the BabyDoor at the Temple, at night, and no questions were asked. There was a bell by the Temple door, and when it rang at night, we all knew that another baby had arrived. The smallest babies lived in a separate BabyHouse until they were able to walk, and the little ones lived in a big dormit, all together with some from the Third Age of Childhood who tended to their needs until they could work. Even very small ones were put to work picking berries, sorting and unknotting embroidery threads, peeling and chopping food, cleaning steps and so on. I wondered how the little boys were brought up in the OutFort, but I did not want to interrupt Tarik, so I held my tongue and listened on.

'I chose the path of metalsmith and learned to make arrows and sword blades, discs for the horses' armour and so on. Alongside this work, I worked on my archery and I did maintenance work on the OutFort. I was eventually selected to go with my OutCommander, Gabra, to the Queen's Court whilst he had a meeting with the Queen.'

My companions, like me, were fascinated by this insight into the life of an OutRider. The way that they dressed and their speed on the horses and their undoubted skill with weaponry had stopped us all from thinking of them as people just like us and had set them apart. Now we were learning about their lives and how they thought and acted. There were so many questions which I had for them; I wanted to know how they made the discs on the horses' armour of such a uniform size and shape; I wanted to know how they learned to kill with no thought to their pain; –how to obey orders without questioning- and then I realised that, until I too had left the Temple, I had also obeyed orders without questioning. Although in the Temple we were not required to hurt or to kill, I had done my fair share of unpleasant tasks, and done them thoughtlessly, bound to do as the Priestesses asked us. It sounded as if the OutRiders, far from being so very different to us, were in fact quite similar.

'When we arrived, I was told that we would be doing some work for the Queen. I should not expect to see her, and we were to work on the Queen's Audience Chamber, a place to which her subjects might come to petition her on matters of importance. I think that only important courtiers could make petitions.' added Tarik hastily, as he looked around at us, my companions open mouthed at the thought that it might be possible to petition the Queen, and already mentally drawing up a list of issues with which to confront her. 'The chamber itself was hewn out of stone underneath the Queen's Chamber, and our job was to make a curtain of metal discs such as are found on the horses' armour, so that no person could enter or leave the chamber without it making a noise. It was done so that the Queen would know when someone was there. It took some days to cast and beat out the discs, but eventually we were ready to put up the curtain, and my OutCommander left me in the chamber to thread them onto wire of honeygold. Honeygold is a special metal, which carries sound very clearly.' Ambar used his hands impatiently, and I thought perhaps this was the sign for 'Hurry up'. Tarik did not speak often, but when he had the floor to himself, he enjoyed the chance to explain things in detail.

Tarik pretended not to notice Ambar's gesticulations, and continued with his story.

'You understand, of course, that the Queen would not be in the same room as her subjects, so the petitioners would remain in the Audience Chamber and the Queen would be in her rooms above. I had not realised this when we were making the curtain of discs, but now I understood it. They clearly could not hear me – unsurprising as I was not yet threading the discs on but merely placing them in rows ready. It is very careful, fine work.' I could imagine Tarik doing careful, fine work. And yet, he was not an incapable warrior; he fought cleanly and crisply, as I had seen for myself. I pondered on the different sides to his nature and wondered again why he was telling this story and why it was so important to me and my companions.

'The Audience Chamber was hewn out of the stone walls of the palace, as I have said, and there were channels carved into the rock which carried the sound from the Chamber to the Queen and from the Queen to the Chamber. I could hear voices talking to one another, hushed voices, and yet the shape of the Chamber and the angles of the tunnels down to it meant I could hear the conversation as if I were right next to it. They began to talk of the Queen, that she was getting too old to govern, but that there was a way to continue ruling without her, as long as the next Queen did not realise that her time had come and that she could claim her throne. If she did, all the power and riches that had been built up by the Queen would be for nothing, for a new Queen would clear out her Palace and begin a new community of courtiers and advisers. This was the way it was and had always been and yet they wished to remain in their places at the Palace, reaping their rewards and living in luxury, for they had all been there for many years, ever since the Queen was crowned almost seven ages ago. One of them said "We must stop the Maid at all costs. She must be made to stay in the Temple until we can take her. Once we have the brooch of the Queen, from her, we will send her for service with the Angels." I was much disturbed,' confessed Tarik. 'I could not move for fear of alerting them to my presence. Fortunately for me, my OutCommander arrived at the door to the Chamber at that point, and they stopped speaking, as he told them we were ready to put up the curtain. I did not hear another word whilst I was at the palace, but I was curious.' Tarik looked around at us, a little defiantly. Like me, he had been brought up not to question, merely to do, and felt some guilt about his perceived betrayal of his Commander and his Queen, even by the simple act of observing his surroundings.

'I heard no more whilst I was at the Palace,' continued Tarik, 'and I did not tell my OutCommander what I had heard. I should have done, and yet if I had, I might not be here today. And I do not know whether I should be glad of that or not, for I have betrayed my Queen and my RiderForce, and if they find me, I will have to fight to the death.'

'Why?' asked Ashtun, breaking the silence crisply. 'If you have not told anyone, then none of your fellow OutRiders knows, and you can carry on as you were before, riding around the countryside fighting and intimidating people. For surely we would not have noticed if you were an OutRider who was loyal to the old Queen or this other new Queen you heard tell of.' He laughed, a little bitterly. 'We do not, after all, normally talk with either OutRiders or Priestesses aside from to beg for favours. Who cares about your loyalty, and why is it any of our concern? We do not care who is Queen, for the same thing will happen to us regardless; we will still have to pay taxes in our crops and give up our harvests and our work for nothing!'

Tarik looked taken aback. It crossed my mind that perhaps he had felt more secure with our group than he should have done. Gladia and I had, after all, been with them for longer than the others, and had seen them working and talking together. Perhaps we understood that they seemed very like other people in many regards. For Ashtun, however, they were the enemy; they always had been, and they might remain so. I sensed that he would like nothing more than to wear their armour though and fight with their weapons on the back of a horse. There was something in the hungry way in which he looked at them that made me feel that, in some strange and incomprehensible way, he was jealous of their lives.

Benakiell frowned. Like me, he had too many questions which lay unanswered. Why were Tarik and Ambar together, and how did they come to know one another? The others did not know that Ambar was the very merchant who had traded me the little bee pendant, but this made me question even more. How did Ambar know the ways of the OutRiders, to the extent that he knew their language and rode their horses as if he were joined to them, and yet he was a merchant and a traveller? Were there many OutRiders who masqueraded as ordinary people of the Outer?

'Maids are thrown out from the Temple every month or so,' mused Benakiell, running his thumb through his wiry beard, making scratching, rasping sounds. 'And each time, the OutRiders collect them up before they go further than a day. Surely by now this Maid must have been picked up anyway?' He looked at Ambar and Tarik calmly. 'You OutRiders must know how famed you are for finding people and making them vanish. Surely this new Queen cannot be a Temple Maid, anyway? A royal child would be kept in a palace, not in a Temple with the rest of the Drabs.' I winced at his words inside but managed to maintain a placid face. Benakiell knew what he was doing and had not betrayed the secret of me being a Temple Maid, even though I had hurt him and angered him by my actions earlier.

Ambar spoke then. 'The Queen we seek is not the daughter of the Queen. She is the daughter of the Queen's daughter, Paradox. The Queen had three daughters who died or disappeared at the age of Maturity, when they might have their own children. It is said that one of them was with child when she left the Palace secretly. They say she was found dead three weeks later, but without child. It is for this child that we seek.'

Gladia's eyes snapped, with their old spark. 'This sounds like an old story with no substance, based on air and fancy thoughts! Even if this child of the Queen gave birth to a child, you assume too much in this noble quest of yours!' She stretched out her hand, still bruised and grazed, and began to count off the points. 'You cannot know what happened to this child. Maybe it was loved and cared for by its father and other family. Maybe she was not with child. Maybe she was with child and the child died as she did. Maybe that child has been taken to another land. Maybe the child survived and then died. And maybe,' she paused, for greater emphasis, 'maybe that child was a boy!'

Achillea gasped at this final point. It had seemed obvious to me, but apparently not to her, for she seized on this point. 'Why you could be looking for the wrong person altogether! It could be a boy! Why do you not search for a boy?!'

Ambar and Tarik conversed again, silently. It was beginning to really irritate me, and, try as I might, the emberjar of my mind was catching light. Unless I was very careful, the sparks flying in my mind might lead us into more trouble and I had already been the cause of so much. I cast my eyes to the ground, for supposed modesty, but mainly because I did not want Ambar to see my rage.

'We do not understand your language of the hands, brothers,' said Benakiell mildly, just as I was about to say something similar, but probably in a more incendiary way. 'Can you not share your thoughts with us? It feels to me as if you are sharing some and not all your story. And why do you tell this story to us? I see that you, Tarik, have some disagreement with your comrades in the OutRiders and that may have been why you have disguised yourselves and why you fought the other OutRiders to the death back there. We do thank you for your kindness to our friend Gladia, after you hurt her so badly, but I think it is time for us to go back to our little lives in the village now. It sounds as if you have more important things to do in this world, with new Queens to chase and to find, and OutRiders to evade, and all manner of things. Why,' he chuckled, 'it sounds like the sort of story I used to hear my mother tell around the fire under the Paradox tree!'

Ambar looked around at us. Perhaps he had hoped that we would all join him on this quest of his to find the new Queen. We all looked back at him with varying degrees of resentment, pity, disdain and, in the case of Ashtun, a little envy. Inside my mind, however, I was asking questions of myself faster than I could answer them, and it took me all my might not to speak of the bee necklace which he had made sure that I had, and the brooch left to me by my mother. It was more important to me now to be with my friends from Mellia. We were all tired of excitement and wanted to go home. And even while I thought this, I became aware that I now called these people my friends, rather than my companions, and Mellia was now my home.

'Why are you in such a rush to find this Queen?' asked Achillea. 'If the old Queen is ill or dying, and this child cannot be found, surely they will just find another to rule?' She laughed. 'I am sure there are many who would be happy to pretend to be the grandchild of the Queen if they knew they would become the Queen and live in a palace with all their needs tended to! Why, even I could manage to lie about in a bed with silken sheets all day, with Ashtun here bringing me pomegranates on a plate!' She giggled at his exaggerated frown.

Ambar paused before he spoke to us.

'The child we seek is not a boy, nor yet a child. The Queen cannot birth male children; the Goddess has made it so, for the Goddess and the creator of all things could only be a woman to bring forth new life where once there was nothing. That at least is what the Priestesses of the Temple tell us. If the Queen's daughter gave birth to a child who lived, there is no doubt that it would be a girl. And since this happened a full three ages ago, the one for whom we seek is not a child but a young woman, one who is in the First Age of Adulthood, just like Talla and Achillea here.' He waved his hand gently in our direction. His hand lingered in the air, almost caressing it. I did not dare to look at him. They had all heard Tarik's story where he had overheard them talk of the Maid in the Temple, and they must have known that whilst he included Achillea in his gesture and in his words, the aim of his words pointed as surely toward me as his arrows had to the OutRiders who tormented Gladia.

I looked up to Benakiell who stroked his beard thoughtfully as he put together all these new items of information. Gladia's eyes widened, taking in the impact of his words, and already I could see her too trying to put together the pieces of this broken vessel of information. Ashtun looked down at the floor, his jaw working furiously, grinding down on his teeth to stop himself from saying anything, while Achillea seemed not to have grasped what everyone else had; that the Maid they were seeking might be me. Of course, I was still the only one who knew about the brooch, and about what the little bee did to me.

Achillea yawned loudly and reached for her netela, turning towards me briefly as she raised it to her head and winked. 'I am tired now,' she complained, 'and Gladia is worn out by all this talking. Let us return to Mellia so that as we think about this story and look out for runaway Queens we can at least be in our own homes. We all have jobs to do, not least Talla who is our village Beeguard, and Benakiell and Ashtun who need to get back to their dwelling making. This is the time of year to harvest the building reeds after all.' I noticed that she had not mentioned her own work but was so grateful to her for trying to move along from the news which Ambar had given us that I did not mind.

Ambar frowned. 'You cannot just go back to Mellia and carry on with your lives, harvesting reeds and building huts! The Queen's OutRiders will not stop searching. They will come again and again to Mellia. They will have already been there while you were travelling, and they will know that two Maids of the right age have left to travel. By now, they will be stopping and searching all those of the right age wherever they find them, and if they are suspicious, they will take them. Wherever you go, you will still be in danger!'

Benakiell stood up and brushed the dust off his robe. 'We cannot stay here, and we cannot return home. What is your suggestion then? We will have to take our chances, I suspect. Gladia and I are too old to be wandering nomads, and until they find this would-be Queen for whom you search – who may not even exist – you say they will continue to search.'

'I will fight them all off!' declared Ashtun, who seemed to become more and more like the OutRiders with every moment. I wondered again whether he wished he could be one, rather than an apprentice for Benakiell, who glared at him wordlessly. Ambar and Tarik signed again silently, their fingers flashing so fast that I could not keep up with them. I was determined to learn this language and understand it, for I could see its uses.

Tarik spoke aloud then, in that precise and slow way of speaking that he had. If I had to listen to him for too long, I felt I might fall asleep, so soothing and dull was he. 'There is a place to which you can be taken. It is a sign only of our great trust in you, and our belief that you are important to the life of this land and its Queen. There is another who lives there, who has also been wronged by the Queen's OutRiders, for she is very important to this quest too. She used to live there with many, but they have all left or died. We found her there and she has offered us shelter in our travels before. It is hidden near the mountains, two days ride from here, and we can rest there and take time for you to learn more about the cause for which we fight. It is a small place, and certainly not built by any Angels, like the Temples, but there are several old dwellings there, and we can rest there safely.'

The Angels. This was the second time they had mentioned them, and I wanted to know more about them. In the Temple we were often told about how the Temples were built by Angels overnight, carved out of solid rock and left for the Priestesses to fill with life. The Goddess was said to dream of the Angels, and they would appear to do her work in the world and disappear just as quickly. I wanted to ask Ambar about them, but he was looking at Benakiell, and obviously viewed him as the leader of the party. I felt the glow of anger. Always the same. Even if I might in fact be the next Queen, it seemed that an older man would always be the one who decided things, even though we lived in a land governed by a powerful woman. Benakiell surprised me by turning to Achillea, rather than anyone else, and asking her what she thought about this idea. Perhaps she was more sure of her response, for she answered immediately that she would be glad to go there if she but knew that when we got there she could sit still and rest and never have to ride a horse again. Then he turned to Ashtun for his answer, who answered yes, of course. He wanted to be with Achillea, and I could see he was seduced by all this talk of fighting and defending, and spending time with these men from whom he could learn so much. Gladia, too, was happy to go somewhere safe where she could continue to heal and rest, and where she could sit and stitch under a tree. I realised then how cunning Benakiell was; by asking everyone in that order, he arrived at me last and with everyone else wanting to go, I felt as if I could choose nothing else, and gave in with resignation. Ambar and Tarik relaxed with relief once this decision was made and quickly went to saddle up the horses, leaving us to pack up the gourds and the carrysacks.

CHAPTER 20

Besseret, as it was known, was nestled at the foot of two mountains, in some scrubby forest, far from any worn traveltrails and it had been uncomfortable travelling there. It was close to a stream and was a loose conglomeration of dwellings, all made from mud and reeds, waterproofed with paradox oil and with their roofs covered with tree branches. Unless you knew how to get there, it would have been hard to spot from any main trail. It had once been a moderately sized settlement, looking at it, although it was clearly neglected now, and I saw Benakiell looking speculatively at the roofing. There were a dozen or more dwellings of varying sizes in the main part of the village, and a few more set further apart. I noticed there was smoke coming from one of them.

I worried about how easily my travelling companions had fallen in to trusting Ambar and Tarik, even though I was aware that the little bee pendant showed me no flashes of anger or fear from them but a warmth. It seemed very suspicious to me that they should trust these men, who had, after all, injured Gladia. Gladia herself was fatalistic about her injuries and her treatment, and now that she had arrived in Besseret, where she could sleep in a dwelling house on a woven mat and rest from her travels, she seemed even less aware of danger than normal. I had suggested to Achillea that going to this village might be a trap, that they might be planning to turn us over the Queen's OutRiders, but she shook her head and laughed.

'Talla! Why do you always think the worst of everyone? They may have this quest for the Queen's grandchild in their heads, but I think they mean well enough. I am looking forward to being still for longer than a day,' she confessed. 'I need to wash and to plait my hair and to eat fresh food. It will be well, Talla, it will be well.' She laid her small hand on my arm and I felt a deep warmth from her. She seemed oblivious to it; I checked to see if I had inadvertently left the little bee pendant on under my robe. However, it was safe in my underpocket, along with the brooch and I could not understand how this feeling, which I had only previously felt while I held the little bee or at the Empath Erayo's could have manifested itself. Still, the warmth comforted me, and I felt reassured by Achillea's faith.

I suspected that Benakiell knew a great deal about this land of ours, Oramia; the existence of many different places like Besseret, and bigger towns and cities, and even other lands. He seemed quite relaxed and unmoved by being in different places, and had travelled widely, as a merchant when he was young. His past was not much known to me, save what he had told me of his wife and their life before she died. I thought sometimes that perhaps Benakiell had been something like Ashtun when he was young, something of a firebrand. The glint in his eye when you disagreed with him and the bold way in which he set himself towards a goal made him someone who I was glad I was not opposing in a fight. It still seemed odd that these places existed which were unknown, I mused, and the next day, when I was sitting picking through a basket of dates to take out the stalks and bits, I said as much to Ambar who was, as usual, sitting on the stone nearby, available to talk but quiet unless I spoke. He laughed, when I said this, and I didn't like it. It always seemed to make me angry when people laughed at me because it felt like they were looking down on me. I felt my lack of life experience in their world acutely. Sometimes I thought of how I could do the same to them were they to come and observe my life in the Temple.

'Why are you laughing at me?' I asked him sharply.

'Talla, just because you do not know something, it does not mean it is not so. Many people know of the existence of these places, and many people know of the existence of all kinds of people; not just OutRiders and TempleMaids, and citizens of the Outer, but others from many lands.'

'But nobody has told me!' I burst out. 'And why should people not know about them?' I very nearly blurted out that the Temple Maids who left the Temple should be told of them so that they would always have a place to come to when they left, having heard so much that seemed sinister about the ways in which they were picked up after leaving and never seen again, but realised, just in time, that this might alert him to my previous life.

Ambar spoke to me sharply. 'Well, and why, sister Talla, should you know everything or be told everything? And even more, if you would just calm that rage you keep so well-tended in your heart, you would understand that if everyone knew about Besseret still being here, then that would mean the Queen's OutRiders would too, and the point of us being here would be lost, as would those who will be spending some time here. You may have led a quiet life in the village tending your bees,' and he raised his eyes to look straight into mine, 'but there is very much more in the world than that which you know. We are all born to a small life, and it is our responsibility to learn about the lives of others. Perhaps you will take the time to get to know the one who still lives here and learn from her.' I lowered my eyes, ashamed of my outburst, and finding his searching look discomfiting. Perhaps Ambar sensed my embarrassment, for he stood up and asked me to follow him as he wanted me to meet somebody.

We walked down the path, with him walking slightly in front of me. I watched him walk, his legs moving easily and fluidly, his arms swinging freely, his bow slung on his back with his quiver, as usual. I was so comfortable in his presence and yet he made me feel awake and sharp and almost confrontational. I knew that with every relationship I had built up – with Gladia and Benakiell and Achillea – there was a similar feeling of warmth and a corresponding irritation which often passed, but Ambar intrigued me more. I caught him looking at me occasionally when he thought I didn't notice, and his eyes were soft and searching. I wondered how I looked at him. His hand brushed mine and I felt the channel of warmth between us. He turned to me and spoke.

'I am taking you to see Maren, the one who lives here still. She is a Beeguard too, but I should warn you, she has little sight – at least not through her eyes.' He smiled. 'She seems to see enough though. I thought you might like to spend some time with bees again. Although,' he added, 'I would rather that we were doing something to find the new Queen than hiding here talking to bees.'

I didn't answer but continued to walk. We were moving towards a dark granite outcrop. I could see a small dwelling built up next to it, and the hanging log beehives in the paradox trees nearby. As we got closer, I could see the bees flying to the lavender bushes planted nearby. The air was hot around us and the sound of the humming bees was soporific. I pulled my netela over my head to shade my eyes and wished I had stayed at the dwelling rather than coming along to see this woman. I did not feel comfortable with making new acquaintances. I thought that the more people who met me, the more likely it would be that one of them would realise that I came from the Temple. My friends from Mellia were different, but new companions could not be trusted. I could have been sleeping in the shade, instead of walking in the sun.

'I will leave you here now, sister Talla,' said Ambar abruptly. 'Maren is expecting you, but make sure to call out to her before you arrive so that you do not startle her, since she does not see and does not know who you are yet.' Ambar had a way of making me want to do what he suggested, even while he often infuriated me, expecting me to follow his bidding mindlessly. It had been the same in the Temple. The High Priestesses brooked no argument or disagreement. Any attempt to suggest an alternative was met with some implacable quoting of the Aphorisms of Ashkana with whom nobody could argue. I wished that I too could be someone that people would want to follow the direction of. I saw a figure sitting by a hive which had been lowered to the ground and I called out softly, 'Sister Maren, it is I, Talla. Ambar has sent me to visit you.'

Maren turned to face me, and I was pleased she could not see the expression which must have passed over my face. Her eyes were a milky white colour all over, covered in a sticky film and although she turned to apparently look at me, they passed right through me, opaque and mysterious. Her skin was pockmarked with pits and scars, as if she had been splashed with pain. She was a spare, but wiry person, evidently accustomed to her fair share of heavy work, for her sinews stood out. She wore a light blue robe, with no ornamentation, and a matching netela which was arranged loosely about her face. I thought perhaps she used it to hide her face from others, knowing what the sight of it might make them feel.

FLAMMEUS

'If you are done looking at me, please come and sit in the shade, sister Talla,' said Maren, drily. 'Ambar told me that you are a Beeguard in your home village, and that you have a natural skill with the bees, the messengers of the Goddess. Perhaps you can help me with this hive, for the bees need to be moved so I can get the honey. I can do it without much sight, as I can do most things, but it will be good to share it with a fellow Beeguard.' I felt my objections and apathy melt away, and an enthusiasm return to me. In truth, I found the endless sitting and waiting and small talk difficult. I had worked every day of my life from the Second Age of Childhood, and it was more comforting to me to be busy. I had not had chance to draw designs or use my pouncet box for Gladia for quite some time and I felt aimless and without direction. I sat down next to the beehive.

The hive was made of a hollowed-out log sealed at each end with a plug of palm leaves. There were small holes to allow the bees access to the hive. The hive was humming with the sound of the bees, and while odd bees were still crawling in and out of the hive, it seemed peaceful enough. I hesitated. Although I had withdrawn honey in Mellia without issue, these were not my bees. It was traditionally done with smoke which made the bees confused. I had not done it like that, the bees having simply moved aside for me to take the honeycombs out. Next to Maren was a small pierced gourd. I had not ever seen such a thing, so I asked her about it. She explained that inside the gourd were crushed leaves of the Lippia bush which, aside from being a tasty addition to a stew, caused a calmness and a happiness to descend upon the bees. It made them feel sleepy and replete, unlikely to sting. The gourd was pierced all around, like my pouncet box or an emberjar, and I was interested to see it. Maren ran her fingers over the shell, smiling slightly.

'I invented this because I could not control the fire so well after I lost my sight. I needed a way to put the smoke into the hive. The bees have always listened to me and the smoke just makes them quieter for me. Since I lost my sight, I hear them and can judge their mood even better. I do not like too much smoke in any case.' A shadow crossed over her face and she closed her eyes briefly, wincing. I waited for her to continue. The beehive hummed quietly next to me, and I laid my hand on its surface. The wood was warm and weathered, there was no roughness on it. It was as if it were something that were not alive and yet alive, in the same way that the Temple seemed to me to be a living thing, even whilst it was only a building of stone. The sound of the Maids singing and chanting to the Goddess had the same comforting hum to it, and I wondered if that was why I was drawn towards Beeguarding.

Maren felt for the end of the hive where it was blocked off. I wasn't sure whether she wanted me to help so I waited for her to tell me what to do. She asked me to take out the leaves gently and then began to hum. I could hear the bees in her voice; she had copied the different pitches and rhythms in the hive, beginning with the low noise of the workers, then the more musical tones of the pollen gatherers. As she hummed, the bees in the hive took up her rhythm until it seemed like they were singing in harmony, just like the Priestesses in the Temple. When Achillea sang, her voice rippled and gurgled, it caught at the senses, but this music was less personal and more communal. The way in which the sounds blended together was like the sound of breathing or a heartbeat, visceral. It was like the music of the body whereas Achillea's singing was the music of the soul. Maren asked me to place a coal from the fire into the gourd. As I moved, the bees' humming in the hive rose up, but Maren lifted her own humming tone and they settled again. Keeping bees happy was important for the sweetness of the honey. They made the honey anyway, but if they were unhappy, although the honey tasted sweet, it left a bitter aftertaste. In the same way, if they fed off sweet scented flowers the honey was warm and flavourful. The Physics in the Temple used honeysalves to treat pain. They kept the salves in small earthenware pots and rubbed them into the skin around the pain. It seemed to work especially with those in their seventh age whose bodies were aching and tired from too much work. But work was, as Ashkana reminded us, the purpose of life, and however old you might be, there was always useful work that could be done. Even those who could not walk could sew, and those who could not sew could prepare food or wash clothes. They could tell stories to the children, or could even rock the littlest ones, the babies who were left at the doors of the Temple and who lived in the BabyHouse. There is always work that can be done by all.

I returned to my task and carefully placed the charcoal into the gourd, and it began to produce a thick, pungent smoke. The scent was like lemons mixed with woody herbs and I recognised the scent from the tea used by the Physics at the Temple. The tea made people calmer and soothed their agitations and I saw why Maren had chosen it to make her smoke. The smoke itself was thick and almost blue as it trickled out through the holes in the gourd and Maren guided it, with a practised hand towards the top of the beehive log, humming quietly and moving it gently down. The smoke, perhaps because it was so heavy, dripped downwards rather than upwards and soon enough, I could see little wisps of it fading out through the small cracks in the hive. Maren gradually slowed down the tempo and volume of her humming until everything was silent, and the bees too had ceased to hum. She took out the gourd and laid it by the side of the hive and reached into the hive to take out the honeycombs. She pulled out the stick frames- there were three of them – and gave them to me to lay in the open clay dish she had ready. I was ready for the stinging that might accompany the removal of the honeycomb. I sympathised with the bees for all their work was being stolen away from them and I could not blame them for stinging the thieves, but these bees made no move to sting and just crawled placidly over the honeycomb which lay, oozing sweetness, in the dish. All the while, Maren continued her low hum and then she dipped her hand in the honey and waited for the bees to crawl up on to it, asking me to ensure that all the stray bees were on her hand before putting her hand over the entrance to the hive. The bees crawled off and went back into their home willingly, ready once more for the main door to be shut and to begin to work again.

After I had secured the hive and pulled it back into the tree, I poured the pure golden honey into the gourds that Maren had lined up ready. There was plenty of honey and it was thick and clear and tasted wonderful; sweet and scented with the scent of lavender and thyme. There were more than a dozen gourds, all told, and when I had finished stopping the necks of them with folded leaves, Maren suggested that we could drink coffee. There was an earthenware pot on her fire where the coffee was bubbling gently, and I poured us each a small cup of coffee. It was hot and thick, full of power and just what we needed after our labours.

'You have worked well with the bees, sister Talla,' said Maren. 'Brother Ambar says you have the gift of Beeguarding, and I see that he is right. Perhaps while you are here, I can teach you even more to take back to your village when you go.'

'How long have you lived here?' I asked, curiously. I had had the idea that this place was a good place to settle for a short time, where people might just stay for a little while before they moved on to another village, safe from the eye of the OutRiders, who seemed to have so many people to look for and chase that they could not possibly keep track of all those whom they searched for. It did not feel like a place where people had lived despite the dwellings. I should ask Ambar if this were true, but I still did not trust him. I knew he would answer the question, but how would I know if he told me the truth? It seemed a better idea to ask others.

'I have lived here for years,' replied Maren, to my surprise. 'But I am the last one left from the village that used to be here. They left me here for dead, when they had finished with me, but I survived. I have lived here for many years now and would not think to change.'

'But why did they want to destroy the village?' I asked.

'It was me they wanted to destroy.' Maren's milky eyes scanned around her uselessly, but nervously. It seemed that she was remembering what had happened. She gripped the clay beaker more tightly and sipped her coffee. 'I did not die, but they took from me the thing which I needed. Without my sight I cannot see the ones whom I tried to protect, nor identify those who did this to me.'

I wanted to ask my questions, to find out the things I wanted to know. There was so much I suddenly wanted to know about Maren – who she was, who she was trying to protect, and what had been done to her, but I felt the little bee pendant glowing with warmth, and something stopped my tongue. Instead I waited, sipping my own coffee. The doves cooed in the branches of the tree overhead, and the bees settled back into their daily life, visiting the flowers and dancing with one another on the way to and from the hive.

'Can I hold your hand?' Maren asked me as we sat there, and I placed my hand into hers, feeling the warmth I had felt when I was held by the Empath. I could feel Maren felt it too, and as her face relaxed, her feelings drained into me. I felt confused and bewildered; I felt my eyes sting and water, I felt warmth and I felt again the spark in my emberjar mind. I felt a rage that was not mine but rather Maren's and I understood that, despite her outer calm, inside she was angry with those who had done this to her. I sat and held her hand for some minutes, silently, until she spoke again.

'I will tell you my story. I tell it to you because I need to tell it to someone before they come back and find me again. Ambar has said they are searching for the new Queen. They will be out everywhere looking for anything that may be important to them, and they may see that in me, if they remember me from so long ago. My story begins some three ages ago, when I was something like your age myself...

'I have not always been blind, as I told you. I am blind because of what I have seen. My eyesight was ruined by them so that I could not witness again that which I know to be true. It stops me from knowing the truth.

'I was not always a Beeguard either, although I always used honey in my work. My mother was a Beeguard, but I had always wanted to be a Birthmother and I learned my trade with Hortensia. A Birthmother's job is to bring a child into the world, to be the mother of its mother as she becomes a mother. It is indeed a gift from the Goddess. My mother's skills were useful in my work; honey can be used to soothe the mothers in the birth and to hush the painful cries of a little one, beeswax can be used to rub and stretch the skin and to heal wounds and to give food and warmth to babies whose mothers milk has not yet come. The humming I use for the bees is soothing too; for a labouring mother, the rhythm and the music of the bees is calming.

'Hortensia had birthed many babies. She could turn a baby inside the mother and deliver babies who were born feet first. If a baby died, she could treat the mother with remedies which eased her pain.

'We were some distance from Exodia when it all happened. We had travelled there to stay for some time, as we usually did, moving around from place to place to serve the mothers. We had already birthed four babies and had been given goods as payment for their safe delivery; food and spices and cloths and gourds and clay jars for our ointments and unguents. We were at the resting place one afternoon when one of the women from the village came to us to say she had found a young woman on a forest path as she walked home from gathering fruit. The woman was labouring and in distress but could not walk and was holding on to a tree trunk for support. She had begged the village woman not to tell anyone and to leave her alone but the woman, Anglossia, came to us for advice, being kind-hearted.

'We packed our things – clean cloths, threads, honey and honeysalve, bitter-orange and poppyjuice, gourds of water and cold flatbreads and hastened to the place Anglossia showed us in the forest. When we got there, the woman was leaning against a tree, biting down hard on a twig so that her cries could not be heard, and her eyes widened with fear when she saw us. Anglossia told her quickly that we were Birthmothers and had no motive save the safe delivery of her child. It was clear the woman was fearful, and we had seen this before; perhaps she had been with the husband of another woman or had not received the Goddess's blessing on her child, though she looked well clothed enough to have afforded that.

'I unwrapped a cloth and made a shelter of it over the tree branches some way from the path so that she could be private and comfortable. She spoke in a low voice to Hortensia. I laid out the potions and the jars and the kapok pods and waited quietly as Hortensia walked her in, talking to her all the time. The labour was long and painful, but the woman bore it quietly, biting the twig and taking honey between the movements of the baby. Hortensia talked to her throughout it, and she was evidently of good birth from the way she spoke and acted, and from the softness of her skin, although that had recently been scratched and dirtied. Hortensia asked about the father of the baby and the woman said only that he was no longer present and that it was up to her to care for and protect the baby. The way she said protect like that made me think she must have some secrets. Hortensia asked her what we could call her, trying to find out her name and she told us to call her Paradox, like the tree. We never knew if that was her real name or not. She repeatedly asked how long it would be before the child was born. When it was clear that she had entered that quiet moment before the real work began and Hortensia told her it would not be long, she made Hortensia promise that she would take the baby to the Temple, as a gift for the Goddess. She said they would not think to look for it there. Hortensia asked what to do should the child be a boy, and the woman smiled a little faintly and said she had not considered that. She did not want to care for the child, that much was clear, although it seemed to trouble her. We were used to helping mothers who could not keep their babies and were grateful we lived in a land where even the youngest of us had a place and a purpose, whether protecting the land or nurturing it with worship.'

Maren continued to talk to me about the birth. I was grateful that she was blind, for the things she told me so matter of factly shocked me. I did not know how babies were born, since no one at the Temple ever had one, and all the babies that we saw appeared at our doorstep or in the Temple as gifts for the Goddess. The ordeal that she described sounded horrifying to me, but she spoke of it as if it were perfectly normal. I tried to imagine my own mother giving birth to me. I did not understand how anyone who would go through all that pain and suffering would not want to keep that which they had sacrificed. There again, perhaps it was too strong a reminder of pain, and that was why so many babies appeared at the Temple door. I sipped my coffee, pondering the story of the birth, which Maren seemed to relish in ever more elaborate detail as I quietly shrank back from the whole awful process. I would have resolved to never give birth myself, but I was confused by all the different stories I had been told were truths. Could a TempleMaid have a child? I had been told it was impossible, that they all belonged to the Goddess, but what if they ran away like I had? Did that mean the Goddess no longer protected me and that somehow suddenly one day I might find myself having to go through this same process? And how did the baby grow anyway? There seemed to be something from the relationship of a man and a woman that made a baby grow, but I did not know how it might happen. I returned my attention to Maren who was describing the moment that the baby was born.

'We were expecting a big baby, for the mother's belly was big, and we thought there would be difficulty for her birthing it. I bathed her in honey water and Hortensia encouraged to move around on her hands and knees.

When the baby's head could be seen, the mother drew up all her strength and gave birth to a small baby. It was a girl and she lay quiet for some time as Hortensia tended her, breathing gently into her mouth and rubbing her with a netela until she cried, when she wrapped her in the cloth and brought her to her mother. Her mother lay spent, breathing rapidly, and moaning slightly, and even though I tried to get her to look at the baby, she waved her aside and shut her eyes. I thought she was going to deliver the afterbirth and I was ready to help her as she finished the birth but instead of the afterbirth, she began to strain again and scarce a moment passed by before another baby was born. DoubleSouls. I had never been at the birth of DoubleSouls before and called Hortensia quickly away from the first baby to attend to Paradox, who was struggling to give birth to another baby, spent as she was. Eventually the child was born; it was another daughter. A similar size but a different face, with different eyes. The first born had a mark on her which showed us the difference between them, should we forget. By now Paradox was muttering incoherently and feverishly and was losing blood rapidly. Hortensia was tending her, and I saw Paradox pin something to one of the babies' cloths and whisper closely to Hortensia. Hortensia nodded and began to move quickly, swaddling the babies in cloths and wrapping them up. She left the mother on the floor on her mat and I had never seen her treat a woman with so little apparent regard. I protested to her that the mother was too weak to leave the shelter, and the babies too small, that they might die if they were to go so soon but she told me she had to care for the babies and take them with haste to the Temple, and that it was not safe to keep them with the mother for she was being pursued. It was very hard for me, sister Talla, to understand that Hortensia cared more for the babies than for the mother, and as a good Birthmother, it went against our teaching. The Goddess favours none more than the women who gave birth to women.

'I stayed to care for the mother, and Hortensia took some simple supplies and left the physic and a gourd of honey with me. She embraced me and told me that she would see me soon, but I never did see her again.'

Maren looked down and a tear trickled from her milky eye. I felt uncomfortable as if I should not be here, should not be listening to this story which hurt so much in the telling. But this was no reason to stop the flow of the story. I wanted to find out more about this mysterious event and how Maren had ended up unable to use her eyes. I could not see what it had to do with the birth of the babies, but then there were, it appeared, so many things which I did not know. I was beginning to understand that the more I knew, the more I realised how much I did not know. The wider my world became, the wider my thoughts roamed.

Maren looked down and wiped the tear from her face with her netela and then took some coffee, drinking it slowly while she composed herself. There was a bird in the Paradox tree which sang regardless of the tale which unfolded beneath the branches of the tree. It was a joyful but insistent song and it reminded me of the singing in the Temple. Beautiful, but constrained. When Achillea sang, she sang free, and every time she sang it was different. The bird and the TempleMaids sang with one repeating voice. Maren began her story again.

'I tended to Paradox for the next few hours. I gave her honey and herbs to stop the bleeding, but she was very weak and drifted in and out of consciousness. I became anxious about how I could get her better and well enough to move her to a place where there was water and better shelter and gave her sleeping herbs. As

I sat near her, I heard footsteps and the sound of horses. There was nothing I could do, so I remained where I was, hoping that they would move on. The OutRiders did not always have difficulty with ordinary people, and I hoped they needed to be somewhere else. But they came to the shelter and roughly tore it off leaving me blinking in the new light of the morning which had dawned without me seeing it. I begged them to allow me to cover Paradox with the cloth, but they pulled me away and roughly tied me to a tree.

'They tried to wake her roughly, but the herbs were strong, as I had known they would be. It was a kindness to her to give them to her; her babies were gone, and she was very fragile. They slapped her face and threw water on her. One of them casually pressed a hot ember from the fire on her foot, but she did not move. Only the slight rise and fall of her chest showed that she did still breathe. In all this time they ignored me, not speaking or looking at me at all. After some time, they talked amongst themselves, some gesturing towards her, and some towards me. I did not know what to do. I tried to tell them she was ailing, probably dying, and that she needed care, but they behaved as if I did not exist, talking over me in both our words and in that silent language they use amongst themselves.

'They began to move her in the cloth, one man at each end, carrying her to the horses. I cried out in concern for her but the guard who was with me slapped my mouth and told me to hold my tongue. I could only think that this must concern the father of the babies, that he must be an important man to have the OutRiders at his bidding, but they seemed more concerned with Paradox herself. They slung her in a cloth between the saddles of two horses and their riders mounted and they galloped away. It looked quite beautiful, you know. The horses ran in perfectly stepped time together, carrying Paradox on the cloth with the sun rising above them. It was the last beautiful sight I saw, and the last time I saw Paradox.

'They left behind one OutRider; he wore a helmet with a mesh over his face and he spoke only to ask me questions. Over and over again, he asked me questions, but from the beginning he only talked about one baby. He asked me where the baby was again and again. I never told him they were DoubleSouls. I hoped that the Mother Goddess would protect them and Hortensia until they came to a place of safety, for I knew the OutRiders would not go into the Temples and that the Priestesses would protect the babies once they were under protection of the Goddess. Besides, I really did not know where Hortensia had gone with them. There were Temples in every direction. I was young then and thought to outwit the OutRiders – and so I did I suppose, but at great cost.

At first, I told the OutRider that there was no baby, that I was but a poor servant girl and knew nothing of what my mistress had done in the tent with Paradox. But he became angry. I had not seen this anger before, Talla. It was not angry as the fire is angry; crackling and leaping, flaring brightly, but angry like a hot coal, so angry it looks dead, and you are taken in by its quietness and then it burns you harder than you ever thought possible. White ash rage it was. The angrier he got, the quieter he got, and the more purposeful his movement. I was still tied to the tree and he began to build a small fire in a clay pot, using kindling that lay around. He reached to a pouch on his belt and took out some small twigs and added them to the pot. I was terrified, sister Talla. I do not want you to think that because I can tell you this story so calmly that I was calm at that time too. It is only the passage of time which has calmed me, the passage of time and the music of the bees and my own company. I was very angry for many years, but it's burnt out now. He held my head over the pot, so the smoke filled my eyes. I closed them tight, but the smoke permeated everything; it trickled under my eyelids and into my nostrils. He held my head there for a short while, although it felt like a long time and then removed the pot and quenched it with dust, keeping his masked head to one side.

'My eyes made tears to add to the ones already falling through my pain and panic. The stinging was unbelievable, like a thousand bee stings. And all the time he did not say a word. I could not rub my eyes since I was tied so tightly to the tree. When I tried to open my eyes, they would not open at first, and then I felt that they had opened but it was still as if my eyes were shut, for I could see nothing but faint traces of dark and light. Only then did he speak to me, still in that angry quiet voice. He asked again about the baby and in the hope of saving myself, I told him there had been a baby girl but that she had been taken away by my mistress, I knew not where. I was so frightened, for I could see nothing, certainly not the OutRider's face but I thought that I felt him smile in a satisfied way. He told me that in any case, I would never be able to identify the baby if it had any distinguishing mark about it, nor would I be able to identify him since he had made me blind, and then he unsheathed his sword. I heard the scraping glide of metal against metal and I believed that my time was done, and that he would kill me, but he only cut the cloth ties which held me to the tree and then without another word mounted his horse and rode away. I could hear the jingling of the horse's armour as he rode away into the stillness. And then a new life was begun.'

Maren looked up at me, and even though she could not see, I felt her eyes on me. She smiled wryly. 'Sister

FLAMMEUS

Talla, I can feel that you are shocked by my tale. It happened long ago, three ages past now and I have grown from the young girl I was then to a woman of wisdom and knowledge. I have learned much from what has happened to me. I have learned about the casual cruelty of strangers but also about the kindness and compassion of others; as I stumbled around the forest, not knowing where I was going, but heading towards the vague light in the east, Anglossia, the woman who had showed us the way to Paradox found me. She too was in a terrible state, for the OutRiders had burnt down the village where she lived. The other dwellers had fled and left her behind, burnt and disfigured. It was this village here, where now you seek refuge, where we sought refuge ourselves. Slowly, Anglossia and I began to work together to rebuild a home. We used her eyes and my knowledge about honey to start again. The bees came to the flowers she planted, and we learned together how to tend the bees and then we could use the honey too. Of course, I could no longer bring babies into the world, being blind, and there was no likelihood of my having my own babies, nor of Anglossia having her own. But I could not see her scars and she did not care if I could see or not, so we lived together, contented for many years, keeping to ourselves and helping each other with the things we each could not do. We loved one another deeply and we were enough for each other. A couple of years ago, Ambar found us, and we were terrified, but he reassured us, and traded honey from us for the goods which we needed. Anglossia died last year. She had ailed constantly since they had burned the village, really, and life became too much for her.'

Maren bowed her head and the tears slipped from her sightless eyes as she spoke of her beloved partner, Anglossia. I did not know what to say to her. I had no training in listening or sympathy. When the Goddess took someone to her, it was no occasion for sadness. We had few chances to make good friends, for work was the essence of our lives and work was how we were judged. There was no encouragement of developing friendship or loyalty to anyone save the Goddess and so there were no close friendships in the Temple. If friendships did grow or become too strong, Maids were moved to other fields of work; Gardeners became Cleaners, Stitchers became Physics. Work was work and more important than friendship. Yet, still we hungered for small human kindnesses, despite them being discouraged. We learned to phrase things in work terms; complimenting one whom we liked on the quality of their cleaning or asking for their advice. In the first age of childhood, we ran and laughed and played and learned our lessons and in those first seven years our friendships ran their course as we played and disagreed with each other, pouting at the Priestesses Mothers as we pleaded our cause or explained our actions. Even then, though, praise only came for good work or good study or for devotion to the Goddess. No one ever said to me that they cared for me, or loved me for who I was, only for what I did.

Now, witnessing Maren's renewed grief over the loss of her companion, I felt the warmth from the little bee necklace and a pity that I had not had this kind of closeness to another person. The only close bond I had been encouraged to feel was between myself and the Goddess. I had been told that no other relationship was important, and yet that was not true. So much of what I had been presented with now seemed to be untrue, or at least a matter of choice rather than fact. Perhaps I was incapable of being a real friend to someone because I had not learned how to be a friend when I was a child.

I reached out my hand towards Maren and enclosed hers in mine. I remembered holding hands in the First

Age, and the feel of another's hand was comforting now, to me, even though I was meant to be the one who was comforting the other. We sat quietly for some minutes, and then Maren composed herself, busying her hands with tidying the coffee beakers, deft despite her lack of sight. I asked her if there were any other small tasks that I could do for her while I was with her. I wanted to ask her a lot of questions about the babies, and the rest of her story but I had only just met her, and I needed to do some thinking of my own. Maren too, appeared to need space around her and so I took my leave of her, and wandered back down the path towards the dwellings. Like other dwellings in our land, they were highly domed and thatched with straw that was now grey and faded from the sun. The mud walls were coated in Paradox oil, and I thought about the young mother with the DoubleSoul babies who had said her name was Paradox, like the princess.

I wondered why she had chosen that name. The Paradox tree was grown everywhere, and it was said that the Goddess herself had planted the first Paradox tree. The wood was strong, the nuts were crushed to make the Paradox oil, which was used for the waterproofing of homes and, of course, in cooking too. The trees themselves were large and provided excellent dense shade from the hot sun. The fruits were sharp but tasty, hanging like pendulous, green plums. It truly was a miraculous tree; Ashkana said 'Be like the Paradox Tree; be useful in every part'. As little ones we used to play with the nuts and make bouncing balls out of the tree sap. I found myself walking towards the Paradox tree at the end of the path, suddenly fascinated by this tree which I had taken for granted all my life, thinking anew about how amazing it was that the Goddess had provided such a useful tree to us. I remembered that the Physics also used Paradox leaves and oil in making medicines as well as in salves for the skin and the hair, but I had last worked in Physic a long time ago, before I chose my forward path, and had no real knowledge of it. Perhaps there might be someone with more knowledge than me. I resolved to speak to Gladia about it. I reasoned that if anyone on the Outer would know about these things, it would probably be Gladia; she seemed to know about most things that happened in the world. And if not Gladia, then Benakiell, who knew as much, but about different matters. At the Temple it seemed right that we each had our own job and learned only the things relating to it. And here, in the Outer, too, men and women had their different and special jobs. But I wanted to know everything and try everything.

CHAPTER 21

When I got back, Gladia was sitting quietly under the Paradox tree. I felt envious of her; perhaps it was her age, but she seemed to absorb the difficulties she faced and not let them bother her. All of the obstacles I faced in this world made me so full of rage – at other people, at the Temple, the lies I had been told, the way in which everyone sought to control me and my actions – and yet here was Gladia, who had suffered terrible pain at the hands of the OutRiders, and was only just recovering, able to let it go, and sit peacefully. I resolved to try to learn from her. My mind was always busy, always curious, always searching. Perhaps if I were not so busy, my mind could be open to the different possibilities and explanations there were for the many questions that swam in my mind like minnows in the margin of a stream.

Gladia looked up as I approached her and smiled brightly at me. 'Did you enjoy your time with Maren? I should get to know her too, since we don't know how long we will be here.' She looked wistful for a moment, doubtless thinking of her cosy dwelling back in Mellia, and wondering how long it might be before she could return to her quiet life of embroidery and village chatter. I told Gladia some of what Maren had told me, glossing over the descriptions of torture, since Gladia had so recently been through a similar ordeal. I explained that she had been blinded to stop her from being able to identify the child. Gladia tutted her way through the story of Paradox, and at the end of it, I asked her if she thought Maren's blurred sight might indeed be permanent or if there might be a Physic who could make a remedy to bring back her sight. She looked at me, her eyes opening wide as she understood what I was asking. If we could restore Maren's eyesight, we could help her to identify the baby, the purported heir to the Queen who might be found and could stand as witness. She frowned. 'What about asking Tarik? He knows about the herbs of healing. Mostly it's the wounds of battle, of course, but even so...' I wasn't sure about trusting them.

'Could you ask him when he next poultices your wounds? Without telling him they are for Maren? I have an idea I would like to try, before he gets too involved, just in case it doesn't work.' Gladia was such an open person that she was surprised by my subterfuge but, in the end, she agreed to ask Tarik some questions about which herbs could be used to draw infections in wounds, and which could be used to cleanse. Then I went in search of further information.

Benakiell was peeling the bark of a fresh, slender pole. He could not seem to stop himself from wanting to make things all the time. He would have been a good TempleMaid I thought to myself and the thought of Benakiell in a drabcoat made me smile.

'You look cheerful, sister Talla,' he remarked, putting down his knife and smiling back at me. 'Do you have a question for me? You always have a very determined look on your face when you are trying to solve a puzzle.'

I didn't like the idea of other people being able to surmise what I was going to do just from observing me, and I resolved to try to develop more of a blank face, such as that borne so well by Ambar.

'I wanted to ask you about the Paradox tree. It seems to have so many uses in our lives. I know you use it in making dwellings,' I saw Benakiell begin to frown, and knew that he intended to head me off as he did not wish me to hear any details of dwelling making which were considered a strictly male occupation and thus not open to discussion or questioning. 'But I don't need to know about that at all. I was just interested in how it was used in Physic; what kinds of ointments it was used in. I was interested in making some ointments with my honey, for Gladia,' I continued hastily.

Benakiell looked at me sharply, but then smiled at me. 'You are an eager learner, Talla. Are the bees not enough for you, along with all the habits and traditions of the Outer? You must know some of the ways we use the Paradox tree for treatment though. Everyone knows the simple remedies.'

'Remember that I am not long in the Outer, Benakiell,' I reminded him. 'The Temple was even more strict than the Outer when it came to keeping our work separated. Ashkana said that only with complete concentration on one job could we give of the best within us. I fear she would not approve of me.' I finished, smiling up at him. He chuckled and acknowledged that I had made a good case for him to share his knowledge with me. I hoped he would tell me something worthwhile to use for Maren's poor eyes. I knew it had been many years since she could see clearly but helping her to see was the only way I could think of to be absolutely sure of the identity of the future Queen. I thought it could be me, and what she might see when she saw me, and how I could be identified. There was of course no reason why it should be me, but too many parts of the story seemed to fit together, like water melting into sand. And I had the brooch which I had been told my mother had pinned to my covering, and Maren had talked about the mother pinning something to one of the baby's cloths. I was consumed with curiosity and fascination. I settled down beside Benakiell on the hard mud veranda of the hut where he was working.

'Well,' he began, 'I can only tell you what I have learned myself. It would take a master Physic to know everything that can be made from the blessed Paradox tree, but one of the reasons that we always grow them around our villages is because they are so useful. We can use them in all aspects of our lives and work – I use it myself, as you said, in making dwellings, but you asked about physic. If only my wife Velosia were still here; she was such a wise Physic. But I will tell you what I know, nevertheless; who knows, perhaps your idea of making more salves and tinctures with your honey would be a good one, for it sweetens everything. You will know that Paradox butter can be used for a whole host of ills, from keeping your skin soft – which I know all you ladies like to do.' He looked at me, his eyes twinkling, and I realised this was something else I did not know. In the Temple, Paradox butter was only used for muscle and joint pains and skin complaints in the elderly Priestesses, and not for beautification.

Benakiell continued smoothly, 'The main treatments are made from the leaves, the roots and the bark. You can use the fruit and the flowers and the sap, but not for medication. If you infuse the leaves, you can use it for cleansing a wound, or as a tea for treating stomach-ache. You can use the leaves, as you know, for making soapballs; you just mix the leaf tea with some of the Paradox butter and some beeswax. You use the roots for toothtwigs, to clean the teeth. You can boil the roots and grind them to a paste to treat loose bowels, and the OutRiders use the paste for saddle sores on their horses, I believe – I think that's what Ambar said, anyway. What else...' So far, he had not mentioned anything about eyes, but I did not want to direct him. I hoped there might be more to say, otherwise we would be relying on Tarik's knowledge. I preferred not to rely on one person's word. As Ashkana said, 'One worker does not make a job.'

I waited patiently, and Benakiell continued, 'Now the bark of the Paradox tree can be used in a few different ways. You need to cut it very fine and then steep it in hot water – Velosia used to soak it for over a night and a day; she swore it made the very finest infusion – then you can use it to treat sore skin, or to bathe a woman in childbirth, or to bathe an infected wound. You can also use it to bathe the eyes, especially if you are attacked by a Spitsnake, or anything else that makes the eye milky. I really can't remember any more; will that satisfy your curiosity for now, for I need to return to my work?' Benakiell stood up to signify that the conversation was at an end, but I didn't mind, for I had learned something of worth here. Now I needed to 'Put together the work of many, to perfect the work of one,' as Ashkana had said. The longer I was away from the Temple, the more I pondered on those Aphorisms of Ashkana which had been taught to us as small children who barely understood what they meant, until we could chant them all off by heart.

I could only speak to Gladia the next day to find out if she had managed to discover anything more from Tarik; there just seemed to be no time in which we could talk alone. When I finally got her alone, I wanted to know if she had found anything out, but she insisted on talking first about this and that, the tastiness of the flatbreads and honey we had eaten for breakfast that morning, the possibility of the rains arriving soon, the question of when we might return to Mellia and her dear home. It was like she was blowing on the fire of rage in my mind, determined to infuriate me by prattling on, but I urged myself to remain patient and to listen to her carefully, having resolved only the previous day to be more like her. Eventually, I could restrain myself no longer, and asked her if she had found out anything about which other plants were used by Tarik in his wound physic.

'Ah yes, I did ask Tarik about what he used in some of his dressings; that one he uses for my wounds is excellent, and the one for my bruises which have nearly faded away.'

'Which flowers does he use then?' I burst in, impatient and wanting to test out my idea. Truth be told, I was impatient about everything now. Nothing was settled, everything was up in the air and I just wanted to go forward with a plan without all the hiding and the shadows. If I could just fix on something that I wanted to do and follow it through, I would be happier. I was tired of hiding in this deserted village with other people who were hiding, all governed by what we had been told by Ambar and Tarik. Gladia and Benakiell were happy to trust them, as was Achillea, and Ashtun just wanted to become them, but I felt more ambivalent. When I first met Ambar, I found him very charming and attractive, and I thought he liked me as a person. Now I knew more about what he was looking for, I couldn't help wondering about his motives in protecting us and in keeping us in this isolated village and about whether somehow he already knew who I was, and that was why he had traded the little bee necklace with me.

I had so many more questions than answers and the many levels of the story that was unfolding kept tangling with each other so that I did not know where the beginning of the story was nor where it might end. Focusing on doing something that I could make a difference with, helping Maren with her smeared and filmy eyes was comforting. If I could untangle the strands of her story, maybe they would lead me to being able to untangle some of the other strands of the story too. It was like Gladia's gourd of embroidery threads, which were frequently tipped out in a messy ball. I found it soothing to sort them out and reorder them. Gladia was telling me the name of the flowers Ambar used, and I had not heard any of them. I asked her to say the names again and excused my inattention by pretending that I did not know the common names for them, since we used other ones in the Temple. Subterfuge was becoming more normal to me now.

Gladia told me that the flower that Tarik used for cleaning away the sweet, sticky infections in wounds was a small insignificant flower, usually purple and white. It could be made into a strong infusion by crushing it and steeping it in a covered earthenware pot for a week. The water had to only just cover the flowers so that it would be strong enough to use at the end of the week. I asked Gladia if she had seen it growing around the settlement, and she confessed she hadn't, but added cheerily that she had not been looking for it, and then asked me what my interest in it was. Gladia was much more astute than she appeared, and once again she had spotted me when I was trying to be unobtrusive. She was such a good reader of people. This was something I need to practice more; the little bee could bring me channels of empathy when I wore it, but it was more of a direct link to a person's emotions. Gladia, on the other hand, just seemed to know when people's behaviour was a little different to normal. I hoped that she would just think that it was because I had been brought up in the Temple and didn't know very much. I told her this, vaguely, and she seemed to accept it and suggested I should ask Achillea to show me some Eyebright flowers. I almost laughed when she told me the name of the plant; I could have worked out what it did just by knowing the name of it! I smiled and told her I would do that and would call on Achillea and suggest a walk.

Achillea was sitting on a flat rock watching Ashtun, who had persuaded Ambar and Tarik to teach him how to use a bow and arrow. They had set up a target on a tree, made of straw, and were firing arrows into it. Ambar and Tarik hit the target every time right in the middle, but Ashtun was much more inaccurate, hitting the edge of the target, the centre of the target and the surrounding trees with equal chance. Achillea laughed merrily whenever he missed the mark, but I could see that he was irritated by her mirth. I could understand both their viewpoints; he was desperate to improve his skills, to work hard at them and Achillea finding it funny was distracting him and making him feel aggravated. Achillea, on the other hand, was trying to lighten the seriousness of his attitude and trying to stop him from feeling so aware of his own lack of skill. Ambar and Tarik were also trying to take it seriously, and I wondered why they would invest all this effort into teaching a man of the Outer to use a fighting bow and arrow – ordinarily reserved for OutRiders – and if they were preparing him for our defence if we were raided by OutRiders again. I left this to boil in my mind for a while and smiled and waved to Achillea and asked her if she would like a walk out to the beehives near Maren's hut. She readily acceded, and we walked off, leaving the men seriously focused on their lesson.

As we walked along, I asked Achillea why Ashtun was learning to use the bow, and if she thought he would master it. 'Ash has always wanted to learn the bow,' she told me. 'In fact, I think if it were his choice, there is much about being an OutRider that he would like to master, although he is not mean and nasty like they are. He is very protective and likes to make people feel safe, especially me. He finds our life in Mellia very boring, and although he works with Benakiell and owes him much for giving him a job, he is not excited by making dwellings for the rest of his life.' She smiled rather ruefully. 'I am perfectly happy in Mellia, with visits to Sanguinea, I think. But yes, I think he will learn to do it well. He is already improving despite me laughing at him, and now I have gone away he will improve even more.'

Once again, I was surprised by Achillea's insight into people's behaviour. It seemed to me that she could accept the person she was without that relentless voice inside her head that was inside mine, that voice which constantly exhorted me to get better, to improve, to learn more, to do more. Achillea understood more about people than I did, and, for all her fluffy and light exterior, she was self-aware in a realistic way. The Outer was so difficult to navigate for one such as me, who had been raised in the closed, structured life of the Temple, with its simple but rigid rules, and its lack of emphasis on our feelings, training us instead to give of ourselves in service. And yet, from my own experiences, at least, it seemed we all had these feelings inside us; they just needed to be awakened.

As we neared Maren's dwelling, I told Achillea a little of her story; not all the details, but I told her of her previous career and of how she came to lose her sight after the birth of the babies. Achillea was fascinated and wanted to know more immediately, firing questions at me. She was intensely curious about the birth and about the job that Maren had been doing. When I told her of my plan to try to make a salve to ease Maren's eyesight, she clapped her hands. 'Oh Talla, what a kind thing to do for her!' and I felt immediately guilty for, truth be told, I really wanted Maren to be able to see for my own reasons. For some time now, I had become convinced that I was the TempleMaid whom the OutRiders wanted to find, the child of the Queen's daughter. Maren's story had simultaneously upset me and sparked my interest. I had the brooch, and she had described Paradox pinning something meaningful on to the blanket of one of the babies and had also told me that she could identify the first born of the DoubleSouls, the one who would take over as Queen.

When I thought about the possibility that I could be the next Queen of our land, it almost took my breath away. How would I, an unknown Temple Maid become a Queen? And why had Paradox had to flee? And why were the OutRiders looking for me so diligently? Unlike Ashtun, I had no real admiration for the OutRiders, although I had to admit that their horses and their armour were impressive. I could only believe that they wanted to do me harm and prevent me from claiming the throne. I almost laughed aloud at the way my mind was running along such dramatic lines, but it gave me something to think about, and I was sure that if I could clear Maren's eyesight enough, she would be able to look at my brooch, still hidden in my underpocket and identify me as the child they searched for or not, for she had not mentioned anything more specific that could identify the first born child. She had been insistent that she was the only one who could identify her, but the brooch could have been associated with any baby and then Maren's identification would be useless. There was also the matter of the second child, my sister. I was convinced that this child must be dead by now, for surely I would know if there were a sister of mine alive in the world. They were searching for me by name. I knew by now that the OutRiders did collect the Maids who left the Temple, so it could just be that they were unusually diligent in my case, but I was sure that there was more to it. I had a sudden urge to confide in Achillea, longing to share all my thoughts with another person, to stop me from feeling so alone, but I bit my tongue and instead told her of the flowers for which we were searching. Straight away, she knew the flowers which Gladia had told me about and told me they often grew with other flowers favoured by the bees.

We walked along the path a little way from Maren's dwelling and across towards the fields. We could see her sitting under the Paradox tree in the shade but carried on towards the flowers. I wondered if her companion, Anglossia, had been responsible for laying out these areas full for flowers for the bees. When she was alive, she had acted as Maren's eyes, and I pondered again on how frustrating it must feel to be Maren, and the sadness she had experienced in her life. This time I resolved to clear her milky eyes not for my own reasons, but for her, so that she could live her life more easily and happily. Suddenly feeling happier myself, I looked again at the flowers, storing away the ideas in my mind, to try out myself for my own bees.

There were four square beds of flowers, standing proud from the red dirt, with stones encircling them to prevent the soil from being washed or blown away. In the centre of each bed was a small flowering tree; two were jasmine flowers and the other two were coffee trees, all of them smothered in fragrant white flowers. Surrounding them were varied clumps of other flowers; roses with white and yellow flowers, lavender, big pink balls of tiny flowers, small fluffy purple flowers and large yellow flowers with flimsy, delicate petals. Whoever had planted these flowers had observed their bees well for they were all crawling with bees, busily working. Achillea looked around for the flowers that Gladia had told me about and found some at the front of one of the beds. They were numerous but insignificant, small and white with a purple throat, and I was relieved that I had Achillea with me, for I would not have had her confidence. In the Temple, when we were in our Second Age of Childhood, we were taught the common names of the plants we grew in the Temple grounds, and of the plants which provided the scents we dedicated daily to the Goddess, but beyond that, it was only those who had been put to work in the physic of the Temple who knew any more. It seemed such a waste to me that there was all this knowledge out here in the Outer world and that the Temple did not make more use of it, teaching the Maids more and more so they could do more and more in the service of the Goddess. In the Outer, there did not seem to be much formal teaching of youngsters, but they all knew things that were important for life and living; ways to look after themselves and how to talk to others – all things in which I felt woefully inadequate.

'Come on, Talla,' urged Achillea, placing a large handful of the flowers in my basket, 'help me pick some more!' We continued to pick the flowers, listening to the lazy sound of the bees on the other flowers until I judged we had picked enough to fit into a large gourd.

'Shall we go and tell Maren now?' asked Achillea, excitedly, looking forward to delivering good news to this woman whom she scarcely knew but felt so much for. I guessed that in the time since her mother's death, Achillea had depended on others very much but missed having someone to care for herself. I pondered on the right time to tell Maren of my plan but could not find a good enough reason for Achillea not to tell her about it, so we walked back to her dwelling and, as we got close, Achillea raised her voice to give Maren some warning of our approach.

Maren seemed happy to see us and showed us the honeycombs she had harvested earlier. They contained very pale honey, which Benakiell had told me was very much in demand, as it was purer and sweeter than any other honey. I asked her if I could have a little of the beeswax from the honeycomb and the honey that surrounded it, and explained what I hoped to do – to make the salve out of the honey and the eyebright water and the Paradox tea that might cleanse her eyes and allow her to see clearly for the first time in over twenty years. Maren smiled rather sadly as Achillea joined in with the explanation excitedly and said 'I do not hold out much hope of this working for me. I have tried almost every kind of salve, tincture and unguent to try to heal my eyes, but the smoke of that tree will not loosen its grip on me. They truly did not want me to see again in case I found the child.' Achillea's face fell, but I asked Maren if she had, in all those attempts, ever tried anything of the sort that I had planned, and she confessed she had not. She agreed that she would try our mixture when we had made it, and we left, feeling optimistic.

As soon as we returned, I put the eyebright flowers into a large gourd and weighted them down with a large flat pebble and then covered them with water mixed with a little white honey. They would need to be steeped for at least a day before I could use them on Maren, so once that was done, Achillea and I went back out again in search of a Paradox tree to take some bark from. That was easily achieved since there were several Paradox trees around the village, and we then returned to the dwelling and put the bark in a small earthenware pot and poured boiling water over it and covered it up. We had just finished doing that when Gladia arrived, huffing and puffing from the effort of carrying a basket of beans up from the gardens, and we made coffee as I told her about our efforts in the salve making. She smiled at us, a little patronisingly, and said that she was glad we were amusing ourselves in little games whilst the rest of them were working on the important jobs in life, such as finding food for us to eat. Achillea laughed merrily, but I felt guilty for not working harder. I had been raised by the Temple to see my worth in my work, and now felt useless. Even though I knew that I was trying to help Maren, a voice whispered sourly in my ear that I was really doing it for my own selfish reasons. To my surprise, Gladia's face also crumpled into a grin, and she patted my hand and told me not to take her words to heart, for it was but a joke. Something else to try to understand; when people were being serious and when they wanted to laugh. Laughing was not normal to me; the little ones in the first and second ages of childhood could laugh and giggle with impunity, but by the Third Age, we were taught by the Priestesses to swallow our laughter and gradually reduce it until by the time we reached adulthood it was no longer instinctive and was not heard around the Temple. Yet, when I heard others laughing here in the Outer, it lightened my spirit, and on the occasions when my own mouth twitched, and I had chuckled at something Achillea had said or done, I could feel my spirits rise too. It was a real gift this, like the gift of the Empath, this ability to make others smile and laugh.

CHAPTER 22

Two days later, I woke up to a bright dawn, and wandered outside the dwelling, to sit in quietude. The sky was a light, bright blue, tinged at the edges with orange, like the petals of the flowers in the garden. There was a faint scent of dew on the dust, and the doves spoke soothingly to one another in the branches of the Paradox tree. The bees were already out and about, searching for the newly opened flowers that were full of nectar for them. At my feet a small ant busily moved along the fine, sandy dust, scurrying this way and that, waving its feelers in its constant search for food. It moved towards a conical depression in the dust, and I watched it idly. As it reached the edge of the pit, its legs disturbed some fine grains of sand, and it lost its grip and tumbled to the bottom. I leaned forward to see what might happen next, and to my surprise, saw two small claws quickly snap out of the sand and grab it, dragging it under. After a few small movements under the sand, the cone returned to how it had been; the ant was gone, as was its tiny predator. I sat back, surprised by this swift interaction and, as I looked up, saw that Ambar was standing there, watching me. He smiled at me, and, remembering how it lifted the spirits, I smiled back at him, even though I was a little disconcerted to see him there, watching me.

'You have found an antlion!' he chuckled, his eyes taking on a faraway look. 'I remember playing with those as a boy in the OutFort.' It was the first time he had referred to his childhood, as far as I could recall. I wanted to ask him lots of questions about what life had been like in the OutFort, if it was like it was for we Maids in the Temple, but I bit my tongue, for he had already begun to speak again, as he squatted down in the dust next to me. He was very close to me, and I could feel the heat from his body and his breath on my arm as he spoke. 'Do you know what to do with them? Did you perhaps play with them too when you were a girl?' I confessed that I did not and couldn't recall ever seeing them before. Probably they had been there, but I had never interacted with them.

Ambar cast about, seemingly searching for something and finally plucked a small stalk of grass with a feathery top. He settled down, right next to me, and I tried to discreetly squirm away from him. I was not accustomed to people sitting so closely, especially men, although I had seen Achillea and Ashtun sitting very close to one another. Ambar seemed unruffled by my moving away and leaned over towards the dip in the sand where the creature he called an antlion lived. He began to tickle the edge of the cone with the grass, causing the sand to start trickling down into it. I leaned forward, unable to resist my curiosity, and watched as there was a twitch at the bottom of the hole. He tickled the sand again and once again there was a movement. Quickly he scooped his hand into the dust of the dip and brought his fist back up triumphantly.

'Hold out your hand,' he commanded me. I tentatively stretched out my hand, in a shallow cup shape, and he poured the sand quickly into my palm. I closed my hand around it and felt a scrabbling tickle in my palm, under the sand. I carefully opened up my fingers and brushed the sand away. There in the middle of my hand was a small, grey beetle with those same large jaws or claws I had seen before. It was furiously spinning around, trying to burrow into my hand. It tickled my hand and its dogged refusal to stop trying to bury itself down made me laugh again, and Ambar joined me, as I gently poured the creature back into the sand and watched it shuffle itself quickly away.

'We learned so much from watching animals like this as youngsters,' said Ambar, still laughing. 'Their fierce unwilling to give up taught me a lot about persevering even when the task ahead seems impossible. Who knows, if you left it in your hand for long enough, it might eventually get through! Just because someone else sees your task as impossible does not mean you should be defeated.'

I was struck by his words and contemplated what I had learned from the bees that I tended both here and in Mellia. They worked together for one common goal, each contributing a small part, with no care for being recognised as the best. They had reinforced the importance of work; of being busy and working hard. They hummed and danced their way through their daily tasks, taking joy from each flower they visited, even though they might visit many in one day. They reserved their stings for when they were in real danger, only becoming angry when they felt that they or their task was truly threatened. I could certainly learn from them, just as I could learn from the antlion. I was about to tell Ambar this when Tarik ran up the path towards us, startling me. He remained standing, the risen sun behind him glaring all around him so that it looked like he was glowing, and made urgent movements with his hands, speaking in the silent language. His fingers flew over one another, and his chest heaved from the effort of running. Ambar rose suddenly from where he was sitting, and said quickly, 'We need to go and help one who is in trouble. Where is Ashtun? We will take him with us!' With that, he and Tarik ran off down the path towards the place where the horses were waiting.

I felt abandoned. I had been enjoying the warmth between myself and Ambar, and had felt myself softening towards him, feeling his charm and easy-going manner. I had even been on the verge of confiding in him about the potion I was going to try on Maren and the reasons why. In my mind, I could imagine myself even telling him that I thought it could be me who was the Queen for whom he sought. Now I felt irritated and restless by his abrupt departure and by the overt way in which he and Tarik used their sign language when they did not want us to know what they spoke of. The Priestesses used to use long, difficult words to each other if they did not want us to know what they were saying, when we were young children. It felt as if Ambar had judged us as being not clever enough or trustworthy enough to speak to about certain subjects, and as the ember of rage began once more to glow inside my mind, I was pleased that I had not disclosed anything further after all. I got up and went to check on the Paradox bark which was steeping in the gourd, and the Eyebright flowers in theirs. The liquid surrounding the bark was now a rich, orangey brown colour, and there were small bubbles rising to the surface, which I knew meant that it was ready, so I took out the bark and put the pot to one side. The eyebright flowers had turned into a mush under the stone, and some of the liquid had been soaked up, but nevertheless there was a good amount of the eyebright and honey solution, which was a light, cloudy green in colour. I picked up the two gourds and went in search of Achillea.

Arriving at her dwelling, I could hear her singing from the path, and went to the other side of the dwelling where I found her, washing her netela, and singing as she worked. In that moment, she reminded me not of an owl as she usually did, but of the bees, humming joyfully while they worked. She stopped when she saw me and cheerfully called out her greeting, wringing out the netela as I arrived. I showed her the two solutions and asked her what she thought we should do next.

FLAMMEUS

'I think we need to make them stronger; they look very weak,' she said doubtfully. 'Why not boil them for a little while to make them stronger, like we do to make the coffee stronger?' It was a good idea and I was a little irritated that it had been Achillea who had thought of it, but I agreed, and we poured the two together into a pot and set it over the fire. We watched it carefully as it reduced until it was around a quarter of the volume it had originally been, and the colour was a rich dark brown. We then rather dubiously added the white honey and beeswax that Maren had given to us and stirred it in until it had melted through the liquid and then left it to cool. While we were waiting, I asked Achillea if she knew where Ambar, Tarik and Ashtun had gone. She hadn't even realised that Ashtun had gone anywhere, let alone with the OutRiders, and was quite alarmed when I told her that they had ridden off quickly on some secret adventure, and that all I knew about it was that someone else was in trouble and needed their help. She began to worry about Ashtun immediately, and I tried to reassure her, whilst privately thinking that it was unlikely they would have taken him with them to any dangerous event, having seen his efforts with the bow a few days before. I was curious about why Ambar and Tarik were putting so much effort into persuading Ashtun that he was one of them, one of their group, and a little scornful of how quickly he had lost his inhibitions about them and become close to them.

It seemed to me that people all wanted to belong to some group or other and that all the world loved to divide itself up into groups; Maids and OutRiders, Dwelling Makers and Birthmothers, adults and children, men and women, rulers and ruled. One could be a member of many separate groups and each of them would lay claim to your allegiance. But where should one's highest loyalty lie? I, myself, could lay claim to a few different groups; Maid, woman and Beeguard, and I intended to try to learn many other skills; perhaps even riding a horse although it was supposedly forbidden to me. I realised that I was also a member of two other groups; the Inner (as I thought of those of us who were not of the Outer – those of the Temple and the OutFort) and now also the Outer, since I could not return to the Temple. Then, I realised that Achillea was telling me something and I had no idea what she was saying, absorbed as I was in my musing.

'And Benakiell tells me that it is me who is always dreaming!' she exclaimed, in exasperation. I shook myself and focused on Achillea, who was showing me that the salve had set in the little gourd in which we had poured it. She held it under my nose for me to sniff and showed me how well it had set. Achillea was excited by our ostensible success, but I knew that success would only be real if the salve had any real effect on Maren's eyesight, and cleared up the film of fog on her eyes which had been there all these years. It seemed unlikely that my idea for curing her eyesight might work, when she had tried so many different remedies already. However, it was worth trying, and, as Ashkana told us, 'Some work is completed after a brief time, and some work requires constant effort. Until we try, we do not know.' Achillea was eager to take the salve to Maren for her to try, so, persuaded by her enthusiasm, I picked up the gourd and tied it to my waist string and we set off back to see Maren, feeling hopeful.

There were dark clouds in the sky, threatening rain. It was hot, heavy and ominous. The rains always came after the dry, hot season and the plants were all thirsty and ready for the soil to be replenished. We had only had a few brief, heavy downpours so far, which had quickly sunk into the red earth and vanished. We had seen the dark curtains of rain clouds being pulled across the plains to the east but, somehow, they always seemed to rain themselves out before they reached us. I hoped that this time they might come to us here. In the Temple, there had always been extra prayers and exhortations to the Goddess to feed her children by bringing the rain. When we were in the First Age, the Priestesses who cared for us used to tell us that the rain was the tears of the Goddess as she wept over us, her unruly children. I remember asking the Priestesses why we wished for the rain, when it meant making the Goddess sad. As usual, when they had no answer for my impudent questions, they sent me away to work pulling out weeds or scrubbing burnt pans, my questions buzzing in my mind, trying to understand what the truth really was. I pointed the clouds out to Achillea, asking her if she thought it might rain today. She wiped her netela over her forehead, wiping away the droplets of sweat which had beaded there like dew, and replied that she longed for the rain to cool us all down and that perhaps we should sing to make it rain. I did not like to sing anything when Achillea sang, for her voice was so sweet that it made me feel self-conscious. In any case I could not sing like she could, I could only chant the rhythms and cadences of the Temple which I found pleasing and soothing, like the hum of the bees. I was content to listen to Achillea singing as we walked along to Maren's dwelling.

> 'Come, rain, come to us, hear our pleas;
> Soak into the earth and feed the trees.
> Join to the water of the river and the lake;
> Spill your clouds for the Goddess' sake.'

The wind got up suddenly, whipping round and bending the long stalks of dry grass that remained from the hot season, and whirling the red dust off the path so it stung against our arms. We both laughed, struck by the timing, and continued to Maren's home. We called out as we approached her dwelling and she raised her hand to us in greeting. I told her that we had made the salve for her eyes and she smiled wryly.

'I do hope that you will not be too disappointed when it does not work,' she said, and I was struck by her thinking of my disappointment instead of her own. Perhaps she had just become so accustomed to her smeared vision and to remedy after remedy failing. I thought of how each time she must have had her hopes raised, only to realise that it had not worked, and, eventually, experience had taught her that the result would almost certainly be that her eyesight remained unchanged. For all that the people of the Outer came to the Temple filled with hope that the Goddess would fulfil their dreams, give them a child or a harvest or a new husband, Ashkana made it clear that hope was not an emotion in which she had much faith, preferring as she did to trust in work. 'Hope will not get a job done,' was a popularly snapped line by the Priestesses when some Maid or other muttered about hoping the work would be done soon.

Achillea described the salve to Maren, telling her excitedly what we had put in it and it made me smile wryly to hear her join her name to mine as if we had both come up with the idea when it had all come from me. Then I recalled that it had actually been her idea to concentrate the solutions down and make them into a salve and I let go of my need for recognition. Maren asked how she should use the salve, and I paused, not quite knowing what to say, since I had not thought this far ahead. It was important to get the salve into the eye, but I knew that having something that waxy in the eye would smear it even further too. What if I made her very limited eyesight even worse? To my surprise, Achillea told her very simply to take some of the salve on her fingertip and to rub it along her eyelids and along the line of her eyelashes until it held her eye shut. Maren obediently put her finger in the salve and did as she had been directed, murmuring that the salve at least smelled nice and was so creamy that it might take away her wrinkles if nothing else! We all chuckled together, and then I hung the small gourd on one of the pegs on Maren's dwelling wall so that she could find it easily as she felt her way around. She offered us coffee, but it was starting to get windier, and we thought that the rain might come down heavily, so we took our leave and hurried back along the path to the dwelling, trying to get there before we were soaked.

We could smell it in the air; the slaking of the dust and the peculiarly delicious anticipation it brought with it. We picked up our robes and ran along as the first few fat drops began to fall, pretending to run to get out of it, but really just exhilarating in it finally falling. Amidst the rain and the kicked-up dust, the winged ants rose up as if from nowhere and added their frantic bodies to the stirred-up air. The bees were nowhere to be seen, preferring to stay in the warmth and sweetness of their hive, but the birds which ate the insects had emerged, even though the rain was heavy and pounding down. They stayed close to the ground, hopping between the raindrops and gorging on the ants before they could fly off into the rain laden sky. We reached the dwelling and collapsed wet but full of the energy of the rain, and happy to be using the salve on Maren. I felt grateful for Achillea, that she chose to spend her time with me and that she lent me her sunny personality and her placid nature. When I had first met her, I had dismissed her as lazy and self-indulgent, coming as I did from the Temple, where judgement rested on one's inclination to work. I was learning slowly that there were more important things in life, although I still believed that work was the way in which we found our place in the world. I was turning these thoughts over in my head as Achillea hung her sodden netela up to dry out and trying to come up with the right words to use to express my gratitude for her companionship when down the path came Ashtun, running fast, streaked with mud and what looked like blood, calling for us.

He was panting for breath, steaming in his robes in the warm wet air. On his back there was a bow, and casually to his side was a quiver of arrows. He looked for all the world like Ambar, wearing the OutRider armour we had previously stripped from the dead OutRiders who had so violated Gladia. I had never seen him in this armour before, and I was taken aback by the appearance of one who I knew had never been an OutRider wearing their trappings with such ease and so little care. Achillea, too, stood with her mouth open, looking at him as if she did not know him, or as if she had seen a phantom. We both opened our mouths to start asking questions, our mood altered from our previous light-heartedness, but he cut us off brusquely.

'There is no time for your questions now! You must come with me. Ambar needs you to be there, both of you, for there is one who has grave need of you. Bring your physic, bring your honey, come now!' His tone was peremptory, and we were both shocked into silence by his high-handed attitude towards us and quickly gathered the gourds and hurried after him. He did not pay any attention to Achillea's wide eyed and questioning look but strode in front of us, blood trickling down his leg from a scratch on his calf. The raindrops mixed with it and smeared his legs even further. The mud splattered up from the path as we hurried along it and soon the hems of our robes were a deep brownish-red colour, the same colour as the mud and the blood on Ashtun's leg. He led us to the dwelling where Ambar and Tarik stayed and pushed aside the reed screen at the doorway.

THE FIRE
CHAPTER 23

Ambar sat cross legged against one wall; he was grazed and muddy too. Tarik sat next to what appeared to be a large bundle of rags on the mat, offering it water. When they saw we had arrived, they both came to the door hastily and motioned us out again. Ashtun walked off and sat against the wall, scrubbing at his legs with a rag, and Tarik followed him with one of his gourds of salves, urging it on him to soothe the wound on his leg. After we had been hurried here so urgently by Ashtun, I could not understand why we had been instantly ushered out of the dwelling, but Ambar began to speak, quieting our questions. He had a way of speaking which made you want to listen, and to be quiet; a quality I found both admirable and annoying.

'We need you to tend the wounded woman we have brought back. She is ailing in both body and mind. We had to rescue her from a bitter attack. She will not let a man tend to her, or even touch her and cannot speak to us. We need to question her; she has come from the Queen's OutFort and she may have valuable information for us regarding the Queen and the hunt for the heir,' Ambar said, urgently.

I stared at him. The questions as usual swam to the top of my mind; fish questing for crumbs scattered on the surface of my thoughts. Why was she wounded? Who had wounded her? Why could a man not tend to her? Why did Ambar and Tarik need to speak with her so urgently? And, most importantly, why was there a woman at the OutFort when they were reserved for the male OutRiders, just as there were no men in the

Temple which was reserved for Maids and Priestesses? And why, in the name of the Goddess, did he choose me and Achillea for this onerous task, when neither of us were accustomed to tender caring for others? Surely Gladia would have been a better choice? And what had happened to those who were fighting? I opened my mouth to begin the interrogation I had planned, but Ambar merely pushed the screen aside again and unceremoniously pushed us into the darkened dwelling, pulling the reed door shut behind us.

Although it was darker than usual outside, due to the steely rain clouds, it still took a few moments for my eyes to accustom themselves to the gloom inside. The only light came from the openings high up on the wall, so I pushed my netela down and took down the small clay bowl of oil and lit the wick with an ember from the fire and brought it over to the woven mat on which the woman who so resembled a bundle of rags lay. She was curled up like a baby or small child, her face turned to the wall, mostly covered with a tatty netela. Even in the dull light, I could see that her robe was torn and dirty, with blood stains and ash on it. I looked at Achillea, helplessly. She bustled over to the fire and placed a pot of water on it to warm, saying brightly, 'We'll just get this water nice and warm and then we will clean you up and you will feel so much better.'

There was no reaction from the woman on the mat, save for a small convulsive movement as she drew her clothes even closer to her. I sat down next to her back, not wanting to prevent her intent to turn away and placed my hand on her shoulder in what I hoped was a comforting manner. I could feel her bones through the ragged cloth. She was holding herself tightly, wound up like the threads on one of Gladia's rolls of embroidery threads, tight enough to snap with just a little pressure. We stayed like this in silence for a minute or two, and gradually her shoulder eased a little against my hand. It did not take long just to warm up the water enough that we could bathe her wounds, and Achillea brought the clay pot over to the mat with a couple of clean old rags that Tarik stored there for the purposes of cleaning wounds. Briefly, I admired his organisation; the foresight that meant he had washed out and dried the dirty rags so that there were always dry rags here to use if they were needed in an emergency.

'We are only going to clean your feet and legs, sister,' reassured Achillea, soothingly, as she dipped a rag in the water, and I did the same with the other one. I followed Achillea's lead and gently patted the cloth to the woman's feet. She winced and drew them back. I brought the oil lamp a little closer and saw that the soles of her feet were slashed with many deep cuts which looked as if they had been made with a knife. They had stopped bleeding for the most part, but any movement of her feet set them off again. I looked across to Achillea, shocked at the intent behind the wounding, and she shook her head warningly as she saw I was about to begin with more questions. I told myself off; always wanting to ask questions and find out answers even when there were people hurting. Achillea put the rag in the warm water again, this time leaving it wetter and began to clean the foot, holding it firmly, despite the woman shrinking away from us. Together we cleaned her feet, and her legs up to the knees. Her legs were bruised and grazed, but there were none of the deliberate cuts we saw on her feet. Once the wounds were clean, we stroked on a simple beeswax salve which soothed and protected the cuts whilst also stemming the bleeding. Achillea took more clean rags and together we bound her feet loosely so that they were comfortable. Her body had now stopped its convulsive shuddering and she lay passively, still curled up but less highly strung. We needed to tend to the rest of her injuries, but I did not think she would let us; as soon as we had reached her knees she had drawn her legs back up into the tight ball, wrapping her arms around herself and fiercely covering her whole head with the netela. I went to the reed screen and slipped outside quietly, as Achillea sat at her feet humming soothingly to her as one would to a fevered child.

I strode over to Ambar and Tarik who were tending to their own cuts and bruises and those of Ashtun. They opened their mouths to speak, but I was resolved to do my speaking first.

'I do not know the story of that woman yet, but I will find it out. I do not know what your connection is, but I will find that out too, I promise you. Before then, she must be made to sleep so we can tend her wounds. Tarik, you must give me something to make her sleep straight away, like you gave to Gladia. She is very thin and needs to eat and drink, but she will not. The physic must be mixed with white honey to make it taste sweet or she will not take it. Even then, I don't know if she will take it; she is terrified of something or someone.' I glared at them all, daring them to question my judgement, but, to my surprise, they did not, and Tarik went over to his saddlebags, and selected a small gourd half full of a musky smelling liquid. He passed it over, along with a clay pot of white honey and a stirstick and I carefully mixed the two together. I looked around for some means of getting the woman to drink the potion as she lay there in her curled-up state and had the idea of using one of the hollow reeds that Ashtun had left by the wall. She could use this to suck up the liquid without moving. Without looking back at the men, I marched back to the dwelling and entered again. I went around to her other side, where her face was and explained to her that she should drink the drink through the hollow reed, so she did not have to move. It seemed that she hesitated, as if to try and refuse it, but she was very weak, and she needed to drink something, so she sucked it up feebly, the netela still covering her face. Once she had had a few sips of it and realised that it tasted sweet, from the honey, she drank of it more deeply and finished all that was in the gourd. I took the empty gourd away and went to join Achillea at the other end of the mat. We sat there for some time, Achillea still humming soothingly until the woman began to breathe more heavily and eventually, we could see her body softening as she fell into a deep sleep.

I explained to Achillea that we needed to tend her wounds while she was in the deep sleep, and once we were sure she would not wake up soon, we moved the reed screen to one side to allow more light into the dwelling. Ambar and Tarik came to the door but Achillea shooed them away.

'If she was found with OutRiders, who knows what they may have done to her,' she scolded. 'Look what they did to Gladia!' The two flashed secret messages to one another and then walked away, over to Benakiell's dwelling where we could see the outline of Ashtun. I asked Achillea if she wanted to go and see Ashtun, but she refused, confiding in me that she felt angry with him for going to fight with Ambar and Tarik, no matter what the reason was.

We went to tend to the woman. Her robe was filthy too, but I realised that it was, in fact, a drabcoat. Like mine, it had been sewed from strips of left-over fabric. This woman had once been a Maid like me. Carefully, we untied the string at the waist and slid the robe off her. What we saw took us both aback. Achillea gasped out loud at the sight. The woman was very thin, and her bones showed through her skin, except for a rounded mound at her belly which Achillea whispered to me showed she was having a baby. There were scars across her chest and on her back, some were older scars, and some were recently made welts. There were bruises everywhere. We worked our way up from her knees, wiping off dirt and smoothing salve on her wounds. Achillea went out to Gladia's dwelling to see if there might be a spare robe there for her. She needed a larger robe to keep her comfortable with her wounds and her belly, and Gladia wore a larger robe than either of us, being comfortably built herself. I decided to wipe her face, and carefully slid off the netela.

We had left it covering her face out of respect for her feelings, since we were washing over her whole body as she lay there. Her breathing was stertorous, and slightly ragged and I did not think she would wake. In any case, now we had almost finished our task, it would not matter so much if she did stir. Her netela was little more than a dirty strip of cloth, and I moved it to one side as I prepared to clean her face. Her eyes were shut, but the delicate skin was already purpling around both eyes, and her lip had been split at the top. I shifted the netela off her hair. Her hair was knotted and dirty, but there was something familiar about the way that it looked, and its unusual tone. I was sure I knew this woman, but I could not think of one who was so thin, and could not think that I could know her, since she was having a baby. I was ashamed to admit to myself that I had never studied the faces of those around me at the Temple in any great depth. I was so used to the Priestesses having their faces covered and identifying people from their daily allegiance and their work assignment that without those clues I was not sure who it might be. As I sat and gazed at her beaten face, trying to work out who she was, Achillea returned with a robe that Gladia had had with her in her items from Sanguinea. It seemed so long ago that we had set out first from Mellia, and then from

Sanguinea, and I wondered fleetingly if we would ever return to Mellia. I did not have many possessions there; mostly food, honey and salt and a soap ball, so it would not matter much to me if I did not return, although my drabcoat was still there, hidden. Gladia and Achillea, however, had gathered and stored all manner of items over their lives in Mellia and not getting them back would be a loss to them. At that moment, I was just pleased that Gladia had more than one robe and that she could lend this one to our unknown woman. We dressed her in it loosely and I looked at her once more. Perhaps if her eyes were open, I might see more of her soul and be able to tell who she was. We left her sleeping and went out, leaving the reed screen halfway across so that she felt neither shut in nor exposed to view, and went over to where the others were sitting.

I sat down heavily on the mat outside the dwelling and leaned against the wall, pleased to be back outside. The air was fresher and cooler since the heavy rainfall. I wanted to know what had happened to the woman, and why this had happened again. I had gathered from Gladia and Achillea that this violent treatment of women was expected from the OutRiders, but at the same time I did not feel like it was an ever-present threat, even though Gladia had been viciously attacked. I did not properly know or understand how the men and women of the Outer related to one another, but they lived together in generally peaceful conditions, and this violence was coming from the OutRiders, who lived in the OutForts, with no women nearby. There was nothing like this in the Temple. When the Maids were young, of course the Priestesses would discipline them; sometimes a child was slapped, sometimes they were sent to their bed with no dinner or made to do chores in punishment for not obeying the word of the Priestesses implicitly. Because we all lived in a place where everybody did as they were told, disobedience was unusual, as was punishment. It was punishment enough to know that the Goddess disapproved of you. The people of the Outer had many more squabbles and arguments and I was learning that was normal, but I had not yet witnessed any cruel aggression such as had been endured by the unknown woman, except at the hands of the OutRiders.

'How is she?' asked Gladia, sighing heavily. 'I haven't seen her, but Achillea told me she was in a bad way.' They all turned to look at me. I looked at Achillea to answer but she dipped her head and leaned against Ashtun's chest wearily.

'Before I tell you how she is, I want to know what happened,' I said, surprising myself with my own firm tone. Ambar and Tarik started using their fingers again, but this time it was Benakiell who stepped in.

'Enough of that,' he said with a steely tone. 'Don't get your story straight first. We will ask Ashtun instead. Ashtun, tell us exactly what happened; you were there, after all.' Ashtun looked dubiously at Ambar and Tarik, but Achillea poked him sharply and he began his story.

'We went out because Tarik had seen there was trouble over that way.' He waved his hand vaguely in a western direction. In my head, I immediately questioned how Tarik had found out that there was any kind of trouble anywhere, but I held my tongue since I wanted to know what had happened. 'We found two OutRiders who were...' he shook his head, looking embarrassed, '...erm...making sport of the woman.'

'Making sport?' Gladia exploded angrily. 'What kind of sport can you mean if this woman was so badly hurt? The sort of sport that they put me through too?' Ashtun hung his head, too ashamed to answer. Benakiell glared at Ambar and Tarik. He remembered what had happened to Gladia too and did not wish to think of it happening to another.

Ambar shook his head firmly. 'Brother Ashtun thinks to protect the sensibilities of the womenfolk. What they were doing to her was not sport, nor yet what was done to sister Gladia. They were using her bodily.'

'What do you mean?' I asked, angrily, the spark of anger in the emberjar of my mind glowing brighter. 'What exactly were they doing?' Everyone looked at me. Everyone looked embarrassed, everyone looked away. It must be some phrase which I had not heard in the Temple. How was somebody used bodily? What could they have done to her to affect her in the way in which she was affected?

'Gladia will explain to you later,' said Ambar, smoothly. 'This woman was badly treated, there is no doubt. We dealt with the OutRiders, although they fought hard. But this woman; we do not know who she is, but she came from the Queen's OutFort from the insignia on the uniforms of the OutRiders. She may have valuable information for us regarding the search for the Queen's grandchild, and the health of the Queen, and how things are at the Queen's Court. She may have heard gossip from the OutRiders, but,' and he broke off, frustrated, 'she will not speak with us! She asks only for a Maid of the Temple, one from the Goddess and will speak with no other! Sister Talla, we rely on you to find out what we need to know.'

I stared at him, wordless. This man, the one who so charmed me with the antlion, the one who had made me laugh, and melt inside thought it more important that I should find out the answers to his stupid questions than that the woman should be tended to and cared for until her distress had lessened. I stood up, no longer able to sit in this place and walked back to the dwelling and the injured woman. Achillea remained there with the others, and I heard a low rumble of voices as Benakiell began to lecture Ambar. I walked over to the reed screen and sat down beside it, listening for the woman inside. To my surprise, I saw Gladia heave herself up from where she was sitting and walk over to me. She sat next to me and patted my hand kindly.

'Don't worry, Talla, I have not come at Ambar's bidding to explain things to you. Only that I too could not sit there any longer as they focus on their politics and their plans and forget about the people. I don't always agree with you, but this time I do. She needs understanding, not questions. What she has been through is not something to be soothed with a draught of honey, but her burden must be shared, or borne by another for a while until she is strong enough to bear it herself. Do you remember how you shared the feelings of Empath Erayo? Maybe you could do it again for this one. It seems she was a TempleMaid, so perhaps you might understand her better. You can listen to her, and she will want to speak to you. In this time, you are the one she needs. If there is anything you do not understand, then come to me, and I will tell you the answers to your questions. And now,' she stood up again, her joints creaking, 'I am going back to my own dwelling where I shall make my stew and do my sewing away from all this.' She waved her hand vaguely in the direction of where the men and Achillea sat, and then, with a brisk pat on my shoulder, she turned and left, walking stolidly and determinedly towards her dwelling. There was a faint moan from the woman inside the dwelling, and I hastened to see if I could help her. It seemed that I had been appointed by all to this task, and I could not help feeling like I had at the Temple when I had been selected to clean the floor around the statue of the Goddess. It was the hardest, longest job to be given, as everyone wanted to be close to the Goddess, to stroke her and to leave offerings for her which all had to be cleaned up every day. It was an honour to be chosen, but it was an onerous task, and barely worth the effort for the honour involved. I wondered if this might be similar.

When I entered the room, the woman was sitting up, cowering up to the wall, the grubby netela once more pulled across her face. 'Who are you?' she asked me, her voice quavering. 'I want to go back to the Temple. I need to go back to my Goddess; she will care for me when no one else will.'

I spoke to her gently, telling her that she was safe and that I was here to help her.

'Are you...are you Talla? Surely it cannot be true? Why are you not in the Temple? Do you not know me? I have changed, I suppose...I am Bellis...' Her voice trailed off, uncertainly. I went over to her, slowly realising who it was that was here. She dropped the netela awkwardly, and I looked into her eyes. It was indeed Bellis. Last seen as she was ejected from the Temple following her Choice, in which the Temple had rejected her and manipulated her into being thrown out. Bellis who was so plump and indolent, she who loved the Goddess so much that all she wanted to do was moon over her statue and devote her life to her as a Priestess. Bellis with the sunny smile and the dreamy eyes. She was much changed since then, even though it was less than a year ago. Gone was the shining dreaminess and her plump and foolish amiability had been replaced by terrified eyes, unkempt hair and a low and stuttering voice. Let alone the fact that she was so thin as to be almost a skeleton, save for the belly. I did not understand how she could be having a baby, as Achillea had assured me she was. Everyone knew that the Maids of the Temple could not birth children. The babies came to us from the Goddess and were left at the gate. Only the Outer women could have babies. But that would have to wait for another time; for now, it was important to tend to Bellis. My head was spinning round, trying, as usual, to work everything out. I determined to focus on my task, as I would have done in the Temple, and I went towards the gourds where there hung a gourd of honey from Maren's bees which I took, along with a wooden spoon. I drew a cup of cool water from the clay pot which stood in the corner and went to sit next to her.

'Take this honey,' I said, 'It will soothe you and give you strength until I can find you some food.' Bellis looked at me wide eyed, like both child and old woman, and I dipped the spoon in the honey and fed her with it, like a baby. She took three spoons of it and some water and then her eyes began to flutter again, and she lay down again on the mat, curled up but not quite so tightly and slept, exhausted.

I stayed with her for the next day, only leaving her to get food and to wash and use the wastepit, and I slept in the dwelling with her. I ignored Ambar's questions and told them I needed to stay with Bellis, although I did not yet tell them that I knew the woman they had found.

I had never been this close to a human being. I do not mean physically close. The Temple got you accustomed to preserving only a small space of your own and understanding that there would always be a Temple Maid somewhere nearby. But, although there were many people there, living in the Temple, we did not share each other's lives, even though we worked together to achieve our work. This was different. It felt as if the personal space around Bellis had been shattered like a clay pot and that we were inhabiting the same broken space. I did not understand it because I did not even like her when we were both Maids in the Temple, if truth be told. I had sneered at her inside my head when she was in the Temple and had dismissed her dreams of serving the Goddess for the rest of her life as the pointless ambition of one who was both indolent and ignorant, one who wished to do nothing for the rest of her life.

I told Bellis that Achillea was my friend and Achillea came in to help with cleaning and dressing her wounds, especially the ones on her feet which were so painful. When Achillea arrived, she was even cheerier than usual, and I could see that she helped in a different way to the way in which Bellis needed me. Bellis needed me there because I knew her life. We had both been brought up in the Temple in a certain way of life and she knew that I would instinctively understand her without the need for explanations. But Achillea knew how to soothe and raise spirits. She sang and hummed as she warmed the water and cleaned the rags, and she brought her comb and eased away the tangles in Bellis's hair, prattling about the birds and the flowers. She also brought me the news that she had been to see Maren and that the eye salve had not made her eyes worse and seemed to be soothing them a little. She suggested to me that once Bellis was more recovered, it might be good for her to be seen by Maren. I reminded her drily that Maren could not see, and that was the point of the salve, but she pushed past this sharp retort and gestured to the mound of belly on Bellis.

'She can feel, though, can't she,' she whispered. 'Remember, Maren was a Birthmother, she can tell us when the baby might be born by feeling Bellis's belly.' I agreed this might be useful, feeling a little abashed that I hadn't thought of it myself. I had never considered of how babies came into being when I was in the Temple. For us, they simply appeared on our doorstep every few weeks, they were gifts from the Goddess. I knew that the women of the Outer were blessed by the Goddess and gave birth to the babies, but I did not know that those from the Temple could also give birth. The Priestesses had told us that our lives were given in service to the Goddess in other ways; we looked after the babies for the Goddess; we did the work. I had only been in the Outer for a little time but I had already seen that here on the Outer there were plenty of babies and children who were cared for and brought up happily, and so it puzzled me that so many must have found their babies difficult or unwanted as we had been assured by the Priestesses. And now I knew that it was just as possible for Maids of the Temple to have babies as it was for the women of the Outer. What I did not know was if Bellis understood exactly what it meant for her to be having a baby. I made some brief excuse and pulled Achillea outside with me and explained my worry to her. She looked at me, wide eyed.

'How could she not know? It is plain to see,' she answered. I tried to explain to her that it was different for Maids of the Temple, that we were brought up knowing nothing about babies except that they were left at the Temple. We all knew we had been left at the Temple for the service of the Goddess, and in our world, we did not birth babies, nor did we ever see women who were with child. Achillea's owlish eyes widened even further.

'You must talk to her more, Talla, she obviously trusts you because you know what it is like to be a Temple Maid.'

I didn't tell Achillea that I had known Bellis in the Temple. I did not want her to know. I had become a different person whilst I was with my companions and I was concerned that they would want to ask Bellis all about me and how I had been in the Temple. I agreed to go and speak to Bellis and try to find out what had happened to her and what she knew about the baby.

Achillea went back to her dwelling. The others had not spoken to me, perhaps on the advice of Gladia or Achillea. I felt glad not to speak to the men. Whatever Bellis had been through it had involved her being badly treated by the men of the OutFort, and I was still angry with Ambar and Tarik because of their behaviour when they rescued Gladia. Even if it had been their only option, as they had explained, I was unsure and wary of them. That feeling had started to fade, and I had begun to enjoy Ambar's company again, and now I felt unsure all over again. I decided to go and see if Bellis was ready to talk to me of her ordeal, so that I would know more and be able to do more. Ashkana had once said, 'Knowledge is only necessary if it completes a job.' That was usually used by the Priestesses if we Temple Maids had asked one too many questions, but it made sense to me now. I could not complete my self-appointed job of working out who the missing princess was, and of understanding how this world in which I lived worked, if I did not have the knowledge with which to do it. Perhaps it was possible for those like Erayo to follow feelings as their currents ran deep through all people, but I did not have her instincts, just waves of understanding followed by even more waves of incomprehension. I needed to know and understand everything, so I went back inside, and once Bellis had eaten, I gave her a cup of coffee and asked her to tell me what had happened to her.

'Tell me everything, Bellis,' I urged. 'Leave nothing out.' She raised her eyes to me, and I could see they were already brimming with tears. 'It will help you,' I said, more gently, and reached out for her hand, while holding on to the little bee pendant with the other hand. Tremulously she nodded and began her story.

CHAPTER 24

When I first left the Temple, I didn't know what to do, I mean, nobody told me what to do or where to go. I just didn't know what to do. I tried to stay at the Temple, but the door was shut and there was no handle on the outside so I thought maybe I could go and find another Temple and pretend I had lost my memory and they would take me in. I've never been clever, not like you, Talla. I really thought the Goddess wanted me, I tried so hard to worship her and to oil her feet. I made prayers and things and I thought she was looking after me, especially when I saw the scroll on Choice day, it was so beautiful, I thought the Goddess made it herself...

'Anyway, I walked along a dirt path for a really long time and then I stopped under a tree for a rest. I was so tired from crying, and the sun was so hot. So, I sat down under the tree and leaned against it and, before I knew it, I was asleep and then I was awake because they came for me. These men came, and they grabbed me. They had uniforms on, and you couldn't see their faces. They just grabbed me and tied me up and put me on a horse. I had never been on a horse before. They never spoke to me, just picked me up and put me on the horse and rode for miles and miles and miles with me. They took me to a big house inside a big fort and just left me there in a room like a dormit. There was a mat and a pot of water and nothing else. I was left there on my own for ages, and I tried to pray to the Goddess, but it didn't feel like she was listening to me.

'The next day, this woman came to my door and grabbed me really meanly and tightly, like the Priestesses used to do when we were in the Second Age and did something wrong; really hard and mean. I tried to ask her about going to a Temple and she just laughed at me and told me I was an Angel now and I had to work. I tried to talk to her, but she didn't talk, she just pushed me out into the courtyard. There were lots of other Maids there, Talla, lots and lots of them, all wearing their drabcoats. I didn't see anyone I knew but it was so hard to tell, I wasn't allowed to talk to anyone and when I tried, she slapped me. They pushed us out with baskets and then we had to work. We had to carve out the buildings of the new Temple. They gave us metal chisels and rocks and we had to chip away at the rock to make the building. We had to put the stone that we chipped away in our baskets and when they were full, we had to carry them away and dump it and then come back and start again. Every day the same for the first few weeks. Then I got chosen by the soldiers and got moved to another house. They told me I was still an Angel, but I had new work to do, I had to make people happy. When they first told me, Talla, I was happy myself because I think I was quite good at making people happy, or at least making the Goddess happy, don't you think, Talla?

'But it didn't make me happy. I cried every night until the AngelMother slapped me and took away my food. She told me this was my work now and I should do it well, that the Goddess was watching me and was displeased. We still had to work in the day, but we finished before the others and then they would take us back to the house and wash us and make us wear these special robes that were just loosely made with holes for your head and arms. There was no belt or underpocket or other covering. We had to lie down on a mat and the AngelMother would lift the robe and lay it over our faces, so we could see nothing, but all our bodies could be seen, with no covering. Then the OutRiders would come in and lay on us and use our bodies for themselves. They would beat us if we cried, and some would beat us even if we didn't cry because it made them more excited. We were not allowed to speak, just to lay there and wait for them to finish. And then the next one would come in. All the way to seven and then there would be a bell and we could put the robe down and go back to the washroom and put our drabcoats back on and go to sleep. Every day, Talla. Every day I cried and shouted and every day I got less food and tried to be quieter. Sometimes when we lived in the Temple, I wanted more food, it was such a pleasure to eat and I know now that we lived in a kind of heaven in the Temple, Talla. There was plenty of food, and beautiful things and the Goddess to praise, and no OutRiders or Angels. I was so tired all the time, so bruised and broken.

'I started being sick every morning and I got weaker and then the AngelMother told me I was having a baby, and I was happy because it meant the Goddess was listening, do you see? It meant she really was there and she had chosen me to have a baby so I could go back to the Temple, and then the AngelMother told me it changed nothing, that it would grow inside me, but I must still work and if it died, it died, and I must still work and if it was born, it would be taken away from me and I must still work. I didn't say anything, but I didn't want that to happen, I wanted the baby to live in the Temple like I did, away from these horrible people, from the OutRiders. I wanted to run away and go back to the Temple and I thought if I could get away, I could go back and beg for them to take the baby.

'I didn't know what to do, Talla, I was growing bigger every day but because I was sad and tried to argue with them, they took more and more food away from me. Some of the others tried to save food for me and give it to me but it was so, so hard and then they told me I wasn't doing the extra work any longer and I had to go back to doing the stone carving. I thought I could run away while we were emptying the stones from the baskets, and I did do well at first, Talla, I did my best and I hid behind a big rock and waited until they went home and then I started walking, following Flavia the star. I walked such a long way and then I started to feel lightheaded and dizzy and I stopped next to a tree and lay down, and then it was morning and I had only been walking for a little while when those two OutRiders found me to take me back.

'They told me I had to be punished and took me on a horse to some big rocks over there. They told me I had no life outside of being an Angel and they had come to take me back, to remind me of my place and to make sure that I never ran away again. And they took their little knives out and they cut my feet so many times, over and over. It hurt so much that I fainted, and when I could see again, they had laid me on the dirt and put my drabcoat over my head again. I thought it could not be worse than in the AngelHouse, but it could; they were shouting and hitting me and would not stop. When one had finished, the other started again and I thought I would die, Talla, and then your friends came and shouted out at them and they stopped and ran for their bows but your friends chased them down and they fought each other and then it was all quiet, and then your friends came towards me and I was so frightened of them that I fainted again and they must have picked me up and carried me here on their horses. And then I have been dreaming of it ever since, Talla, when I shut my eyes and when I open them. The only time I did not was when you gave me the physic and I knew you meant me no harm, for you and your friend bathed me and soothed my wounds and did not shake me and ask me questions about the Queen's OutFort as your friends did, and I know nothing about anything; they kept asking me about how the search was going and if the Queen was still there and what the OutRiders were doing, and all I can say is that they are building places out of carved stone and using TempleMaids like empty vessels, and maybe they always have and we just didn't know!

'I ache all over, in my bones and in my head and in my heart. There is no escape from any of it. I am not clever like you and I don't understand any of it. I don't know why it happened like that, and at first, I thought it was my fault, that it was a punishment, that I had done something wrong to displease the Goddess but then there were so many Angels there, so many TempleMaids being used like beasts of burden. So many working every hour, day and night, for no reward save living another day. We can't have all displeased the Goddess. But surely this must be nothing that the Priestesses know about? I cannot believe that our Priestesses could know that such a dreadful thing was happening to the Maids who leave the Temple. After all, it is the Goddess that guides your hand in the Ceremony of Choice, so they have no bearing over it...

'Oh Talla, I am so tired now, I cannot talk about it anymore. There is a dark cloud inside my head that pushes down on me, so I am exhausted to even talk of these things; I know there is a child inside me, so I know I cannot give in, for the Goddess gives life to every child, but I need to be in nothingness, to sleep and never to dream   again...

CHAPTER 25

It was very hard for me to listen to Bellis's tale without interrupting her with further questions and exclamations. My mind was glowing white hot, like a piece of metal in a fire, so hot I almost could not examine it too closely for fear of hurting myself, so I took refuge, as I usually did, in doing small repetitive tasks to distance myself from the heat of my own anger. I attended to dressing Bellis's feet, having heard of the OutRiders cutting into them to stop her from running away. I warmed water and washed the dirty rags with a soapball. I put honey on flatbread for her to eat, and made coffee for her to drink, whilst I thought of her being starved into submission and at the end, I gave her more physic to make her sleep, unable to do anything else to soothe her misery. She fell asleep quickly, her body hungry for empty rest, and I sat with my back against the warm wall of the dwelling, my mind racing. I could feel the sun through the polished clay of the walls and I wanted to go out into the brightness of the sunlight and let it burn away the pictures which Bellis had put inside my head, and could not now take away, but at the same time, I wanted to stay here in the dimness, where the sound and the light were muffled and where there was nobody else.

I had to find out what was really happening. I had so many questions which I could not answer myself because my knowledge was so limited, and I was determined that I would not be sent away with half-answered questions or shadowed replies. I was sure that they had all hidden something from me. At every turn, I got half answers and vague responses. Somehow the areas which seemed to exist within themselves, with only limited interactions; the Temple, the OutFort and the Outer were all connected together in an insidious web, and if I understood the puzzle of this, I might understand all the other puzzles and riddles that had arisen so far. I got up and left Bellis in the dwelling and pulled the reed screen across to afford her darkness and privacy whilst I was gone and walked over to the dwelling of Benakiell. He was the first of these others whom I had met, and of them all, he was possibly the most measured, even though I had seen the spark of anger and irritation behind his eyes too. I marked him as one who would not tolerate the kind of treatment to which Bellis had been subjected. But when I got there, instead of the quiet talk I had envisaged, they were all there, talking animatedly.

Achillea got up as soon as she saw me and came over to me, asking me how the woman was, and if she seemed any better, and if she had told me yet what had happened to her. I told her that I needed to talk to everyone about what she had told me, and she nodded understandingly. As soon as I sat down though, the questions began; could she speak about the Queen yet? Did she know if they were still searching for the Queen's granddaughter? Was she well enough to speak to Ambar and Tarik? I felt angrier and angrier at their persistent questioning which showed no concern at all for Bellis, but only for the answers to their own questions. I had to speak my truth to them and make them understand what had happened to Bellis and what it meant for our world. The questions continued. I listened to none of them, but their incessant nature fanned the flames of my anger until finally I could bear no more and stood up and shouted at them in my loudest voice.

'Be quiet, all of you! How can you think that your stupid questions are more important than her? Do you know what has been done to her? Do you know how she has been damaged? Do you know anything about her apart from what you think might be useful? Well, do you?' I looked around at them. Gladia looked back at me, levelly. Achillea's eyes widened and she looked concerned. There was a corresponding spark of anger in the eyes of Benakiell. Ashtun flushed and looked down. Ambar and Tarik looked at each other and lifted their hands to start their secret communications, which incensed me even more.

'Stop that right now! You will NOT speak with your hands to each other. There is no more time for the keeping of secrets! There will be NO secret speaking from you two with your hidden plans and your questions which never end! I will find out what everyone knows about what has been happening in our land and if you don't tell me, I shall leave this place and all of you and find out for myself! Because what I have heard is worse than the thought of dying.' I took a deep breath. I knew what Bellis had told me was the truth, but they did not know what she had told me, and I wanted to see if they would tell me the truth about what had been happening in our land. I did not know how long it had been happening for, nor to how many, but from what had been detailed to me, there seemed to be an efficiently planned system, for want of any other description, which must have taken some time to evolve, and I did not believe Ambar and Tarik knew nothing about it. They used to be OutRiders themselves and, I realised with a sickened feeling, they may even have taken part in such horrors. I took in some more deep breaths and looked around again before I began to speak.

'First of all, where do the babies come from? Those who are reared in the Temple and the OutFort? Maybe our friends from the Outer could start and tell us what they know. I will also tell you what we from the Temple know.' I looked towards Gladia and Benakiell, but to my surprise, it was Achillea who spoke first.

'My mother told me that they used to come from women on the Outer who gave them up willingly. Sometimes, women have too many babies and can't look after them all, or sometimes a mother may die in childbirth and the father cannot rear the baby on his own. Sometimes women have them without someone to look after them, I suppose. But I don't know anyone who has taken a baby to the Temple. I heard that the OutRiders steal babies from people on the Outer because they don't give them to the Temple and the OutFort anymore! Gladia, do you know anything about it?' They all knew that Bellis was having a child, and perhaps they thought I was wondering what might happen to her baby.

Gladia shut her eyes and shook her head, mute and weary. I looked across to Benakiell, who reached over and patted her hand kindly. 'Time to let it go, Gladia,' he murmured. 'You may find peace for the telling of the story.' Achillea looked confused and turned to Ashtun but he was gazing away in the distance, impatient with my questions, and not looking at anyone, least of all me.

'I know something of parts of this story,' Gladia began, tentatively. 'It all happened a very long time ago. When I was very young, I loved someone, but when I found out I was going to have a baby, he left the village the next day, and never returned. My parents told me that I had to give the child to the Temple when it was born, as I could not look after it on my own and I was a disgrace to them.' Her voice wobbled, all these years later, as she remembered what had happened. 'After I had the child, I was very ill, and they took the baby while I was sick and left her at the Temple. That would have been four ages ago now. I never had any more babies, and that always seemed unfair to me, that the

Goddess had so many babies and I had none. It has been a great sadness to me all my life. So, I do know that some babies are left at the Temples by women of the Outer, or their families. But I too have heard that babies are stolen. Because there are always so many Maids in the Temples, and new Temples keep on being built, and so do OutForts. And there are more and more OutRiders everywhere.'

I looked at Gladia with pity. She never knew her child and she would never know what had happened to her; did she grow up to be a Priestess or was she pushed out of the Temple to endure the sort of life that Bellis had described to me? I understood now why she needed so much to see the Empath Erayo; to leave her some of the feelings she had from that event so long ago, but which still hurt her now. Benakiell obviously knew her story, and probably had done for some time. He shook his head, partly as if to dispel the story from his head but partly to indicate to me that he did not intend to speak. I chose to speak myself, next.

'In the Temple, we were told by the Priestesses that the babies were left at the Temple because they were chosen by the Goddess to serve her in the Temple. We never considered what might happen to baby boys. I was always told myself that my mother left me on the steps of the Temple, with a note asking them to look after me.' Ambar and Tarik looked at each other meaningfully. I realised I had let slip a part of my story which, until then I had kept quiet, but I was so angered by what Bellis had told me that I no longer cared. I turned to them and looked at them both, daring them to drop their eyes from my fury, but they did not, which I think now was to their credit, although at the time it just incensed me more. 'And what of you two?' I asked them, keeping my voice low and steady, 'What do you know of the babies? For, if you are like me, you are one of those babies! What tales do they tell you in the OutFort of the babies and from whence they come?'

Tarik stirred his foot in the red dust and began to speak. 'I was indeed one of those babies. In the OutFort the baby boys are sent to us from the Temple when they are still young and just able to walk after their first year. They are looked after by those who cannot battle. We were told as youngsters that the Goddess chose us too, that we were chosen because we were brave and noble, and that our parents had given us up in service to the Queen and Oramia and that it was our duty to fulfil their expectations in us.' Ambar said nothing and continued to glare at me.

Benakiell broke the silence, stroking his beard and saying reflectively, 'So, if the baby boys come to the OutFort from the Temple, then the Priestesses of the Temple must know about how this system works. Did you know you had baby boys in the Temple, Talla?'

I didn't. But then I recalled that the youngest babies were kept together in the BabyHouse where only the Priestesses went and cared for them, and even the Maids were not permitted to go. We were told that it was because tiny babies were closer to the Goddess, but I realised, horrified, that what Benakiell said was true, that the Priestesses must know that the baby boys went to the OutFort because they raised them for their first year and then sent them away to the Fort. Whenever you saw the babies, they were wrapped up in long gowns and in any case, they all looked the same to me; it would be easy enough to look after the boy babies along with the girl babies while they were still so small and unable to talk. The shock must have shown on my face. It was hard for me to try to face what I was beginning to understand; that far from being the innocent parties who wanted only to raise pious, Goddess-fearing Temple Maids, the Temple knew and understood that the boy babies were being sent away and brought up to hurt and to kill; they were part of the system. Worried about what else I might find out, I continued with my questions, spurred on by the thought of Bellis and what she had been through.

'And so, I turn to my next question. What do those on the Outer know of those who are called Angels?'

Benakiell answered me this time. Ashtun was still steadfastly gazing into the difference, Gladia was lost in thought, and Achillea scrunched up her nose, listening hard to what Benakiell had to say. 'Well, it's another of the silly stories they tell in the Temple isn't it?' he said, scornfully. 'More evidence that the Goddess is all powerful and merits all the offerings they demand for her. They say that when the Goddess sees need, she sends an army of Angels to build the Temples and to make the country strong again.'

'There are lots of songs about Angels,' offered Achillea. 'In the songs they are always beautiful and powerful, and always succeed in their tasks.'

'We Maids were told the same things,' I confirmed. 'We were told to be grateful for their service, for they built the Temple in a few short weeks, and that only a few were chosen to be Angels by the Goddess. But perhaps those who know the OutFort and the OutRiders best,' I looked at Tarik and Ambar meaningfully, 'can explain to us exactly what an Angel is, and what an Angel does?'

They looked at each other in consternation and said nothing. Before they had the chance to confer with each other, I spoke again. 'Perhaps I can spark your remembrance, if you have forgotten such a trivial part of your life? The Angels,' I turned to face the others, and I know I must have looked fierce and angry, because that is how I felt, 'used to be TempleMaids like me. If the OutRiders had caught me when I left the Temple, as they were meant to, I would have become an Angel too. And all those stories about the Angels building the Temples? Oh, they were true. Because once the OutRiders gather up the Maids that are pushed out of the Temple, they don't take them back to the Temple, as you might have thought – or even as those Maids might have thought, no, those Maids become the Angels! And it seems they have two very special jobs. They are the ones who build the Temples and the OutForts and carve them out of solid stone, working all day every day to make them!' I stopped for a moment, to catch my breath, suddenly visited by an image of myself marvelling at the smoothness of the walls of the Temple and pondering on how the Angels had achieved it. Now it made me feel sick to think of how it had been made; that the Temple we used to glorify the Goddess was a monument to the suffering of others. Gathering myself, I prepared to tell them the worst of what the Angels were made to do.

'But that is not the only thing the Angels do for the OutRiders, is it? You,' and I motioned towards Ashtun and Benakiell, and Gladia and Achillea, 'may have thought that what happened to the woman who was rescued yesterday was because of the actions of some unusually cruel and heartless OutRiders. You may have thought it was something that some soldiers do sometimes to hurt and subdue women they have found who run away from their service. But, in fact,' I could hear my voice raising in both volume and in pitch, 'the other duty of the Angels is to be "used bodily" by the OutRiders whenever they choose. Every day if the OutRiders wish! They use the Maids as a service over and over. They never speak to them or look at them. The women mean nothing to them! And when a baby comes, what do you think happens to it?'

I looked around breathlessly, my eyes sparking with the rage which was boiling over in my head. 'Well, I will tell you; the babies go to the Temple! And then it starts again, and when a girl reaches the age of Choice, the Priestesses choose if she stays in the Temple to carry on the system or if she is thrown out into the world to be picked up by the OutRiders and taken for use by them! Over and over again! And this system,' I spat out the words at them, 'is known about by all the OutRiders, and probably all the Priestesses for all I know! One thing I do know is that none of the Maids of the Temple know that this is what happens to those whom the Goddess apparently chooses to leave the Temple! And before you start asking me how I know all this is true and such, the woman who was rescued used to be in my Temple. Her name is Bellis and she has told me everything. Temple Maids do not lie to other Temple Maids, especially one as simple and devoted as Bellis was...' At that point, I could bear to speak no more and buried my head in my hands, weeping in large, clumsy sobs.

In the Paradox tree, a dove called intensely to its mate. The cicadas had begun their song again after the rains and the bees hummed contentedly. But nothing would ever be the same again. I could not unknow what I now knew. I could never again be that person whom I was just the day before. I felt as if someone had picked up my head and smashed it against a rock and then put it back together, too hastily. Gladia and Achillea got up from where they were sitting and came to sit either side of me, Gladia patting my back and Achillea stroking my hair until I regained some control of my emotions and was ready to look up into the void of the silence.

'Poor Bellis,' murmured Achillea. 'What she has been through. No wonder that she is so disturbed and frightened.'

Benakiell leaned forward and looked at me kindly. 'I am sorry, sister Talla, for all that you have found out. You are so young, and finding out what people are capable of can still shock even me, in my advanced age, so you will be struggling to make any sense of it, as indeed am I. Can you tell us more of what your friend told you about her life?' His gentle enquiry pushed me away from my thinking and back to what I needed to focus on. I related back to them all that Bellis had told me about her life after she left the Temple, and their shocked faces told me that this was not something that they had known about before. Ambar and Tarik, however, had immobile faces, held rigid and unmoving. In their haste to show no emotion, they betrayed their knowledge of this practice, and I turned on them both, still furious.

'You knew that this happened! You told us yourselves that you used to be OutRiders! Maybe you took part yourselves! For you knew what they might do to us if they took me with them when they were hurting Gladia! All this time, you knew what they might do if they caught me after I had left the Temple! How could you? How could you be part of something which treats people like they are nothing more than a tool to build with or a pot to eat from? Did you think that because we were trained to work to give glory to the Goddess all our lives that we would be grateful for the work you gave us when the Temple no longer had any need for us? Did you ever think about what it might do to our hearts and souls? Like me, Bellis knew nothing of the lives of men and women when she left the Temple. She knew nothing of the ways in which a woman can be used by a man nor of how a baby comes to be. And neither did I! And to take advantage of that is wicked and evil. I cannot even look at you anymore!' I could not rub out the picture in my mind of Bellis lying on the floor with her robe over her head and of Ambar and Tarik waiting in a line outside the dwelling, waiting to take their turn. I took some moments to gather myself again, and then explained to them what the nature of Bellis's visible injuries were; the wounds on her feet from the cuts and the bruising and swelling from the beating and told them that I wanted Maren to feel Bellis's belly to see if she could help us with the baby that would be born, though we did not know when yet.

Gladia heaved herself to her feet and said that she would make coffee for us, and Achillea asked me if she should go and get Maren now. I knew that, like me, this had been very hard for them, and that they could not bear much more without a break from it. And, like me, that break came from being busy. I sat back against the wall, spent with anger and distress, still trying to make sense of all that I had heard while they both went off to do their tasks.

'It seems to me, sister Talla,' said Benakiell, conversationally, yet with a real steel to his voice, 'that we should hear what Ambar and Tarik have to say in answer to your accusations. For it is fair to be balanced when we seek the truth, is it not?' He turned towards the two who used to be OutRiders. 'Come now, brothers, tell us what you know of this, and let this be an end to secrets between us.'

I was grateful for Benakiell's intervention. My head was not yet steady enough to phrase my own thoughts. I watched them as they spoke, trying to divine if they were telling us the truth. They both started talking at the same time, and then both stopped, confused. Eventually, Ambar began.

'I am sorry that you had to find out these matters in this way. It was never our intention to mislead you; rather we thought it might be too disturbing for you. We wanted to protect you from this.' I was not convinced by this smooth response but held my tongue, waiting for him to continue. 'We have not been in the OutRiders ourselves for some time now, but we were, and we did know about those they call the Angels, and about what they were used for. It is part of the reason why we search for the granddaughter of the Queen, to bring forward a change in our land, for things have been getting worse and worse. Why else would we have rescued the one whom we now know to be Bellis from these men and delivered justice unto them?' Ashtun was nodding eagerly here, the most animated he had appeared for a long time, so it appeared that he was taken in by this explanation. Benakiell was pondering, as he stroked his beard. I was irritated by them both seeming to give more weight to the words of the men than to my own words.

'Things have been getting worse for how long? And what does worse mean? And you both became men in the OutRiders. Did you make use of the Angels at your OutFort? How many times? Did you beat them and punish them if they tried to escape? How does that make you better than any of the rest, and how can we, the women here, trust that you will not do the same thing to us?' I burst out, accusingly. Ashtun stopped nodding for the first time, as he thought about Achillea. We had all seen with our own eyes how the OutRiders had treated Gladia.

Tarik took up the speaking this time, in that quiet way of his which was more calming. 'Like all who have lived in an OutFort or a Temple, including you, sister Talla, we have made use of the labours of the Angels. For although there is a select group of OutRiders who build the Queen's Court, much of the other stone carving work is done by the Angels. Before we became men, we were kept away from seeing any of the Angels or being told anything about them. We too marvelled at the work it must have taken to carve the Temples and the OutForts out of solid stone and thought it must be a kind of ancient magic. As for the other...' His voice trailed off and he looked to the earth, ashamed.

Ambar took over again, intent on showing himself to be superior to his fellow OutRiders. 'It was a long time ago now. We did not know then what we know now, and we were told as we became men that it was how we would become stronger warriors and that it was a sign of manhood. We lived amongst men, without women around us; we only saw women when we traded or were in the Outer, but never knew them as people. Like the Maids in the Temple we were raised to be absolutely loyal and hard-working and not to question anything. We did what we did because we were ignorant, at least in the beginning. Later, we realised that things were getting worse; harsher and harder. There were more punishments, more Angels, more encouragement for OutRiders to inflict harsher and harsher penalties as the Queen clung tighter and tighter to her ebbing power and her cronies hung harder and harder on to their benefits. I know that many have been hurt and some have been killed. I do not say it is right, only that it happened, and we cannot make it unhappen. All we can do is to try and find the new Queen and hope for a better way forward.' Ashtun started nodding vigorously again, carried away by the rhetoric from Ambar who had always seemed so skilful at using his words to convince. I recalled how he persuaded me to trade my honey for the little bee necklace, and all that had happened since.

It seemed as if I was the only one who felt for Bellis. To the OutRiders, she was an Angel, and I knew what they thought of them, and to the people of the Outer she was just a Drab, one like I was until they got to know me; they could not feel for her; she was too distant. But to me, even though I hardly knew her in the Temple, and had even despised her, she was the nearest I had to a family and I wanted her to feel better. Gladia came back with her coffee pot and the small clay beakers as we sat there in silence. I took mine and then, instead of staying with them, I told them that I needed to check on Bellis and took it with me as I trudged back to the dwelling where she slept. I was so tired. When I entered the dwelling, Bellis turned over sleepily and asked if it was morning. The sleeping physic had confused her, but I left her to wake up properly as I sat and drank my coffee and pondered what I should do next.

CHAPTER 26

As I swallowed down the last bitter dregs of coffee, I saw Achillea walking back with Maren. Maren was carrying a long stick and Achillea was leading her with it. Although Maren could determine light and dark and see vague large shapes, she could not see stones in the path or low hanging branches or where the path might go, and this was a good way for her to have some confidence in where she was walking, for all she had to do was to follow Achillea. I had not often seen Maren venturing beyond the small dwelling and garden where she had lived for so many years, and since she had lost Anglossia, she must have struggled to be able to choose when to go places instead of having to rely on others to offer. I rose to greet them as they arrived. Achillea had evidently taken the time to walk to Maren's to become bright again, pushing what she knew about Bellis to the back of her mind, and concentrating instead on what could be done for her practically.

'I have asked Maren if she can try and examine Bellis or listen to her and try to find out if the baby is alright and when it might come, but she is a bit worried in case she has forgotten all that she learned so long ago,' she told me. I assured Maren that whatever she knew was likely to be much more than any of the rest of us knew, and that Bellis would talk with her if I vouched for her. They had both been badly hurt by OutRiders and so they had something in common. I went inside and talked to Bellis, who was by now lying quietly on the mat, awake but drowsy still, and she agreed to allow Maren to help her.

Maren came in and introduced herself to Bellis softly. She asked her if she could feel her belly to see if the baby was alright, and when Bellis agreed, she gently lay her hands on her and moved them around, feeling for the unborn child. She smiled as she stroked the belly and spoke to Bellis.

'Your baby is well; you must feel it move quite a lot now; it is close to being born.' Bellis looked both frightened and proud at the same time. 'I didn't really know that was what that strange feeling was,' she admitted. 'I don't know anything about babies; none of us from the Temple do.' I refrained from explaining to her what I had worked out; that in fact the Priestesses, at least, must know that the Maids they expelled from the Temple went on to have babies because of what was done to them by the OutRiders, and that I had worked out that babies were made by having a man and a woman together which explained why we, in the all-female atmosphere of the Temple knew nothing of these things. Also, I had seen with my own eyes the lengths they went to in trying to ensure that the right Maids stayed in the Temple and those they saw as unimportant or useless were sent out to what they must have known would be a horrible fate. It made me feel ill to think of Priestesses like Asinte choosing who to protect and who to discard.

Achillea looked concerned. 'How long before she has the baby? She does not look very big in the belly compared to some I have seen.' Maren told us that the baby would be born at any time in the next few weeks, that sometimes babies came early when their mothers were beaten, and that the baby would likely be small anyway as Bellis had not been given enough to eat because of being punished by the OutRiders. She told us we should feed her as much as she needed to eat, and continue to add the honey to her water, and that we should try to get her to walk around more. Achillea explained to Maren about Bellis's feet and we tried to think of how we could help her to walk around a little, perhaps by padding the rags with kapok fluff. Bellis thanked Maren and then turned to me and Achillea and thanked us too. 'It is the first time since I left the Temple that I have felt like anyone cares,' she said, her eyes filling with tears. 'Thanks be to the Goddess.'

'Praise Her Name,' I responded automatically. Maren rose to leave, and I rose with her. 'How has the salve been, sister?' I asked her, thinking more now about whether she might help to birth Bellis's baby rather than whether she could identify me as the granddaughter of the Queen. I had thought that the royal brooch, as I now knew that it was, might identify me as the new Queen, but now I had realised what kind of system the old Queen had put into place, I did not want any part of it, and was now hoping that there would not be any defining sign on me that Maren could identify. She assured me she was continuing to put the salve on her eyes and that it had in fact soothed the itching in them a little, so that she was happy to continue to use it even if it did not clear her eyesight. I left Achillea talking brightly to Bellis about babies and food and walked over to Gladia to tell her what Maren had said and to ask her advice on what we should do next.

'You know,' Gladia said reflectively. 'My own baby would be older now than Bellis, if she still lives. Perhaps my child has had the same terrible things happen to her, maybe she has a child herself, or maybe she is living in a Temple somewhere, as a Priestess, doing her work quietly, and knowing nothing of the beginning of her life. We must care for Bellis and protect her from harm. She is your sister and my child.' And then, as if realising that she had shown too much of her hidden side, Gladia poked me roughly on the arm in the same spot that she always poked me and told me to get on with washing the rags and to stop dilly-dallying and talking when there was work to be done. She reminded me that despite everything that had happened and what we had learned, there were still jobs to be done that would not do themselves, especially when there were young people to do them and allow their elders to rest! Smiling at Gladia's attempts to put us all back where we belonged, I went and attended to the washing, as she suggested, pondering what to do next and knowing that I needed to speak again to Ambar and Tarik despite my ill-feeling towards them and their lives.

When I went to see Ambar some time later, after I had gone over things inside my head numerous times to try to keep calm, he was tending to the horses. I watched from some distance as he trimmed their hooves with his knife and dug out stones from them and ran his hands over them, presumably checking them for injury. He stroked them gently and murmured to them and they leaned in towards him, affectionate. I was wrestling in my mind with what I had learned about him and Tarik. They had done bad things, and the Aphorisms of Ashkana had no ambivalence on this; Ashkana briskly dismissed those who did bad things as being unworthy of the light of the Goddess. But, as I now knew, the Priestesses, who were held up to us all as examples of those blessed by the Goddess, took part in a practice which was very bad. Nothing seemed simple anymore. Could a person be both bad and good at the same time? Could someone believe they were good but be doing something bad? Ambar cared for his animals well, he had rescued countless people from the OutRiders, he had spent long days searching for the new Queen because he believed it was right. He was thoughtful, and charming. And yet, I could not forgive what I had heard from Bellis. He had been part of a system which treated the Maids or Drabs or Angels (who were one and the same thing) as a resource to be used and cast off as one might plant and sow and harvest a bean plant and then cut it down when it was no longer of value. Sighing, I walked closer and raised my hand in greeting. Ambar looked up but did not say anything, continuing to tend to the horse. I walked over to the horse and began to comb my fingers through its mane, awkwardly trying to show willingness to engage. After some time, Ambar began to speak.

'I know we are looking at what has happened through different eyes. But we both want an end to this system that has grown, and an end to the power used by the Queen and her court to such bad effect. It was not always so. They say that until the Queen's daughter, Paradox, was with child and ran away, that everything had worked well but that the Queen could not bear to think of ceding power to her own daughter, and her court did not wish to relinquish their benefits. That was many years ago and things have got worse and worse. I heard about the past from my OutCommander. It was he who first told me how things used to be, back when I was in the Third Age of Childhood. It is what set me on the path I am now on. I know that you want to protect your friend and I know that you hate all of us OutRiders, but we are not all the same. Even though we are raised to be soldiers, to have no feelings except a desire to protect the Queen and follow her orders, we nevertheless are different. I do not know why. Just as you are different from your fellow Temple Maids. I know that you are in some way a key to this. I think you are the child of the Queen's daughter. I know that the baby was taken away by Hortensia, because Maren told me.'

I started, surprised by how much Ambar seemed to know of what I thought I had worked out for myself, and held secret. He continued, 'I also know that the baby was taken to your Temple because what went with it was the brooch of the Princess – well, a part of it. And I know,' he looked up, straight into my eyes with those melting brown eyes of his, 'that you have the brooch somewhere here, although I have not yet seen it. Maren told me that the Princess Paradox pinned something to the blanket of the child, and that must have been the brooch. Shortly after you left the Temple, the OutRiders were informed by that Temple that something valuable had been stolen by the Drab known as Talla. They were all searching for you, and so were we, but I had an advantage over them. They wanted you dead, and I wanted you alive. You see, I had the other part of the Princess's brooch. Remember the necklace with the bee on it, which I traded you for some honey? That bee was originally on the flower part of the brooch. It has a seeking metal in it which means that when they are with each other they click into place, and they seek each other out. It is like magic and it's how I found you in Sanguinea; it pulled me to you. If you show me the brooch, and put the bee with it, they will interlock, and if the brooch is yours, then it must mean that you are the daughter of Paradox.'

I was silent for some time, pondering on what he had told me. He had certainly filled in some of the gaps in my knowledge, and I now knew how he had found me in Sanguinea. For a long while, I had wondered if this could have truly been a coincidence. He had been more honest with me today than he had been on countless other occasions, but this did not endear him to me further. Rather, I became angry again at the way in which he had deliberately charmed me and traded with me to make sure I had the bee necklace. But just as I was thinking about this, I wondered how then he had traced us once he had given the bee necklace back to me? Perhaps I was too hasty, forever jumping to conclusions and attributing blame where perhaps there was none. In a world where I had just discovered that everything I had relied and trusted in had not been true, it was difficult to become a trusting person again. Besides, it seemed that although Ambar knew some of the story of the Queen's daughter Paradox's child, he did not know that she had birthed DoubleSouls. Even if I had the brooch, it did not mean that I was the child destined to take over from the ailing old Queen for even DoubleSouls are ordered and one must be born first. Only Maren held the key.

Ambar began to speak again. 'We must ask Bellis urgently about the Queen's health for she came from the Queen's OutFort and she may have heard or seen something vital. We must know whether we still have time to find the rightful new Queen or whether the Advisors have plotted some other Queen, for the old Queen herself does not wish to have her grandchild in her kingdom. She has already put into motion plans to prevent it, for I think she believes she will live forever. It is very important!'

I don't think I had ever heard Ambar speak with such fervour, but I did not trust him, and I wanted him nowhere near Bellis in the fragile state in which she found herself. If she did know some information that might aid us, I could see that it might be helpful, so I suggested, rather brusquely, to Ambar that if he told me the questions he wanted answering then I would ask Bellis them and report the answers back to him when I had them. He was not happy to relinquish control of the questioning, but I think he knew that I would not let him interrogate Bellis. So far, she had not even seen the men in the camp, not even Benakiell who seemed to me the least threatening of them all, though now I was starting to see all men as potential attackers, having heard Bellis's story.

FLAMMEUS

There was one more question of my own that I had for Ambar before I left him to his horse, however. 'If your tale of the brooch and the bee is true, how came you by the bee? For surely if the brooch belonged to the Lady Paradox, the child would have had the whole brooch and not just the flower?' I asked, looking at him fully in the eyes. Ambar's eyes flinched, although his face did not move at all, save for the slight pulsing at his jaw. He paused, collecting his thoughts. The sun was hot on the back of my neck, making my skin prickle with sweat. It felt oppressive again, full of rain and the threat of thunder. The whole situation made it feel even more oppressive; there was such threat and heaviness everywhere. For a fleeting moment, I wanted to turn around and walk away from everything. But my Temple training reminded me of my responsibility to work and I waited for Ambar to respond, hoping that what he had to say would resolve my questions about Paradox.

'I do not know how it is in the Temple when you are growing up. In the OutFort, you are assigned to an OutCommander during the Third Age of Childhood. You are in a group of seven and you do everything with your group, under the guidance of your OutCommander. Sometimes you are lucky, as I was, to come to know your OutCommander well, and to develop a close bond with him like a father and a son.' This was not the same as in the Temple. In the First Age of Childhood, you were assigned to a single Priestess who cared for a small group of you until the Second Age but after that, the only groups you were part of were the different work groups that you joined, or your fellow Maids, those whose day was the same as yours. I was intrigued by what Ambar had told me and wanted to know more. I had imagined that life in the OutFort might be similar to that in the Temple, except for the tasks, but it seemed there were distinct differences.

'My OutCommander, Palus, was a good soldier, and a good man, too,' continued Ambar. 'He taught us to expect the highest of ourselves and to always question if we were doing the right thing. On the day before I moved to my new OutCommander, as an OutRider and a man, Palus called me to him and gave me the bee. He told me that he had once loved a beautiful woman, the Lady Paradox, that she had broken her brooch of inheritance and given him the bee and kept the flower herself as a sign that they belonged together. He told me he had originally been her guard, to stop her from seeing other men but had come to love her himself. He told me that he had been sent away not long after that, to another OutFort and had never seen her again. He asked me to look after the bee for he felt he was in sharp danger. I was sent away the next day with the rest of my OutForce, and never saw him again; I heard that he died in battle, but in truth, they tell you that everyone who dies, dies in battle, and he may even be living in another land. It is part of the way it is; we are OutRiders, so we die in battle; we are never killed or are ill or run away. I never forgot him and when I first heard the story of Paradox from Maren, I knew that he must have been the one who was the father of her child.' He looked at me again, his eyes gentler now, and kinder. 'It could be that he was your father, sister Talla, and a finer father you could not hope to find. Please try the bee in the brooch if you have it, and at least we will know if his story was truth or not. We want different things, you and I, but I think we both want to know as much as we can.'

'I will think on it,' I responded, determined not to do his bidding straight away, and went back to rest in the heat of the day, the sweat trickling down my back. I sat beneath a Paradox tree, where the shade was deep and dark, and closed my eyes.

CHAPTER 27

I was woken up some time later by the pattering of the first few raindrops falling on the glossy, wide leaves of the tree. The sky had darkened again, heavy with the promise of even more rain. I looked around but could see nobody, and did not, in any case, feel like speaking with anyone. I heaved myself up and headed inside. I couldn't resist taking the brooch out from my underpocket and examining it. I could not see a point where it might have been broken, but maybe it did not need to be broken to be split in two parts; possibly the two pieces just slotted together ingeniously. I reached for the bee pendant, which hung around my neck, and felt the warmth from it. The metal got warm very quickly compared to the kind used to make armour and knives. I held it in my hand for a few moments. It was the same size and shape as a real bee, cunningly fashioned, whereas the brooch was a more symbolic flower. It was, of course, the cipher I had seen on the shields of the OutRiders and I realised now that this meant they were the Queen's OutRiders, looking for the brooch of the Queen's daughter. They must have been told that the brooch was missing along with me. And that meant that someone at my Temple, the place where I had grown up, had told the OutRiders and the Queen that I had gone along with the brooch. There was no affection between us in the Temple; there was no time to pursue friendship, and it was, in any case, discouraged; 'Work is your closest and most reliable friend,' and 'Time wasted in idleness can never be recovered,' were the admonishments of Ashkana. I knew them all so well that I had never questioned them, just memorised them and absorbed them and repeated them, convincing myself of their worth. But this meant that someone who knew me had chosen to betray me, knowing what might happen. My whole world felt very shaky now. It felt as if I was walking through sand or mud rather than on a steady stone path.

Hesitantly, I held the metal bee over the brooch as if it were hovering over a flower and I felt a pull between the flower and the bee. I moved it nearer and the pull became stronger and stronger. I let go of the bee and it snapped down to the centre of the brooch, over the red stone and held fast to it. It seemed like magic. I turned the brooch upside down, but the bee did not drop off. I shook it hard and still the two remained linked together by an invisible force. I scrutinised it closely. The feet of the bee rested in small dints in the stone which I had not previously noticed. I wasn't sure that I wanted the two of them linked together like this, whatever it proved. They were, to me, two separate things; the pendant and the brooch and were better staying that way. I poked my fingernail under the bee and pushed upwards. I pulled on the cord of the pendant at the same time and the two separated again. I re-examined the bee and saw that the underside of the creature and its legs were made of a different type of metal. I held it over the flower brooch again and it hovered slightly and locked into place once more. I was fascinated. I knew that Tarik had worked with metals for the Queen. He had told us of the metal listening threads that the Queen had in her rooms, and I wondered if he knew of the properties of this metal. There was so much I did not know. In the Temple there was very little metal, and we rarely had metal traders coming to the Temple; only those who traded knives and metal vessels. The OutRiders used a lot of metal in their weapons and their armour and were clearly skilled in its uses. I wondered who had put it together. It was an ingenious invention and I found myself admiring the careful thought behind it.

So now I knew, according to Ambar, that the brooch which I had left the Temple with did indeed belong to the Lady Paradox. I had been told that I had been found with the brooch pinned to my blanket by the Priestesses. But I still did not know if I was the first born or even if I really was one of the DoubleSouls born to Paradox. Perhaps the brooch had been left on a different baby and my own mother had seen it and moved it to my blanket to try to ensure I was looked after well. Only Maren could identify the firstborn of the DoubleSouls. Patience would be necessary as we waited to see if her vision would clear enough for her to be sure of whatever it was that identified the child. If Maren's sight was recovered and she could indeed identify the firstborn of the DoubleSouls, it would answer Ambar's questions and fulfil his search and push forward the advent of a new Queen. But would we ever know who the other DoubleSoul was? We did not even know if they had been left at the same Temple. I cast my mind back to try to think which of the Priestesses might know if two girl babies had been left on the same day, or even if they had been left together.

Priestess Saphna had often told me of the time when she had found me at the foot of the Goddess, with the brooch and the note, but she had never mentioned finding another baby at the same time. There again, even if I had been found with another, the Priestesses would not have told me so, especially if they suspected we might have been DoubleSouls or sisters. There was no family in the Temple, only the family of the Maids and Priestesses under the motherly care of the Goddess. 'The Goddess is your work and your rest, your family and your friend; you need no other.' I really wanted the chance to be able to ask questions of the Priestesses at the Temple but could not figure a way to being able to do that. I could not just walk back to the Temple, for they would know who I was if they could see me, even if I did look different now with my hair neatly braided and Outer robes and a netela.

I parted the bee from the flower once again and replaced them, the bee around my neck and under my robe, and the brooch pinned to the inner section of my underpocket. I needed to think through my next step carefully. There were so many loose and tangled threads to this web, and no single one of them seemed to go to the centre of it all. Each one led to another, and only if I understood or resolved all of them could I hope to see the full picture and understand everything. I decided to go and tend to Maren's bees because they soothed me and helped me to think in a more orderly way. Watching them all moving with a shared purpose, but each with an individual task made me examine things more dispassionately, without being guided by emotion. I walked down the path towards Maren's. I could feel Ambar watching me as I went, and I drew my netela over my head more, keeping my head down. I needed some time alone.

The fallen rain still lay in droplets on some of the furry leaves in the flower gardens where the bees were busily working. Some of them had come to the water and were lined up, drinking it, reminding me of tiny goats at a stream Others were moving from flower to flower, collecting their bee dust from the flowers and carrying it on their legs like baskets of flour. Once their load was complete, they would fly back and take their harvest inside the hive where it could be made into honey and beeswax by those who worked in the hive. I wondered if it was always the same ones that went out for the bee dust, always the same ones that made the beeswax or the honey, always the same ones who guarded the hive from intruders. They seemed to have a variety of tasks, just as we humans did. I mused on the OutRiders, always aggressive and ready to defend or attack with their arrows and sharp knives, just like the sting of the bee. Perhaps we from the Temple were the honey makers, the sweeteners of life, and those of the Outer were the workers; those who persistently went out and gathered the bee dust and the water, continually bringing in the materials to make the honey but never benefiting as much from it. After a while, I stopped trying to make patterns in my mind, stopped trying to listen to all the conflicting voices of explanation in my mind and just watched them as they moved around their world, busily fulfilling their destinies. I spent some time clearing dead grass from around the flowers and replacing the stones around the flowerbeds so that they looked neat and orderly. Everything seemed calm, despite the constant movement of the bees.

Maren was the key. Even if the Queen died or put into place another Queen, I still wanted to know how I was connected to the brooch. I had lost the security of life in the Temple and I was sure that there would be no return to the Temple. I did not want to be part of a system which serenely sent Maids out into the world with no interest in their final destiny. The fatality of believing that if the Goddess willed it, so it should be, did not sit well with me; how could a supposedly benign being require for young women to be taken and treated as objects, especially if, as we were told, we were made in the image of the Goddess. Maren knew what identifying mark was on the first-born child and would be able to swear to it to confirm the new Queen. If the salve that Achillea and I had made did not sufficiently clear her bleary vision, that would not be possible, but I thought that if I had the courage to tell her of my search, and why I needed to know the answer, she might tell me what the sign was so that I might know if it were indeed me or not. I hoped that she would understand.

I talked to Maren over a beaker of coffee. I noted how much surer she was when she was making it, how she fumbled less, and I hoped this meant her vision was clearing, but I did not mention the salve, other than to enquire if she was still using it and if she still had sufficient of it. She replied that she did with a smile on her lips. She asked me how Bellis was, and said she planned to visit her later. 'It is so good to feel useful, sister Talla,' she said, a little ruefully. 'I can tend the bees well enough and make enough honey to trade and grow enough to eat, but since I lost the companionship of my dear Anglossia, I have been lonely, and I have always missed being a Birthmother. There are some things I can still do, just by using my hands, but there are other parts that I need my sight for. When I met Bellis, it reminded me of just how much I enjoyed helping the mothers and their babies. Although I am not everything she might need, I am at least something, and I can help her in the ordeal which lays ahead, for it is always worse when a mother does not properly know she is carrying a child, nor yet what led to its growth.'

We spoke of Bellis and her injuries and Maren asked me about her personality. I found it hard to say much of what she was like, because we were not encouraged to become close, so I could only go by the little I had observed. I told Maren about Bellis's love for the Goddess and her devotion to her to the detriment of her work. To my surprise, Maren brightened when she heard this and told me that this augured well for her child because it showed her nurturing and loving nature. I stored this away to ponder later. I could see that not all the judgements I made so rapidly were accurate, and it taught me to not always heed the first thing that I concluded.

FLAMMEUS

We sat for some time talking, until, eventually, I was ready to bring up the issue of the mark on the first-born child of Paradox. Maren had been adamant that she would not describe it, and after all she had been tortured by the OutRiders and yet said nothing, and had not even said anything to Ambar, despite his honeyed tongue, so what chance would I have in persuading her? I decided to tell her the story of me and the brooch. She was amazed that I had this brooch and asked if she could see it. Reluctantly, I took the brooch out of my underpocket and placed it in her hand. She traced over the golden petals and the deep blood-red stone. She held it in front of her eyes as she tried to focus on it and breathed in sharply. This was, she believed, the same pin which Paradox had pinned on the blanket of one of the babies. I took in a deep breath, relieved to feel some of the parts of the story becoming woven together, fitting closely in and out of each other. So, the brooch was definitely associated with the babies of Paradox. But was it also associated with the first born of the DoubleSouls?

I asked Maren if she knew, but she reminded me that it had been Hortensia who had dealt with the babies after their birth; Maren had seen them, and had seen the identifying mark on the elder before she was swaddled, but after Paradox had spoken to Hortensia so urgently, Hortensia had done everything else with the babies, including leaving their mother with Maren while she hurried away with them. By now, I realised why Hortensia had been in such a hurry to leave with the babies; Paradox must have told her that she was the Queen's daughter and asked her to take the babies away to a Temple straight away before they could be found and killed by the OutRiders. And it had worked. I wished that Ambar's OutCommander had never told him of what had happened; that the babies had been left to take their chances in the Temple as any other girl child had to and that I had never been dragged into any of this. If only I had not been so curious in the Temple; if I had not found out how to scribe and read, had not worked out the trick, had remained in the Temple and become a Priestess! But I was where I was, and I needed to make Maren understand the importance of the identifying mark. I asked her if, now she had heard my tale of the brooch, and felt its shape for herself, she might consider telling me of what the mark looked like on the first-born child, so that I could see if it were me.

'It seems such a strange thing that I would deliver a child of the Queen's daughter who might then grow up and come to see me with the brooch,' Maren pondered slowly, trying to work out whether she should tell me or not. I assured her that even if she told me what the mark was like, she was still the only person who could attest to it. If she only told me where the birthmark was found on the child, I could check for myself. If it were a mark on the arms or legs or any other part of the body which I could see with my own eyes, then I already knew it could not be me, for there were no blemishes on my skin, save a scar I had incurred as a child, falling out of a tree. She thought for some time and then told me that she would reveal to me where on the body the mark was to be found. I waited for her with some trepidation.

'The mark is to be found on the child's back, between the shoulder blades,' Maren said, gravely. 'Is it you, sister Talla, are you the child?' I had to confess I still did not know, for there was no way of me seeing my own back. Maren's eyes were not clear enough to distinguish such a mark on my skin, so I would have to ask another. But who should it be? If I asked Achillea or Gladia, they might want to know the whole story, and I could not ask the men, so I resolved to ask Bellis. She would likely be able to do such a task for me without asking too many questions. And I felt easier with her seeing the skin on my back than anyone else, since she was a Temple Maid. I thanked Maren for her trust in me and she smiled back at me. 'Go, then, sister Talla, and answer your question of yourself, for until you do, I feel you will not rest easy.'

Returning to Bellis, I was excited to find out the answer to my question, although with each step, another problem seemed to arise in my mind until it was boiling like a pot on the fire. From the time I had received the brooch from Lunaria, I had felt like it was entwined with my destiny, and now, I might finally find out what my future life might be like. I tried to remain calm, calling out to her softly as I entered the dwelling. She was sitting up on the mat, her feet freshly dressed, eating the last of a flatbread and honey. It seemed that someone else had been tending to her while I had been busy with my own questions and actions. She showed me a small piece of fabric with a flower sketched out on it and a needle threaded with blue thread and explained. 'Your friend Gladia has been to visit me. She has showed me her stitching and let me have this little piece of cloth, so I can learn to do it too!' Momentarily, I felt a flash of something akin to anger; I had seen Bellis as my own, and now she was making friends with others whom I had also seen as my own. From having had nothing in the Temple to now feeling like I had things, whether they be netelas or friends, I did not want to share my things. Perhaps there was something to be said for the practice of having no possessions or friends, for you could not feel the pain of losing them.

I looked at the stitched flower and saw that Bellis was already more adept at stitching than me. My jealous feelings subsided, and I was happy that she had something to take her mind off her troubles. I praised her efforts and she told me that Gladia had told her that if she showed some promise, that Gladia would give her some things to stitch so that she could start to make a living for herself and the baby which was coming. It was good of Gladia to do that, and I thought again of how she had lost her own child and how she still grieved. She might be just the right person for Bellis at this time, and Bellis might, in her turn, be the right person for Gladia to care for. I asked Bellis if she could do something for me and explained that I wanted her to examine my back, between my shoulders. Curious, she asked me why and I told her, rather impatiently, that I would explain later. I told her that I had asked her because she had been a Temple Maid and I was more comfortable with her seeing my skin because no other had seen it. Her face, which had brightened when she showed me the stitching, fell again, and I realised that what I had said had hurt her, since her own skin had been seen by too many and in such dreadful circumstances. I stammered an apology, but she waved it away and asked me to turn my back to her and then raise my robe up to my shoulders. The robe of the Outer was more tight-fitting than the drabcoat of the Temple and I hitched it up warily, concerned it might split. She directed me near the doorway so that the sunlight fell on my back and bent close to it, presumably looking intently at it. She stroked my back with her warm hand, and it felt so soothing. No person had ever touched my skin there before, and it felt like the warmth of the sun on my back.

'What is it that you want me to search for, sister Talla?' asked Bellis.

'Is there a dark mark on my skin on my back, between my shoulders?' I replied, knowing that this might be the answer to so much. She bent forward again, scrutinising my skin and then laughed.

'Don't worry, Talla, there is not so much as a tiny blemish on your skin; it is as clear as the running water.

There is nothing there, not even a tiny spot, you lucky thing!' And there it was. I was not the child for whom Ambar sought. I was not the future Queen. I did not know who my mother was. I was just a Temple Drab. I felt crushed, as if all the things I had been working for were for nought. My head seemed fuzzy for a moment, and then I was aware that Bellis was speaking again. 'Not many do have those marks, but I remember seeing one in just the place you mentioned, funnily enough, on Lunaria. Do you remember Lunaria, Talla? Always doing the right thing, and always in the favour of the Goddess! I used to long to be her!'

I pulled down my robe hastily and turned to look at Bellis, scarcely believing what I was hearing. 'What shape did this mark take?' I asked her, to try to get a specific description to return to Maren with.

'It was the strangest thing,' Bellis continued, glad to have provoked such interest. 'It was in the shape of a bee. I know, because the day I saw it, I had gone to wash and didn't realise someone else was in the washroom; you know what I am like, always busy thinking of something else, and Lunaria was there and she was just going to pull up her drabcoat and I saw the mark and I called to her to stop, that there was a bee crawling up her back and went to scare it away and then I saw it was just a birthmark on her back! Isn't that strange! I would never have remembered that if you hadn't asked me to look at your back!'

It began to make sense to me. The new Queen was not me, after all. It was Lunaria, even though the Temple had given her a different day of birth to mine. She had the mark on her back, and I knew in my bones that this would be the defining mark. Maren had said nothing at all to me of the shape of it, but the fact that it was a bee was surely very significant. I would know for certain when I confronted Maren with the shape of the birthmark. But how might I get Lunaria and Maren together so that Maren could verify that she would be the next Queen? Did this also mean that Lunaria was my sister? Did I have somebody somewhere whom I could call my own? Or was I just another baby from an unknown place who had been accidentally endowed with the burden of the brooch?

As usual, there seemed to be more questions that arose from a single answer. The only ones who might know the answer to that would be the old Priestesses who were actually there on the night that me and Lunaria were left at the Temple; even though we had been given different days of birth. I knew that the Priestesses tried to balance the Temple Maids so that there were even numbers for each of the days of the week, so that the Goddess was served in equal measure every day, so it was quite normal for a day of birth to be randomly assigned. I had been told that my birthdate had been given to me because it was scribed on the piece of paper pinned to my blanket with the brooch. But if Lunaria was separately wrapped, there would be no reason to give her the same date. In fact, the Priestesses did not have Maids with the exact same birthdate. They did not, after all, know the exact date a baby was born, only the date on which they had arrived at the Temple. I was deep in thought, and hardly heard Bellis as she asked me why I had wanted to know. I stuttered some vague response about being curious because Maren had told me that some babies were born with marks on them. 'I wonder if my baby will have a mark like that,' murmured Bellis, absently. I made some excuses about consulting with Maren and left Bellis hurriedly, nearly bumping into Gladia who was puffing up the path towards Bellis as I hurried back to see Maren.

FLAMMEUS

I almost ran back, my bare feet leaving small puffs of red dust as I followed the path. The birds made small satisfied noises in the branches of the Paradox tree and although a few small clouds floated across the deep blue sky, there did not seem to be a chance of rain today. I called to Maren as I arrived, and she turned and smiled in recognition of my voice as I came close to her. 'Have you answered your own question?' she asked. 'Are you the first born of the DoubleSouls of Paradox, daughter of the Queen?'

I answered slowly, 'Let me ask you this, sister Maren; was that special mark on the first-born child in the shape of a bee?'

Her jaw dropped, and she began to breathe more rapidly. 'Is it you? Praise to the Goddess that you are alive, and you are grown to a woman who can take their rightful place in the world!' She looked quite overcome and fanned herself with her netela.

It was confirmed to me now that it was indeed Lunaria who was the rightful heir to the throne. I had to find a way to let her know and to get her out of the Temple and to the court of the Queen so that she could begin her rule when the old Queen died. I also realised, in that moment, that I was going to have to trust my travelling companions with all my knowledge in order to make this happen. It would take more than just myself to accomplish this task. 'Many hands make short work of a long job,' as Ashkana had said.

'No, sister, it is not me,' I answered Maren, 'but I know who it is, for she was a Maid like me in the very same Temple.' I told her swiftly what Bellis had told me of the bee shaped mark on Lunaria's back, and she raised a trembling hand to her eyes, almost as if she could see the mark now, imprinted on her eyelids. In some ways, the OutRider who had tortured her into near blindness had achieved the opposite effect to his intent, for although he thought that taking her sight away would make her unable to certify to the veracity of the child, it had burnt the image of the birthmark on to her eyes as one of the last things that she saw. She must have pondered often on these last things she saw clearly and so knew the mark even better than she might have if she had been left to carry on with her life unhindered. I told her that I planned to go and find Lunaria and bring her to safety.

CHAPTER 28

I formulated a plan as I walked up to Ambar and Tarik's dwelling. It was crucial to speak with Lunaria about the meaning of the birthmark but finding a way to speak to the Priestess she was now would be difficult. It had to be me who spoke to her, but if I returned to the Temple, they would call the OutRiders to come and take me away, no doubt believing I was the one for whom they sought. So, I needed to get into the Temple without being seen and to spend time with Lunaria on her own in order to tell her of the situation and get her out of the Temple and to the Queen's Court. I would also require protection, so Ambar and Tarik would be necessary partners. I needed to think of a way to enter the Temple with my face covered, and suddenly an idea came in to my mind which was almost too outrageous to try but which I truly believed I could carry off; I could disguise myself as a Priestess visiting from another Temple. That meant I could wear a veil which would shield my face from recognition by the Priestesses and Maids at the Temple. It would also mean I would have access to Lunaria, as a fellow Priestess. The OutRiders would be assumed to be my guards, perhaps. I would need to take with me another woman, though, since Priestesses never travelled alone, but travelled with either a fellow Priestess or with a Temple Maid. Perhaps Achillea could be persuaded to be my Temple Maid.

When I arrived at the dwelling, I called them all and they slowly arrived from the places where they had been; Achillea and Ashtun strolling along, hand in hand, Gladia emerging from Bellis's dwelling, Benakiell moving from his spot in the sun where he was cutting strips of cane from a large pile of reeds and Ambar and Tarik walking over from the place where the horses were tied up. They all looked at me curiously, and I supposed that they may have seen me going up and down to Maren's dwelling and wondered what I was doing, especially in view of my outburst the previous day. In Ambar's case, he may have been wondering if I had tried to put the brooch and the necklace together yet after his explanation to me. They sat and waited for me to start speaking.

'I have news of the utmost importance for us.' I spoke quickly but clearly, as if I were addressing in the Temple, and began to tell them what I had found out. It was important to make sure they fully understood what the story thus far was, and only then might they understand what I would ask of them next. 'We have heard much from Ambar and Tarik regarding the Queen, since they used to work in the Queen's Guard themselves. We know that the Queen is dying and that they seek her daughter's child, if she lives, for she will inherit the throne. We also know that the OutRiders have been searching for me diligently since the day I left the Temple, and, indeed, if it were not for your friendship and efforts on my behalf, they would have easily found me. I do thank you most sincerely for all that you have done for me.' I looked around and Benakiell inclined his head briefly, rubbing his hand through his beard, as was his custom. 'However,' I continued, 'I have not told you everything that I could have done.'

Ashtun glowered at me resentfully and turned his head away. Achillea frowned but looked straight at me. I took out the brooch which I had held tightly in my hand, and showed it to them, telling them the story of what I had been told as a child, and of how Lunaria had come after me and given it to me as I left the Temple. I then recounted to them all the story that Ambar had told me of the bee necklace and the brooch and I took the bee pendant from around my neck and showed them how the two seemed to magically link together without any kind of fastening pin, attracted to each other, like a bee to the honey of the flower.

I glanced over at Ambar's face only after I had shown them the two pieces and told them the story. His face was like a sky over which passed dark clouds blown by the wind. I sensed he was angry with me for telling them all the story he had told me alone, but at the same time I could see that he felt relieved, and indeed vindicated, that I did have the brooch and that the two did fit together. I told them about what Maren had told me about the DoubleSouls birthed by Paradox, and they were all shocked by this revelation, especially when I told them what had ensued; the pinning of the brooch to the blanket, and Hortensia leaving with the babies before the OutRiders came, and the torture of Maren so that she could never identify the child. Gladia interrupted at this point, her brow furrowed with concentration.

'But why would they do that? Because you could not identify a grown woman from a baby's face, and surely the baby who had the brooch pinned on their blanket must have been the older one? And does that mean, sister Talla that you are the one who will be Queen? Because I don't know what to think about that! I don't fancy you giving me orders, that's for sure!' She finished with a twinkle in her eye, and a chuckle, and with some relief, we all laughed together, before Benakiell brought us back to her question.

'Do you know why, sister Talla?' he asked, looking at me straight in the eyes, disconcertingly. 'Why was it important to cloud her vision?'

I explained to them then about the birthmark that Maren had seen on the body of the first-born child and heir to the throne. I did not know why the OutRider had done that to her eyes since she had said nothing about the birthmark, but perhaps he was simply making certain, or perhaps his OutCommander had told him to kill Maren and he preferred to maim her. But the important thing was that Maren could still identify the firstborn by virtue of the mark, and if the salve that Achillea and I had concocted worked, then she would be the key in the inheritance of the throne.

Achillea became quite excited now, and burst out, 'Oh Talla, show us the birthmark, you must have it! Imagine you being the next Queen! It is so exciting!' I smiled at her enthusiasm, feeling a little pang of loss for all that Achillea would have enjoyed, had it been me who would inherit the throne.

'It is not me, Achillea.' I said firmly. Everyone looked at me, aghast and confused about why I had taken so long in telling this story in which I had no part. Ambar sat up straight, just as mystified.

'We must keep on looking then,' he said wearily. 'There must have been some mix up or perhaps a deliberate muddying of the waters. I don't know where to look next; the bee and flower piece were what I was depending on. We cannot survey the whole country for a Maid who has a birthmark that matches the one Maren saw...' He lapsed into thought, his head dipping lower.

'It isn't me. But I do know who it is.' I said quietly. His head jolted up as if he had been stung by a bee. Everybody looked at me. I continued. 'It is Lunaria. The one who gave me the brooch when I left. She has the birthmark. I asked Bellis to see if I had a mark in the place Maren described and I did not, but it reminded her of having seen the exact one on Lunaria's back. So, we must get to Lunaria before anyone else finds her!'

'But how can we do that? She is a Priestess with a veiled face, we cannot take all the veils off all the Priestesses in the Temple of the Goddess's Blessing until we find one with a birthmark in the right place without word getting to the Queen's Guard!' Tarik exclaimed in frustration, surprising us all with his outburst.

I explained my plan. 'The only way this can work is if I can get to talk to Lunaria without anyone knowing it is me,' I asserted. 'If I can get inside the Temple and speak to her, I am sure she will listen to me, especially when I tell her what Bellis has told me. I will disguise myself as a Priestess from another Temple so that my face is covered too when I enter the Temple. Then, when I am alone with her, I will speak to her openly. If we all work together, I am sure we will succeed, especially if it is as important as Ambar and Tarik have convinced us it is.' My face was flushing as I continued to speak, to explain my plan to them. After I had told them all I had thought of, there was a long silence, during which Ambar and Tarik continued to converse silently. I ignored them, because I felt as if I knew more than they did, as if I was finally in control. I knew how to solve a question and I was the only one who could carry it off.

'Surely a Priestess would not travel alone, Talla,' Gladia pointed out. 'We could not let you go back to the Temple alone, in any case.' She settled more comfortably on the mat, breathing out heavily, and picking up her stitching from the mat next to her. I cast her a grateful glance, pleased that she had moved the conversation on to more practical matters, as was her wont.

'Indeed not, Gladia,' I responded. 'If the disguise were to be successful, I would need to take with me a Temple Maid and some OutRider guards who might lend authenticity to my presence there.'

Gladia chuckled. 'Well I don't think they would believe I was a Maid, at my age, and they wouldn't believe it of Bellis since she's heavy with child, and, as we all know, Temple Maids do not have babies!' She looked at me, her eyes twinkling, and so full of mischief-making that my lips curved into a smile before I knew it. 'It seems our dear Achillea will have to learn some obedience and humility, after all!' she continued, smiling even more broadly.

Achillea pursed her lips, unsure whether to be excited at the thought of being included in the plans, or disdainful of having to disguise herself as a Temple Maid. Eventually, she said, 'But we have no drabcoat for me to wear, Gladia, since Talla left hers in Mellia, and they won't believe I am a Temple Maid without one!'

Gladia's smile grew wider. 'Ah yes, that's true, Achillea,' she affirmed, and I felt crestfallen suddenly as I had not thought of this when I was making my plans. Perhaps we could make one of torn up rags? 'But do not worry,' continued Gladia, 'you can wear Bellis's instead!' Of course! I felt real relief that this problem had been so swiftly dealt with by Gladia.

Achillea's nose wrinkled in disgust. 'But Gladia, it's so dirty and horrible and covered in rips and blood and all sorts.' Then she stopped, conscious suddenly of how she sounded, complaining about wearing Bellis's drabcoat when Bellis had had to go through the ordeals which had led to its state of disrepair. 'But,' she carried on quickly, 'I can wash it and maybe we could all help to stitch it back together well enough.' Gladia threw Achillea an approving look and she smiled back, happy that she would only be playing the part of a Temple Maid rather than having to live the real life of one.

Ashtun leaned forward. 'I don't think I am happy about Achillea being put in harm's way like this,' he muttered, and I did feel a pang of sympathy for him. He cared about Achillea, and of course he did not want her to come to any harm- neither did any of us- and I think that he felt a little unimportant now, having played his part in the rescue of Bellis which had now been superseded by more important events. Achillea looked at him fondly, 'Well, Ash, it's not up to you to decide that for me, is it?' she asked sweetly. 'We are not married after all, and I have no parents, so I make my own choices in this world.' He subsided grumpily.

'And what about you?' asked Benakiell, who had followed this plan with keen but quiet interest thus far. 'How will you find the garb of a Priestess here in Besseret? For they wear the veil over a coloured robe and how can we make those things here?'

I had thought about this too, and I turned once more to Gladia. I explained that I could describe the Priestess veil to her, and she could make one, and I could draw a pattern on the edge of it and she could stitch it for me. 'We just need to find a way to colour the robe,' I mused. Gladia affirmed that she would do her very best to work with me on producing a Priestess veil but did not know what to do about the colouring of the robe, as weaving and the associated skills were only practiced by the men of the Outer and she knew nothing of their processes. Why was there such a hunger to withhold knowledge, I wondered, with each group holding it tight to themselves, maintaining what power they had with it. Surely the world would be a better place if all people could learn all things? I frowned, deep in thought, and then Tarik intervened.

'I think I may be able to assist in this regard, sister Talla,' he said. 'As you know, I worked with metal-smithing for the OutRiders, but I also worked with plants in developing physic for healing wounds and the like, although I had never thought to do what you have done to make the salve for Maren.' His words of praise brought a sweet feeling to me, like the first taste of honey, but before I could savour it for too long, Tarik continued. 'I know that marigolds can be boiled with cloth to make an orange colour. Would that colour be acceptable for a Priestess?'

I assured him that it was indeed an acceptable colour for a Priestess to wear, the colour of the day Aureus, the day after my own day of Flammeus, and the scent of orange blossoms. I turned to Gladia and asked her if she could stitch simple, small, white orange blossoms around the bottom of the veil and the robe if I patterned them for her, and she readily agreed, pleased I was not asking her to stitch anything more complicated, like the tiny flowers of lavender. Achillea volunteered to go to Maren's garden and pick all the marigolds there were, in order to dye some fabric. Luckily, Gladia still had in her pack two plain robes which she had acquired in Sanguinea to take back to Mellia to adorn with stitching and return to market, and a dozen or so plain netelas which could be easily joined together to make a Priestess veil.

Throughout all this planning, Ambar had listened keenly but had not spoken once. I turned to him now, fully aware that I needed his support if my plan were to have the smallest chance of success. I knew that I had betrayed his confidence in me about the brooch and that I might have made him angry. In the back of my mind, I still worried that he would return to the court of the Queen with us all as captives. I decided to try to address the practical issues and leave the issues of trust and feelings to one side; they were already smearing my judgement. 'Do you think you and brother Tarik could be the Priestess Guard?' I asked him. 'For it may be that, as well as for the sake of appearances, we will end up in need of your protection and your fighting skills, especially if we persuade Lunaria to come away from the Temple with us.'

His mouth curved into a slightly scornful smile, as if he was surprised I had even asked such a thing, and said, 'Yes, sister Talla, or should I say Priestess Talla – or what name should we call you, for I am sure that your own name will cause consternation if we announce it so.' I had not thought of this before, but swiftly I came up with the name Neroli which was another name for the orange blossoms and would be most appropriate for the colour of the robe. It felt as if Ambar and I were playing some sort of game of skill and tactics, where each of us would make a move and then the other would try to outdo it. Ambar was intent on pointing out things I had not thought of, and I was just as intent on solving his puzzles and proving that everything was in my grasp. 'You do know,' he added conversationally, 'that all Priestesses carry with them a scroll of Permission when they travel to other Temples?'

The others all stopped and gaped, for it was well known that none but the Scribes and Readers could write and read, and none of us were Scribes or Readers. Or so they thought, for I had never told them of my ability to scribe or read. Ambar was looking at me, half in despair at finding a fatal flaw, and half in triumph for the same reason. I had seen these scrolls before, when Priestesses visited the Temple, and I was cleaning the High Priestess's quarters, so I knew they were very plain affairs, merely stating the name of the visiting Priestess and that the travel had been agreed by her High Priestess, and the purpose of the visit. I would have to think carefully about the wording, but I was sure if I practiced it with a fine charcoal stick, I could make a passable copy. I took a deep breath and told them all my secret; that I could both scribe and read. There was more gaping.

Benakiell showed the most interest and leaned forward and muttered, 'I should have known. She is indeed someone of many talents. I can cut a fine reed pen for you to use Talla.'

I gratefully thanked him and turned to Ambar, happy to have overcome his final barrier. He smiled at me briefly and then said, 'Well, there appear to be no more reasons why we should not try Talla's plan. And I do not believe there is another way. This may be our final and only chance to put in place the rightful Queen. Maren must certify her to be the Queen's heir; we must not forget that most of what we do depends on her being able to see enough to verify the birthmark which has so far only been seen by Bellis. I should remind you all that if we fail, there will be certain punishment or even death.' He looked round soberly. We all looked back, undeterred. Ambar continued, 'Ashtun and Benakiell, can we rely on you to protect those left behind? Tarik and I will accompany our sisters Talla and Achillea to the Temple. You will need to take care of the camp here at Besseret while we are away. We may be some five days in total, as it will take us two days of travel to get back to the Temple of the Goddess's Blessing. Gladia, can we rely on you to care for Bellis and for Maren, and to ensure that the salve continues to be applied to Maren's eyes? It will take us some time to get everything ready, perhaps two days. I wish I knew how things were in the court of the Queen, it might inform the speed with which we have to work. Did you ask Bellis?' He turned to me expectantly, and I had to answer that I had not asked Bellis his questions. He sighed in exasperation, and, feeling guilty, I muttered that I would ask her when I next visited her. We agreed that we would not tell Bellis or Maren the true reason for our journey away and would instead tell them that we had gone to fetch supplies.

FANNING THE FLAMES
CHAPTER 29

I was still averse to asking Bellis all the questions about the Queen's Court which Ambar wanted to know, but I knew that it was important to find out how much time we might have left, so I went to visit the next day. She was sitting outside more now, although still unable to walk much due to the wounds on her feet, and her eyes followed the men warily when they walked near. She spent much of her time with Gladia who was continuing to show her how to stitch and, I had to admit, rather grudgingly, that she had a neatness and a patience which I lacked. Achillea had come back from the gardens with a basket full of marigold flowers and Tarik showed me how to steep the flowers in water overnight and then break up the flowers with a stick and boil them up in a large pot. We left the plain robe and the two netelas steeping in the pot for some time before hanging them out to dry on the bushes. I watched them blowing in the breeze like huge butterflies and wondered why the people of the Outer did not dress in these beautiful bright colours every day. I, who had been surrounded by colour in the Temple in some ways, and yet deprived of it in others, in the muddy greys and browns of the drabcoat I wore every day, and forbidden from wearing colour, thought that to wear colour freely must be a wonderful thing. My only experience of being clothed in colour was on the night before I left the Temple when I had worn the warm and fiery robe of Flammeus, which had been my one chance to see what it might have been like to have chosen the Temple.

Perhaps it was only my upbringing which made me see colour in this way; for the people of the Outer who saw and lived freely with colour every day tended only to use colour in the embroidery of their robes, though perhaps those from other lands wore robes of different colours. Tearing myself away from the bright clothes, I went to sit next to Bellis, asking her how she was. She brightened when she saw me and welcomed me, showing me her stitching, I praised her work, and she laid it aside as we talked.

I did not have the subtlety that others had when addressing difficult questions and instead asked Ambar's questions outright. 'What did you hear of the Queen, sister Bellis, when you were kept at her OutFort? Did the AngelMothers talk of her at all, or even the OutRiders you saw? I am sorry to ask this of you,' I added hastily, seeing how her eyes clouded over as soon as I mentioned the AngelMothers and the OutRiders. 'But it is crucial, and it may help us to stop what happened to you from happening to others. Anything you may have heard of the health of the Queen or her plans could be crucial. You are such an important person to us being able to help them.' I had deliberately added this last sentence, knowing how much Bellis had wanted to be an important member of the Temple, and hoping that this small flattery might make her more likely to tell me what she knew. She frowned, pulling her thoughts together.

'I don't really, know, Talla, I mean nobody really spoke to me about anything except to tell me what to do or where to go; some of the Angels did talk to me a bit but it wasn't encouraged; it was like the Temple in that way, talking wasn't really allowed in case it stopped us working hard. I did hear that the Queen was very ill, and she was in her bedchamber. The AngelMothers talked about it; they said she would die soon and there was no new Queen to replace her.' She paused, wincing slightly, and I watched in peculiar fascination as her whole belly lifted and shifted like a boiling pot. Bellis laughed at me and told me that, as she now knew, it was the baby moving inside her, settling down. I had never been so close to a woman carrying a baby and it was very strange to imagine a child moving around beneath the surface of the skin. It didn't seem to me that Bellis had added much to what we already knew, but as I prepared to go and tell Ambar what she had said, she spoke again, 'I did hear the OutRiders speaking to each other, the ones that captured me. They said that there would be a big change in the world when the month of Ashkana comes.' I pondered on this; I was a little unsure of what month we might even be in, lacking the regulation of timing of the Temple. There were seven months, each of seven weeks, each week of seven days. The months took the names of the days, and each month there was a special day named for the day on which the numbers aligned. I had been told I had been born on Conflagration Day. Conflagration Day fell on the first day of the week of Flammeus in the month of Flammeus. In addition to these seven months, there were three intercalary weeks named for the Goddess and the Prophets Ashkana and Asmara. These weeks were spread evenly through the year. This could be very useful information for Ambar, if he knew what month we were in now. I thanked Bellis for helping me with my questions, and then changed the dressings on her feet. They were much better, the honey-soaked rags had healed the angry infection and inflammation, and I encouraged her to leave her feet out in the sun for a while before I dressed them again.

Achillea was hanging out the grey and brown patchworked drabcoat that had been worn by Bellis out on the lavender bushes. If clothes were light enough, spreading them to dry on a sweet-scented shrub was a clever plan, filling the cloth with the smell of the flower. Achillea wrinkled her nose at me as I walked towards her and gestured to the garment. 'How on earth could you bear to wear it, Talla? It has taken me an age to scrub it out against the washrock!' I smiled. I knew what she meant, in a way, for the drabcoat was unflattering, with its lack of colour and ornamentation, and its cut. But it was practical, you could move easily in it, its size was adjustable to a large degree (although not made, obviously for women who were with child), and I had enjoyed its anonymity. Nobody noticed you wearing a drabcoat, though I suspected this would not suit Achillea, who took great care with her appearance.

It seemed that Achillea was much engaged in the task ahead of us and took her forthcoming role as a great opportunity to question me about all aspects of being a TempleMaid. Prior to this, I had been rather reserved about what life was like in the Temple, and now I really had no excuse for not answering her questions. She assured me that she would use all the information I gave her to play her part with greater accuracy. I told her as much as I could, showing her how to walk with her eyes cast down, and warning her not to look anyone in the face, even the Priestesses whose faces could not be seen, because, be assured, they could still see you. It would be most difficult to get Achillea to give the impression of working all the time since she was not inclined to do this in real life, and I considered what Temple job she could be said to do. Eventually, we decided that we would say that she worked as a Physic. She had thought of the idea for the salve for Maren, and she had a good knowledge of the flowers and herbs in her mother's garden which had grown for the bees, but which all had other uses. Indeed, I thought, perhaps this was why honey was such a healing substance; because it contained the nectar from all these flowers of the Physic. I left Achillea to collect up some herbs and flowers to dry and make into concoctions and salves to carry with us and went on.

Benakiell looked up from his whittling when I walked over. He was sitting in the shade of a Paradox tree, a small bundle of reeds at his feet, concentrating on trying to fashion the shape of a pen which I could use to write the Scroll of Permission. I had never used a pen and ink before, although I had seen the Scribe in the Temple using a pen to scribe and ornament the Scrolls of Choice. I had myself only used fine charcoal sticks to write with although usually I just used a stick in the sand, since it could be easily brushed away and hidden. I asked him how he knew how to make such a thing, and he smiled.

'You are not the only one who holds their knowledge close to their heart, sister Talla. In my younger days, when I travelled more, I even journeyed to other lands, and saw there how some of these things were made. We can learn so much from seeing how others do things. Much of what I know best is what I have learned from people who are not of this land, from people who do not live like us, but who have so many interesting things to teach us. I should like to travel this world again one day,' he concluded wistfully, and laid the pen he had made on one side. 'You can only use a reed pen for a while before the ink makes it soft and unclear, so I have made you a pile of them! I will make the ink too. I have seen it made with crushed charcoal boiled hard with berry juice, so I will have some ready for you to try by the end of the day. But I am struggling to know where we will get the parchment from.' Something else which had not occurred to me, but luckily, I still had the parchment I had brought with me from the Temple in my underpocket. 'The Goddess seems to be guiding your luck, sister Talla,' observed Benakiell, his eyes twinkling at me again when I mentioned it. 'You have been thinking ahead without even realising it!' I smiled back at him, feeling happy and secure in his support for my endeavour. I suspected he would have liked to attend the Temple with us, but he recognised that his role was here in Besseret, protecting the others. I could learn a lot from Benakiell, and I suddenly longed for a time where I could just sit on the step of his dwelling in Mellia and ask him questions about his travels and all the things he had seen and learned and the places where he had been. Perhaps one day I would be able to do that, after all of this was over.

Later that afternoon, when the orange robes and netelas had dried in the sun, I gathered them up and went to visit Gladia to show her how to join the netelas to make the veil of a Priestess. I had seen them in close quarters before, when I was working in the clothes cleaning block, where the clothes were washed weekly. The drabcoats were all stewed together in a big vat over a fire with water and a large soapball. It didn't matter if the colours ran together after all. But the Priestesses' robes and veils were washed individually. Each Priestess had two robes and two veils so that one could be worn while the other was being washed, and they were particular to each Priestess, not shared like our drabcoats were. I had seen how the veil was made so that the Priestess could see out, but it was difficult for anyone to see in. The veil had a slit cut in the top where the eyes were which was then covered over with carefully knotted threads dyed in the same colour as the veil. I had peered through one of these nets once, and it was easy to see through them after a while, for the threads were so close that they blurred and vanished as you looked out. Once we had cut the required shape out of one of the netelas, I drew a pattern for Gladia using a stick in the dust. We laid out the orange dyed threads into the pattern, and Gladia's nimble fingers knotted them together easily enough. For all her plumpness, and her lack of inclination to movement, Gladia's fingers and hands could move quickly, and she knew how to work with threads. These people, whom I was getting to know better and better, kept on showing me new levels of who they were. I did not feel like I had the same levels of being as they did. I had been brought up in the Temple like so many other Maids, and in exactly the same way. We believed in the same things, we were taught the same readings of Ashkana, and I assumed the Priestesses all learned the same sort of things from the Prophet Asmara's readings. And so, perhaps, if one had the same upbringing as so many others, one felt as if there were no real layers to one's being. But the people of the Outer had all lived varied lives, and all their experiences had blended together to make a unique person – much like one could get a unique colour by mixing different dyes and colourings.

I had one small strip of parchment left after removing the larger piece which I needed for the Scroll of Permission, and I drew out a design to pounce for Gladia to stitch along the hem of the robe, the sleeves and the veil. It was so satisfying to know that I only needed to draw out one section of the design and then use it repeatedly until the pattern was done. Because we had dyed the cloth orange from the marigolds, I chose a design of simple white orange blossoms. Often the embroidery work on the robes of the Priestesses was more complicated than the work that Gladia could do, but we did not have the time to make anything more ornate; the important thing was to complete the disguise as quickly as possible. In any case, it gave me a valid excuse for asking to see Lunaria; I would ask for her expertise in making me a new more ornamented

Priestess robe, since she was such an accomplished embroiderer herself. Everything was coming together well.

Ambar and Tarik were working on the horses and on polishing and waxing their armour. Ashtun was working with them, looking for all the world like an OutRider himself as he sharpened the edges of his arrows against a stone. Ambar was teaching him what to do should they find themselves under attack while we were away. Benakiell still sat under the tree with his reeds, reluctant to learn any tactics from the OutRiders, and happy to rely on his own heavy club and knowledge of the world. I was sure that nobody would come to Besseret anyway, but it was good to know that Gladia, Bellis and Maren would be safe while we were away. I felt excited because we would be travelling again and doing something new. Doing the same things every day had its appeal and made me feel safe and grounded, but there was also a hunger in my heart to learn more about my world, to meet new people, to find out new things, to learn new skills. And I was eager to find out more about who I was, too.

Over the next day, we all worked on our tasks. Achillea had to be persuaded to remove her braids and leave her hair with no beautification, save a quick comb through, which displeased her enormously, and she grumbled about how long it would take her to get her hair back to her exacting standards when we returned from the Temple. I worked hard on planning the wording of the Scroll of Permission, and Ambar told me some of the wording that he himself had heard from some of these scrolls. I was beginning to see how, more and more, the ability to scribe and to read were powerful tools. I knew that not all the Priestesses could read and write, for we only had one Reader and Scriber in our Temple and I assumed it was the same for the other Temples. Ambar told me that it was similar in the OutFort, but that in the Queen's court many more people had the ability. And I could see how important it could be in sending messages that you did not want others to read. I supposed that the silent language used by the OutRiders was the same kind of thing – a way of communicating things to other people which you did not want everyone to know. I even asked Ambar about the silent language, but he brushed away my questions and said that it was unique to the OutRiders. I was surprised that he still identified himself as an OutRider since he was in opposition to the Queen and her Court who were clinging on to power at all costs, but, when I thought about it, I was not sure where I belonged either. Was I a Maid of the Temple or a woman of the Outer? I did not belong anywhere, and perhaps it was the same for him, for almost all the skills of fighting he had learned in the OutRiders were not needed here in the Outer. We held onto the things which we knew, in the face of all the things of which we were ignorant.

When I had the wording right, I collected the reed pens and the ink from Benakiell and began to practice using the pen, dry in the fine red dust initially and then using the ink and the pen on the back of a patterned piece of parchment so that I knew how to manage it. I had to make this right, because there was no more parchment and besides, we had no time to acquire more. Benakiell led me to a mid-height flat rock. 'When I have seen others scribing on my travels, I have seen that they scribe at a flat or slanted surface, standing up or sitting down, for it helps to steady the pen – and perhaps the thoughts,' he said. He asked me if he could stay and watch me and I was happy for him to be there. Benakiell was interested and curious, like I was, and he watched keenly as I moved the reed pens over the surface of the parchment, offering me the best cut pens when the one I was using started to get soggy. When I had finished, I read it back to myself. There may have been the odd character which looked slightly wrong, but I made sure to put in lots of curlicues and trailing lines, so that these errors were less obvious. Benakiell looked at it with admiration when it was dry and ran his fingers over the script. He asked me to show him a word, so he could learn it, and I showed him the word Temple. He copied it carefully into the dust with a spare reed pen and then practiced it a few times until he knew it. I promised that I would teach him more when I returned, and I did not doubt that he would be a quick and able student. I wished I had had somebody who could have taught me, instead of having to work it out for myself but there was no time for regrets now. I rolled the parchment carefully and set off towards Gladia to see if she had finished the stitching yet which had to be done by dawn the next day, when we would be setting off.

Gladia was sitting out under a Paradox tree when I got there, her lap full of orange fabric, busily stitching away. She had a big task to complete, and I was once again grateful for these, my friends, who had willingly joined in with me in the hope that my plan might succeed. When others support you, you feel braver and more successful, and when they doubt you, you doubt yourself. She showed me the completed veil; the grille at the front was carefully stitched in place, and there were entwined orange flowers stitched around the bottom. 'Try it on,' she urged me, and I placed it over my head. It felt heavy, even though the cloth itself was a light cotton, no different from a netela. I realised how focused the Priestesses must become; for all the peripheral world was cut off from them and they only saw what was in front of them. The grille was at exactly the right level for my eyes; as I got used to it, the threads in front of my eyes seemed to blur and soon I was almost unaware of them. Gladia shuddered. 'I don't like that, Talla, and I don't mind saying it! How can you ever have the measure of somebody when you can't see their eyes? I don't know how you Maids coped in there!'

'We did not know any different,' I pointed out to her, and she nodded her head thoughtfully and returned to her work.

CHAPTER 30

The sun was just rising as we prepared to leave Besseret. The dark of night had already turned to purple, with pink glowing in the east. There was a faint smell of dew on dust. Birds were singing. Gladia had made her fire early and wisps of wood smoke curled through the air, mixing with the smell of freshly brewed coffee. Ambar and Tarik were speaking to Ashtun, leaving last minute advice. Achillea and I looked at one another. She was wearing Bellis's drabcoat, stitched together once again, freshly washed and dried, looking much neater and more attractive than I ever did in a drabcoat. Her hair looked unfinished without its braids, and I realised how quickly I had become accustomed to the small individualities that defined my friends. When I finished my breakfast, I placed the veil over my head. I had tried to argue that I could leave it off while we travelled, but Ambar and Tarik did not agree and reminded me of how much depended upon my disguise, so I reluctantly agreed to wear the veil now until we either succeeded or failed in our mission. I looked out at my companions through the veil, and, because they could not see my eyes, they began almost immediately to avoid looking at my face as they spoke to me, even whilst I could see them and their reactions to things. It was like being able to see people without them seeing me, and I thought about how the Priestesses always knew what was going on in the Temple and realised now how that might have come about. We just did not notice them, even though they moved around in bright colours, just because we did not see their faces. I was concerned that my voice might be recognised at the Temple by those who knew me. We were taught to speak in a particular way at the Temple; modulated and balanced, with no inflexion for emotion. The Priestesses spoke in much the same way, but more forcefully. Since I had been living in the Outer, I had been trying to put a lightness in my voice which I had noticed from Gladia and Achillea; a quickness of speech, and now I had to try and return to something that might appear more like a Priestess. I found that if I tilted my chin downwards somewhat as I spoke and kept my mouth tight, it made my voice deeper, so I practiced speaking like this, and hoped that the impossibility of me appearing to be a Priestess from a distant Temple would mean that any similarity to the Temple Maid who had left might be overlooked.

Ashtun and Achillea made their farewells; he looking askance at her new outfit, for which she teased him, laughing at his preference for her to be dressed up and ornamented and joking that when she was old, he might not find her so appealing. Achillea was able to stay happy despite the circumstances, and I envied her this brightness of life; she did not waste worry on things she did not believe she could change. Benakiell came over to me as I sat on one of the horses connected to Ambar's horse by a leather rein and joked that he was speaking to a Priestess for the first time. Ambar tucked the Scroll of Permission into his saddle bag alongside our provisions. We carried gourds of water, and on one of Tarik's horses hung smaller gourds filled with our hastily put together concoctions, decoctions and salves, as well as some small gourds of Maren's honey in case we needed to show evidence of our ability to trade. Ambar and Tarik wore their oiled leather armour and had polished their horses' metal bridles and decorations and carried their bows and arrows on their backs. Achillea sat on a horse linked behind Tarik and I sat on mine behind Ambar, decorously riding side saddle, as befitted a Priestess. We said our goodbyes and, as the sun rose in the sky, pushing back the pink in favour of the blue, we headed off back towards the Temple of the Goddess's Blessing.

Little was said until we stopped at noon beside a stream. Gratefully getting off the horses, Achillea and I walked to the small stand of trees leaving Ambar and Tarik to guide the horses to the water. The animals bent their heads thankfully to the stream and drank deeply as we made our way back. We had taken four of the five horses, leaving one for Ashtun in case of emergency. As well as the archery, he had been working more with the horses, riding them and controlling them, as well as tending to them. Should we succeed in persuading Lunaria to return with us to Besseret, she would ride with Ambar so that he could guard her. I longed to remove my restrictive veil, but it was not safe to do so; we could not know when another group of OutRiders might come by. We had agreed to say that I came from a Temple a long way distant, beyond the Okoh mountains. Benakiell had come up with the location, as he said it was one of the furthest places he had been to during the time he had travelled around our land. Mostly, the Temples were visited from only the Temples that were within a day's travel, so we felt this was a good choice. After eating, we continued on our way.

I looked around me at the landscape as we moved through it. We travelled through grassland and shrubby groups of trees; their occasional shade was welcome in the building heat, and at one point we stopped to gather some fresh wild Carissa fruits, enjoying their fresh tartness. But for all I tried to enjoy the passing scenery, and to try to move with the horse as Ambar had suggested, sitting on it sideways with my Priestess robe was uncomfortable, and I longed to stop. I tried to think through every eventuality of what might occur on our arrival at the Temple, and of what the best way of persuading Lunaria to come with us and not alerting the other Priestesses at the Temple might be. I was torn between announcing myself to her once we were alone in the Temple, and not telling her anything at all except that she was to come with us to our supposed Temple and then revealing the truth once we were far away from the Temple. I did not know how much the OutRiders were still searching for me, or how many times they had revisited the Temple since my departure, nor what they had told the Temple about me or the brooch. It felt like I was trying to weave a cloth from cobwebs and thistledown, insubstantial and fragile.

Ambar and Tarik had planned to keep us away from people as far as possible, and so we were taking a more circuitous route back to my Temple. It would be extremely difficult to answer the questions of other OutRiders or curious people of the Outer, so we planned to sleep outside, in a small forest which Ambar and Tarik knew about. They were well versed in travelling the terrain and knew all manner of ways to get to places, able to keep it all in their heads, for they never consulted a chart of any sort, contenting themselves with occasional discussions involving drawing diagrams in the dust and looking at the position of the sun and the mountains. Eventually we arrived at the place they had chosen and Achillea and I got down from the horses, stretching our aching bodies.

Tarik took out two large cloths from his saddlebags and began to make them into shelters by tying them to the trees and weighting the edges down with heavy stones. He worked quietly and efficiently while Ambar led the horses to some grass. Achillea took out the emberjar and built us a fire to make us some coffee and to heat up the flatbreads we had packed to bring with us. We ate simply, boiling up dried beans and tomatoes to go with the flatbread. Eating with the veil on was difficult; I had to raise it off my face slightly and then put the food in my mouth quickly before getting the food all over the veil. This was a skill I did not think I would like to work on, and it made me feel even more vindicated in my decision to leave the Temple. A life condemned to wear a veil forever was no life for me, but I reminded myself of what had happened to Bellis when she left the Temple and realised that this was no life either. It made me even more determined to ensure that we got Lunaria to the court of the Queen. After we had eaten, we retired to our sleeping areas, and finally I removed the veil, keeping it close to my head while I dropped asleep, listening to the sounds of the bushbabies and the owls in the thicket.

The next day, the skies were a sullen grey. It was warm and the heat was building, and it seemed a thunderstorm might be on the way. We were all quiet, even Achillea, who had stopped trying to engage me in chatter from Tarik's horse, and instead sat silently, rehearsing some of the stock phrases I had taught her to say; 'As the Goddess wishes it', 'Blessed be the Goddess', 'As it is told' and 'Yes, Sister'. Most of the time, the Temple Maids were merely told what to do and these responses were an acknowledgement that we had heard the order and would fulfil it. There was no other real choice of answer. It was not a known thing in the Temple to disobey the orders of the Priestesses, and in any case, we had been raised to believe that what they asked of us was the will of the Goddess, so we did not think to quibble.

I was already weary, even before we set off; the ground had been as hard as dry earth always is, and I missed my sleeping mat. I tried to think through what I knew about Lunaria and how she might react to the news I had to tell her, and I became increasingly convinced that if I told her while we were still in the Temple, she would turn me over to the Priestesses. Not through malice, but through her desire to do the right thing as directed by the Goddess. Perhaps she lacked that spark in her mind which I had, and which seemed to burn brighter and brighter the longer I stayed away from the Temple. In the Temple, it would be strange to behave in this way, suggesting different ideas, finding new things out, but in the Outer, it was normal, a way of making one's way through the world.

As the sun dipped down towards the west, we neared the Temple. We were approaching from behind it, so we did not pass through Mellia. That would have been unwise, since Achillea at least would have been recognised by those who still lived there, and were presumably, still waiting for our return. I wondered if they worried about us. We stopped a short distance from the gates to the Temple and went over our plans for the final time. As was traditional, Ambar and Tarik would present the Scroll of Permission at the Gatehouse. It would be taken to the Reader who would confirm its contents with the High Priestess and then they would return it to Ambar. Often, the same scroll could be used several times, especially if a Temple was seeking some item that was rare or difficult to find with ordinary trade; perhaps a certain medication or a piece of fine embroidery. If all was well, then we would be admitted to the GuestHouse and begin our efforts to find Lunaria. Ambar and Tarik would remain at the Gatehouse unless we summoned them, perhaps to bring our goods to us. I reminded them that my name was Priestess Neroli but advised Achillea to merely call me Priestess so that my name did not slip out inadvertently.

'I wish you well, Priestess Neroli,' said Tarik, gravely. 'Be constantly aware of what is happening around you; that veil will allow you to observe things even where people may not think you watch. And sister Achillea, keeping your eyes to the floor will mean you will hear more. Remember that we depend on you, that we trust you to complete this most important of tasks.'

This small speech made me feel even more anxious, truth be told, although it was intended to boost our courage, and I just wanted to get on with the task in hand. We turned the corner and there, I knew, was the Temple, behind the stone wall with the pink light of the sky glancing off its polished stone exterior. I marvelled at its beauty and its intricacy, all the while remembering that it had been made by those Angels. Not armies of heavenly helpers sent by the Goddess, but discarded Maids from the Temple, forced to work their fingers to blood and bone and to be the slaves of the OutRiders, and who were sent there by the Priestesses themselves. I clenched my jaw beneath my veil and we rode on at a measured pace until we arrived at the gate.

CHAPTER 31

We dismounted from the horses at the Temple Gate and composed ourselves, waiting for the Priestess of the Gate to attend to us. From underneath my veil, I scanned the Temple and the grounds, feeling a pang of familiarity as I followed the lines of the dormits round towards the Temple itself and saw the Priestess house, the Guesthouse and the Babyhouse. I thought of the babies who were being cared for in there, and of the journey that awaited the baby boys who would move to the OutFort when they finished their first year, and of the lives of the baby girls who might become Priestesses or who might be rejected and be sent out to be captured and become Angels. It was a good thing that I was veiled, for otherwise the Priestess who came hurrying towards us might have seen the snap in my eyes.

The Priestess wore the colour of Viridis. There were several Priestesses in my time who wore Viridis; Adia, Gelila and Layla and some others who I could not remember, even though it had only been a few months since I had left. I realised that it did not matter much what they were called; we never saw them, and they could have been replaced by anyone else and we Maids would never have known.

'I greet you, Sister,' she said in a low voice, slightly out of breath. 'We did not expect a visitor! Do you have a Scroll?'

'Blessed be the Goddess,' I said in an equally low and moderated voice, tilting my chin down to alter my voice and nudging Achillea slightly who dutifully echoed my response. 'This Rider has the Scroll,' I continued, gesturing towards Ambar. 'We have journeyed from afar, to visit your Temple for we have need of your expert seamstress. We have seen the skill of Sister Lunaria on a veil which we had sight of some months ago. As you can see,' I waved at the hem of my robe, 'our own Stitchers do not have her fine skill yet, and sadly we lost our best Stitcher who joined the Goddess after her seventh age.'

'Blessed be the Goddess,' came the response from the Priestess. 'Sister Lunaria is indeed a Stitcher of some prowess. My name is Priestess Gelila, and you are?'

'I am Priestess Neroli,' I answered, 'and this Maid is Achillea. She works as a Physic. We have some medicaments and some honey we brought with us to trade should you need it. We will await the Reader.' Ambar proffered the Scroll of Permission and Priestess Gelila took it and bustled off. Achillea and I sat on the stone bench and Ambar and Tarik waited at the Gate with the horses. I pressed Achillea's hand comfortingly, as I saw her twist her drabcoat anxiously.

In the event, it was very easy. Gelila reappeared some minutes later, carrying the scroll, which she returned to the OutRiders, and gave them instructions on using the Gatehouse and stabling their horses. After they had left, the Priestess led us down the path towards the Guesthouse. She was brisk, but hospitable enough, and told us that the evening meal had already taken place but that a Maid would bring us coffee and water for washing. I was relieved that the meal was done with, since I did not wish to be closely examined by too many people, and I knew that after sundown, it was the habit of the Priestesses to retire for personal prayer and reflection. The room she led me to was much more luxurious than the dormits in which we Maids had slept, with a bed frame raised from the floor and some woven covers. There was a mat in the corner of the room which she pointed out to me and told me that it was for my Maid to sleep on. I nearly laughed aloud, as Achillea stolidly kept her eyes to the floor, but I could sense her seething soul. I had never travelled out of the Temple until I left it, and so I did not know about these differences between the Maids and the Priestesses, but it was certainly educational. I was learning a lot from this visit already. Priestess Gelila asked if we needed anything more, and then told us that we could see Priestess Lunaria in the morning, when we could discuss what we needed from her, and if she would be able to stitch it for us. I thanked the Priestess for her assistance and blessed the Goddess, and then Gelila turned to me and asked, in an interested way, 'So what is it you do in your own Temple, sister Neroli?'

For a moment my mind went blank. I had not thought that I, as a Priestess must have a role to play in the Temple too, but then I suddenly realised that I did have a skill, and moreover it was one which only one other in the Temple could identify, and that was reading. 'I am the Reader at our Temple, sister Gelila,' I replied. 'It is to be hoped that none visits our far-off Temple while I am away, but I think it unlikely; we have only received one visit this past year.' She inclined her head towards me graciously and blessed the Goddess, murmuring that my Temple were indeed lucky to have me there as a Reader. There was much of this elaborate talking done by the Priestesses, who complimented one another incessantly. She left shortly afterwards, and Achillea busied herself with arranging the gourds of physic we had brought, hanging some of them up on the hooks on the wall, and stacking the rest by the wall. There was a tap on the door a few minutes later and a Maid came in with coffee and water. She was a Maid who worked in the kitchens with the cooks, by the name of Elida. She was solid and hardworking, and I recognised her face from under my veil. It was strange to see one I knew, and yet for them to be seeing me as something I was not. She gave the things to Achillea and scurried out, banging into the doorframe in her haste to leave.

I sat down cautiously on the raised bed. I had never slept on such a thing before. Achillea threw a look at me, and I patted the bed next to me. She came and sat down next to me, and I saw that the door had a simple locking mechanism on it of a weighty wooden peg on a leather band which could be slipped through a hasp on the wall, so I got up and locked the door quietly. With a sigh of relief, I took off the veil and flung it on the bed, exasperated by its continuous presence. Achillea laughed, for now unguarded, and lifted her legs up on to the bed, enjoying the feeling of being almost carried by the stretched leather straps underneath the mat. I poured the coffee and we drank it and ate some dates, happy to be out of the way of others and able to be ourselves.

We were weary after two days of riding, and when we had eaten and washed, we went over our plans for the next morning, and our hopes for persuading Lunaria to come away with us. I knew that the next morning we would be woken at daybreak by the sun shining through the pierced windows high up on the wall. During the morning hours, the Temple was open for worship and prayer of the Goddess, and I thought it would call more attention to us if we did not attend, so I reminded Achillea about what she should do when we visited the Temple. We would try to attend as early as possible, avoiding the Gathering when most members of the Temple would attend after they had eaten. We would try to attend Temple early and then eat and ascribe it to different Temple timetables. I knew from visits we had had in the past that every Temple in Oramia set its own local timetables, so this should be the best way of planning our visit. Lunaria would have already been told that a visitor wished to see her about some stitching and would be available to us in the morning. At last, we lay on the bed, which was plenty big enough for two, drew up the covers, and slept.

The light flooded in through the pierced walls, along with a cool breeze which seemed to indicate it had rained in the night, although I had not heard it – one didn't ever hear the rain fall on the roof since the whole of the Temple had been carved out of stone. For a moment, I was unsure where I was – was I in the Temple, or in Mellia, or in Besseret? It had been a very comfortable night's sleep on the raised bed, and I had every intention of trying to replicate its structure when I had a place of my own again. Achillea and I saw to our dressing and washing and crept quietly along the dark corridor towards the Temple to complete our daily devotions in as much isolation as possible.

There was one other Priestess in the Temple, wearing the colours of Flavus. It could be old Saphna who was the Priestess who had found me as a baby. It might be useful to exchange some polite niceties with her and try to hear the story again, but it was impossible to tell whether it really was her since there were three who wore Flavus when I had left the Temple and by now there may well be more. Come to that, Saphna might have gone to the Goddess herself; she had seemed old to me even as a child. She did walk with a limp on her right side though, so I might be reasonably sure of myself if she rose. I had told Achillea before we arrived that only the Priestesses were allowed to pray on the dais beyond the Goddess, and she obediently went to sit at the feet of the Goddess in silent contemplation. The Goddess was clad in Flavus which explained the presence of the Priestess; on the day of your colour, the Temple was always attended by Priestesses and Maids of that colour.

I walked serenely past the Goddess into a part of the Temple I had never set foot in before.

You could see into the Priestess's area from where we Maids sat, but I had not appreciated the fineness of the carving of the piercings in the walls from there. There were patterns carved into the stone; sarcelly crosses and spirals and lattices, which spilled the sunlight into the area. The Priestesses sat on formed clay benches, unlike we Maids who sat on the floor, and I duly sat on a bench, bowing my head and going over my plans for the day rather than attending to the Goddess. The scent of yellow jasmine wafted through the Temple, and I saw a Maid had appeared and was oiling the feet of the Goddess as the day began.

After I had been there some time, the Priestess dressed in Flavus stood up, her bones creaking audibly, and I could see the familiar way of walking of Saphna. I waited until she passed me and then rose to greet her. I was a little worried that she might recognise my voice, so I made sure to try and make it deeper and slower than I usually spoke.

'Blessed be the Goddess this day of Flavus,' I said to her courteously, acknowledging her superiority on this day.

'Praise be,' she responded. 'You must be our visitor from afar,' she continued. 'We have heard that you seek the stitching of Lunaria. She has such skill; I am not surprised that you wish to make use of her talents. Do you know, I was the one who found her as a baby?' I nearly tripped over my robe as I heard Saphna say this. I had heard her talk of finding me, but she had never mentioned that she found Lunaria too. Perhaps she found both of us at the same time and I was the other DoubleSoul to Lunaria, which would mean I was her sister. I breathed in and calmed my voice.

'Indeed, sister? Perhaps she was left in a well stitched cover or some such, as a sign of her future stitching talents!' Saphna allowed herself a small, dry chuckle which rapidly turned into a cough. I waited for her to finish her paroxysm and then told her that we had brought physic and honey with us, and that I could perhaps help her with her ailment. She thanked me, and then returned to the subject of Lunaria.

'She was left on the same day as another baby; I found them both. One of them had a gold brooch pinned on her wrapping cloths and one of them was just wrapped in an old blanket but I can't remember for the life of me which one was which. One was Priestess Lunaria, and one was a Maid called Talla. She stole the brooch when she left after Choice, you know. Asinte was very cross with me because I was the one who had told Talla the brooch came with her. I didn't know really if it was her or Lunaria, but Lunaria was always so skilled at everything as a child, whereas Talla never really shone at anything...' I had to dig my nails in to my palms to stop myself from making some sort of angry retort to Saphna. I wanted to ask her more questions, but she tailed off, as if aware that perhaps she had told me, a stranger, more than she should have done. As people got older, their tongues got looser, it seemed. At the Temple, the older Priestesses spent more and more time with the babies in the BabyHouse until they were cared for in the same way as the babies; safe, fed and sheltered until they went to be with the Goddess.

I filled the silent gap which had bubbled up with some complimentary remarks about the beautiful Temple and the ornate piercings in the walls, and Saphna's face brightened again as she guided me to the meeting room. 'And here is our Priestess Lunaria, with some of her stitching. Her fingers are guided by the Goddess herself!'

'Blessed be the Goddess,' I responded automatically, and 'Praise be,' echoed Achillea, playing her role impeccably. The Meeting Room was a large chamber whose doors opened out onto a balcony, allowing the sunshine to stream into the room. Lunaria sat on a clay bench near the doors, stitching a blue veil. I wondered if it was frustrating to have to stitch whilst looking through the grille in the Priestess veil. I found stitching frustrating enough without a veil and felt sure I would soon throw it to the floor in disgust if I had to try to stitch so finely with a veil on.

'Thank you, Priestess Saphna,' said Lunaria. The old Priestess turned to leave the room, once again coughing. Achillea moved towards her instinctively, as she would have done towards Gladia or another older woman of the Outer, to lay a friendly hand on her shoulder. I hastily moved towards Lunaria at the same time, so she did not see what would be considered a transgression by my Maid. Achillea stayed herself quickly and Saphna left the room. I moved over to Lunaria and sat on the bench alongside her. Achillea sat on the mat at my feet, as she had been told to do.

'I am told that you seek stitching for your Temple,' Lunaria began. 'I can show you some of the veils I have stitched already, so that you can see my work. It is a great honour that you have heard of my stitching so far away as your Temple is.' She took a selection of veils out of her basket and laid them out next to us. I evinced interest in them, picking them up and examining the stitching. I had no knowledge of how this transaction should progress. The only experience I had of trading was that one occasion in Sanguinea when I had traded some of my honey. I knew that trading between Temples would be different to the barter and banter of the trade in the Outer. I picked out a veil that was in a deep crimson red, my own colour of Flammeus though I had no assigned colour now that I was one who belonged nowhere. Even though I had only ever worn the colour once, before I left the Temple, and before that I had always been clad in the drab, I had an affinity for it, which must have been borne of so many weeks of tending to the Goddess, of smelling the rich spiciness of cinnamon bark and of laying the rich red fabrics over the Goddess. I passed my fingers lightly over the embroidery of small red flowers in the shape of stars and curving tendrils in a slightly different tone of red. It was indeed very fine work, much finer than Gladia or Achillea could achieve. It had all been stitched by eye, and so did not have any of the regularity that my pounced patterns had. I, who had been so proud of their regularity and form, now wished for them to be more like this; creative and flexible.

'Do you have new Priestesses at your Temple?' asked Lunaria, curiously. 'For I see you look at the veils of Flammeus rather than Aureus for yourself.' She looked at my veil rather critically, and I was conscious that I did not want her to closely examine the hasty embroidery on it. I sighed dramatically behind my veil and told my story again of the lack of an expert seamstress in our Temple, and that our Maids were still untrained in stitching and we only had one Priestess with stitching skill left who was very young. I saw my way to trying to persuade Lunaria to leave with us, to go to my supposed Temple to aid us for some weeks. Temples did occasionally have visiting Priestesses, often with special skills that may be lacking in other Temples, like Physic and Scribing. I took an instant decision and spoke with what I hoped was the right degree of authority.

'Sister Lunaria, we have great need of your skills, at the Temple of Blessed Work at Semaya, as you can see from my own garb.' I gestured to it disdainfully and felt

Achillea bridle in resentment of my apparent disdain of the work of Gladia. I prodded her slightly with my toe under my gown, and she subsided into obedient silence. 'Would you be willing to travel back with me for a period of a month, so that you can help us to replenish our woeful veils? You could also teach your skill to our new Priestess such that she might do better work. We have a Priestess who is a skilled Physic, some of whose work we have brought with us, and there is some excellent honey which we trade for with the Outer traders who tend the bees near us. It is said that the white honey has especially good properties, and we use it a lot in our own remedies. In return for your skills, we could offer the services of our Priestess Physic to your Temple for a similar time, and she could bring with her all the salves and remedies you might need.' I paused for a moment. It was so difficult to know what Lunaria was thinking without being able to see her face, and whether she was swayed by my appeal to her skills.

Eventually she spoke. 'I am honoured by your request, Priestess Neroli, but I can only accompany you with the permission of High Priestess Asinte, as you know, and I will need a Permission Scroll to travel with you. Our Scribe, Priestess Abssina is having trouble with her joints and it takes some time for her to scribe at all at these times.'

I thought quickly. 'Sister, we may have some salves and tisanes for sister Abssina to take to aid her recovery, we have brought with us some of those items. Achillea, do we have the honey salve and the willow water?'

Achillea was not expecting to be addressed and almost raised her head to speak to me face to face, but remembered herself and answered demurely, 'Yes, Priestess Neroli, we have both of those with us.'

'We can certainly leave those with your Priestess to aid her recovery,' I continued smoothly. 'As for the scribing of the Scroll, the Goddess is blessing us all, for I am the Scribe and Reader for our Temple, and I can scribe your Permission Scroll myself, if you have the pens and inks.'

'Blessed be the Goddess,' murmured Lunaria, 'for she has blessed your request indeed. She must be guiding your path for the good of all.'

'Praise be,' I responded, rolling my eyes under my veil, for it was I and not the Goddess who was guiding the path.

Lunaria stood up, placing the veils back into the basket, and I stood up with her as she said, 'I will go and converse with High Priestess Asinte. She may wish to speak with you herself later.'

'I thank you, Sister Lunaria,' I replied. 'I will spend some time in the Temple, praying to the Goddess that she continues to guide our way.' And with that, I pushed Achillea towards the door, which she duly opened for Lunaria who glided out, looking much more self-assured and confident than I had ever seen before. I was amazed at how she had changed from someone who had been shy and biddable only a few months before to someone who was sure of herself and her status in the Temple. How quickly she had become someone of power. Was this all it required? A change of clothes to identify you as one of those who made decisions which affected those beneath you? I wondered if Lunaria already knew about what happened to the Maids who left the Temple, and at what point the Priestesses became fully complicit in the web that I had discovered.

Achillea and I walked towards the Temple again and as we passed by the Gatehouse on the way to the Temple itself, I told her quietly to go and see Ambar and Tarik and tell them what had ensued since we had left them the day before, and to bring back three small gourds of white honey as a pretext for her visit. As she went off, I walked over to the tree beside the Temple and sat beneath it, challenging myself to be calm. I looked around me, feeling comfortable in the familiar surroundings. So many times, I had swept these paths according to the seven-step rule, internally cursing the red flowers that dropped from time to time off the tree under which I now sat. Now I did not have to sweep them up, I looked up through the feathery leaves to the same flaming flowers, which perched above like a cloud of butterflies, and appreciated their beauty. After a few minutes, Achillea re-emerged from the Gatehouse with the honey gourds, and we walked back into the Temple once more.

We sat in the Temple for some time, pretending to be in deep prayer to the Goddess. I suppose, in truth, I really was petitioning the Goddess, for our mission's success depended on the success of my hastily put together plan. I pleaded with the Goddess that she would guide Lunaria and Asinte to agree to my suggestion and allow us to get away from the Temple with Lunaria. The rest of the plan would have to follow on as it did. At length, I rose from my bench and beckoned to Achillea and we walked from the Temple towards our room, wondering when we might hear if my plan had succeeded. If it did not, I would have to further contemplate the possibility of revealing everything to Lunaria and throwing myself on her mercy, but I liked this idea less and less. Lunaria's duty and loyalty clearly lay very firmly with the Temple, and, until she was away from it, she would be unlikely to choose to follow me.

We had almost reached the room when a Maid, whose name I had forgotten, came to tell us that Lunaria was awaiting us in the Meeting Room, so we retraced our steps and went back to the Meeting Room. Lunaria was standing when we arrived and was accompanied by High Priestess Asinte. I could not help feeling awed to be standing in Asinte's presence as an almost equal. I greeted her calmly, and she returned the greeting in a business-like tone. It became clear that she did not intend to stand on ceremony but was only here to make sure she acquired as much as possible in any forthcoming trade. I repeated the suggestion I had made to Lunaria, offering her the three small gourds of white honey which Achillea had fetched as an example of the goods I could offer her. She dipped her finger in the top of the gourd and took her finger under her veil to taste the honey. She paused as she savoured the taste, and then with very little negotiating, she agreed to the deal, so long as I scribed the Permission Scroll for Lunaria, which I agreed to, asking her to provide me with a parchment and a pen and ink. Asinte assured me that Lunaria could direct me to the working room of the Scribe Abssina, and swept out, asking Lunaria to ensure she had veils for every colour we required, and a good selection of embroidery threads. Lunaria turned to me after Asinte had left and said quietly, 'It seems that I am to come to your Temple at Semaya after all, sister Neroli. I hope that you will offer me some assistance as we travel, for I have never left this Temple in my life, and never thought to. I am only recently become a Priestess, so everything about my life is new and different. You must be well accustomed to travelling in this world of ours and will be able to guide me, along with the guidance of the Goddess.'

I nearly laughed out loud at the thought that I was an experienced Priestess used to travelling from one Temple to another, but I inclined my head and murmured, 'Of course, Priestess Lunaria. We will travel at dawn tomorrow for it takes some days to get to Semaya. I will prepare the Scroll of Permission from your High Priestess. Achillea here will assist us both until we return to Semaya where you will be more settled.'

Lunaria showed me to the familiar room where Priestess Abssina worked. She was not there, but there were part-finished Choice Scrolls around the room, some with those beautiful illustrations such as I had seen on Lunaria's scroll, and others which were untidy and scrappy. I recalled the trick of the Scrolls of Choice and affirmed to myself that the Priestesses must know that something bad happened to the Maids who left the Temple, otherwise they would not try to skew the choices by offering the Scrolls with the beautiful pictures on them to those they wanted to keep. It made me feel so angry that they did not care in the least about those whom they judged to be lacking, and I banged into the writing frame, ill-tempered. I found a box of ink pens, carved from hard wood, with metal nibs, which wrote a deal more smoothly than the reed pens which Benakiell had so carefully crafted for me. I copied the wording of my own Scroll of Permission (which I had written for myself), and used a black ink again, even though I was tempted to use some of the coloured inks which Abssina had in gourds hanging on the walls; dark blue and purple and red. I just wanted to get it finished and given to Lunaria by evening so that she could show it to High Priestess Asinte, and we could leave before anyone realised that we were not who we said we were. Prior to leaving, I folded some parchment and put it in my underpocket, should I require more later on.

I made the scribing last longer than it should have done, keeping Achillea with me. By now she had become quite sullen, obviously uncomfortable and irritated by our visit to the Temple, and I knew she longed to get back to her own life, to braiding her hair and singing, and talking to whomever she wished, to spending time with Ashtun, away from this all-female world. I had purposely worked past the time of eating in the evening so that we could eat alone in our room. The same Maid brought us some flatbreads and some bean stew, with water to drink and two pomegranates. I had never seen whole pomegranates in the Temple given to Maids, so this was something else that the Priestesses kept for themselves. The Maid made sure she brought the pomegranates only to me, looking darkly at Achillea who pretended to fiddle with the gourds again. At last she had left, and we were alone, and ready to prepare for what might be the riskiest part of the trip so far.

CHAPTER 32

We left behind us almost all the physic we had brought, most of which belonged to Tarik. We also left behind the white honey, which I suspected might go towards the comfort of the Priestesses rather than the Maids. There was much that I wanted to ask Lunaria about the matter of how life changed for a Maid when she became a Priestess, and whether she knew all the details of how much the Priestesses were in partnership with the OutRiders and in thrall to the Queen. I kept on telling myself to just get to the next step of the plan, not to think too much about how Lunaria might react when she saw me again, how she might react to the news that she was probably the new Queen of the land, and what might happen when we escorted her to the court of the Queen, and how to get her in to that court so that she might be declared the rightful heir to the throne.

Achillea and I made our way to the Gatehouse in the pink dawn of the new day. I spoke quietly to Ambar and Tarik, telling them swiftly that we would indeed be taking Lunaria with us, but that she had no knowledge of who we were and that we were ostensibly heading for the Temple at Semaya. Ambar nodded quickly and conversed silently with Tarik. Lunaria bustled towards us, a Maid carrying her baskets for her. I had thought that Asinte or the other Priestesses might come out to bid us farewell, but it seemed we did not merit that importance. I welcomed Lunaria politely and explained to her that she would ride behind Ambar since she was unaccustomed to horses. Ambar stood the horse by the mounting stairs and helped Lunaria to sit on the horse. I could not see her face, of course, but from the way she turned her beautifully veiled face from one side to another, I felt that she was excited by the adventure, but also apprehensive and fearful. I walked to the side of the horse and gave her the blessing of the Goddess, for her protection and to ease her mind. I could see her shoulders relaxing, and wondered at the power I had, being able to stop someone from feeling frightened just by saying some words. And yet, Lunaria would say that power came from the Goddess, not from the speaker of the words.

Tarik tied Lunaria's baskets on to the back of his horse and then Achillea and I mounted our horses from the block. Priestess Gelila emerged from the Gatehouse and opened the gates, bidding a short blessing to Lunaria as we rode out. It seemed remarkably easy to have engineered the trickery we had used in order to get Lunaria away from the Temple, but I understood that there was much still to do. I had given Achillea the message to pass on to Ambar and Tarik as she took the items to pack on the horses that we should keep up the pretence for today and as we camped overnight and wait until we got to Besseret before we told Lunaria. I had thought it through and surmised that if we were stopped by any other OutRiders, it would do us well to have Lunaria lending her voice to ours, that we were an innocent group of travellers, moving from one Temple to another. It would also be easier if we were in Besseret so that Lunaria could hear Bellis's testimony for herself, and so that Maren could confirm the birthmark that showed that she was the Queen's heir. It would be a long ride and a tedious time for both Achillea and me since we would have to maintain the disguise which was already causing us both irritation and discomfort. At least we did not have to do very much conversing while we rode. Ambar and Tarik concentrated on the riding- they both had not only their own horse to control but also mine and Achillea's which were linked to them by their leather straps, and Ambar had the added difficulty of trying to manage Lunaria who had not ridden on a horse before. I remembered how I had felt after my first riding experience and felt some sympathy for her when we stopped, and she moved painfully and stiffly off the horse.

'Do not worry, sister Lunaria,' I assured her. 'You will get accustomed to the riding; I felt the same way when I first was on a horse. The Goddess will protect and nurture you.'

'Praise be,' she responded, rather tiredly. 'From the way that you look so comfortable, you must have a lot of experience. How long have you been a Priestess for?'

Slightly taken aback by her question, I had to think quickly. 'Around 5 years, by the grace of the Goddess. But I have not travelled so many times. Semaya is a long way from anywhere, so most of the time we are very quiet. We do not have as many Maids as you do at your Temple though. We live a very quiet life there.'

'Your Maid Achillea is very quiet herself,' commented Lunaria. 'Perhaps she is a little shy of having travelled. Is it her first time out of the Temple? She is blessed to have the opportunity to travel with you, sister Neroli, to further see the works of the Goddess.'

'Ah yes, Achillea is a very shy person. She works very hard in the Physic at our Temple, however, don't you Achillea?' Achillea turned to me, her head still lowered obediently, but I could feel the quiver of a smile on her lips as she answered, 'Yes, Priestess, Praise to the Goddess.'

Ambar and Tarik made camp again and after a quiet repast we went to sleep, our tent a bit too snug now that it contained three, even though none of us were the comfortable shape of Gladia. Ambar and Tarik took turns to sit up on guard through the night. I slept near the edge of the mat and could see the shadows by the fire flickering as they walked up and down. The fire ebbed and flowed through the night, dying right down to glowing embers and then flaring up with the addition of more kindling. It put me in mind of our quest; that there was an ever-present spark within me that needed answers to my questions. Sometimes it lay quiet, but still glowing, and other times, when things happened, it crackled and spat. I lay there in the night pondering the fire and the paradox of being warmed and comforted by it and yet being scared by it.

The next day was much the same as the first; we purposely did not engage in much talking, since it was not the Priestesses' way to talk in front of anyone who was not a Priestess except in reference to the Goddess or her will. Besides, Lunaria seemed to need all her effort to sit on Ambar's horse. I wondered idly how it felt for him to be riding the horse carrying the future Queen, the focus of all his questing. I did not have any doubt that Lunaria was the next Queen; Bellis had been clear in her recollection of the birthmark and so was Maren, and surely it was a unique thing to have a birthmark in the shape of a bee. What I still did not know was how Lunaria would react to the news we had to impart to her, and how we would get her to the court of the Queen.

It was a relief to recognise the outcrops of rocks and trees near to Besseret. Before we arrived there, Ambar and Tarik stopped the horses. Tarik addressed Lunaria respectfully and told her that he planned to go on ahead to make sure that our dwelling place for the night was ready, and that he would be accompanied by Achillea who would make sure everything was appropriate for the comfort of Priestesses. I thought with some envy of the raised bed in which I had slept at the Temple. The real reason, of course, was to warn the others that we would soon be arriving. We had discussed this before we left, and we were agreed that Bellis and Maren and Gladia would remain in Bellis's dwelling until they were sent for, and that Benakiell would keep watch over them. Ashtun would stay in the stables until Tarik took the horses, when he would return. We might need all three of the fit young men if Lunaria took objection to us once she had heard our story. We planned to take Lunaria into my dwelling and allow her to rest and compose herself before we told her a story which she would doubtless find incredible and unbelievable.

Tarik took off at a quickened pace towards Besseret, leading Achillea on her horse. She would by now be longing to put on her normal clothes and tend to her hair – and, of course, to see Ashtun again who would have worried for her. I did not understand their attachment to each other; there was much about relationships on the Outer which I struggled to comprehend, but I could, by now, understand how much one could get used to the presence of others whom you trusted in your life. I reminded myself, too, that I had not known either of them for very long whereas they had known each other for years. I was looking forward to removing my veil and to being able to see the whole world with my eyes instead of having to move my head around to see through the threaded grille in front of my eyes. The short spell of wearing the veil had taught me some things though. I was confirmed in my choice to leave the Temple – at least insofar as it had turned out for me. If I had left the Temple and been scooped up like Bellis and taken to be an Angel, I doubted if my outlook would have been so positive. I had also learned that we discover a lot from people by looking at their eyes, and that the Priestesses withheld their eyes from the world because it gave them an advantage of power. They could look at the eyes of others even though others could not look into theirs. It made it easier for them to tell lies and to avoid telling the truth. After a short rest, we continued our journey, walking with the horses to Besseret.

CHAPTER 33

Lunaria remained in the dwelling, resting and apparently conversing with the Goddess. I had made my excuses that I needed to go and use the wastepit and wash. I think she was happy to be left alone for a while and seemed quite bewildered by the turn of events. Luckily, because she had not travelled outside the Temple, as very few Priestesses did, every new experience could be explained as just the way it happened on travels, which she accepted without question. I suspected she would feel even more bewildered before long.

Achillea had already changed back into her normal attire and was looking much happier. Although she had not braided her hair neatly yet, she had combed it and smoothed it so that it looked cared for once more and she had put on her brightest netela. She sat near Ashtun, and they looked often into one another's eyes as Achillea had been unable to do to anyone while we had been at the Temple. They were immersed in their own private world where their communication was just as mysterious and silent as the silent language of the OutRiders. I spoke with Ambar and Tarik about how we could begin to tell Lunaria of the momentous changes that might now take place in her life, but we kept on disagreeing and getting mired in details and plans for how to react depending on what her response might be. In the end, I went to fetch Lunaria to bring her to eat food with me first, as it seemed likely to be a long evening.

Ambar and Tarik came at the end of the meal and stood some distance away. Lunaria asked me why they were there, and if it was normal for them to be there, whispering to me that she had not much experience of dealing with men and that they made her feel uncomfortable and had no place amongst Priestesses. I told her that they were there to help me to explain something to her, and she looked around, apparently even more uncomfortable from her nervous shifting and frequent head turning. I sighed. There was no easy way to descend into this story, which, I freely admitted to myself, sounded increasingly unreal and unlikely. However, Lunaria had no means of escape from Besseret, so she would have to listen to the full account, even if she did not believe it or wanted to have nothing to do with it. If she was the next Queen, she would have to get used to a lot of other things in a short time too. I reached up to my veil and pulled it off, in front of her.

'Sister Neroli, what are you doing?' she asked, aghast. 'The Goddess protect you! You are her Priestess and she requires you to wear the veil.'

'No, Lunaria,' I said, looking straight at her. 'For I am not Priestess Neroli. I am one whom you used to know, only a few short months ago, when I left the Temple. Since then, I have found out much of importance about this our land, and much that is important about you. Do you know me?'

She peered through her veil at me, puzzled. In only a short time, she had become accustomed to not recognising people by their features but only by their veils, and of taking no notice of those who did not wear a veil. I could not tell, of course, if she recognised me or not, now that my veil had gone. It was not so very long since we had last seen one another on that day that I had left the Temple, on the day on which she had pressed the brooch upon me which had started everything in this story.

'I am Talla. I left the Temple some months ago. It was not long after you had your own Choice Ceremony and became a Priestess. You must remember me! You gave me this brooch when I left!' I pulled out the brooch from where it was clipped, under my robe and showed it to her. She moved her head closer to it, unable to see clearly in the dim light and through the veil.

'Talla,' she said eventually, wonderingly. 'But the OutRiders have been searching for you to bring you back to the Goddess. The Priestesses have been waiting to hear that they have found you. Priestess Asinte told me to give you the brooch so that you could be more easily found, for the Goddess did not intend you for a life outside of the Temple, any more than me. You made the wrong Choice somehow. The Priestesses did not understand it, for the Goddess is never wrong.'

I looked at her in exasperation. There was too much to explain to her, and too little time for her to take it all in. Swiftly I reached forward and pulled the veil off her head. She cried out in alarm and distress and covered her face with her hands, peering out above her fingers. I pushed her hands away impatiently and made her look me in the eyes so that she could see the truth of what I told her. Her green eyes flecked with amber and fringed with long, curled eyelashes flinched away at first but gradually she began to calm down.

'I need you to listen carefully to what you are about to hear, Lunaria, for it is very important that you should understand. Some different people will tell you lots of different things, but you need to listen to them all, and there is a lot of listening to do. We will try to be brief, but there is much to say,' I warned.

'I do not understand at all. Are you not a Priestess? Did you not become a Priestess at another Temple then? Are we not travelling to Semaya? Do you have no need after all of my embroidery skills?' Lunaria queried, looking crestfallen. 'I must return then to the Temple immediately.' She made as if to get up, and reached for her discarded veil, which lay like a dead animal on the floor, but I placed a staying hand on her arm and she settled back down, agitated but listening.

And so that long evening began. The shadows lengthened and then subsumed everything into darkness, the frogs' singing rose above the chirps of the cicadas, and the fire provided welcome light. Ambar began by relating the story of Paradox, the daughter of the Queen and her romance with an OutCommander which led to her running away, pregnant with DoubleSouls. He told her of the subsequent birth of the babies and the attack of the OutRiders, and of Hortensia taking away the babies along with the brooch, and of Maren being the witness to their birth and the means of identification of the future Queen. Lunaria looked at me wide eyed, wondering if I was the future Queen, but I asked her to wait until the end before she asked her questions because I was worried that she would distract us from the task in hand. When Ambar had finished his part, I took over and told Lunaria what had befallen me since I left the Temple, and of how the OutRiders were searching specifically for me. I told her of the great kindness of Benakiell and Gladia and Achillea, and the others. I told her about the little bee necklace that Ambar had given me and how it snapped magically on to the flower brooch and showed it to her as proof of the relationship between Paradox and the OutCommander. She handled it wonderingly, under the flash and flare of the snapping firewood.

Ambar continued with his account, telling of how the old Queen had deteriorated as she aged and how she clung desperately to power, fully resolved that no heirs would take over her land, and sending out her OutRiders to try to find the Maid who had the brooch, as it was told that she would be the new Queen. He explained to Lunaria that the Queen neared death and that, for the land to flourish, it was important for the intended heir to take the throne, rather than the set of greedy courtiers who managed the country currently. The new Queen must be in place when the old Queen died; it was the way that it worked; the new Queen would arrive at court, she would be certified by a witness and the old Queen would be sent to a Temple to spend her last few days close to the Goddess. I watched Lunaria's face as she listened to Ambar speaking. Her eyes never left his face as he spoke, and I could see him catching her eyes, as she caught his. Her skin was smooth and clear, and her hair, freed of the veil, tumbled in dark curls all around her. Her green eyes were beautifully framed by those long curling eyelashes and her nose was fine with a slight uptilt. I knew that in this world of the Outer, Lunaria was indeed beautiful.

I wanted to tell Lunaria about the deceit visited on everyone by the Queen, the OutRiders and her own precious Temple. It was important to me that she should know what had been happening in our land of Oramia. Ambar persuaded me that it would be better to tell her in the morning, when the light would be bright enough for Maren to look at Lunaria's birthmark. I did not even want to consider the possibility that Bellis had been wrong about the birthmark; that she had mistaken Lunaria for another or that she had not seen the birthmark. I had every intention of making sure that Lunaria knew all about the Angels and I was resolved to introduce her to Bellis and see if she remembered her and prove everything I knew to her. I shifted restlessly. Ambar seemed to be talking for the sake of talking, rambling on about the protocols for a new Queen and other things in which I had no interest. Lunaria, on the other hand, appeared to be fascinated. I looked around and everyone else was as bored as I was, so when Ambar paused for a moment, I seized the moment and said loudly 'It is getting late now, and sister Lunaria has had a long and tiring day. Let us go and sleep and talk again in the morning.' Relieved, Gladia and Benakiell stood up to leave, as did Achillea. Ambar continued to watch Lunaria, clearly entranced by her, his eyes barely leaving her face. Sourly, I wondered if he was attracted to her good looks or her future station in life, recalling how much more interested he had seemed in me when he thought I was the next Queen, and how all that charm was now being lavished on Lunaria.

The men worked out between themselves a guard rota, and Ambar told Lunaria that they would be keeping watch overnight. She thanked him lavishly for his efforts. I almost snorted out loud. Perhaps I had also learned to not trust, as well as to trust in this world of the Outer. In the Temple, there were no choices about whether to trust or not trust someone; things simply were as they were. Wearily, I prepared myself for sleep, once again having to share my dwelling with another person. First Achillea and now Lunaria.

All I really wanted was to spend some time on my own, perhaps with the bees, in the garden. Or to sleep in the dark silence of the night with only the starshine for company. I realised I was starting to feel resentful of Lunaria and reminded myself that there was still the high chance that she could, in fact, be my sister. Not just my sister, but my DoubleSoul. I felt no kind of kinship with her, but then I did not really know her aside from her skills in embroidery, and her devotion to the Goddess and duty. I asked her how she felt about what she had heard from us that evening, and she replied that she did not know what to think, or what she should think and that she hoped that the Goddess would guide her thoughts. She seemed disinclined to light conversation and, remembering how I myself had struggled with that when I first left the Temple, I bade her goodnight and lay down on my own mat, regretting again that I did not have one of those raised beds that I had experienced at the Temple, and assuming that Lunaria felt the same.

The next day, I rose with the sun. I may have lacked sleep but to spend some time with no other person around me was worth more than sleep. I walked down the path, dampened with dew, towards the gardens. The air was clear and sparkling, and already the birds were singing. I sat on the flat rock by the flower beds, watching the bees begin to crawl out of the hives, warming their wings in the first sun. There was so much that was uncertain in my life and in the future of this land. At least in the Temple all was secure; there was nothing unexpected, things progressed in a preordained manner, and if it had not been for my discovery about how the Temple did run so well, and how it sourced the Maids, I might have been wishing to return to it. It was important to resolve something to take us forward and it was most important to confirm who Lunaria was. Once we knew that, all the other possible plans would be affected. I walked to Maren's dwelling. She was also awake, blowing her fire into life to make some breakfast. As I walked towards her, preparing to call out to her to alert her to my presence, she waved to me, smiling. 'Good morning, sister Talla!' I was amazed. She had recognised me as I walked down the path! I rushed towards her, asking about her eyesight. She beamed at me, her eyes watering but clear of the milkiness that had afflicted them for so many years of her life. 'Oh, Talla, I have been longing for your return, I could not wait to tell you how successful your salve has been! Two days after you left, I woke up with a lot of sleep dust around my eyes. I rubbed it away, and it was as if someone had just washed my eyes clear! It is not yet fully healed but already I can see better than I have in over twenty years! I am so thankful for what you have done for me!'

It was a wonderful feeling to know that Maren's eyes had been healed, and that the salve we had made had worked so well. Now she would be able to tell us all if Lunaria was the first-born child. I wished there had been a clue for the second child. I did not think I would ever find my own place in life, not even if I were Lunaria's sister, and the other child. If only I had had a birthmark too! I embraced Maren warmly, leaning slightly on her as if to share my anxieties, and then told her that the time had come for her to examine the one whom we thought to be the first-born child of Paradox, daughter of the Queen and heir to the throne of Oramia. She agreed to come up the path to my dwelling when she had eaten and washed, and I made my way back up the hill to find Lunaria sitting outside the dwelling, in her Priestess's robe, but without her veil.

Lunaria was looking around her, apparently enjoying being able to see so well, and it occurred to me that it must be a little like it had been for Maren; to be able to see clearly where once you had been restricted. I smiled at her and wished her well for the morning.

'Praise to the Goddess,' she replied to me.

'Praise be.' I responded automatically.

'You would have made a good Priestess, sister Talla,' she said. 'Would you like to return to the Temple? I am sure they would consider it, although the Goddess never makes mistakes in the Ceremony of Choice.'

I snorted, and at her pained expression at my disdain for the Temple, I began to explain to her how the Scrolls of Choice worked. Her perfectly smooth brows wrinkled.

'But the Goddess guides the choice of the Scribe Priestess,' she began. 'Why else would the Temple separate out the Maids, for I am sure that all who sincerely wish to serve the Goddess would be welcomed.'

'Do you remember one called Bellis?' I asked her. She told me that she thought she did, and I reminded her of how Bellis had wanted to stay in the Temple so much and yet had not been chosen. I had every intention of introducing her to Bellis later that morning, but, at that moment, Ambar and Tarik arrived, bringing flatbreads and honey. Gladia came along with her coffee pot, and we ate, enjoying the food in the freshness of the morning. Just as we finished the last crumbs and licked our fingers of the last delicious drops of honey, Maren came up the path. Achillea looked at me, wide-eyed, and I confirmed to her that Maren could now see well enough to get around more and to recognise people and things. Ambar smiled fleetingly. He knew that this meant that we were one step closer to knowing the truth about the child of his OutCommander and of Paradox; a story that he had been searching for an end to for many years. I introduced Maren to Lunaria, and Maren peered at her, wonderingly, pondering on whether this was the child who she had helped to deliver all those years ago. I spoke to Lunaria as she eyed Maren suspiciously, wondering who this new person was and what she was doing there.

'Sister Lunaria, this is Maren. She was one of the Birthmothers who helped Paradox, the daughter of the Queen to give birth to the DoubleSouls, whom the OutRiders seek to harm on the orders of the Queen so that the heir cannot take her rightful place at the head of the kingdom. Maren can testify which of the DoubleSouls will be the new Queen, if we can but get her into the Palace. We think that that person is you, Lunaria.'

'Me?' Lunaria trembled. 'Why would it be me? I know of nothing to mark me out from any other Temple

Maid or Priestess, and, in any case, I thought they sought the owner of the golden brooch that you have. Is that not what you told me last night?'

'The child was born with a mark which shows they will be the next Queen. The OutRiders tried to blind Maren so that she would never see it again, but we have made her a salve so that she can see better and better. And there is one other here, who left from our Temple, who has told us that you have a mark in the right place. All we need now is for Maren to be able to view the mark and tell us all if it is you that we seek!'

Lunaria gaped at us, as we sat there surrounding her. 'Who is here from the Temple? You know they tell us as Priestesses that once someone leaves the Temple, the Goddess takes them to herself and we will never see them again, so how can it be that first you, Talla, and now another one who has left the Temple can be still here? Something is going wrong.'

'Oh, something is definitely going wrong,' I ground out, trying to remain calm in the face of her naivety. 'But we can talk about that later. And I promise you that you can meet the other one from our Temple later. But for now, we must resolve this issue, for it has far reaching consequences.'

Lunaria looked at me again, uncomprehending. 'You need to come with me and Maren and Gladia into my dwelling, so that Maren can examine this mark.' I stood up decisively and extended my hand to Lunaria who grasped it and stood up, still looking bewildered. Maren came over, and after a degree of puffing and grunting, Gladia heaved herself up from the mat and we walked over to the dwelling, out of sight of the men. We had agreed that Gladia would be a good independent witness to the birthmark and Maren's reaction to it since she had never met Lunaria before yesterday.

When we got inside, I asked Lunaria to sit facing the wall so that the light from the light space in the wall fell on her back and yet she was still modestly hidden from the eyes of others and explained to her that we needed her to lift up her Priestess robe so that we could see her back. Wordlessly, she lifted the robe and pulled it up to her head, keeping it modestly pinned to her sides so that nothing more than her back could be seen. I could even see from where I was that there was indeed a birthmark on her back, in a place where she would never have seen it herself. I wanted very much to get close to it and see for myself what the shape of it was, but I motioned to Maren to come forward so that she could say what she saw and affirm to it in front of witnesses who had not yet seen it themselves. She stood in front of Lunaria's back and then knelt to look more closely at the mark. She raised her hand and lightly ran her fingers over the mark.

The tiny flecks of dust danced in the light, golden. In that moment, all was silent; there were no birds singing, no hum of conversation. I held my breath.

'There is no doubt,' Maren spoke finally. 'This is the first born of the DoubleSouls of Paradox. This is the mark I saw on that day that she was born. It is the mark of the bee. Look for yourselves!'

Gladia and I went towards Lunaria, who sat there, motionless, as we peered at the skin of her back. The mark itself was a very dark brown, almost black against Lunaria's lighter skin and it did look exactly like a bee crawling up her back, complete with wings and stripes. Gladia was wordless in amazement, and so was I for some brief moments. Gently, I pulled down Lunaria's robe and helped her to her feet. She was dazed. So much had happened in such a short time to her, and although at the beginning I had fancifully imagined myself to be the child who was sought so eagerly, I know now that I would have found it too big a burden; that it needed someone who was strong in faith and in duty, and that person was not me, but Lunaria. I walked with Maren, Gladia and Lunaria to the door of the dwelling, and Ambar came rushing up to us, asking what the outcome was. Maren spoke.

'There is no doubt. This is the child first born of the Princess Paradox, the one whom I witnessed being born and who was taken away by Hortensia before the OutRiders of the Queen could kill her and her DoubleSoul sister. She bears the exact mark in the exact place and my eyes have seen it. Sister Lunaria will be the Queen of our land if the Goddess wills it.'

'Praise to the Goddess,' responded Lunaria obediently.

Ambar dropped to his knees in front of her, and bowed his head, pledging his lifelong allegiance to her and to her protection. Tarik did the same thing. I looked on, amazed. Lunaria was dazed but gracious in her acceptance of their fealty, as if she were born to this life, as indeed, I suppose she was. I wondered how another might have reacted. I stepped forward to her. I did not know what the right way was to behave in front of a future Queen, for I had never met one before, but I did not think that a title should make a lot of difference to the essence of the person.

'Lunaria, we must make plans regarding this, for, as we told you, the old Queen is close to death, and you must arrive at the Court and be declared before that happens. We will help and plan what to do next, but you must know some things before you arrive at court and at the office of Queen. There are things you must know before you take power,' I told her abruptly, sensing my opportunity to explain to her about the Angels.

Ambar stepped in, a little too smoothly and adroitly for my liking. 'There is surely time for that later, sister

Talla,' he murmured, his eyes not leaving those of Lunaria. 'We can take some moments now to celebrate finding the one for whom we have searched for so long.'

Everyone else murmured in agreement, and Gladia bustled off to find coffee and dates. Achillea, in her sunny, fluffy way wanted to talk to Lunaria about what she might have to wear as the Queen. Benakiell looked on from a little distance, a small smile on his face, perhaps contemplating a more settled future and a story to tell others. Ashtun was hovering. He had no link with Lunaria as I and Achillea did; he had not seen the birthmark as Gladia and Maren had, he was not an OutRider like Ambar and Tarik and yet he longed to be. I could see that he wished he could do what Ambar and Tarik had done, wanting to belong to that brotherhood of men to which they belonged, and perhaps that was what he really yearned for - a sense of belonging. As for me, I did not know what I felt. One part of the quest was over, and yet, another, more difficult one remained. I was relieved that we had found the right person, but there was a part of me that wished we had not. Was I envious of Lunaria, and her sudden importance not only in the world but also in the eyes of Ambar? Perhaps. For I still had no place in this world, and belonged nowhere, like Ashtun, even though I had worked so hard for this outcome. But I resolved that I would continue to work just as hard until the end of it all. The anger I felt towards the way in which the system had changed to make use of people as objects still burned brightly in my mind, and I was determined to explain it all to Lunaria, at the right time. But Ambar was right. There was time to rest and celebrate our achievement before we moved on to our ultimate journey.

CONFLAGRATION

CHAPTER 34

The sun beat down on us, its heat wilting; rains brewing again across the plain. We were a silent party, riding across the grassland toward the Queen's Court. Inside each of us lay a spark of determination to succeed in our mission – to get Lunaria into the court of the Queen where she could be declared the Queen's rightful heir and where she could not be harmed. Ambar had explained to us that the OutRiders swear their vow of loyalty to the Queen, but that when an heir is found with a proper claim to the throne, their loyalty will immediately switch. It is their job. He believed that those who sought to kill the Queen's grandchild were those who were part of the old Queen's court; her trusted emissaries and ambassadors who did not want to lose their grip on power. They were greedy for all the good things that came to the Queen's Court. They were obsequious and flattering to the old Queen in exchange for helping her to maintain her powerful grip on Oramia. Once Lunaria was lawfully declared to be Queen, the OutRiders of the Queen's Court would protect her from these people of the Court. His explanation seemed flimsy to me, but I already knew about the blind agreement and continuance of old tradition by the Temple, so perhaps it was not too far a stretch. Besides, we had no other choice but to be led by Ambar. This was his world, not ours; we were only there because we had a role to play in the unfolding future.

It was now some five days since Lunaria had been told by Maren that she was the rightful heir to the Queen and would be Queen herself, all things being well. There had been much discussion, argument and planning for this day. Lunaria, rather aggravatingly, seemed to take everything in her stride, her amenable and dignified nature being perfect for assimilating each day's new discoveries in a calm and modest manner. If she were my sister, which I doubted more and more, simply because we were so unlike one another, we had not inherited the same sort of temperament. Indeed, whereas I continued to seethe and burn regarding the plight of the Angels and the appalling manner in which they were treated, Lunaria had listened to my story, and that of Bellis, gravely and respectfully and had promised to examine the matter further should she indeed become Queen, if the Goddess willed it. Bellis had been amazed to see Lunaria again, and even more amazed to hear that she was the one who would be Queen. But Bellis's surprise was small in comparison to that of Lunaria who struggled to comprehend that Bellis was having a baby. This, more than Bellis's abuse at the hands of the OutRiders, and in certain knowledge of elements of the Temple, seemed to sway her. I quizzed her on what she had been told or what she knew as a Priestess about the Angels, but she never gave me an exact answer, murmuring that she was not sure that she should share the training of a Priestess with one who was not a Priestess. I pointed out to her that soon she would herself no longer be a Priestess, but she was not swayed, and eventually I gave up asking her.

We were a party of seven; me, Lunaria, Ambar, Tarik, Achillea, Maren and Ashtun. It was clear that Bellis, in her advanced state of pregnancy could not travel anywhere, and indeed, Maren was loath to leave her, except that she would be leaving her with Gladia, who was so capable and practical, and to whom Bellis clung like a child. Gladia herself was very happy with her maternal role towards Bellis, and spent much time caring for her needs and talking with her, laughing and busily bustling about. Benakiell had volunteered to stay with them just in case anyone came to Besseret and they needed protection.

Ashtun was happier than I think I had ever seen him. He had been allowed to ride one of the horses and wear some of the old armour we had taken from the dead OutRiders, and he had spent much of the five days practicing his arrows so that he could play an active role. It was clear to me that this was what he longed to do, and I wondered why the OutRiders did not simply ask among the men of the Outer if there were those who would wish to join them, rather than raising them from being babies, but I suppose that they were better able to mould the babies into the soldier they wanted, rather than trying to change a ready-made man. Achillea had to reprise her role as a Maid, much to her disgust. However, she could see that where there were Priestesses, there had to be Maids, to make the party look right, and there was no other candidate. The veils of the Priestesses meant that they were the easiest disguise to wear to enter the Queen's Court. We were fortunate that we had Lunaria's basket of stitching with us, which she had brought in order to clothe the supposed Priestesses of the Temple at Semaya, and we selected a robe for one born on the day of Viridis, and a matching veil delicately embroidered with intertwined leaves for Maren to wear. It was crucial that she should be able to declare Lunaria as the rightful heir, and as the witness to her birth. Lunaria had also suggested I could replace the orange veil which Gladia had made with one of the same colour, but which looked finer, and reluctantly I agreed, feeling disloyal to my friend Gladia and the efforts she had made to stitch it. Gladia, however, took it well and suggested that she could remake the veil into a smock for Bellis's baby, and the two of them happily began to plan the outfit.

Tarik had remained his usual calm and precise self as he instructed me on where the crucial things were to be found in the Hall of the Queen, since he was the only one amongst us who had spent any real time there, having been there installing the special communication curtain which he had told us about. He was the one who had heard the plans of the members of the Queen's Court to have the Maid who escaped with the brooch of the Queen killed and the brooch taken from her and given to some pretender to the throne who would keep them in their positions of luxury and indulgence. So much had happened since we had heard that story, and yet it had only been a couple of months. Within the Queen's Hall there was a scroll which had to be read when a new Queen had been verified and which would validate Lunaria as Queen. That would be my role. When I reflect now, my skills of reading and scribing had proved to be crucial, even though I had not read anything that was of my choosing. But I treasured my skill, especially as even Lunaria, the one who would be Queen could not read or scribe. It made me feel important and special.

Lunaria rode with Ambar once more. He was taking his role as her personal protector very seriously, but, even more than that, it was clear to everyone that he now felt a special bond with her. His melting eyes focused on her face and his voice became more warm and charming whenever he spoke with her. Achillea kept on trying to have a conversation with me about it, nudging me every time they looked at one another and likening them to herself and Ashtun. I had found Ambar charming and interesting myself, easy to talk to and funny, and I was increasingly left out and discarded now that I was no longer the first born DoubleSoul. Inside my head I still thought about whether I was the second DoubleSoul, but it seemed that particular child was not important to this story. When this was over, I planned to go somewhere far away from both Temple and OutFort, where I could find out more about my world.

Sweat trickled down my face under the orange veil, streaking down my nose and over my lips until I tasted its saltiness and pressed the veil against my skin to soak up the sweat. I called to Maren who sat with Tarik, and asked her how she was feeling, and how her eyes were. She called back that she was faring well, that she was enjoying it in fact, and that the veil took away some of the glare from the sun, so her eyes were comfortable. Once again, I was struck by how the same thing, in this case the veil, could make one person feel restricted and hemmed in and make another feel secure and comfortable. Ambar had coached Maren in what she had to say, in response to several preordained questions which were asked officially of anyone who claimed to witness the birth of the next heir, and she had learned them easily, sounding composed whenever he asked her the questions. Whether she would sound the same when we were in the Queen's Court, I could not tell, but it seemed that Maren was both courageous and pragmatic from the life story she had told us all, and I was sure that she would fulfil her role well.

Bellis had not been able to help us very much with any other knowledge of the Queen's Court, since the Angels were all held near to the OutFort which protected the Queen's Court. The Queen's Court itself, we were told by Tarik, was found at the top of a very steep and rocky outcrop, which was well protected at all points by the OutRiders. Along with the scrolls of permission for myself and for Lunaria, I had added another one for Maren, giving her the name of Priestess Betula and using some of the parchment I had taken from the Temple. The Permission Scrolls were a powerful tool, for there were so few readers in Oramia that, as the Priestesses in my Temple had discovered, those who could not read them were easily fooled. Even the Queen's Court treated the Priestesses and the Goddess with respect and any visiting Priestesses would have good reason for the arduous trek to the Court. Tarik told us that Priestesses brought especially beautiful and valuable items to the Queen's Court for her enjoyment, and so we had brought some gourds of Maren's honey and some finely embroidered fabrics from Lunaria's basket. Once we were given entry, all we had to do was to get into the main Audience Chamber and declare Lunaria's right to the throne in front of the Queen's Chancellor. Like all plans, it sounded simple in the speaking.

We stopped an hour later, as we reached a wide stream. No doubt it would get even wider as the rains continued to fall, but for now it was cool and pleasant to be there, off the horses in the shade of the Paradox trees which grew some distance from the bank. There were a few reddish rocks by the river, and some reeds, amongst which we could hear the sounds of the birds; small brown ones which crept up and down the reeds, and then in the water there were those with longer legs, strutting about trying to collect frogs and small fish. The men took the horses to the stream to drink and to cool off their hooves and took the opportunity to refill our gourds with fast flowing water from further upstream. The landscape was becoming hillier on this second day of travelling, and the stream came down from a rocky little hill which was itself on the flank of even higher mountains. Tarik assured us that we could get to the Queen's Court outcrop without going over that mountain first, and that although the way around the outside of it was longer, it would be easier for both us and the horses. In any case, once we arrived at the Queen's Court, the horses would have to be left in the stables at the OutFort at the base and we would have to ascend on foot. We would ride a little further today and then make camp so that we were rested for the ascent the next day.

We sat under the Paradox trees watching the horses in the stream, not speaking, each of us thinking our own thoughts, or just resting. Achillea was the only one of us lucky enough not to be wearing a veil, and she looked her normal happy self, humming away like a bee about the flowers. There was a sense to me of it being the last day of an old life, that after this day, nothing would be quite the same again, whatever ensued.

CHAPTER 35

The next day, we rode at a sedate pace toward the OutFort, at the foot of the cliffs which led up to the Queen's Court. This would be our first test; if the OutRiders allowed us to progress towards the court, along with the goods we had supposedly brought for the Queen. I hoped that perhaps human greed might mean that the OutRiders would let us through, especially if we insisted they could have their own gourd of honey as payment for their troubles. The Priestesses wielded power purely by their presence and we would be relying on that; the presence of three Priestesses would surely lend authenticity to our trip. Tarik and Ambar agreed that it was a good idea to stick with the story that we came from Semaya, and that they came from the OutFort near there too. It might explain our supposed lack of knowledge about the Queen's deteriorating health.

Having ridden around the foothills, we now came upon a flat plain which stretched out before us. The grass was still brown and dry here and the ground was littered with stones and boulders all in the same sandy red colour. We necessarily had to slow down so that the horses could pick their way over the rocky land. The thorny acacia trees punctuated the view with their scratchy shade. Rising high in front of us was a large rocky plateau with steep cliff edges showing the yellows, oranges and reds of the sandstone. It was too steep for any trees or vegetation to grow. It looked like it had been built there, but it had not, although the OutFort at the base certainly had been.

The OutFort Gatehouse was a curious building to look at. I had, of course, never seen one before. If any of the Priestesses at my Temple had been to one or seen one, they would never have described it to us anyway, and ever since I had left the Temple, I had been steering well clear of the OutRiders. It was very different from the Temple buildings, being square and of three levels. It was built in alternating layers of flattish stones, evidently gathered from the scattered plain, and wooden beams laid counter to them, which must have come from the large trees in the wooded mountains around here. I tried to take in as many details as I could from behind my veil, for which I was thankful, since it allowed me to indulge in my curiosity. I thought that Benakiell would be interested in this kind of construction of dwellings.

We halted at a stone wall, and dismounted from the horses, and Ashtun moved them to the shade of a scrubby thorn tree. We stood quietly together, hopefully sending out a dignified impression while Ambar and Tarik went into the Gatehouse along with the three Permission Scrolls. All we could do was wait and be grateful that the veils masked our anxiety. I noted that Tarik had loosely tied a couple of small gourds of Maren's honey to his waist belt, and when they finally emerged, the gourds had gone.

They went over to Ashtun and the horses and then brought them over to us, so we could mount them from the standing rocks. We did not know whether we were riding to leave or to go through the gateway towards the Court of the Queen, until they turned the horses and we headed towards the massif. Another obstacle had been overcome. Once we were some distance from the Gatehouse, Ambar relayed to us that we had been successful, but that the OutRiders had warned him that we may yet be turned away when we got to the Court. I caught sight of some of the buildings of the OutFort as we went around the corner, and I felt a pain in my heart, and a warmth from the little bee necklace as I thought of where the house of Angels might be, where there would be other Maids like Bellis, going through pain and suffering every day and with no one to care for them. I hoped that if we were successful in our mission that I might return here and free them.

There was a small fenced area with shade trees and stone troughs of water where one could leave the horses. It was tended to by a group of around eight youngsters in the second age of Childhood, from the OutFort. Like the Maids, they were already well trained in their work, and confidently took the reins of the horses from Ambar and Tarik, with little interest in the rest of us. Ambar flashed them something in their sign language and one of them smiled widely, his teeth flashing white in the sun. They wore a sort of leather tabard, presumably a precursor to wearing full armour like Ambar and Tarik did. We loaded up with our gourds of water, honey and Lunaria's basket of sewing. One of the boys peeled off from the group and headed towards the edge of the cliff. Ambar waved us on.

'This boy will guide us up to the Queen's Court; you must follow the person in front of you and we will keep to a given order. The boy first, then me, then Priestess Lunaria, then Achillea then Ashtun, then Priestess Betula, then Priestess Neroli and finally Tarik will be at the back. You must follow exactly what the person in front of you does; the way up is perilous and steep, but the footholds are safe and marked to the boy who leads us. There is no other way to the top – at least not for us.'

I looked up above me. The walls of this stone island rose sheer from the plain. But we had no choice than to follow the boy who skipped nimbly ahead of us, around to the eastern edge. Here there was a narrow channel or gorge which had had stones filled into it in a series of steep steps which took us about a third of the way up.

The steps were not comfortable, being too high and too steep to move up easily, and we were soon puffing our way upwards. Only the boy and Ambar and Tarik seemed impervious to its strains. It was, at least, shaded within the gorge passage upwards, for which I was grateful. Maren, in front of me, clearly felt the strain, being the oldest one there and frequently stopped to catch her breath. Luckily, the boy must have often been up and down this path and was content to go up slowly, step by step. Eventually, we arrived at a narrow ledge where there was space enough for the eight of us to stand and catch our breath.

I looked out over the plain, the straggly trees now just grey-green splodges against the grass. In the distance, I could see the spiral of smoke rising which showed there was a village there, and further back were the purplish-grey mountains. Achillea passed me the gourd of water and I murmured, 'Blessed be the Goddess,' gratefully. The water was brackish by now, but it was so refreshing that I longed to drink it all, reluctantly handing it back to Achillea who was playing her role of helpful Maid and taking the water to each Priestess in turn before drinking it herself. I noted that I had dropped down in the hierarchy, being the last of the supposed Priestesses to drink, after Lunaria and Maren, but ruefully acknowledged to myself that I probably was the least important one.

The boy gestured upwards, and we prepared to continue our journey, which now wound us around the cliff on a narrow path along the stone, worn down by the feet of countless hundreds of those who had gone before us. It was right on the edge of the cliff and it was not wise to look anywhere but at the path. I had glanced at it, but it made me feel dizzy, and it was difficult enough to see well through the veil, so I cast my eyes downwards and plodded on. There was no sound of cicadas or birds here; there was no vegetation growing on the rocks, and the only sounds were the sounds of our stertorous breathing and the sound of the occasional dislodged pebble trickling its way down the cliff. We continued in this way for some time until we reached the end of the path. We were still not at the top of the climb, but the path had run out. A platform had been carved out of the stone, allowing us all once again to catch our breath and to drink. The boy spoke silently to Tarik and pointed upwards. The rock face was pockmarked with small hollows, some marked with a red clay dot, and there were thick woven grass ropes hanging down from the top of the cliff next to them

'From here we will climb,' announced Tarik gravely. 'You must only place your hands and feet in the marked places, and you can use the ropes to help yourselves up. We will climb slowly. It is not as steep as it looks.' We looked upwards at what appeared to be a vertical rockface, but, by now, we were all grimly determined to make it to the top. It felt like a very long climb to the top, but perhaps it only felt that way, and it really was not as bad as my memory paints it. Had I been wearing a robe I could hitch up, and had I been without a veil, I might have enjoyed the challenge. As it was, I concentrated on placing my hands and feet in the marked rock hollows, following Maren's steps and we finally reached the top of the climb. I could not help but wonder how we would descend the cliff, and how much harder it might be.

Finally, we sat at the top, breathing deeply. There were trees growing there, at the top. I looked around, curious. It was like a land uplifted from the plain. There were large trees and buildings. I pondered on how they had built this place. The boy flashed us all a sudden smile and skipped off around the corner, presumably on his way back down again. As he went, he must have alerted the guards that there were visitors, as a group of around eight OutRiders came towards us. They were dressed in the shining armour made of interlinked metal discs which we had seen before. Their armour was polished, and their buffalo hide shields emblazoned with the symbol of the Queen – the interlinked flower shape which was the exact double of the brooch. I still had the brooch, I suddenly realised, along with the bee pendant, separate from each other, one around my neck and one in my underpocket. I wondered why Ambar had not taken them away from me, but perhaps it was to protect Lunaria before she could take her rightful place as the Queen's heir. Ambar stood up, as did Tarik, and Ashtun joined them after a short hesitation, standing back from Tarik. Their fingers flashed as they communicated. I stood with Lunaria, Maren and Achillea. Achillea kept her eyes to the floor but kept darting her glance upwards to see what was happening. I watched carefully, grateful again for the protection of the veil.

Ambar waved his hand towards us, presumably explaining our supposed excursion. Tarik produced the Permission Scrolls with a flourish and one of the OutRiders took them off to be examined and presumably read by the Reader. I thought there must be many Readers at a place as important as the Queen's Court, although, until I left the Temple, I had no idea even of the existence of a Queen, nor indeed of the amount of power she wielded over not only the Temple but the OutFort. From what I had understood from Tarik, the Queen's Court was, like the Outer, a place where men and women coexisted, and where the Queen, at least, could produce children, to perpetuate the line. I wondered how this was achieved, given that there seemed to be no marriage in the Queen's Court, nor any man who ruled like she did. She was a mirror to the

Goddess; the Goddess ruled over things spiritual, and she ruled over things that were of the land, and yet both laid equal claim to the people. I wondered if the Queen even believed in the Goddess. Maren and Lunaria walked over to the flat rocks by the trees and sat down in the shade, and Achillea followed them. After a while I joined them too, not wanting to stand out, even though I could see less of what interested me from there.

It was a lengthy time that we sat there, and Ambar and Tarik sent Ashtun over to us, ostensibly to guard us but probably because otherwise one of the OutRiders from the Court might understand that he was not a real OutRider, especially if they tried to converse with him in the language of the OutRiders. He stood near us, sullenly, stationed closest to Achillea. At last the OutRider returned and conversed silently with Ambar. Ambar was always the leader in these conversations. Tarik had shown himself to be intelligent and careful and precise, but he did not have the charisma of Ambar or his skill for making you feel that he was only interested in what you had to say. Ambar strode over to us, outwardly unhurried and calm, and made an announcement. 'Sister Priestesses, Maid, we are commanded to enter the Court of the Queen with our offerings.'

'Blessings of the Goddess,' responded Lunaria clearly, and we all followed suit with our praise for the Goddess. Inside my mind, I added a fervent prayer to the Goddess that she should watch over us all in this endeavour. I did not know if I truly believed in the Goddess anymore, but old habits meant that I relied upon the Goddess when there was no one else to rely on. Achillea picked up the heavy basket of embroidery again, and the gourds of honey. We did not gather honey in the Temple, nor did they in the OutFort; it was an occupation which was only performed by those of the

Outer. I pondered on why this might be, for honey was so prized by all, I was puzzled that more did not become Beeguards. Achillea had told me once, when I first started staying in Mellia, that her mother had told her that the bees would not make honey for those whom they did not respect, and now I felt this might be true and might be the reason for there being less Beeguards than other professions. Perhaps the bees knew something we did not know and had little respect for both the Temple and the OutFort with their cruel practices. Maren nudged me forward and I realised I had been standing still while the others had begun to make their way through the stone entrance towards the receiving hall.

The Temple was made of stone, carved out of solid rock, by Angels. This Queen's Court was also made of stone, but it was made of carved blocks of stone, a harder greyer rock than that of the cliffs, which must have been carried up here. The central building was large, with a very high doorway, arched at the top, and bolted with fine, elaborate bolts attached to a deep red wood. There were windows and cross shaped light openings around the top of the building, too high to allow anyone access, but nevertheless letting in the light. Beyond this hall like building, were further stone buildings, and beyond them buildings made of stone and wood in the style of the OutFort. At one end of the hall was a more elaborate carved screen window, and I surmised this might lead to the chamber of the Queen which Tarik had told us about, from where she could hear the conversations in the hall.

The OutRider led us towards the door and turned the handle to let us in. We followed him inwards to the far wall where there was a long table, on which were placed a variety of ceremonial objects. Tarik had told me that this was where the Queen's Scroll was kept, in a silver scroll holder which was placed against a stand, polished and gleaming. It was a beautiful creation, elaborately chased in a pattern of interwoven flowers and honeycomb patterns. There were other items on the table; a carved wooden box said to contain the original scribing of the Aphorisms of Ashkana, according to Tarik, a box made of almost transparent crystal and several other pieces which had importance to the status of the Queen. My interest, however, was in the scroll, as this was what I would have to read out to begin the procedure by which Lunaria would be made Queen. On the scroll were posed several questions that had to be answered by witnesses in the presence of the Queen's Representative. According to history (and again, according to Tarik, who appeared to have taken in a lot of detail about the history of the land, although he assured me that all OutRiders had to learn about the history of the Queen and her protection) this ceremony was normally planned and undertaken quietly within the Court, with barely anyone even realising that power had been transferred. It was important that the land should continue as it always had done, without a change or a break. I wondered how anything ever changed. Perhaps things changed so very slightly that nobody was aware of how they had changed, but surely someone must have realised how wrong the system of the Angels was.

I edged a little closer to the table. The OutRider who had escorted us inside went to stand by the huge door. He moved, like all of them, with a sort of lazy arrogance, a knowledge of his own physical power. He did not watch the men of the group, nor indeed we who wore the veil of the Priestess, but I could see him closely examining Achillea, who was standing modestly between Lunaria and myself. His eyes occupied themselves in travelling up and down her, as if he were assessing her suitability for some task or other. I remembered what Bellis had told us about how she had been treated; like an object made for use by the OutRiders, and I felt myself growing angry again.

There was another doorway at the end of the hall, below where the more elaborate window had been. I caught a glimpse of the metal curtain described by Tarik which was behind a dark blue woven curtain pushed to one side by the Queen's Representative who had now arrived. For some reason, I had thought it would be a man, perhaps an OutCommander, and was unprepared for the figure of a woman who came through the curtain. She was heavily built and of a good height and did not wear any type of clothing that I had seen before; she was of neither the Temple nor the Outer. She wore no veil nor netela over her hair, and her robe was richly coloured in a dark pink with a deep border, finely embroidered in dark blue, and a similar pattern embroidered around the neckline and cuffs. Her mouth was held closed, in a thin, firm line, and her eyes were sharp and alert as she cast them over us. Ambar bowed down in front of her and introduced us as a party of Priestesses who had brought with them gifts for the Queen and her Court. Her eyes gleamed avariciously, and she demanded that we show her our gifts. Achillea began to show the gourds of honey, which the Representative tasted, by dipping her finger into the honey, instead of using the tasting twig offered to her by Achillea. She even hooked her finger as she brought it out of the neck of the gourd so that she could get more. She could not resist running her tongue over her lips afterwards, the flickering movement reminding me of the lizards who sat motionless on the rocks in the sun, waiting for the flies to land.

'This honey is certainly good; we will take it for the Queen; it will bring her pleasure.' She waved her hand at Achillea. 'Put all the honey over there by the curtain, girl. I will take care of it personally.' I thought I knew what that might mean. She had every intention of keeping the honey for herself was my interpretation. Achillea picked up the honey gourds and trudged over to the curtain with them, scowling once she got past the Representative, who had now moved on to examining the embroidered cloths that Lunaria had brought in her basket. She flicked through them, examining the backs as well as the fronts of them and holding them up to the light. She returned to a light blue cloth of Azureus which had a pattern of tiny white flowers on it intermingled with dark blue birds. 'This is fine work. I think I ... the Queen ... would like some more fabric like this to make a gown in this style.' She preened slightly, smoothing her hand over the work on her robe. 'Which one of you is the embroiderer?'

'It is I,' Lunaria answered, quietly. The Representative snapped her head around and glared at her. 'You, Priestess, need to address me as Excellency. You owe me respect.'

Ambar stepped smoothly between the Representative and Lunaria and Tarik pushed me hard towards the table. I had barely seen their flickering fingers, but I suspected that the OutRider on guard at the door had caught the end of it because he began to advance towards us.

'It is you who should be showing her respect!' said Ambar. 'She is your Queen. You should be kneeling to her!'

'There is no new Queen,' retorted the Representative, spitting the words out. 'The old Queen made sure of that. And since I am her Representative, I take her role. Whoever this imposter is, she has no right to be the Queen. There is only one who could be the Queen and there is no way to know who she is!' She turned and beckoned the OutRider on the door who advanced towards us, drawing his knife. Maren dropped to the floor in terror, as did Achillea who was next to the indigo curtain. Ambar blocked Lunaria with his body and drew his own knife. They must all have them secretly hilted on their person, a second weapon to use when the bow could not be. I was rooted to the spot, standing behind Tarik, but I still managed to grab the Scroll Holder and saw that the top was also sealed with beeswax, impressed with a similarly complicated pattern.

Then, with no warning, Ashtun suddenly rushed towards the advancing OutRider, brandishing his own knife, charging towards him, bellowing his rage. The OutRider sidestepped him and then grabbed him round the neck, forcing him to the floor. Then in a swift, single movement he stabbed him in the throat. He did not look back but continued towards Lunaria. I tore the seal off the Holder, beeswax scattering everywhere and pulled out and unrolled the scroll with trembling fingers, unable to do anything else, transfixed at the sight of Ashtun who lay there, having flailed briefly on the floor before all movement ceased. Tarik took out his own knife which I noticed now was strapped to his wrist in a manner which allowed it to be quickly withdrawn. It had three blades on it, each facing in a different direction, and each a different size. He flicked his wrist and the knife flew through the air toward the advancing OutRider, hitting him in the neck. His knees crumpled, and he too fell to the floor. Before the Representative had time to make a noise, Ambar moved to stand next to her and said quietly, but menacingly, 'You have to listen, now. Talla, read the Queen's Scroll.'

Achillea was still curled up next to the curtain, shaking. I did not know if she was even aware of what had happened to Ashtun. She seemed to have withdrawn into a closed state. I noticed that Ambar had called me by my real name, but it did not matter anymore; either we would succeed in our mission or we would all meet the same swift end as Ashtun. I looked down at the Scroll, ready to read it out loud.

'These are the questions which must be answered in order that a new Queen can begin her reign,' I began, my voice quavering slightly. 'They must be read in front of the Representative of the Queen. If the questions are answered satisfactorily, allegiance must be given to the new Queen from that minute onwards.

'Is there a witness who was at the birth of the new Queen? Let them affirm it.'

Maren got up hesitantly, and then threw back her veil and, looking straight at the Queen's Representative, said in a clear voice, 'I am the witness to the birth of the Queen. I was the Birthmother when Paradox, the daughter of the Queen gave birth. She birthed DoubleSouls, and Lunaria was the first to be born, because she bears the sign. I believe that Paradox died after the birth, for she was taken away by the soldiers of the Queen.'

I moved on to the next question quickly. The Queen's Representative stood with her mouth slack, looking at Maren disbelievingly. I could hear quiet, suppressed sobbing from Achillea.

'Does the new Queen bear the mark of the bee?' We were all amazed at this question, for it seemed to foretell that the daughter of the Queen would have a birthmark in the shape of a bee. The scroll had been written when the old Queen was first made Queen, and so her own daughter Paradox must have had the same mark. She could not have known that the firstborn daughter of Paradox would have the exact same mark – unless all Queens had it, perhaps.

FLAMMEUS

Maren stepped forward again, her voice a little stronger, her eyes averted from Ashtun who lay in a heap, diminished by death, deep red blood pooled under his head, and from the guard who likewise lay dead, sprawled on the floor. She took a deep breath and spoke once more. 'She bears the sign of the bee. She bore it when she was born, and she bears it now. The Queen's Representative must see it now in the presence of witnesses.'

I admired Maren's initiative in getting the Queen's Representative to look at the mark herself, so there could be no doubt. At this point, Lunaria too, threw back the veil from her face. It dropped to the floor, crumpled and empty, like Ashtun. Maren walked over to Lunaria, and Ambar turned his back for her modesty. Maren untied Lunaria's robe at the back and eased it down over her shoulders so that the Queen's Representative could see the birthmark. There was silence while she examined it carefully.

Ambar asked finally, 'Does she bear the mark of the bee?'

The Representative answered, with some disbelief in her words, 'Yes she bears it.' Maren replaced Lunaria's robe and tied it up gently, with shaking hands.

I looked down at the scroll, my sight suddenly blurred with tears, to read out the final question. Maren put her hand comfortingly on Lunaria's shoulder. I focused on the script, which was elaborate and not easy for me to read, especially through my tears.

'Does the new Queen hold the Brooch of the Body and the Necklace of the Mind?'

We all looked at one another, bewildered by this question which sounded like a half-finished riddle, but then I realised exactly what was meant by it, and said clearly, 'Yes, they are here. I will place them into her ownership now.' The Brooch of the Body was the golden brooch which bore the shapes of the honeycomb, the emblem of the OutRiders, the bodies who protected the Queen, and the Necklace of the Mind was the little bee necklace, the necklace which had first warmed for me and opened the channel in my mind that allowed me to feel the feelings of others. I thought that perhaps now that I no longer owned it that I might not sense those connecting feelings anymore, but it was time to give it back to its rightful owner. The brooch, which I had been told all my life had been left with me, was not really mine but Lunaria's and I still had no idea if she was my sister or not. I bent down to access my underpocket and took out the brooch and took it to Lunaria and pinned it on her purple robe, over her heart. Then I slowly took the little bee necklace off over my head and held on to it briefly as I placed the leather loop over Lunaria's head. Instead of letting it hang loosely around her neck, I held it over the brooch and the magical substance pulled them together until they snapped together, the bee and the honeycombed flower together.

'And now,' said Ambar in a clear and triumphant voice, 'do you acknowledge and swear unending loyalty to this, your new Queen?' The Queen's Representative blinked, completely dumbfounded by the swift unfolding of events. She could only agree if she wished to be spared, for all the conditions had been met, and she knew that it would be pointless to resist. She dropped dramatically down to her knees in front of Lunaria and bowed her head.

'I acknowledge and swear absolute loyalty to my Queen,' she said, and as soon as she had finished speaking, both Ambar and Tarik did the same thing, pledging their loyalty to Lunaria, who was now my new Queen too. But I did not kneel; I did not know what my place was in this world yet, and I was not of the Temple nor of the OutFort, nor yet of the Court of the Queen.

Instead, I rolled up the scroll and placed it back into the scroll holder, with its broken seal, and went to Achillea who lay, still curled up on the floor, weeping silently, unable to look at Ashtun who was there, but had gone.

I knelt beside her, unsure of what to say. I had never really liked Ashtun, but I had not really known him. Achillea had loved him, for perhaps he showed to her, or she saw in him something hidden from the rest of us. I had never seen a person that I knew dead. I patted her back awkwardly, and she raised her face to me, her beautiful, large eyes red with weeping, overflowing with pain, her face streaked with shining tracks of despair. She raised her arms to me and drew me down, nestling in my arms and resting her head against me. We sat like this for only a few minutes until I became aware that the hall was filling with people. The main door had not opened, so they must have been coming from behind the curtain, and they must have known to come because the special curtain, which Tarik had told us about, had allowed them to hear what was happening. I rose to my feet, and Achillea rose with me, still clinging to me. I tried to steer her past Ashtun's body without her looking too closely at it, but she started to sob again as we went past.

Ambar was still standing by Lunaria who was looking out at the people who had assembled. There were many who were dressed like the Queen's Representative in rich, ornate robes, both men and women, all well-nourished, superior and anxious. One came up to the Representative and whispered in her ear.

Ambar quickly addressed him. 'There will be no whispering in the face of your Queen! Speak your message for all to hear!'

The man turned to him. He was small and rather round, like a busy squirrel, bright eyed, and with a grey beard and fine moustaches. He wore a deep green robe with golden edging and an interesting skull cap in white. He spoke in a reedy, finicky voice.

'I am Parvez, I was the Physic for the old Queen. I came to tell the Representative that she has gone to the Goddess, just as the new Queen came to us.'

There was a murmuring. I wondered if she had died before or after hearing Lunaria was the new Queen, and whether she had died in joy or sorrow, in that knowledge, or even if she had died naturally. It occurred to me that it was possible that this was my own grandmother, and of course that of Lunaria, but we were not accustomed to the notion of family in the Temple and so we had no attachment to it. I went to Tarik and prodded him. He turned to me, surprised by my presence, and apparently as transfixed as everyone else at being in the presence of their new Queen.

'Can you please organise somebody to take them away?' I hissed, gesturing to the bodies which still lay on the floor like old sacks. 'It is distressing Achillea, and indeed all present, I am sure!'

Startled, Tarik looked up at me and then at Achillea with concern and murmured, 'Of course, of course...' He went to the main door and called for the OutRiders to come. I pushed Achillea towards the back wall, beyond the table, and got her to sit down next to the wall. I beckoned Maren over and she came to sit and comfort Achillea while I went over to Lunaria and Ambar.

I pushed my way through the members of the court who all moved aside for me. When I reached Lunaria and Ambar, I was very upset about poor Achillea and that no one had thought to say anything about Ashtun's death – or indeed the death of the other soldier, and I angrily asked Ambar what he was going to do about it. His eyes flashed in sharp rebuke to me, for not showing due deference to the new Queen Lunaria, but I was beyond weary, and wanted only to be gone from this place and these people. Whereas my life in the Temple had been too regulated, and the same every day, my life since then had been too different. I no sooner became accustomed to one thing then another thing had to be learned or performed or understood and I was too tired to care any more about what Ambar or indeed the Queen thought about it. Ambar was about to speak, when Lunaria came forward and spoke first instead.

As soon as she opened her mouth, the whole hall fell silent in deference to her.

'Both of these men have given their lives in the service of the Queen; a very high price to pay. One of them had been raised in the ways of the OutRiders and as a warrior, but this man here,' and she pointed to Ashtun, 'was not a trained warrior, and yet he gave his life to protect me. His devotion to his land and to me as his Queen were commendable. May the Goddess embrace them both as they return home to her. Ambar, can you ask the OutRiders to take them for washing and for preparation for their return to the Goddess with the utmost respect?'

Ambar immediately bustled off to do as he had been asked. I was impressed with Lunaria's calm responsibility and dignified authority. Perhaps the Goddess really was guiding her steps through this new world, for where she had appeared naïve and ignorant before, now she seemed to know exactly what to do and how to speak.

'And now,' continued Lunaria. 'My companions, and indeed I, are weary and need to rest and to eat and drink. After that, I will converse with all of you about the next steps. Perhaps there is a private room to which we can go?'

The Queen's Representative came forward and indicated the indigo curtain which hung at the end of the room. I went over to Maren and together we helped

Achillea stumble out of the room and made our way to the private chambers beyond the curtain where we could rest and take stock of all the bewildering events of the day.

THE EMBERS

CHAPTER 36

I look back on the days that followed as if through Maren's long-smeared vision. So much occurred and so much changed, and yet so much remained the same. Traditions of life and governance of land are not changed in a single day or by a single person, but life for any one individual can be changed in a single moment forever.

We remained at the Queen's Court for only two more days. Some of us, that is. Lunaria or The Queen, as we learned to call her remained at the Court, of course. It was now her home, her workplace and her life. The old Queen was returned to the Goddess with little ceremony, as was the way with all deaths. Also returned to the Goddess were the OutRider, Antulla, who was killed by Tarik, and Ashtun. Achillea was asked if she wanted his body returned to Mellia, but he had no family there, and she wanted any ceremony over swiftly. Tarik had spoken to Achillea kindly and told her that Ashtun would have been well known if he had been an OutRider, and that his courage had earned him a place in the memories and stories of the great warriors of the OutRiders. The OutRiders themselves did not distinguish between the two deaths; both had died in service to the Queen, and both had died in the hope of protecting their Queen, and so, to the OutRiders, in whom loyalty and duty were paramount, both had died giving the supreme sacrifice. Achillea wept often, but she was comforted by the thought that Ashtun had died bravely and reminded me of how happy he had been to be considered one of the OutRiders. I was not sure if he had been brave or foolhardy, but this I did not say; instead, I tried to keep Achillea busy in helping the Queen to choose new robes to wear from the considerable numbers of them which had been acquired by the Queen and her Representatives.

Ambar had become more distant towards me and Achillea and Maren. He was completely absorbed in enabling the new life of the Queen, and it was clear to all who had known him before this time that he was closing off one chapter of his life and opening a new one. It was equally clear that the Queen relied on him heavily and trusted in his judgement implicitly. By the end of the second day, she had appointed him to be Court Commander, in charge of overlooking the security of the Queen and in charge of the OutRiders of the Court, sending the current Commander away to look after the OutForts on the western borders. It was, as yet, unclear what would happen to the many members of the Court. I wondered where they had been drawn from – were they from the ranks of loyal Priestesses and OutCommanders? They were surely not from the Outer, or from other lands? How could the Queen be sure of their loyalty, given that they had been part of the old Queen's cruel regime? I asked Lunaria some of these questions, but to many of them, she simply smiled and said that she was sure the Goddess would guide her. I was made angry by this stock response and tried to push her for a further undertaking to close down the practice of taking the Maids from the Temple and forcing them into slavery as Angels. Again, she smiled tolerantly at me and said that the practice would be removed in due course, as she explored her land and how it worked. The Court was full of more rules and regulations; one was that one could not raise one's voice in the presence of the Queen. If there was the slightest hint of this, one of the Queen's Guard would step forward to remind you; it made it very hard for me to express my burning anger to Lunaria. She, on the other hand, suited it perfectly, since her voice was calm and modulated like a good Priestess.

I spoke about it instead to Tarik, who seemed his usual self, as he had throughout. He listened to me calmly and agreed with me that the practice should stop, but asked me what I would do with the Angels now? For they could not be Maids of the Temple any more, having been used by men, and it would take much learning and adjusting for them to take their place in the land of the Outer, especially if they came to know about who they were and how they had been used. I reminded him of Bellis's story and of the history of Gladia's baby and of all the individual examples of pain and suffering there must be, and he nodded sadly, and suggested I should try to think of a way to help them instead of being so angry about it. I knew that he was right, and that any angry, injudicious action on my part might end up making things worse for those I wanted to help most. I identified closely with the Angels, although Bellis was the only one I knew, for they reminded me of myself; rootless, belonging neither here nor there, and in need of understanding and patience, and for the Angels, having the wounds of the body and the heart soothed. I felt that I needed to get away from the Queen's Court, for it held too much pain and unresolved anger for me now, and told Tarik that I was ready to leave the Queen's Court with Maren and Achillea, and he went to Ambar and the Queen and told them.

I was called to a meeting with Ambar where he told me that it was unlikely that I would ever return to the Queen's Court once I had left. He told me that although our subterfuge had been necessary, now that he was the

Queen's Court Commander, he would be ensuring that a new way of checking who Priestesses were would be introduced so that no other could enter the Queen's Court in a similar way, because his loyalty now was to his Queen and to her protection. It was difficult to see how he could have been disloyal to the old Queen and yet so blindly loyal to Lunaria, about whom he knew much less than I did. I felt quite dismissed by this man who had once been my friend, and who had relied on me and my expertise for his quest to succeed, and whose words had once come close to melting my heart, and I had a sick feeling in my stomach and no wish to see him again. The Queen thanked me for all I had done for her and asked if there was anything else I needed.

Again, I felt dismissed; used and then discarded, like a pot which once contained sweet honey. Lunaria, who could still be my sister, my DoubleSoul, paid me no more importance than any other person, now. I had spoken to her since her accession and told her more about what I had heard from Saphna and Maren, and speculated to her that we might be sisters, but she remained unconvinced, and having been raised in an institution which had no concept of family ties, it meant little to her either. I asked only for her undertaking that Besseret and Mellia would be left in peace by the OutRiders so that we might continue our lives wherever we might choose to live, and she gave me her promise. I believed her, because there was no reason not to. I did not feel that she bore any of us ill will; it was just that we were no longer a necessary part of her life and she was quite happy that we should go away and not bother her again. It seemed that all our personal sacrifices were no longer important and had been just a necessary part of progress. It was agreed that Tarik would escort us back to Besseret. He would then be moving on himself, to the east of the land, to a new OutFort.

FLAMMEUS

We left early the next morning. I was ready to face the precipitous route back down the mountain, but, to my surprise, Tarik led us to an area on the opposite side of the Court to where we had climbed up. There was another smiling OutRider youth waiting for us who guided us to a large woven structure, like a boat, which was wrapped by large woven ropes which sprawled behind us and which were braced over a large tree trunk. The boy indicated the basket and Tarik told us that we needed to sit in the large basket and we would be lifted down the cliff by a special mechanism. Our faces must have been an interesting spectacle for the boy grinned so widely you might have thought that it stretched all the way round his head. He flickered his fingers to Tarik and Tarik chuckled and told us that the boy said that they had never dropped anyone before. Dubiously we ventured into the basket and I thought how much Benakiell might enjoy investigating this structure and how it worked. I was not so convinced, myself. Achillea sat down listlessly. She was so sad that she had become a wisp of her earlier self; all the singing and humming and light-hearted laughter had gone. Maren had been a great comfort to her and had been able to talk to her about how she had felt when her dear friend Anglossia had died and had been able to provide hope for Achillea that others had survived the death of their loved ones and that, with time, she could too. But, for Achillea, who had lost her father as a young child and her mother as a young adult, the death of Ashtun had taken away her foundations in a strange place, and she needed to get back amongst people that she had known for a long time; Gladia and Benakiell who had acted as her parents to some degree, since the loss of her own mother.

The basket lurched, and I shut my eyes as the boy kicked away the boulders which had been holding the basket to the top of the cliff and we began to judder our way down the cliff face. Tarik told us as we made our slow and bumpy way down that this was the way in which the members of the Queen's Court also ascended the cliffs and that it took many strong OutRiders to haul them up the cliff. Finally, we reached the bottom. It had been an uncomfortable and nerve-wracking journey, but it was over in a very short time, in comparison to our arduous climb up to the Court. At the bottom, we found our horses waiting for us –well, three of them; I guess the rest had been taken to the OutRider stables. Tarik tied all the horses together in a long line, since we were not accustomed to taking control of the horses ourselves, and we set off once more, on the way back to Besseret.

As we rode in to Besseret the next day, weary and silent, having done our part in the work that had been set before us, perhaps by the Goddess herself, I don't think any of us felt, at that time, any particular satisfaction or sense of achievement. We had not ever really thought beyond the next step of the way and now we had reached where we thought we wanted to be, we realised that it was just another stop on the road. Benakiell was the first to greet us; he was sitting under the Paradox tree near where the horses had been stabled, shaping reeds with his knife. He got up straight away, waving to us enthusiastically until he saw that Ashtun was not with us. Tarik quietly explained to him what had happened, in uncharacteristically brief terms, as we dismounted the horses. Benakiell called for Gladia and she came out of the dwelling; like him, she was happy to see us and then full of sadness at the loss of Ashtun. Ashtun had been apprentice to Benakiell in learning the business of dwelling making and so they had worked together each day for some time, and, I supposed, had often talked to one another of this and that. He had no children of his own and perhaps Ashtun was the closest thing he had to a son. Gladia bustled over to Achillea and swept her off. Maren went to check up on Bellis. I turned to speak to Benakiell, but he had walked away to one side with Tarik, deep in conversation. And I realised that I needed to be on my own, for now. I headed off down to the flower garden and the beehives.

I wandered around aimlessly for a while, smelling the flowers and herbs, and then decided to watch the bees as they worked. I lowered one of the wooden hives down from the tree using the rope it was suspended by. It reminded me of the basket we had travelled down from the Queen's Court in. The bees gave a warning hum, but I ignored it and once the hive was laying on the ground, I removed the side slat that allowed access to the honeycombs and watched them as they scurried around. They all had a job to do whether it was making honey or collecting pollen or cleaning the hive or protecting the hive from assailants. Each focused only on its own task, just like we did in the Temple, or how they worked in the OutFort. Here in the Outer, people also had their own jobs to do, but along with their jobs, they learned to do other things like cook and garden and trade. They learned how to talk with others, how to give and take trust and kindness and how to love and look after one another. I could see how orderly and organised the hive was; there was no room for disagreement or independent thinking. I was not a person who could stay in a hive, nor even be its Queen. There was too much to learn and understand about the world, not just in my land but in the lands of others.

In the end, I stayed another two weeks at Besseret. Tarik had surprised us all by staying too. I asked him if he might not get into trouble with the OutRiders, but he smiled wryly and said he thought they had bigger things to concern themselves with. So, he stayed with us, tending the horses and making salves and decoctions. He consulted me and Achillea on how we had made Maren's eye salve and made several more small gourds full. He stopped wearing the armour and became more relaxed, borrowing a tunic from Benakiell. He helped Benakiell to finish thatching the dwellings at Besseret and spent some time fixing more rope on Maren's beehives too and put together two new ones for her.

I had planned to only stay a few days, and had told nobody of my need to leave, but three days after we returned, Achillea came running up to me, calling out, more animated than I had seen her since we returned from the court.

'Talla, Talla, it's coming!' I looked at her, puzzled.

'What is coming?' I asked.

'The baby! Bellis's baby is coming! We need to get Maren!' I accompanied her to fetch Maren, who was excited to be doing her job as a Birthmother again and came dashing up the hill. Everyone was in a fever of excitement – except for me. I cared for Bellis, and wanted her baby to be born safely, but I had no experience of babies, and all the ones I had ever known had been unwanted or abandoned – or stolen, as I found out later. I had never known how much a baby might be wanted before, even one who had been made in those circumstances. I still did not quite understand how the baby was made or how it was born. Maren had told me some details when she told me the story of Lunaria's birth, but I wasn't comfortable with being around when it happened. I fetched and carried for Maren but as things became more fraught, I left her urging Bellis on. Bellis sat against the wall of her dwelling holding on to Gladia on one side and Achillea on the other side, groaning and breathing hard, and I quietly exited the dwelling, heading instead for the horses, where Benakiell and Tarik were feeling similarly.

We talked of this and that as we waited for news. Tarik groomed the horses and then tied them to a new tree within reach of all the fresh new shoots of grass that were emerging after the rains. Benakiell asked us some questions about our time at the Queen's Court and we told him about the basket lifting mechanism which intrigued him. The time passed and all we heard were muffled cries and shouts from inside Bellis's dwelling until there came a time of quiet. Just as we were starting to shuffle uneasily and wondering what this might mean, there was a faint, high, reedy wail, and we knew that the baby was born. You might have thought Gladia had given birth to him herself from the way she came running out and telling us all about him. It was a boy. For some reason, it had never occurred to me that Bellis, a daughter of the Goddess could give birth to a male child. There was some discussion about what his name should be; the way of the Outer was to name a baby after one of his father's family, like Benakiell or Ashtun were but Bellis did not know the baby's father, nor did she want to. The OutRiders called their members a single name of their own choosing, since they did not know their fathers either and eventually Bellis decided to call her son Jember. That name came from an old folksong which Achillea had sung to Bellis, when she had first come to our camp, about an ancient prince who performed many honourable deeds. Jember was a scrawny baby, hardly surprisingly, considering his mother had been half starved, but he appeared to be beautiful in the eyes of all, especially Bellis who looked at him with the same devotion she used to have when she gazed at the statue of the Goddess. Everyone was fascinated by him, aside from me. Even Benakiell, who was normally quite taciturn and serious, could be found making silly faces at the baby who moved his limbs about excitedly in response.

Gladia enjoyed all this tremendously. She was playing an important role in a kind of a family life, which, in reality, she had yearned for for years. Bellis depended on her for advice and support, and Gladia thoroughly enjoyed dispensing words of wisdom, and issuing warnings. She came to sit with me about a week after Jember had been born, as I hung out some washing on the bushes to dry. I had taken to wearing the Priestess dress sometimes. Although it was orange and not red, the colour of Flammeus, it warmed me and made me feel more confident. It was a comfortable robe, and without the veil, it felt more joyful.

'I'm guessing you see babies in your future, too, Talla,' she started, smiling at me in a mischievous way. 'I thought perhaps we might find you a nice husband and marry you off soon, so that you could join Bellis and have a friend for Jember!' I looked at her, horror-struck, until I realised that she was poking fun at me, once again. She laughed out loud, slapping me none too softly on my arm, as she liked to do. I rubbed it better as she continued to chuckle.

'It's been a long and difficult journey for you since you left that Temple, hasn't it?' she continued after a few minutes. 'If it were me, I would want to settle down and be quiet somewhere for a long while, but I don't think you do, even though there are many ways for you to make a living for yourself, here in Besseret or back in Mellia.' I shook my head. I still felt too close to the Temple and the Court of the Queen, and all the reminders it had for me of the paradoxes and injustices of our land, and for all the attachment and security I felt for my friends here in Besseret, I felt within me a need to go somewhere new and start again, without the pressure of the search for the Queen. Yes, I wanted some peace, but I was not ready to bury myself in village life forever yet.

'And what of you?' I asked, turning the question back on Gladia, 'Will you stay in Besseret with Maren and Bellis or return to Mellia with Benakiell and Achillea?'

Gladia looked shocked. 'You are not the only one who seeks a different life, Talla! I intend to persuade Maren and Bellis and little Jember to return home with me. I do wonder sometimes about our friends in Mellia, and hope they are well, and that the village is thriving since we left. It is time to return to our old lives and tend to those who need our care.'

I felt guilty, knowing that it had been my presence there that had led to trouble in Mellia in the first place, and thought momentarily about the Rupicola's dream about me, and how I had thought it meant I might be the next Queen. Probably it had no meaning at all and was just an old woman's dream.

'We shall all go to Mellia,' continued Gladia briskly. 'I have a friendship with Maren which will be good for both of us. I will be caring for Bellis and Jember and helping them to live out here, with us. Bellis can help me with my stitching, or perhaps she can learn from Maren to be a Birthmother.' Her eyes drifted off into the future, and I was amazed at how much of this I seemed to have missed. I had spent so long in thinking about all the events that had happened that I had not spent enough time talking and listening to my friends. I had not lost the warm channel of empathy that had first occurred when I went to see Empath Erayo and held onto the Queen's bee necklace, and I had found it hard to manage all the emotions from Achillea since we had returned. She was distracted by baby Jember and I tried to keep her busy with work. 'If you work hard enough, work is all you need,' as Ashkana had informed us all in the Temple. The trouble was that although I could feel her pain, I could not identify with it, not having experience of it. So, after spending some time with Achillea on our work, I would go and walk around on my own until the feelings died down. I realised now that I had neglected my companions and questioned Gladia more.

'And what of Benakiell?' I asked. 'Will he certainly return to Mellia too?' I knew how much Gladia depended on Benakiell, and what affection they held for each other. Gladia smiled. 'I think he will. He would like to travel again, but he will surely be content to travel in our land, trading and making dwellings, and will come back at the end of each trip. He will search for a new apprentice to take Ashtun's place when he goes to Sanguinea to trade. He is much taken with little Jember, too. I am convinced he will be setting him to work before he can walk!' We looked out over the plain from our perch on the rocks by the bushes, enjoying the fresh air and the new growth all around us. Gladia made life in Mellia sound quite tempting, with the recommencement of normal activity, of trading and growing and working. But I needed to go and explore the world, and I was sure that they would welcome me back to Mellia at any time, should I ever choose to travel back.

'You will take Achillea with you, though,' announced Gladia finally. 'Staying here will only remind her every day of what she has lost, especially with Bellis having the baby, and Benakiell still here. It will be too hard for her to lose you too, so you must take her with you.' I gaped at Gladia and began to shake my head. 'You cannot refuse, sister Talla,' responded Gladia, firmly. 'For, think of what she did for you, and for your quest to find the Queen. She did it willingly, to be sure, and she did it because you are her friend. And she has lost Ashtun forever through the same quest. I am not blaming you,' she added, hastily, 'but Achillea needs to go somewhere else too for a little while. You are a strong person and a hard worker but Achillea will be a good friend to you, which you need.'

I was speechless but could come up with no good reason why Achillea could not come with me, if she wanted to. We neither of us had parents or family to keep us back, and we both needed to start again, in our own way. I did not think Achillea would want to come away with me in any case, but it became clear that Gladia was a better judge of character than I was, for Achillea was relieved to be offered the chance to leave everything behind. Tarik had offered to stay another week until we headed off in the direction of Gabez on the eastern border of Oramia. We planned to stay there for some time before we decided on our future path. Tarik was supposed to be going to the OutFort there, but he was circumspect about it, saying that he would end up where he was supposed to be, in the end. He was less dignified and pompous than he had been, and now that Ambar was no longer there, enjoyed talking about this and that, and devising little amusements for the baby Jember, even though he was only days old and unable to do anything but eat and sleep and cry, from what I could see. Benakiell was pleased that Achillea and I would be accompanied by a man who could protect us in case of rogue OutRiders.

And so here we were. Tarik had returned the horses to the nearest OutFort. I don't know how he managed to do that without rousing suspicion, but apparently, he did. When he returned, he hid the armour in a small cache near Besseret in case he might need it again one day. We had with us the gourds of physic, and a few small gourds of Maren's honey. I had left my pouncing parchments with Gladia and shown her how to trace the patterns with the charcoal. I could easily make some more if I needed to, though I doubted that embroidery would be in my future, or Achillea's. I took, instead, a stock of reed pens carved for me by Benakiell, who continued to practice his letters himself, and a gourd of ink. I had left him a written set of every letter, so he could practice for himself. We had with us a few other small items to trade; some cloth and stitching, the physic, the honey, some fruit.

We said our farewells. Gladia and Benakiell stood back, watching us leave like anxious parents might, as we turned eastwards, and Maren and Bellis waved to us, Jember shrieking in protest or perhaps in delight. I suddenly thought that I might never see them again, and I turned to look back at them, my eyes catching the sun and oozing tears, even when I had finally turned away. It was time to leave.

May the Goddess guide us onward.

ACKNOWLEDGEMENTS

I'd like to thank my wonderful group of Beta readers. Their interest, support and faith in me and my book kept me going through many times of uncertainty and doubt. They have helped me enormously with their feedback and encouragement and I am very grateful.

If you would like to find out more about me and my book, please do visit my author website, or contact me at
https://www.emberjar.com/

The lovely cover art for this book was created for me by Amy Yeager. You can find her pages on Facebook/Instagram.
https://www.facebook.com/tusg.art/
https://www.instagram.com/tusg.art/

If you have enjoyed reading Flammeus, please do take the time to leave a review for me on Amazon or contact me via my website – I really appreciate your feedback.

Finally, my grateful thanks to you, dear reader, for visiting the world of Oramia with me and taking the time to enjoy the beginning of this journey. I really do appreciate it.

A writer is made complete by their readers.

Printed in Great Britain
by Amazon